MY MO AND I

The Epic Story of Grenada

Kamau McBarnette

Island Girl Publishers

ISBN-13: 978-1492907541
ISBN-10: 1492907545

Copyright © 2014 by Kamau McBarnette. All rights reserved. No part of this publication may be reproduced, stored in a retrieval system, or transmitted, in any form or by any means, electronic, mechanical, photocopying, recording or otherwise, without the prior permission of the author.

About the Author

Kamau McBarnette was born in St. George's, Grenada in 1956. He spent twenty-five years as a political prisoner at Grenada's Richmond Hill Prison, following the American invasion in October 1983.

He was educated at the Grenada Boys' Secondary School and taught both at the primary and secondary school level. He was also the Captain of Grenada's most successful steel orchestra, *Angel Harps*.

At various times during the Grenada Revolution of 1979-1983, he was a columnist for the Free West Indian newspaper, served as its editor for a short period, and was also the manager of Radio Free Grenada and the Junior Minister for Information.

For over two decades, he had been involved in teaching inmates to read and write. He is the author of *Operation Desert-Rat*, a short story and poems, and *Forget Me Not*, an anthology of poems. *My Mother And I* is his first published novel, a docu-novel.

Acknowledgements

There is no shared responsibility for the contents of this book, but I must nevertheless express special thanks to Bernard Coard who, in addition to the editorial assistance which he so readily gave, allowed me a peep into his vast repository of knowledge; as well as to Hudson Austin for his similarly invaluable help.

Thanks too, to my Research Assistants, Sule and Madge and to my colleagues Cosmus Richardson and Errol Adonis who, during the writing of much of this book, literally became my right hand when my own was still temporarily decommissioned.

Special thanks to Wilton Thomas and Christopher Stroude. Special thanks as well to all of my other colleagues and friends who may have assisted me in any way, your good deeds are appreciated.

Dedication

To the memory of
my Mother, Myntrude,
Jerome, my father;
To my sisters and brothers
And other relatives, near and far.
To Bernadette
And to Philo, Sule & Ashphil
"The grist in my life's mill."
For Margs, Cassie and Mickey,
Your friendships, my sails they fill.
And to all of my other friends
And sympathizers who let it be known
That I was never alone.

Chapter 1

Cursing and moaning, pounding and groaning were part of my birth; a difficult one. Having to spend a gestation period, which lasted longer than the normal nine months, was indeed a bad beginning. The many weeks of horrendous labour-pains, which this phenomenon occasioned, didn't help either. But my Mother was strong and determined.

And brave and powerful! Whatever the super-human qualities with which she was blessed, my Mother was quite capable of singularly bringing into this world, man, building or machine. Or anything for that matter which was considered vital for her personal enrichment and glorification. Mother was so dexterous in the manipulation of her own DNA, that, even without trying, she rendered Aldous Huxley's "Brave New World" obsolete. More importantly however, she had the wherewithal necessary for the protection of her vast wealth and prestige.

Many of her sons and daughters rushed forth in defense of this prestige and honour. Some were motivated by greed and self-aggrandizement, others by altruistic reasons; though all claimed to be acting in Mother's name. Cardinals Richelieu and Mazarin did. William, Duke Of Normandy, carried the family's emblem across the English Channel, and was nicknamed 'William The Conqueror' in salute of his tremendous feat. But Joan Of Arc was the family's pride and blazed a trail that even Marshall Pétain, Marshall Foch and General Charles De Gaulle had great difficulty following. Napoleon Bonaparte however, did Joan proud when he swept across Europe with a speed, Mach, the Austrian physicist, wouldn't have thought possible.

I hesitate to admit that Louis XVI was also my brother because he thought nothing of the wounds which he inflicted on Mother. But he, along with his wife Marie Antoinette of "let-them-eat-cake" fame, met his comeuppance under the guillotine. Nonetheless, his wife strengthened the argument that both Louis XIV and Louis XV were saints.

The filial love that my Mother felt for Colbert and De Tocqueville was boundless, as it was for Jean-Paul Sartre and Marie Curie. They conducted their lives with distinction and sent Mother's oversized ego into orbit.

I recall one of the many occasions in my Mother's eventful life when she crash-landed into a state of cardiac arrest. Our home was thrown into unprecedented turmoil, splintering its foundation into irreconcilable parts, when the proclaimers of Liberté, Egalité, Fraternité stormed the Bastille. Though it was my very brother who was being violated, to my Mother's everlasting discomfiture, I sided with Dante, Robespierre and the other revolutionaries. After all, they too were my brothers!

Not only was Mother famous for her cuisine but she can boast of having produced some of the world's most accomplished painters, sculptors, artists, scientists and philosophers.

When Descartes died in 1650, it was a sad death. But Du Parquet, my errant brother, thought little of it, and was clearly not moved by any of Mother's teachings which spoke of piety and a time for moaning. He had more important things to do with his time!

He quickly pulled together an expeditionary force, which could have been any modern day posse, declared himself Rear-Admiral, and with sails set for optimum use of the north-east trade winds, headed from Martinique in a southerly direction. All done with such haste that Du Parquet could have had no other intention but simply to escape from the evil spirit of death.

But he had baneful designs of his own! Whatever the plans that had taken shape in Du Parquet's mind, none were in accordance with any explicit instructions from Mother. They were based on what he rightfully thought would have aided the expansion of Mother's economic interests and sphere of influence.

Chapter 2

The distant sun shone radiantly that day as if determined to bring the darkest thoughts to light. Not that Du Parquet needed any prompting given his expansive and buoyant mood: "Well, fellars," he said to his crew, "Santa Lucia it will be for some of you," using the Spanish name for the island that was known to the Caribs as Hewannora – 'The Land of The Iguana.'

> "The rest of us will move further south,
> To the land we heard much about;
> The natives to slaughter, from man to brat,
> If with the land they refuse to part.
> First, try subterfuge and a smiling face,
> Glass beads, metal knives, hatchets and lace.
> That should do to win their trust
> Our intentions are noble, our God is just.
> But if they be, still unease
> Hesitate not, their land to seize.
> Promise God's blessings, his salvation
> Promise a seat on God's right hand;

But better you know it is impossible to tame,
These cannibalistic creatures without a name.
So steadfast by your musket, he who stands
Slave girls like peas, land for plantations,
And those who cross our trading routes
Would discover how well Du Parquet shoots."

His mood definitely called for a 'Carib beer,' a bitter foretaste of his experience with the Caribs – the indigenous people who called themselves Kalinago. But Du Parquet did not yet know it.

Nor did he as yet know that the blue, virgin waters, through which he now sailed, saddled by an archipelago of islands, baby-fresh, lush and green, were to immortalize through its name, the memory of the people whom ill fate placed him against.

Any half-decent nitwit should have had sufficient extrasensory perception to realize this, and on whose side history stood. But such foresight is never found among those whose every action is predicated upon narrow self-interests and the need for immediate fulfillment at any cost; no matter how much it is usually shrouded in godliness. The costs have been known to include the extermination of whole civilizations; ask the Aztecs, Mayas and Incas.

Du Parquet was not about to ask anybody anything. Certainly not after the last several days of travelling which made him even more convinced about the rightness of his mission. He held the fingers of his right hand conjointly, placed them against his lips, then pronounced these islands, "O Earthly Heaven!"

Someone evidently worked over-time, and took extra care in putting together this part of the world. This was no hurried paint-job. The green of varying shades, a display of everything which was crisply-new, untouched, unspoilt and virginal, was delicately tempered by the red, yellow, pink, brown, white, blue and purple flora and fauna charmingly proclaiming their immense diversity. No accident could explain the endless mountains, valleys and plateaus neatly and lovingly rolling into each other, like spouses eager to embrace, yet finding equal satisfaction in delaying the moment.

And when they do finally embrace, and all hell breaks loose, satiated, they find comfort in the arms of each other, tentatively touching and petting while floating on a sea of love. Much like the sea, which was lazily lapping at the numerous stretches of white sand, as if both sea and shore were joyously locked in a flirtatious game. Who was seducing whom remained unclear.

Except in the case of Du Parquet. The sights he beheld were of such intense celestial beauty, they were enough to have given him several bouts of vertigo. But whether he was made groggy by the steady and heavy-scented breeze, or the anticipation of owning a piece of this seemingly eternal chain of real estate, is undecided. He was however, unable to recall riding at anchor off Santa Lucia for the duration of time it took half his expeditionary force to wade ashore.

In his condition of fuzziness, the azure blue skies with puffs of cotton-clouds, typical of a tourist brochure, and the foam-spotted seas, all seemed the same. The many islets, reefs and shoals were way-stations for rest, sight-seeing and the resupply of food and water for persons engaged in long and tiresome journeys. The sun varnished everything in its path, making the land, sea and sky picture-perfect; its gloss wasn't illusory.

My Mother and I

For Du Parquet's part, he was existing in a state of nirvana, and would have overshot his final destination but for one thing: there was simply no other like it!

Chapter 3

A group of wandering Spanish sailors more than one century before, could hardly be considered aesthetically impoverished. They knew top-of-the-line quality whenever they saw it. The green hills and bays, white and black sand beaches, unparalleled scenery, a country completely at peace with itself, conjured up images of Granada in Spain. It was the closest to the genuine article they could get.

For the Caribs it was not Granada, it was Camerhogne – 'Spiritual Home' – of the Carib people. This 120 square miles of serenity they considered hallowed ground and prayed to their many Gods to keep it that way; particularly to Atabeyra, the earth Mother, and guardian of moving waters and childbirth.

Priapos, the Greek God of procreation, would have been envious of the Carib's sexual appetite; but not their birth control practices, which were always based on the community's ability to feed and care for its young.

Nonetheless, little disturbed their obsession for male children who were seen as potential hunters, fishermen, fighters and defenders of the Carib home. The ears, nasal bone and lip of the babies were pierced, their foreheads flattened, in time giving the adults a slanting forehead and prominent eyebrows. This, it was said, did wonders to the shooting-eye; a claim that Du Parquet wasn't anxious to verify.

The bows, arrows and poisoned spears were used both as legitimate weapons of defense and as necessary tools for the gathering of food.

Since they were enterprising farmers, hunters and fishermen, much of their diet contained cocoa, corn, yam, sweet potato, arrowroot, beans, peanuts, pineapples and citrus, guava and papaya. Their staple was cassava, which they grated into flour and cooked over a clay griddle. Cotton and tobacco were also grown. A great deal of their proteins came from fish, of which they had an inexhaustible supply, and the agouti, manicou, iguana, birds and snakes which they hunted.

No wonder the Caribs always exuded robust health. They were rock-ribbed, broad-chested and copper-skinned, with long, straight black hair, regularly washed and oiled. At the sight of what they wore, a European would have thought that cloth was scarce. It could have been a fiercely waged battle between loincloth and apron struggling for the upper hand. The optimist would have scored heavily for apron, while the pessimist would claim that loincloth won by knockout.

The Carib women themselves were natural knockouts, with perfectly toned, well-rounded, tantalizingly proportioned bodies. Their breasts seemed to rejoice in the unfettered freedom which European breasts were denied; and stood out sag-proof, firm and arrogant, as if ready to challenge the fetishes of the imminent intruder. They tied their calves with strips of cotton causing it to swell; this was considered attractive and gave the Carib men cause for pause.

Body-paints were artistically used by the Caribs, sometimes to give prominence to a few well-chosen parts of the body, employing complex and sophisticated designs. It all depended on which part of the body they thought needed the viewer's attention or the desired mood to be evoked. For such occasions as feasts and raids, no time was spared in contriving patterns of red and yellow, black and white.

The jewellery with which they bedecked themselves – necklaces, earrings, nosebones, arm and knee bands – were made from animal teeth, bird bones, fish vertebrae, shells and crystals. Thus bejewelled, against a harmonious mix of riotous colours, they were altogether sightly and gorgeous.

The indigenous people of Camerhogne and the Caribbean were master craftsmen, weavers, carvers and potters. They gave their skills to the production of vitally needed tools and utensils, including the mortar and pestle, which were used for grinding cocoa; and calabash containers.

But they were never able to contain their religious fervor. The images of their many Gods were made of clay, shell or cotton, and were called Zemies; with which they decorated ceramic pots.

At times their religious ceremonies involved the eating of miniscule quantities of human flesh, not as a means of supplementing their diet, but as a ritual act. The Caribs believed, as many other cultures before them and since, that in so doing the essence and admired qualities of the person would be transferred to them. This act was restricted to the cadavers of only their Chief, community leaders, and those who may have shown exceptional brilliance in community-uplifting activities. It was their equivalent of "the body of Christ" as depicted by the Christian Eucharist. It was foolhardy then to believe that because Spanish law permitted the enslavement of cannibals, did it mean that potential slaves were cannibals!

Gods of benevolence and gods of curse were the architects and guardians of the Caribs' destiny. Today it was one of the former on duty; at least for the moments he was able to stay awake.

The Caribs had already completed yet another war-raid on a neighboring settlement. These raids resulted from the intense rivalry between some Carib communities and the ongoing feud between the Caribs on the one hand and the Arawaks on the other – Amerindians who were driven to establish new settlements on the larger islands.

Competition and the struggle for dominance were the grist for the fierce battles which were fought. But they were also used as the staging ground for initiation into manhood and warriorhood.

If it had been a social event, it would have been a stag party, since the women were never allowed to bear arms. Nonetheless, even in the throes of combat their menfolk were unable to forget the high-spirited, ebullient, go-get-'em send-offs which they received. It was always a heartwarming occasion before setting off on the cold seas aboard their ocean-bound, sturdy-built, ceiba and silk cotton wood canoes, measuring between forty and ninety feet.

The Caribs tenaciously defended every square inch of their home, keeping intact its sanctity for hundreds of years. In war they proved themselves adept in the use of decoys and chameleons in the use of camouflage.

It would have been nigh impossible to have seen from the sea the Carbets and thatched homes of the Carib community, inconspicuously nestled between the unshed greenery of tall trees, which were looking up at even taller mountains. Their

Chapter 4

On some other day the Caribs would have been resting in their hammocks, enjoying a brief siesta; relative quiet would have reigned over Camerhogne. They would have refused outright to disturb a scene so ethereal and risk being reprimanded by one of the evil spirits. Or it could have meant that they had been overpowered by their own strain of 'eat-and-sleep'.

Except that the sweet rhythmic sounds floating upon the pepperpot-flavoured gentle wind was alive with activity and merry-making. One would have been at pains to be anything less than captivated and a Philistine to be unmoved.

But moved one did to a scene astir with festivity. It was the feast of Yocahu – 'Giver of Cassava'- a male God residing in volcanoes, whose chest was swollen with pride at what he saw.

The dance wasn't the Spanish bolero, and this was no modern-day, open-air theater. But they offered features of both, nicely wrapped into an attention-grabbing, body-shaking package.

In the center of the large square, perimetered on one side by the carbet, and on another by thatched houses, were the dancers basking in the heat of a ceremonial masked dance.

They numbered fifty and were sub-divided into five groups. Each group had its fair share of men and women, who were themselves individual links in one extensive chain.

Looking up from a circle maintained with geometric accuracy, were colourfully painted masked faces. None wore expressions of melancholy or disappointment. They were facial contortions expertly crafted into perpetual demonstrations of joy, contentment, glee, triumph, ecstasy, enchantment, exaltation, good cheer and well-being. Some laughed, smiled, grinned and smirked. Others had the effrontery to sneer at those gathered around.

But any ridicule felt was softened and rendered neutral by the fierce interplay of multi-coloured masks, which appeared, as heads moved, jostling among themselves for dominance.

The red, yellow, white, green, blue, cream, pink and orange flowed joyously into equally iridescent bodies, swaying, writhing and undulating to the music which was heavy with the beat of percussion instruments.

The musicians too, were similarly decorated and occupied a position close to the carbet and diagonally opposite the dancers. Some sat while others stood; and they each held before them the instrument with which they contributed their individual pinch of melodious salt to the ragtime potpourri.

Bamboo flutes and wooden piccolos sparred and parried among themselves; each musical note sharp but flowery like the tweeting and trilling of birds at the first light of dawn. But they were never so selfish as to refuse to accommodate the little idols used as rattles; its sound, an octave lower than the lively input of the 'shak-shak', the fruit of the flamboyant tree.

The Caribs made music with just about anything they could lay their hands on; and if suitable material was unavailable, heaven knows, they may well have resorted to dancing to their own heartbeats.

But the dancers were also moved by the zanzas and the tock-tock measured sound of sticks, which were being knocked against each other. They were cut to specific dimensions, and each gradation seemed to hold its own musical secret that quickened dancing steps when revealed.

What the sticks didn't succeed in doing, drums accomplished with merely a grumble. Their rich, pulsating rhythms taunted the dancers into actions, which were thoroughly expressive and suggestive. Every moveable part of refreshingly hued, sweat-covered bodies, spoke lustily of emotions felt. It was easy to tell that nimble fingers and the palms of wizards had worked its spell into the thick of the day's festivities.

And into the cadence of the chorus singers. Their voices had a swing that skipped its way merrily across, in and around, the pitapat, pitter-patter, thump-thump of the drums. These teasing, cajoling, but-never-rejecting rhythms of the drummers were responses to refrains, which were vocalizing a life of struggle, sacrifice, hard work, godliness, brotherhood and love for Camerhogne

The songs were delivered with a timbre, which held a sweetness as powerful as love. It was the gel which brought to heel any discordant instrument and gave the final touches to a marketable product; not dissimilar to the way the bandmaster uses his baton.

But like some haughty and pompous people, the drums were determined to have the final say. Throbbing sounds rolled off smooth surfaces and went straight to the heart, as unerringly as Cupid's arrow.

Enough to have set the dancers' feet chipping along. Moving towards each other from a tightly held circle, their hands were upraised in supplication to Yocahu. And until no more forward movement was possible, they twitched their bottoms from left to right as if responding to a drill instructor. Now bending forward, torsos parallel to legs, they reversed their dancing steps; the ultimate show of total respect for, and complete submission to, the "Giver of Cassava."

They were just as thankful to the "Giver of Life" who made possible the boogie-woogie and shimmy which they were now executing in fine style. Heed was no longer paid to any particular formation, but instead, individual dancers engaged in the choreography of their own moves.

There was flinging of hands and feet aplenty. For some this was the moment for plain and simple gyration. Others were manoeuvring their hips into various configurations with such amazing grace and deliberation, one would have thought that they had the whole afternoon for nothing else. Any European press report of this festivity would have carried the headline "Read my hips!"

Throughout it all the expressions on the masked faces never did change. Nor did the colours, which were as gay as the well-articulated body language. There was no let up in the uptempo medley of the instrumentalists. Nor in the harmonizing and perfectly pitched voices of the chorus singers. No change but for the sun which tarried awhile longer than seemed necessary. All was as it should be for the feast of the God residing in volcanoes.

And in his honour a young boy emerged from the sidelines, and in the midst of the dancers, poured the contents of a clay bowl on the ground; a libation of fermented drinks.

Anymore pouring would have been down their throats as they all participated in the drinking and eating that were characteristic of these festivities. The thought of this appeared to goad them into more frenzied activity; certainly they were doing things which they never did before.

But as sudden as an unexpected shower of rain, a cloud of silence drifted over the entire Carib community. One could have plotted its course as it inched along ominously from one end of the square to the other. Dark clouds, clouds thick with dread!

The Chief, Kaierouanne, now standing at center-stage, had the attention of everyone. Not only because all were anxious to hear what he had to say, but also he exerted tremendous influence and commanded the respect accorded popularly elected leaders.

The place was dead quiet! Waves beating against sandy shores hundreds of yards away, could have been distant thunder-claps. The gentle flutter of leaves in winds both soothing and lightly caressing, sounded loud to the ears. It was an ill-wind!

"A ship of the misshapen enemy has been seen drifting towards Camerhogne," the Chief said, his face stern, his bearing soldierly.

He did not need to say anymore. Except for the minds ravaged by senility or still tender and uncomprehending, those words painted a thousand pictures. Snap-shots of fierce battles fought in defense of their homeland raced through their minds. Twice in the last forty-one years they'd had to use every means homes were unadorned. Their exterior unpainted, with all the hallmarks of freshly hewed wood, lent itself to the natural colour and texture of the trunks of trees and surrounding woodland. And the thatched roofs? Nothing but a few withered branches grouped together in the comfort of old age, struggling to stave off the encircling vitality of an otherwise unsmeared forest.

But the thick undergrowth wasn't thick enough to protect entirely its privacy from the inquisitive eye of the sun. It pierced its rays into the barest opening, craning its neck to see everywhere and deliberately creating the kind of shadow that would give one the uncanny feeling that in there lives the gods of curse; or at worse, that some ghostly or evil spirit lurked there.

Elsewhere the sun was on its best behaviour, dressed resplendently in gold garments, and slightly flamed-coloured at its core. If the sun were the queen then the sky was the lady-in-waiting decorously attired in blue. The milk-white clouds were the servants scurrying to relay the royal edicts to the queen's lesser subjects.

And they could not fail to be impressed by this ostentatious display of royal power as the sovereign held court. They stood helplessly by while the sun extended its glittering and glorious influence over the trees, hills, valleys and mountains; over the animals of the wild, and the birds of the air. Everything looked majestic!

Nor were the rivers, streams and springs able to escape the sway of the monarch. Their cool, clear glistening waters carried on business as usual, reciting its often heard mantra of purity, and sang a well-practiced lullaby.

at their disposal to repel the efforts of invading forces. And they were destined to do so again.

Those who did not learn their history by being witnesses to its unfolding did so via the family-tree or the community's Griot. But they all knew that the Chief's words were synonymous with the command, "Prepare for War!"

Chapter 5

Du Parquet couldn't believe his eyes. As far as he was concerned this was the jewel of all jewels and his to be had.

First, however, he had an immediate problem to overcome. There was the sea breeze blowing in fits and starts; unable to decide whether to be an abettor to Du Parquet's crime or an active saboteur. But its indecisiveness delayed his mission and gave him an opportunity to come to his senses; if that were indeed possible.

And judging from his jitters one would have had good reason to hope that common sense was within his grasp. By the time Du Parquet had set forth on his journey, the Carib's image as a fierce and warlike people had travelled half way around the world. He was well aware of the experiences of his forebears and others who had taken to the seas on similarly ill-advised expeditions. Nor was he able to keep at bay his own imagination of what fate awaited him if captured.

Cold hands of fear gripped his heart. The fitful winds could do nothing to stem the tide of his cold sweat, or to ease the discomfort of cold feet. And all of this, despite the hot, sunny weather that was the envy of Siberians.

He raised his head to the sun in search of inspiration, and then he saw it! The pristine landscape beckoned him forth, dealing first a blow to his apprehension. The sea breeze saw what was happening, and in its own self-interest quickly relented, allowing Du Parquet to sail straight into the warm welcome which the Carib's Reception Committee had prepared for him.

The afternoon was fading. The scene was tense. There wasn't now just the fluttering of leaves. Gassed by an increased flow of adrenaline, stout hearts flip-flopped with alacrity.

War-painted Caribs eyed Du Parquet's advance with the same wariness with which the bull watches the matador.

Dressed, as they usually are, in layers of clothing, Europeans always appeared abzocky to the Caribs; and with extreme relish referred to them as the "misshapen enemy."

But Du Parquet too, was doing his own watching for an adversary felt but not seen as they lay in patient ambush.

Poised for action, the Caribs' killer-darts, poisoned-spears and bow and arrows were well aimed. They took deep breaths to steady their nerves as Du Parquet and his crew came off the ship and into range.

The Caribs' hands fell off the 'triggers'! They were dumbfounded by what they saw. "Something just ain't right," they thought. It was not what they expected, and definitely not what they prepared for. What they were now seeing with their own eyes wasn't in keeping with their experiences or their well-rehearsed military exercises. Even the birds were momentarily quiet, and the Caribs' world may have stood still for a few seconds.

Coming off the ship were men covered in swaths of blood-stained bandages, faces screwed-up in pain and misery. They were carried on the shoulders of men, not as battered, but equally, victims of disaster.

Was it one of those unpredictable Caribbean storms? Was there a mutiny on board that had been quelled by further acts of violence? Was this the consequence of a drunken, free-for-all brawl? Or did one of the Gods of Benevolence unleash a pre-emptive strike in defense of the Caribs' interest?

Whatever it was, one must have felt sorry for Du Parquet and his badly wounded and scruffy-looking crew. As they got to the beach, one could hear a chorus of groans struggling to get past their lips. The mere act of groaning evidently caused them more pain.

Their breathing was laboured. Any second could've meant their final breath. Hands were variably held in slings, and broken or injured arms were virtually useless in battle. Their faces were lifeless and tainted with a gray pall. This hangdog and woebegone appearance presented an altogether pitiful sight, sufficient to have provoked tears of sympathy from a stone or to melt a small giant of an iceberg. But the Caribs were never so cold!

Slowly and cautiously they emerged from their well-concealed positions and a formation which made it demonstrably clear just how easily the misshapen enemy would've been netted. An involuntary hiss escaped the dried lips of the would-be captives!

The Caribs, however, were brandishing no weapons. Nothing more dangerous than pleasant smiles; the forerunner to the hastily revised version of the warm welcome about to be executed.

Du Parquet and his crew visibly relaxed as the Caribs drew near, reciprocating with waning smiles of their own, caught between anguish and growing relief.

The extended hand of the Carib Chief, Kaierouanne, was quickly grasped and enthusiastically pumped by no other than Du Parquet himself; anxious to assure all that the new-arrivals were men of peace. Unable to communicate in the language of each other, he quickly pantomimed what appeared to be a scene of immense tragedy.

"We had been adrift for over one week without any idea of where we were. A vicious storm had struck in the middle of the night blowing away a piece of the mast, damaging the rudder, and causing other destruction and chaos. Amidst a valiant effort to save the ship, eight men died and others seriously injured. In the days following, whatever repairs possible were carried out, but in the growing hardship tempers flew, and with it fists, feet and other objects. As you can see, minimal force was used to discipline the men.

"We're tired and our supplies are limited. We beg of you your hospitality until our ship can be made sea-worthy again, and the men have recovered."

Even if Du Parquet had been able to communicate in words their misfortune, nothing said could've been as convincing as his actions. The gloomy expressions remained glued to their faces. Their dejected look and drooping shoulders were as if they were labouring under the weight of the entire world.

The Carib Chief in turn pantomimed his sympathy and their willingness to share their home with men of peace and in need of rest and care.

Abruptly he turned and indicated that they should follow. And follow they did, not the customary brisk pace of the Caribs; but a gait more leisurely out of consideration for the injured, weak and hobbled.

It was an unusual party that made its way by twilight to the Carib's community. The Caribs, anxious, eager and fussy hosts to their perpetual enemy, 'the white man', were all smiles. Their guests ambled along, unsure of their steps and destination, and were a mixture of intermittent moans and groans.

Chapter 6

The birds flew escort overhead, guarding their charges from the clutches of a slowly encroaching darkness. But their evening-song was light-hearted, filled with lots of fun, teasing and good cheer. Intended of course, to lift the mood of men burdened by their own thoughts and unhappy circumstances. Altogether, it was a lively accompaniment which announced to the Carib community the arrival of its unexpected visitors.

A hush descended on the community as authoritatively as the drop of the judge's gavel. Eyes popped out of heads as this motley group straggled in, so unlike the hearty strides of their men after a hard day's work. Man, woman and child looked with disbelief, and in the privacy of their own minds, attempted to fathom this rather strange turn of events.

Already rumours began to make the rounds as murmurs crescendoed into gossip. There were such vivid descriptions of a heroic battle fought; of brave men making mincemeat of an enemy armed with big guns; and for the goodness of the Carib heart, spared the lives of some, that any Hollywood scriptwriter could've been put to shame.

A stickler for truth, Kaierouanne quickly punctured the din with a few shouted sentences of what took place.

Mouths dropped open, chests expanded with immense pride and all eyes looked at their men with newfound respect.

All needed hands set about with bee-hive industriousness to find suitable quarters for their guests, and to make comfortable with the care and attention that is reserved for men of honour.

Soon they were resting king-like in five huts vacated for their use. Food and drink from the interrupted feast flowed ceaselessly and in abundance. Their wounds were attended to with tender hands. Each and every pantomimed wish was treated with the urgency of a command. No five-star hotel could've come anywhere near these five huts!

And soon, too, the guests began to ogle the Carib women. Their pain seemed to have now shifted from their arms, heads and feet, to their crotches. It may have been an agreeable pain, since there were no longer any moans or groans to be heard.

Luckily for them the Carib men did not notice since they were too busy being the good hosts; and were themselves slightly soused by the consumption of fermented drinks.

One who gives willingly experiences a grandness of heart larger than the sum of the individual person. Now add a touch of alcohol to this and philanthropy knows no bounds.

With slurred gesticulations, Kaierouanne invited his guests not only to eat, drink and be merry – unnecessary in the circumstances – but to adopt his home as theirs and to remain for as long as they may wish.

It was all the cue that Du Parquet may have been waiting for. Swooping down like vultures upon a freshly expired carcass, he gathered seven of his men and directed them to return to the ship for clothing and other basic supplies.

Wearing an undisguised look that was leery and eyes that were breasts-crazed, the men were reluctant to leave. The Carib Chief, wanting to be of assistance, offered to send two of his own men along and the use of two small canoes. Du Parquet at first declined the offer, but realizing that this could appear suspicious, quickly changed his mind. The men then left, unhurriedly, seven of them now actively pondering the rightness of Du Parquet's mission.

And in their absence the feasting went on; the guests fanatical in their acceptance of the Carib Chief's invitation. Injured arms appeared to leave their slings as fast as fermented drinks were emptied from clay bowls; and then slyly rushed against exposed womanliness. Feet once hobbled miraculously regained mobility, if only to get in the way of the gentler sex; who chose to regard such rude conduct either as innocent acts or playful teasing by lonely and traumatized men. Many shades kinder than would've been the opinion of their menfolk had they been restricted to the water-cart. As it is, they'd had more than their fair share of insobriety and everything took on a hazy and imprecise appearance. And whether such an excellent repast would come to an end was now also uncertain.

Du Parquet had no intention of being caught unawares. His swansong of the evening was a gift of glass beads and lace to his hosts as a token of his appreciation for the hospitality unselfishly extended. A gift that the Carib Chief graciously accepted, but would've done well to have known the old saying: beware of Greeks bearing gifts!

Meanwhile Du Parquet's seven-man detail, ably assisted by two well-muscled Carib canoeists, made easy work of the several bags which were carried from ship to shore.

When they first got to the bay, it was as quiet as the night was dark; as still as the stillness of a cemetery at midnight and as dark as the underworld. It was the type of night best suited for the work of evil spirits, when they can roam freely without the danger of being happened upon. But whether it was La Diablesse, Jumbie, Mamamaladie or Loupgaroo, it was an experience no one looked forward to.

Even with the sudden rustling of leaves and its unsettling sound-effect, the two Caribs had been certain that they weren't hearing spirits. What they heard were whispered voices floating across the sea from the ship to where they stood in amazement. And it ended abruptly as the rustling of leaves had been unexpected.

If Du Parquet's men had heard, and they should have, there was nothing to indicate; but there was uneasiness in the air!

It was enough to fire the two Caribs into pell-mell and furious activity: Eager as they now were to complete their assignment, leave the bay, and avoid any chance meeting with one of the evil spirits; a petrifying encounter which, it was believed, meant inescapable death.

So across the sea they rowed at break-neck speed. For all it may have mattered, Du Parquet's men sitting in the canoes could have been as light as helium-filled balloons. But they also considered the 'white man' jinxed, and privately were dying to escape their presence.

And so swiftly they moved, they soon found themselves on the starboard side of the ship which was facing the horizon.

Now, they reasoned, it's not unusual that trouble comes in pairs; and if even they may have been hearing spirits awhile ago, it was unlikely that what they were seeing was also spirits. Hearing them is one thing, but seeing them is the unfortunate experience of the damned and cursed. Their natural response therefore, was to engage in an act of self-denial: They just could not be seeing what they were seeing.

But yes, it had to be! There was definitely a light aboard the ship that had been snappishly extinguished. And just as rapidly, a cold breeze sent chills up their spines! In the reflected glow of the light, the angular faces of Du Parquet's men appeared to register the anemic, clammy look of the dead or one who had just seen a ghost.

The Caribs did not wait for answers to the questions their faces asked, but manoeuvred the oars with a dexterity their hands never knew.

They were steadying the canoes in no time at the bottom of the ladder which was on the port side of the ship. And four of the seven-man detail hurriedly scrambled aboard, lit a lamp, and after a pause of several minutes, had the bags expertly delivered into the canoes like stevedores of long service.

But not one word from them about the whispered voices or the light aboard the ship; strange happenings which the Caribs resolved to tell their Chief about. After a couple busy slices of the sea with their oars however, and a hasty return to the community, their experiences were buried and, pro tempore, forgotten in the alcoholic fog of the few remaining drinks.

Chapter 7

Within two weeks Du Parquet and his men had moved into their own temporary quarters, which, they argued, were necessary for the full and complete convalescence of the infirm.

And if their new quarters held any therapeutic value, it showed. In quick time bandages and slings were discarded. Limp steps became purposeful strides in pursuit of its daily routine. Their wounds which were no more than exaggerated blotches of the skin and slight bruises, left nothing behind to confirm their past existence. No more of the dejected look. Faces took on a glow as warm and optimistic as the sun. Here are a group of men, their foxy smiles said, who ran aground on the rocks of adversity and despair, and washed ashore on the beach of good cheer, health, hope and well-being.

The now recovered men wasted no time in getting involved in the hustle and bustle of activity. Constant pounding could be heard. Without the Caribs' permission, new structures were being added and with it came an air of permanence.

There was a growing trek between the ship and this embryonic settlement. And, for awhile, every trip made by the two apparently expropriated canoes appeared to magically increase the settlement's population.

The pollution and desecration weren't far behind. Grounds, which were considered especially sacrosanct, were recklessly defiled. Du Parquet and his men moved about with impunity and without any restrictions, and with the posture of the landed gentry. It wouldn't have been far-fetched for one who didn't know better to believe that the land on which these settlers stood came on the ship.

But they brought with them diseases unbeknownst to the indigenous people; and when the air became permeated with the fetid scents of the rotted, disused and unwashed, the intruders' diseases began to spread. Soon, many Caribs fell ill and their herbal medicines and centuries-old concoctions were of no use. The young and very old began to die of maladies which weren't understood except as the callous work of evil spirits which, more and more, the "misshapen enemy" came to represent.

Understandably so, relations between the Caribs and the Settlers were now extremely tense, and as taut as the strings of a bow.

Two weeks, however, is a long time for even the most affable of visitors to overstay their welcome. Much less five months. But the 'white-man' seemed determined to test to its limit the elasticity of the Caribs' hospitality and graciousness.

Six Carib women returning from the river one afternoon were waylaid and brutally raped by a roving band of twelve occupiers. Enraged, the Carib Chief dispatched two of his Elders to inquire about the motive for this dastardly act. One was summarily clobbered to death, and the other was favoured with his life at the costs of a fractured skull, smashed teeth, a broken arm and ribs.

There is no place in the world where such conduct would be tolerated, and certainly not within the borders of one's country; And even the most benign of peoples would be hard-pressed to take such treatment lying down. Was it not enough to deceitfully exploit the kindness and humanity of another?

To share the warmth of another's home and in return deface and tarnish it with your vile standards? And as if that wasn't sufficient, to set about destroying the home which opened its doors to you, its people and community?

But what conscionable thought has ever had the power of a drug to alter man's wild chase for money and profit; at the expense of lives and whole nations if necessary? What scruples have ever been more important than the needs of super egos?

The world was not about to grow out of its sad history; one in which weapons of destruction allowed persons to achieve what human decency will not permit.

But if these colonizers thought that that was enough to keep in check the righteous anger of the Carib people, then he wasn't on Camerhogne but living in a fool's paradise.

The Carib Chief, Kaierouanne, immediately summoned Du Parquet and pantomimed the riot act: leave Camerhogne within the next two sunsets, lock, stock and barrel, or face the eternal wrath and damnation of the Carib people and all their gods!

Du Parquet in response gave the Chief the full benefit of a sneer more contemptuous than any which the slave-master bestows on his slave. If looks could kill, he would've had no difficulty in conquering the world.

Chapter 8

Stormy clouds of expectation hung in the air. Not the aimless clouds making merry on a bright but uneventful day; not the careless clouds teeming with youthfulness, kissing and flirting with each other; but clouds nonetheless, laden with something sinister and made gray either with age or worries.

And yet it was a normal day in many respects; even though it was hot like hell! The leaves of the trees were courteous enough to genuflect occasionally when the wind bid them to. But in the face of the sun's heat they cringed.

The birds kept up their refrain of "Ka---mau you----tweet---------Kaaamau—youuu-----tweet," though without any enthusiasm; as if they were doing a paid job, and found no fulfillment in it. They, however, were unlike some animals in the wild that had long concluded that the sun was as potentially dangerous as man, and kept indoors.

A sensible thing to do considering the deluge of bodily streams which flowed everywhere. It would've happened anyway in the normal run of things. But a great sweat was being worked-up from increased activity that appeared to change nothing; yet very little could ever be the same again.

The Caribs' "misshapen enemy" seemed to fare the worst, dressed as they were in European garb. Nonetheless, it was a collective discomfort; the one that is no respecter of persons, the classless type.

Even the wind scrupulously rationed itself. When it gave, it did so equally; and when it withheld its services, it was to the detriment of all. Though, to neutralize the sun's roaring guns would've required a greater volume committed to the battlefield.

Maybe this common sauna bath was to be one of the last things to be shared by the Caribs and 'white man.' Their histories were different. Their worlds were, literally and figuratively, miles apart. Two worlds as distinct as Mars is to earth, and unable to converge; to attempt such is to invite the inevitable bloody finale.

One sunset had already gone and there was only one more to go. Never before had a sunset risen, albeit overnight, to assume such overwhelming importance; and invested with the power and authority to decide the fate of a people.

Held on a pedestal, it found its rightful place among the gods, Carib gods and European gods alike; and did nothing to command the respect of the faithful. There were no changes in the sun's daily journey; no quickening of steps, no altering of course, but the same deliberate sauntering from the east to its destination in the west.

Its slightest movement, even a shrug of its shoulder, received computer-speed calculation in time. No one wanted to waste any. In a land where life proceeded at an unhurried pace, time became a precious commodity; worthy of a princely price if sold commercially.

Everyone wished to be on time for sunset for fear of committing the most grievous act of lese majesty. On any other occasion it could've been the busy preparation for the community's ball, or the unexpected arrival of a famous person for dinner. But today Camerhogne was bursting with energy, because no one knew whether there would be time to do what must be done after sunset. And no one was quite sure what this eventide portended.

My Mother and I

The Caribs took to the high ground. Being a somewhat nomadic people, they were weighed down by few possessions; and it was therefore no Sisyphean task to 'pitch camp' further to the north and into the hills at short notice.

Kaierouanne had ordered the move. He did so for three reasons. The hills provided a greater degree of safety, especially for the women and children. It allowed them to make their own preparations away from the watchful eyes of the "misshapen enemy;" while benefiting from the advantage of keeping the enemy under close observation, without themselves being observed.

And worked fervently they did in perfecting their choices. Their canoes were now strategically located. Other Carib communities were placed on full alert. And they now waited with no little anxiety as the sunlight stepped towards sunset, like it was nobody's business.

The "misshapen enemy" was expediting theirs in a way which alarmed the Caribs. Around the settlement that they now called St. Louis, they were building tall barricades with cannon emplacements; which the Caribs called simply "big guns." They appeared to be all armed with muskets and pistols, which were also "big guns." The swords and bayonets were dubbed the "white-man's spears".

They could've been at it for almost the entire day, working with white heat to ensure their own safety. And with every barricade added, and every additional weapon which came into view, the Caribs were better able to fine-tune their own strategy. Their choices became fewer and fewer.

But when the sun entered the home-stretch, St. Louis became silence itself. It was as if in one fell swoop, some unknown evil had smote the Settlers and robbed them of their voices.

There was no one to be seen and no movements whatsoever. St. Louis could've been a settlement hurriedly evacuated to protect lives from an imminent disaster.

Wherever they were, they watched apprehensively as the sun slowly drifted towards sunset. There were but few yards to go and it was taking its own good time, and enjoying it too. A recalcitrant child on an errand for her mother would've loitered less. But aware of where the eyes of the world were now focused, it luxuriated in the spotlight, savoring every moment of it.

Slowly but surely the sun showered the skies with the uniqueness of this phase of its journey; and cast Camerhogne in a glow that was orange and fiery.

The sun moved jauntily as it played to an audience held spellbound by its performance; an audience that experienced a suspenseful uneasiness as the final act drew near.

It could've been several suns doing the same thing at the same time, or the smoldering remains of burning logs which someone carelessly scattered all over. But the heavens were definitely carrot-hued.

Nothing escaped its ambience! Not the yellow-breasted Bananaquit birds or the red-flowered Flamboyant trees. Everything with life was affected and adopted the sun's warm glow as its own.

Now but an arm's length from its denouement, the ill-at-ease audience was treated to a splendid array of colours; orange, yellow, yellowish brown, red, reddish brown, yellowish orange, and quickly repeated again as though seen through a kaleidoscope.

All were completely silent in a disquieting kind of way, as if witnessing the tragic end of an otherwise brilliantly performed play. Or one may have been bidding farewell to a dear friend whom one is not certain of seeing again.

Then the sun took its final bow in a blazing reddish orange and disappeared over the horizon.

Chapter 9

A thunderous applause rang out from the Carib community, but it was not a curtain call. With eyes focused exclusively on the sun, they didn't see the ship of the "misshapen enemy" creeping furtively out of the bay and now in full sail away from Camerhogne.

When they saw the ship under sail, it was their best sight since the arrival of Du Parquet and his crew, and their response was instinctive. They were relieved to see the back of their heads rather than their rude, arrogant and angular faces. And they were grateful for a victory that did not require them to waste their spears, poison darts and arrows on those they found utterly detestable.

But the perceptive Kaierouanne knew something was wrong and counseled vigilance. His Intelligence Network soon told him what he suspected and it wasn't what most Caribs were inclined to believe.

Du Parquet wanted to convey the impression that they'd conceded to the Caribs' ultimatum, and so set sail. In so doing he hoped to lull the Caribs out of their mountainous sanctuary, and into rash actions, for which Du Parquet and his men were suitably prepared.

It was an opportunity, Du Parquet also calculated, to mobilize reinforcements that would surely be needed, if the Caribs' reputation were anything to go by.

The main reason, however, for the quick dash of the enemy's ship was less obvious. The "misshapen enemy" was woefully outnumbered. And against the Caribs' hardiness, Du Parquet had no confidence in his barricades and cannons. Fearing for his personal safety, and along with a skeleton crew, Du Parquet did the next best thing: took flight! Thus, it was a victory of sorts for the Caribs to learn that not they alone were with fears; the occupiers had theirs too.

And much more so for Le Compte, Du Parquet's cousin, who was now in charge. In charge of a settlement that had the lingering feel of abandonment; and only heads peering through windows and doors during the day, told of the presence of its occupants. They were much too old to be living under parental curfew, neither were there any known cases of agoraphobia among the occupiers. It was more like Caribphobia!

A paralyzing fear gradually eased its hold each day the Caribs failed to appear. Then they hunkered down behind their barricades with a good demonstration of bravado; and when no arrows came calling, they chanced a few moments outside the barricades. They became more daring with every step further afield. But no spears paid them any interest, so they ventured into the surrounding woodlands with the spunkiness of a conquering army.

Poisoned darts were more often felt than seen. They cut the air with a swish and embedded themselves in soft white flesh, each choosing its own bull's-eye. They took to their unaccustomed targets with the ardour of a young lover, dispensing with their charms amidst wild protest.

A cacophony of Ahs! Oh God! Ugh! Help! erupted from the forest floor, shattering the tranquility and committing a sin the inhabitants found unforgivable.

To make matters worse the settlers were indiscriminately discharging their muskets and pistols to frighten the Caribs away. But the bedlam this created sounded more like the Battle Of The Bulge, and may have only added to their own panic.

Those who were still able to run found paths out of the forest no one knew ever existed. Closely following on their heels were spears, which for the first time showed some fondness for their former guests. And those who didn't as yet feel the need to stop their mad scampering, did everything to avoid the arrows that desired nothing more than to pay their respects.

It was a horror-stricken enemy who, with due haste, made their way behind the barricades and hunkered down for another confidence-building exercise.

But Le Compte could have as well proclaimed a state of siege. Had they seen their nemeses they would have known where to look; and a Carib in the dark was worth two hundred in the bush; An unacceptable ratio for offensive action. Perhaps, though, it was a "collateral damage" assessment that convinced them that there was no place like 'home'.

Chapter 10

The Caribs kept a silent vigil as the days matured into weeks; fretting at the delay in the war and its apparent stalemate, and wondering "what the hell the white-man doing inside there so long."

They couldn't understand that an enemy armed with "big guns" could be afraid of a people armed with bows and arrows. But with their dignity, national pride and an inalienable right to their land, and the determination of their own destiny, they could hardly have been better fortified.

However, they understood their own fears and kept well out of range of the cannons, occasionally spitting more fire than an abused dragon. But the point was clearly made and the Caribs stuck to their turf.

Kaierouanne held his peace but everyone knew what he was thinking; there was one man who escaped too lightly, and that was Rear Admiral Du Parquet. He badly wanted to administer to Du Parquet's rear the very best of his poison darts!

He knew, however, that the arriving ships weren't going to provide him with another opportunity. They sailed towards Camerhogne swiftly; cutting its waters with the sharpness of a scythe making easy work of a sugar-cane field.

But there was nothing sweet about their arrival. Already they'd won the loyalty of the trade winds, and the hundreds of men aboard. They disgorged so many "big guns" and tons of foods, the Caribs could've fainted; except that the deep hatred and disgust they felt proved to be the correct antidote.

And swore they did to rid their homeland of all these evil scums, as they were seen by the Caribs, even if their gods were to mandate that the fight be continued from their graves.

Presently, St. Louis came alive with militancy. No more the grumpiness of occupiers beleaguered, but the spirit and sparkle of despots in shining armour. And ready to take on the whole world judging from the lively chatter riding astride a reluctant afternoon breeze.

With the strength that comes from numbers and superior technology they hurled themselves back into the woodlands. Their eyes were set on naked genocide and the thirst for revenge oozed out of their bodies.

Cannons belched forth high explosives in volumes equal to a full scale war; saturating the forest with its acrid scent. Muskets and pistols peppered everything within its range. Not even a frog could've lifted its head if it needed a breath of fresh air; in any case, there was none available. The sound of deadly weapons was deafening; and perhaps as lethal as the bullets themselves for one with a weak constitution.

There was no let-up. Vast acres of plants were destroyed. Trees lost their branches with a creaking agony; and those that were still standing had their leaves removed by an autumn of slugs and cannon balls. Life in its natural habitat – plants, insects, animals – was destroyed, to be replaced by desolation. The frenzy came to an end only when they were satisfied that the Caribs as a threat were finished.

Except there were no Caribs there! With fuming rage they combed deep into the undergrowth but without success. However, they were successful in finding their way back to the encampment to plan again, and feeling like a frustrated bully.

Chapter 11

In two days they were back on the trail armed to the teeth and with an order from Le Compte: "The Caribs must be killed; find them and find them fast!" And Le Compte, by the tactics he outlined, thought he was well on the way to achieving his barbarously colonial objective.

Several bands of occupiers entered the forest, as soundlessly as heavy boots on dried twigs would allow. They did so from different points, which formed a loosely drawn arc and extended to as far as their forces permitted. It was inconceivable, Le Compte thought, that the Caribs would break out of his creative application of the deadly pincer. And once cornered he could then roast their bottoms at his own timing. First, though, he had to locate the Caribs; an adversary who had, thus far, remained elusive to both their sights and superior technology.

But the people of Camerhogne knew their country well. They understood the best ways to which its resources could be put to use; chiefly as a means of survival. And defense had always been an integral part of their survival. Defense against the daily dangers of living; defense against the curses of evil Gods, be it in the form of diseases or 'the white-man' whom they thought was curse itself.

They were by no means frugal. It is just that they used whatever they had, efficiently and wisely. A virtue which served them well became a plague for the "misshapen enemy."

Sooner than they expected, the occupiers discovered that the Caribs were far more adroit at finding them than they were at finding the Caribs. And the Caribs found them fast!

This unsettling news came from the direction they least expected: from their rear! As the occupiers were bushwhacking in search of their enemy, the Caribs were creeping up at the backs of theirs. When the occupiers thought that they'd spotted their enemy, the Caribs had definitely seen theirs. And when the occupiers were primed to discharge their weapons, the Caribs were discharging theirs.

'Swosh! Swosh! Swosh! Swosh! Swosh!' arrows leapt from their bows with the agility of leopards and found their targets without much ado. The chorus of oieee's and ah's with which they were received told one that they got something to yell about.

And to run about. Fortified by a small armoury, they dashed in the direction from which the arrows appeared to come; and they did so with blazing guns. They plastered the forest good and plenty, and there was little chance that the archers could've survived. But the Caribs had disappeared as quickly as the arrows had appeared.

For two years the Caribs ran rings around their enemy; harassing them and whittling their numbers and confidence with the punctilious and painful work of a surgeon's knife without the benefit of anaesthesia.

And their means were simple yet sophisticated. No guided missiles, no 'smart' bombs. Strictly lo-tech.

Too often the enemy was startled out of their wits, frightened to death or inflicted with serious injury by objects which fell out of trees of their own whim, or so it seemed. Sometimes too, unusually twisted vines and sharply pointed sticks would take a fancy for the feet of the occupiers, and all they got for their compassion were squeals of anger.

Their steps were irresolute and as unsure as were their chances of seeing tomorrow's sunrise. Ground, which was once firm and compact, would treacherously give way to a bed of punji sticks. The Caribs' 'misshapen enemy' became so paranoid that leaves which rustled too hard were speedily torn from their branches by a hail of bullets; and they would keep on shooting long after the leaves fell to the ground.

That wasn't all, though! The Occupiers had to put up with the Caribs' own rendition of biological warfare. They produced noxious gases by scattering hot pepper over a fire. Or the innards of dead animals were placed in containers and then buried for periods up to four months, depending on the exigencies of war. When they were uncovered, a more evil-smelling, fecal stench to assail the nostril could not be discovered. Perhaps, though, the gods had favoured the Caribs with the most fanatic of all natural allies: Pois-gatee, which the Caribs dubbed "scratchers." It was the flower of a plant that stuck to the hides of animals, the skin of man, or anything with which it came into contact. And when it did, it was with the tightness of a shoe one size too small, and with itches many times the capacity of a crab louse at its worst.

The Caribs knew it and avoided it. Their enemy did not! The Caribs reported to their Chief that the 'white-man's' first baptism in Pois-gatee was about the most hilarious experience they ever had. They just couldn't help laughing even though they risked giving away their hidden positions. And they did, but the enemy simply couldn't be bothered.

There they were, well dug in and with the enemy under close observation, when, without any warning, the 'white-man' performed the fastest striptease ever seen. With clothes piled on weapons they clawed at themselves and scratched with the ferocity of tigers. Heads and toes, backsides and crotches, chests and backs, everywhere became bruised and marked with red blotches. Twenty-five starkly naked men were poised for flight when they heard the uproarious laughter, which burst forth uncontrollably. The next thing the Caribs saw were ghostly apparitions streaking pass their positions, and no one was left standing where, half a second before, 'the white-man' stood.

The occupiers never knew what hit them. The Caribs did! They held their tummies, rolled on the ground and screamed with mirth until their sides ached and their facial muscles cried out in protest and begged them to stop.

But the war was no laughing matter and the humiliation had gotten under the occupiers thick skin. They moved in concentrated numbers and with a fresh determination to wipe out the Caribs once and for all.

Chapter 12

They who were the indigenous inhabitants of Camerhogne and toilers of its soil; They who were the keepers of its peace, resources and natural beauty; the custodians of its rich heritage, were targeted to become cannon-fodder in their own country. Much more than they had already been. When the explosives came their way, more often than not, it was a shot in the dark. But that did not in any way minimize the scorching force with which it tore into bodies, ripping lives and limbs apart. And while the deadly weapons chewed-up all and everything in its path, the diseases brought in by the settlers, which had long opened its own front, sucked lives like a leech.

Throughout it all the Carib women never once flinched in their increased responsibilities. They became doctors and nurses, administering all the known remedies, and even coming up with some of their own whenever it seemed necessary. They set broken bones, applied tourniquets, and suffered with their men in the throes of death.

And they prayed damn hard too, beseeching the gods for all their needs. But while they prayed they did everything to supply their men with enough food; and helped with the constant restocking of bows and arrows, spears and killer-darts.

Whatever else may have been exhaustible, never their love and devotion. They were tireless in their support and loyalty. Their dedication was never in short supply. And they stood shoulder to shoulder with their men, sharing the good days and the bad; and a commitment to face together whatever future the Gods may have decreed.

However, the ravages of war are always more difficult to endure for the less equipped, and the Carib fighters were feeling profoundly its pinches.

They fought heroically, but the enemy's cannons, muskets and pistols effectively neutralised the advantage they had in numbers. What their projectiles did not do, their diseases did; painfully chipping away at an army of skilled and seasoned fighters. And they weren't able to replenish their stock and their ranks at the rate that would have satisfied the needs of the battlefield. Neither were they, with fewer hands now available to plough the fields, able to maintain the nutritional requirements of fighting men.

The war effort had begun to sap their energy. Less alert, less cautious, fatal errors were made. Not once, not twice, but several times the enemy's bullets caught them unawares, perforating bodies and spattering the badly charred forest with the blood of a Nation being systematically devastated.

But here and there the verdant landscape fought back, cleaving possessively to its unspoilt beauty. The wind continued to stir the trees and tall grasses and vines; it still hummed refreshingly, as yet unburdened by the scent of decay and decadence of a growing foreign occupation.

The cool, crystal waters of the rivers and streams on which the sun maintained the golden glitter of its unchallenged influence, were less resistant. They were never able to wash away the vestiges of genocide. Nor the desire to own and control the mountains, valleys and plateaux of fertile land that was Camerhogne.

All Invaders and Occupiers suffer the same misconception: Adam and Eve bequeathed to them the land of their choice to do with as they pleased; and its people to cast into a life of deprivation or death, whichever came sooner.

The Caribs preferred death and the "misshapen enemy" waded into their blunders to hasten its occurrence. It was not long before they discovered the Caribs' sanctuary and struck a decisive blow. They let loose with everything they had, drowning out the wild, frightened and desperate shrieks of a hunted people. Men, women and children were decimated. Weapons discharged in a maddening frenzy brusquely cut short the plaintive and pitiful screams of the bloodied and dying. And when lips were sealed by death, and no longer able to raise a mournful note, for good measure, the occupiers treated the makeshift camp to a fusillade of hell's-fire.

Some who attempted escape were brought down in mid-stride. Others successfully made it downhill and into the anxious and waiting arms of the dense undergrowth.

There was no time to moan; barely enough to regroup and face a hotly pursuing, wretched and cursed enemy.

But the back of the resistance had been broken. With so many of their compatriots blasted sky-high, the Caribs had lost some of their best soldiers and with them the cohesion of a tightly organised fighting force.

Their sudden thrusts, then quick bobs and weaves were perfunctory, as they were driven further and further to the north; until, with more of their warriors wiped out, some taking to their canoes, they travelled to the furthest point and came face to face with ultimate destiny.

Chapter 13

The Caribbean Sea, bathed in a greenish-blue colour, beat harshly against a cluster of sharply pointed molten rocks, jutting out at the base of a precipice whose elevation topped one hundred and twenty feet. One could tell that the sea-god was angry by the amount of foam being spewed all over. Angry, perhaps, by the knowledge that it was powerless to bring to a halt the savage and unjust treatment of the Caribs. Nonetheless, after the rigours of war and the loss of their kith and kin, the Caribs found the scene a welcoming site.

As welcoming a site as were the volcanic mountains sporting a screen of luxuriant vegetation, none of which had lost its verdure despite the environmentally hostile streak of its occupiers.

The trees looked bereft, bowing their heads like a congregation listening to the intonement of a eulogy; Maybe it was because the wind blew as light as gossamer, just enough to let one know it was alive but not enough to instill life.

There was something disturbing about the way the trees kept their bent heads in the direction of the foaming sea; even refusing to chance an occasional glance at the sky.

Pale blue and with the attendant gray clouds, the sky had a distinctly somber appearance. As if its dour mood stamped on heavy clouds would, at any moment, condense into calamitous events that would water the seeds of Camerhogne's future development.

It was an open face, yes, the one the sky wore; as open as if the words "bad omen" had been boldly written across its underbelly.

With the sun told to remain indoors, gloom reigned supreme that day. But very little seemed to have penetrated hearts and minds that were stout and Carib.

They raised their heads to the sky, willing the trees to do the same. Proud heads, like the proudness of a people who'd stood up to the obscene desires of an unscrupulous enemy. An enemy armed with big guns who'd committed larceny on a grand scale. A treacherous enemy. And where double-dealing was concerned, the Caribs considered "the white-man" singularly ambidextrous.

True, they'd been far out-gunned and it pained their hearts that they were ill-equipped to do to their unscrupulous enemy what they so badly wanted to do.

They'd lost their loved ones and that saddened them greatly; but they knew that their spirits were resting comfortably, having done their gods proud in the cause for which they lived, fought and died.

Now, they'd lost everything, their community, their land, their home, and for this they lamented. There was no longer anything worth living for.

They would die together, they decided, with their pride and dignity intact, with the honour of not having allowed themselves to become vassals of the occupier. With the knowledge that their spirit would rise again to haunt eternally all invaders and occupiers of Camerhogne.

And they preferred the hard rocks at the foot of the precipice a few yards away, rather than "the white man's" bullets. It was their way of ensuring that they left behind an inerasable mark on the pages of history; while relegating the enemy to the role of passive observer – rather than active maker – of one of its episodes.

The Caribs were herded together, forty of them, men, women and children, while the Carib Chief, Kaierouanne, led them in prayers to their many gods. For a moment they were as solemn as their surroundings as they gave thanks to their Makers including Atabeyra and Yocahu. They thanked them for the many blessings with which they were bestowed; for life and for a land well endowed with resources and for family and friends both dead and alive.

A special plea was made for the vengeance of all the gods combined to be hurled at the heads of the occupiers with the force of one hundred volcanoes. And finally they prayed to Obiyel Wa' obiran, the deity attending the souls of the dead. They asked for nothing more than to be given eternal rest.

But not before they hugged and kissed each other. Their eyes had a faraway look, seeing and yet not seeing as they gazed upon each other. Then upon the green hills and mountains, and strangely enough the trees appeared to be suddenly waving as a brief wind traipsed across the landscape.

They looked to the sky as if seeking the source of all life; but the brightly plumaged birds were heard more than seen, as they pierced the air with a few melancholy chirps. They may have been punctuation marks for the series of emotions that busily registered themselves on the faces of the Caribs. There were quick flashes of regret, abandonment, courage, despondence and dispiritedness. But, in the end, defiance won out!

Kaierouanne, with a shout that could've been a cry of martyrdom, rushed forward with quick steps and threw himself bodily over the one hundred and twenty feet high precipice. The sound of flesh spattering on the rocks below rose up chillingly and merged with similar sounds, as each Carib, one pace behind the other, hurled him or herself over, while flinging curses at the enemy. It was a sickening and macabre sight!

Chapter 14

By the fuss the seagulls were making, one would've thought that they'd sighted a school of fish and not the pulverised remains of a people.

When the occupiers arrived shortly after, hot, sweaty and out of breath, it was the cawing, hooting and cooing of the seagulls, which attracted them to the location of the Caribs' leap into history.

And what they saw caused their own stomachs to revolt. Just this one part of the Caribbean Sea could've been called the Red Sea because there was blood everywhere. Blood too thick to wash away or too resistant to give up so easily. Blood that spread its redness in an ever-widening arc. The rocks were equally red. But more gruesome were the seemingly endless pulpy bits and pieces of human flesh scattered indecently about. It was possible for the occupiers, in a few cases, to identify parts of the body, especially hands and feet; though by now they'd seen enough.

The horrible sight had told its own story. It was far worse than if they themselves had pulled the trigger. That they may have been able to live with, but not this! Such a messy ending of life was never meant to be. It was an affront to their own values, even as debased as they'd shown them to be.

My Mother and I

In their own minds the occupiers were questioning whether it was worth it. They hadn't felt the sense of fulfilment that they'd expected at seeing the end of the Caribs. It was no victory! But the callous and cold-minded destruction of a whole people and nation.

The events had impacted on them greatly. It was one they weren't likely to forget. They called the site of the Caribs' rendezvous with fate "Le Morne de Sauteurs" and the island they had violently robbed, "La Grenade."

Mother had had enough! She feared that her children may have been playing with a time-bomb, the way some would toy with matches.

In 1674, Mother sent packing those of them who'd formed themselves into a Company and had assumed ownership of the island. The rivers and valleys, hills, streams and beaches, and all within the borders of La Grenade, she now considered her own. The acres of fertile land, tobacco fields, together with its imported slave labour, came under her personal care.

So far so good! Except that the British were devout believers in the notion that to 'thief from thieves' would make God laugh; and soon engaged Mother in the "Mother of all battles" for possession of the island.

For ninety years they threw broadsides at each other with hardly a lull. Cannons, muskets and rifles belched forth in fierce contention; while muzzle-loaders did their utmost to add to the fracas and the totting up of those killed and injured. La Grenade changed hands often!

And while Mother and her antagonist were preoccupied with painting the sea crimson, Yocahu's anger was smouldering; and he thought that this was as good a time as any other to vent his rage.

Unfortunately for those of my family living in St. Louis, they learnt too late that they'd been doing so on top of a volcano; one of Yocahu's fixed places of abode.

He recognised no Statute of Limitations. And where crimes against his own people were concerned, he wouldn't even consider it. Fifty years were sufficient time within which to avenge the deaths of the Caribs. Their souls couldn't find peace if their prayers were not answered.

Neither was Yocahu willing to forget. When Du Parquet and his crew of despots arrived, it was His feast they rudely interrupted with characteristic craftiness. They shared in the food and drink served in His honour; And from that day proceeded to ruin the lives of the people for whom He was partly responsible. Of all the gods, Yocahu felt the obligation greatest on him in ensuring that the unjust deeds of the occupiers received their just deserts.

One fateful day in 1700, amidst the hubbub of war, Yocahu struck! With a growl, which sounded like the peal of thunder, artillery preparation and the snarl of a thousand bulldogs all in one, Yocahu blew his top and sent St. Louis zipping through the air.

For miles his clouds of ashes and dust hung everywhere and coated everything with its grime. The rumble and grumble told all that he wasn't quite through yet; emitting more and more lava as if spitting on the graves of the occupiers with the maximum disdain possible.

When all was quiet, Mother came out of her daze with the same feeling of one who'd just experienced a horrible nightmare. And in a jiffy she accused the British of exploding a secret weapon, a charge that could hold no water, considering the unmaking of St. Louis that had taken place. The land was simply laid bare. Nothing was left of the buildings, nothing of the fields and nothing of its people. As if all and sundry had miraculously ascended to heaven on the wings of a giant tornado.

And in its place everything was new. Yocahu may well have been following in part the Book of Genesis. He worked, perhaps, not with the same expertise of the Christian God, but it was a damn good try!

The topography was different too! Some of the land seemed to have been pushed further back, making mountains out of molehills and hills and hillocks out of lowlands; and each given a gentle curve.

It was a picturesque, circular setting for what, only a short while before, used to be land on which sat the many houses of the occupiers. Now it was a twenty feet deep lagoon, its waters untroubled and richly gray as if sweetened with ashes.

St. Louis had been completely unmade, but the final product had a touch of neatness, elegance, grace and artistry that was the work of the world's best architects and designers.

Just perchance, Yocahu may have also been saying to whomever the cap fitted, that if you must invade and destroy, then the responsibility is yours to rebuild, and with quality resources. If you don't have it, then there is even more reason why you must not invade.

But Mother was in no mood for elementary lessons, neither did she think that the now extinct St. Louis a location suitable for learning.

Pregnant with grief at her loss, she hurriedly gave birth to a new home, less than one mile away and named it Port Royal.

The unofficial respite in the war, which the volcano allowed, only lasted long enough for the completion of very basic engineering works. But as Mother never really stopped fighting to protect and defend her personal domain, so too she worked night and day to strengthen its capacity to defend itself.

And forever testing her own ability to reproduce, five years after Yocahu struck, Mother was again great with child. She was in labour for one year and delivered a sturdy young man whom she named Fort Royal.

Chapter 15

Unfazed was Mother despite the gruelling war being fought over La Grenade. She certainly found time for her illicit affairs and never regretted it. How could she? When Fort Royal proved to be just what was needed to show the British who was really man.

This emboldened Mother. Her amorous activities only grew and where her beaux were concerned she became less choosy; so intent was she to propagate the species.

One year later when Mother again became big with child no one was surprised. During the time that she was expectant, everyone was expecting her to bring forth a quality addition to the family. But Mother had her own plans.

It was a little runt whom she gave the unattractive name of Port Royal Prison. Perhaps that was good enough for a by-blow; and in any event, Mother needed a place for her growing number of captives, slaves and rebellious children.

The British fought bravely but Mother was tenacious. She kept her children in line with regimented discipline, and gave no quarter to the British when she could help it. On the occasions when she lost her grip on La Grenade, Mother fought back with everything she had to regain it. And regain it she did!

My Mother and I

No one knew what got into Mother's head one chilly and windy morn in early 1763, when she decided to append her signature to a peace treaty, and gave La Grenade away to her archenemy.

The British liked no better sport. With the gusto of a freshly made parent she renamed La Grenade "Grenada" and changed the names of Mother's children as well. Port Royal Prison became "St. George's Prison," Port Royal became "St. George" and Fort Royal was named "Fort George" after George III, reigning King of England.

But their stay was relatively brief, caught perhaps, between a G-string and a bikini. If Mother had lost her head she recovered it soon enough, and drove the British out of La Grenade after sixteen years.

Winds of war were gathering speed to blow more violently. Belligerence became the British second name, humiliated as she was by defeat. And pissed-off too by what she deemed deceitful and perfidious conduct on the part of Mother.

Throwing dust into British eyes is one thing; after all, she was Machiavellian enough to throw some of her own whenever the opportunity arose. But King George III felt deeply angered by Mother's support for the American Revolutionaries struggling to gain their independence from England.

If only to teach Mother a lesson, the British were determined to retake La Grenade. Mother resolved not to lose it!

The stage was set for Armageddon when I made my screaming entry into the world.

The imperial sun inched along majestically across a blue, cloudless sky and with the confidence of one assured of life for at least five billion years more.

It had been preceded by a light spatter of rain, like the sacramental sprinkling of Holy Water to keep sacred and spiritually clean all that have been made new.

For a brief spell, both sun and rain had been contending to share their blessings; but now, after having admonished the rain for its rudeness, the sun shone with all the magnificence it could muster.

In a persistent breeze that was as cool as it was pleasant, the sunlit trees held a drunken sway; happily intoxicated no doubt, by the general to-do and excitement of my birth.

Although I was born big there was no need for a caesarean section since Mother was rather broad at the hips.

She lay recumbent and spread-eagled. Her right leg rested tiredly on Fort Royal, while the other found purchase on the tops of Forts Lucas, Aldolphus, Frederick, Nelson, Morne Jaloux, La Grenade and Jeudy. These Mother had given birth to only a short while before in the face of increased British hostilities, and were in compliance with the Norman-Keep Defense System.

But Mother felt incomplete without me. It was one pregnancy which did not lay guiltily on her conscience. Not that she suffered any such pangs about the others. It was just that she saw me as the product of a legitimate need that neither Papa God nor the British could quarrel with.

She laboured in sweat for several months, and the scorching La Grenade sun, showing small mercy on occasions that were few and far between, lent no succour.

Even with excruciating labour pains Mother never stopped pushing. Pushing and pounding, nailing and cursing. Then there was scaffolding, concreting, bricklaying and more cursing. And when the pains became almost unbearable, and the exigencies of war may have forced her to terminate me midstream, she resorted to screaming.

Maybe it was this final scream which jolted me onward. I cleared the cervical passage with lightening speed. Where Mother's screams ended, my own began with élan and heartiness. I shrilled my arrival to all within earshot and they had to take note. But then I was long overdue and held back against my will.

Mother subsided into low moans and groans of relief. She looked at me from head to toe and with a critical eye, in which appeared a sudden gleam. Hereupon she touched and stroked me, tentatively at first, then with the certitude that I'd been made in her likeness.

She had the exalted look of a mother convinced that her newborn is the cutest in the community. Satisfied with the fruit of her labour, Mother designated me "Military Hospital" and directed me to serve all Regiments and Militia; "that's an interesting start to my life," I thought.

Chapter 16

Mother never intended me to prostitute myself, and I want to make it very clear that I never did. But men were nonetheless attracted to me, and who could blame them!

The midday sun held me in a tight and warm embrace, showing to its fullest advantage my unique lines and curves. I stood with an air of dignity, a paradigm of Baroque architecture, and felt a sense of disdain for those around me.

To my back, looking down at me with reciprocated contempt, were Forts Frederick, Nelson and La Grenade: A powerful shield against Invading Forces! But ineffective against the domineering mountain range, always first to greet the rising sun.

Morne Jaloux, unable to hide its jealousy, was willing to greet the sun everyday rather than extend a hand of friendship to me for one second.

My Mother was Caucasian and that would have accounted for my white complexion, but I do not think that was Morne Jaloux's grudge. On the other hand it was obvious to all that more men would come to me rather than go to the mountain.

My own bearing held an aloofness that was impossible to miss, and this had little to do with the fact that, located on a hill, I commanded a view of pictorial Port Royal for which others bitterly competed.

I knew I was special when my brother forts were told, in no uncertain terms, that it was their responsibility to protect me. But such a vainglorious and self-centred thought threatened to bust my head at its seams and brought an unsteady feeling in the legs. In my pomposity I mused of a nobler birth than I had a right to claim, expropriating to myself the airs and graces of a Cleopatra.

This ostentatious conduct only fed the hostility mill of my siblings. Their hatred was unconcealed and vocalized and it wasn't unusual to hear, entangled in the pandemonium of war, the words "Get out of here, you bastard!"

Bastards we may all be, and the occasional projectile inflicting bruises to my unarmored skin was more than enough encouragement to leave if such was my intention. In any event, barring the use of force or some divine act, I had tremendous difficulty in understanding how my removal was to be achieved.

My estranged brothers had their own plans. Some of the projectiles I surmised were deliberately aimed in my direction; so close to my head they passed that very often I found myself attempting to duck. However, I was arthritic and "stiff-necked" or so it felt, and not totally unhappy with this condition since I did not wish to appear intimidated.

But for as long as the British and Mother were unable to curb their mutual animosity, my life remained partially snafued.

Non-combatants have no place in the middle of a war, but there I was dutifully living up to Mother's expectations.

My workload grew in proportion with the amount of high-explosives Mother and the British lobbed at each other. Too often I felt, smelt and tasted the blood of John Bull as he bellowed for my attention and care. Sometimes he was in the summer of life, at other times in the springtime of death; but usually a limb or two would be missing, leaving deep, blood-spurting gaps behind. Many sported gunshot wounds like a sieve, while others were so disfigured that it exhausted scientific know-how to make them whole again.

The sons of my Mother, known to love nothing better than a sizzling affaire d'amour, made full use of my services. They all appeared completely smitten, and an excuse to rendezvous with me wasn't hard to find; especially those who claimed to suffer spasms at the sound of a gunshot.

Many complained of ailments which continue to baffle medical researchers. Some 'experienced' epileptic seizures at the sight of a weapon. For others, simply to touch a weapon brought on "phobic" reactions. And there were those who suffered momentary blindness which appeared to coincide with each tour of duty.

During Mother's many battles with the British, hypochondria seemed by far the most prevalent illness to have struck La Grenade. At times it did better than deadly weapons in ensuring that I was kept fully occupied.

Despite the fact that there had been sibling rivalry within the family and few seemed to like my head, I must try to be fair to my own brothers. Many were brave and decisive fighters and had no qualms about 'taking-out' a battery of muzzle-loaders, even if they were out-gunned. Foolhardy or not, bis peccare in bello non licet – in war one may not blunder twice. Lives and limbs were lost in appreciable numbers; and if the winner of the war were judged on the basis of battles won, then the wounds incurred would have indicated that Mother was heading for a pyrrhic victory.

But Mother was the best judge of this; and it was she who declared outright victory when, one rainy day in September 1783, she again signed another peace treaty and gave La Grenade to the British to do with as she pleased.

For my part the British would never have set foot here again, if their past record was anything to go by. And indeed it was!

In true British form, arrogant feet needed no encouragement in trampling the land and the people over whom was now exercised unfettered power. They took to everything with the mania of monks with papal dispensation to forego their vows of chastity for one day.

Instantaneously the process of bastardization was re-introduced. La Grenade was henceforth referred to as "Grenada," while my brothers and sisters were forced to labour under the burden of English appellations.

And the cruelty, which was visited upon my kin, wasn't only brutish but distinctly British. No step was missed, no eyebrow beaten in exacting harsh reprisal for Mother's misdeeds. Many staggered under the blows of new and murderous taxes, tougher than any Thatcherite poll tax.

Life perverted by colonial rule or any form of foreign domination is almost like being Lucifer's inamorata. The newly oppressed, themselves ruthless manipulators of this power only a short while before, soon made this discovery. Their lands and homes were openly confiscated in an attempt to redress an imbalance, which arose during Mother's reign; except that it was done without even the tact of a Nicodemus.

The conflict between the colonialist and the colonized wasn't without religious overtones. Protestants, now in ascendancy, were looking into every crevice for an excuse to start their own jihad against the Roman Catholics. Whole churches were expropriated by the British and I wondered for what purpose. True, some were put to religious use but I quivered in my boots to think that the precursor to the fabled communists had arrived. None were turned into discotheques because luckily those were not yet in vogue but the new colonial masters were afflicted by a fever of destruction and defilement. With a devil-may-care attitude, icons and artefacts held inviolable were vandalized and otherwise desecrated.

Homicidal taxes, purloined property including churches are one thing; but when physical blows began to make the rounds, some of my brethren became fanatic adherents of the adage "any port in a storm".

Out of fear that their very lives were in danger they hightailed it to Trinidad and took with them all manner of chattel, their slaves included.

For those who did not make it to the schooners in time, I was never one to turn away a man who needed ministering to. And it mattered not whether I went beyond the limit of my function. Every selfless act rebounded to Mother's credit, and every traumatized body and spirit rejuvenated by the kiss of life, calmed my own sensual intemperance.

However, the many who came to me did so in pursuit of their own needs and not mine; though the two, through Divine benefaction, were inextricably bonded.

I pray that you forgive me my imprudence and callousness but I must continue to tell my story as I quest for the truth immersed and distorted by centuries of falsehoods. Often the line between the two becomes blurred and indistinguishable, and one can be mistaken for the other. Especially if what has always been regarded as truth goes by unchallenged. But if we allow our conscience to speak without interference, then the truth and the truth alone shall emerge. So here is my conscience.

I wish not to offend righteous sensitivities; however, I am morally obliged to say that I benefited handsomely from my brothers' suffering and blight. There appeared a remarkable correlation between my fortune and their misfortune. Every additional "cut-ass" expended meant an increase in my profits. And time and time again, in the area of brute force the British demonstrated businesslike proficiency.

Chapter 17

But my cousin, Julien Fedon, was not going to have any of it; He was not about to put up with this intolerable situation. Someone had to leave and it was not going to be him. He, together with his band of revolutionaries and thousands of former slaves, were determined to put the British in their place, which was anywhere out of Grenada, to put an end to slavery and radically improve the living and working conditions of all who resided here.

The ruthlessness typical of the French in their dealings with the Caribs was what the British sought to emulate in their treatment of the French expatriates who took up residence here. But as diligently as they tried they fell way short, though not short enough for the oppressors-turned oppressed.

Fedon, a freed coloured Grenadian, was a descendant of a French expatriate. He owned Belvedere Estate, one of the largest plantations in Grenada, and with it many slaves who were responsible for its large production of cocoa and coffee. He nonetheless treated his slaves with a level of humanity unheard of and frowned upon by some of his fellow slave owners.

The liberal and progressive ideas which he held were bosom-deep, but they were to be ignited by the American

Revolution of 1776. Further, he sought to give new life to the rallying cry "Liberté, Egalité, Fraternité" of the French Revolution, which began in 1789, and which greatly influenced him. Moreover, he could not be any less inspired by the occurrence of the Haitian Revolution which started as a slave revolt in 1791. By 1804 the Haitian Revolutionaries had not only ended slavery there, but had succeeded in ejecting the French and the British from Haiti. Toussaint L'Ouverture, Jean Jacques Dessalines, Henri Christophe, Alexander Sabès Pétion and Jean Pierre Boyer led the Haitian Revolution, but given the approximately 1000 'as-the-crow- flies' miles between Grenada and Haiti, they could only have been my distant cousins.

Fedon and his like-minded freed coloureds had subsequently freed their own slaves, much to the anger of many Plantocrats, and by March 2nd, 1795 they determined that it was time to make their move! Generally, there was a thirst for freedom among the slaves, both former and current, that needed to be quenched. Soon then, thousands took up the call to arms, certain that their cause was just!

With a penchant for left-leaning ideas and for not being afraid to speak out against what was wrong, Fedon proved himself a champion of the cause of the oppressed and emerged as the natural leader among his compatriots.

Moreover, the revolutionaries received unasked for assistance from an unsurprising quarter. Because of the brute treatment meted out to the French expatriates by the new colonizers, Mother found Fedon and his forces to be her natural ally and quietly sought the demise of the British in Grenada. In addition to the crates of arms and ammunition which she smuggled to the 'Fedonists,' she dispatched two of her senior military commanders to provide Fedon with whatever help was required.

No help was required, however, in determining Belvedere's place in Grenada's military history. Situated in the parish of St. John's and travelling down the western side of Grenada, along the unpaved coastal track, Belvedere which means beautiful view, was twelve miles from St. George's. Difficult to gain access to and in turn providing easy access to both the western and eastern sides of the island, it lent itself naturally to the employment of the pincer; a military strategy even the most resourceful of enemies would find extremely difficult to contend with. Belvedere was strategically located. This suited Fedon well as a command post, and so it became.

From there, armed with the latest weaponry, a just cause and Fedon's solemn exhortation of "Freedom or Death," and with its ranks swollen by thousands of freed slaves, the revolutionaries embarked on a mission that was popular and which was intended to crush the Plantocrats and release Grenada from the clutches of British colonialism.

Etienne Ventour, Charles Nogues, Joachim Phillip, Stanislaus Besson and Pierre La Valette also led this legendary struggle, and they too were my cousins.

The successes which they scored were rapid and telling, and in the face of it the Plantocrats and British Colonialists, among them Gahagan, Garraway, Lindsay and Parke, along with La Grenade who was a freed coloured, could only dig deeper. Their quarters in St. George's were running out of space. Many were captured however, as the rebellion advanced. Some, including the British Governor, Ninian Home who was then visiting his Balthazar Estate, soldiers and eighty other 'Whites,' literally lost their heads when the Colonialists repeatedly failed to accede to Fedon's demand to surrender.

By then, the ranks of this rebellion were bursting at its seams with the addition of thousands more slaves who had abandoned the plantations, plantations which were first looted, burnt and destroyed as one of many defiant acts which the slaves undertook on their own initiative.

Victor Hughes, too, another of my cousins, had lots of initiative. He was a revolutionary leader and Mother did not mind when he quietly slipped into Grenada from Martinique to command one of Fedon's battalions. He took charge of the Eastern Front and led and won a decisive and historic battle at a place that was later to become known as Battle-Hill.

It was not an especially sunlit day! The sun, canopied by clear, blue skies was just gathering its strength after a particularly heavy downpour of rain which drenched the earth for twenty-four continuous hours. But the light breeze was sufficient in assisting the trees in drying themselves as they swayed less than merrily.

There was nothing to be happy about. The air carried with it the distinct smell and feel of a country torn by war, and so it was. There was the sometimes distant, sometimes near sounds of weapons of war echoing over the hills and across the valleys. The pah-pah-pahhh of rifles was irregularly interspersed by the boom of a canon, and the acrid scent of ammunition recently used was heavy in the air. There was also the smell and the sound of the dead and the dying.

Lured into a precipitous attack by the 'Fedonists,' the British thought they had the revolutionaries cornered. But how momentarily deluded they were! They were brought to their senses in quick time.

After several days on the march, Battle-Hill was meant to be a way-station. The revolutionary soldiers needed to rest and to do stocktaking of their supplies in preparation for the long and hard days ahead. When this intention was communicated to Fedon by a messenger who rode the last leg of three relay-horses, he advised that two birds be killed with one stone. Hence the plan was made but unfortunately for the unsuspecting British, 'two birds' and 'one stone', when stripped of their euphemism, meant as many British soldiers as were possible with the least amount of bullets necessary.

Though the British soldiers had a camp just one mile away, the revolutionaries were able to slip into theirs with the British soldiers none the wiser. With Fedon and his forces on the move, no one could blame the British soldiers for not wanting to voluntarily show their faces, or take an interest in finding out what was happening outside of their camp. So, in an atmosphere of anonymity, the 'Fedonists' were able to get Battle-Hill battle-ready and rest for forty-eight hours before giving life to their plan to drive the colonialists one step closer to Grenada's exit door.

It was the time of morning when the dark of night and the light of day are still tussling for dominance and then the night reluctantly decides to give up its last shred of darkness to the slowly creeping daylight.

It was a quiet morning but one that was filled with immense promise. General Victor Hughes dispatched a squad of his battle-hardened soldiers with the instruction to get as close to the camp of the enemy as possible undetected. They were to be 'agents provocateurs' of the revolution.

This they did with remarkable success. They beat a path through the bushes, avoiding where possible the often-travelled tracks. Moving with the ease of leopards in their accustomed habitat and with equal silence, they got to within twenty yards of the enemy's camp. The revolutionaries could have gotten closer if they wanted to, but needed to maintain a safe head-start on the enemy.

As things stood, the squad needed to kick up a huge hullabaloo in order to get the welcomed attention of the battened-down British soldiers. The provocateurs did not fire off their concealed weapons because the intention was to draw the soldiers out of their camp, rather than to push them even further in than they already were. So instead, they began a noisy, senseless, seemingly heated argument among themselves, loud enough to attract the eyes and ears of the most uninquisitive.

To the British soldiers cautiously peeping out of a few holes and windows in their makeshift barracks, the revolutionaries looked like a handful of poorly dressed and unarmed rebellious slaves who had lost their way and had gotten into an argument about it. They did not seem to pose any great challenge. Indeed, these slaves, the soldiers thought, were easy prey and should be made to pay for the mounting losses they were suffering.

Two platoons of soldiers left their camp in hot pursuit of the revolutionaries, fully armed and with rifles blazing the way.

A hapless bunch of mere slaves, as they assumed, running away and not firing back, was the kind of enemy these soldiers preferred. So they pursued this squad of revolutionary fighters with gusto.

Schooled as they were by the extremely hard circumstances of their life, the fighters had their wits finely honed. They maintained sufficient distance to be out of range of the bullets aimed in their direction, but close enough to keep the soldiers interested. They led a path that was easy for the British soldiers to follow but which made their return journey shorter, and at the same time allowed for maximum protection from the trees which lined its sides.

Follow, the soldiers did, caring only that their prey was well in sight and would soon be caught. They were already licking their lips with relish, prematurely feeling the pleasure of cutting down these slaves to bits. Lead, the revolutionaries did however, knowing the especially warm welcome awaiting the British soldiers, one they would not have had much time to savor.

But the hunt was on. The revolutionary soldiers did not just saunter back into their camp, it was a frantic dash mainly because the British soldiers were closing in on them and the shots which they discharged came uncomfortably closer, like gunners gaining proficiency at target practice. So the speed with which the fighters entered the confines of Battle-Hill was the same speed with which they were pursued.

Hot on the heels of this wayward and rude bunch of slaves, as the British soldiers perceived them, they felt no need to stop and observe their surroundings. Even so, for the casual observer, Battle-Hill would have appeared to be a disused large yard with hastily built, now abandoned, out-buildings. Errant slaves or squatters could have once lived there. Now, evidently, no one was there except for these few hopeless slaves who were making a mad bid to escape into what, unknowingly to them the British soldiers felt, must have been a cul-de-sac.

Nay, it was not the end of the road for these runaway slaves, as their pursuers mistakenly believed, but it was the end of some sort for the British soldiers, and not one that they looked forward to.

On reaching what was a deliberately placed barricade at the furthest end of Battle-Hill, in one swift, smooth and synchronized movement reminiscent of the best gunslingers of the Wild-West, the revolutionaries turned around, drew their rifles and subjected the soldiers to a barrage of gun fire that left no doubt of their intention. Some soldiers fell instantly before realizing that they had been duped. Others turned, seeking cover, only to discover that they were completely surrounded not by mere slaves, but by men whose reputation as resourceful and unrelenting fighters had preceded them. Men with a cause that even they could not dismiss out of hand.

The British soldiers quickly came to the conclusion that their options were severely limited. Indeed, they had only one, stand and fight. To their credit, they fought well, and at one point seemingly giving as much as they got. Eventually, a few of the revolutionaries were cut down and the fight lasted much longer than any could have anticipated. But being so hopelessly outnumbered, the soldiers' end was inevitable and when it came, it did so fast.

It was not as if the revolutionaries were merciless, but they knew that the soldiers were not about to turn around and leave peacefully, even if they were asked to please do so. Both sides knew what was at stake and both were willing to pay the ultimate price. The soldiers fought to the end and they fought the way soldiers were expected to.

With the post-battle clean up completed and with the 'Fedonists' in understandably high spirits, having just shortened their goal by sixty British soldiers, they continued on their march which they hoped would take them to St. George's where the colonialists' seat of power resided.

But first they had to make what they considered a slight detour and a brief stop. They got to the soldiers' camp as discreetly as the 'agents provocateurs' did, determined to make light work of the rest of the British company that were seemingly hiding-out there. The sound of rifle fire echoing across the valley only a short while before may have had the effect of sending the soldiers deeper into hiding, since rousing them took some doing.

The camp was completely encircled before the soldiers had the slightest idea of what was happening. A British soldier who had to answer one of nature's urgent, belly-grumbling calls in one of the out-houses, stepped outside and screamed heart-piercingly when he came upon one of Fedon's fighters.

He was silenced either by a heart-attack or by the powerful hand that was clamped over his mouth. But by then the sixty or so British soldiers remaining inside had been alerted.

It is amazing how one can be so quickly spurred by the survival instinct. In no time the soldiers were discharging their weapons through every conceivable crack in the barracks. It was desperate shooting, shooting for dear life, and at that point they had nothing more important to hold on to.

The 'Fedonists' were lucky to hold on to theirs but they had the advantage of surprise, and the time to satisfactorily conceal themselves.

Wooden, makeshift barracks though, do not offer the best protection against audacious fighters who had been further inspired by Fedon's exhortation, "Freedom or Death." Soon, amidst the din, the agonizing cries of the injured and dying could be heard, and with every splintering caused by bullets coming and going with terrifying ferocity, the cries increased.

It did not take long, then, for a hastily made white flag, apparently unaided, since no one could have seen the hand supposedly holding it, to show itself through one of the few windows, waving beseechingly.

The revolutionary fighters ceased their firing immediately and realized that the British soldiers had done the same. But the soldiers who were walking out of the barracks with their hands held aloft, the internationally recognized sign of surrender, did not look as defeated as one may have expected.

They needed to be watched closely, something that the 'Fedonists' were not about to forget as they permitted the soldiers to attend to the injured and bury their dead.

With their captives suitably bound and numbering twenty, the revolutionaries were soon able to resume their long march, hoping for similar success when they came upon the next contingent of British soldiers or the next British outpost in St. David's. And as they walked, a revolutionary song of triumph, sung with fervor and at the top of their voices, resonated over the hills and valleys.

Chapter 18

Elsewhere the 'Fedonists' were hitting the enemy equally hard. Fedon's forces were marching down the western front like the conquering army they were, and with each advance they made, the more the colonialists quivered in their pants.

Yet they had little choice than to throw everything at the advancing army. Wave upon wave of British soldiers were thrown into battle and the revolutionaries dutifully took the fight to them. With the localized knowledge of the terrain, however, the 'Fedonists' were always two or more steps ahead of the British. Often, then, the revolutionaries were waiting for them in places where they least expected. This obvious advantage provided the 'Fedonists' with a favourable death-ratio of five to one.

So they came in droves and were defeated in droves. Many were killed in battle, more were captured and later executed when the British intransigence and refusal to surrender continued. And when there was disquiet among those who felt moral abhorrence, Fedon responded with "C'est la guerre" – that's war, it cannot be helped. Fedon was in absolutely no doubt that, given the chance, the enemy would do just the same.

My Mother and I

It was not going to be too long before Fedon was proven right. It was now almost one year since this band of determined revolutionaries, actively supported by thousands of former slaves, took up their historic mission. Having already captured most of the island, Fedon's troops were, for the past two weeks, sitting on the outskirts of St. George's, commanding both the eastern and western approaches to the city. Yet the colonialists and the British soldiers stubbornly refused to allow the pincer to be closed. They had inherited the products of some of the most brilliant sappers in the world, so with several forts and other military fortifications, robustly constructed and at their disposal, they were not going to budge easily. They, after all, had everything to lose, including their lives.

Meanwhile Fedon's forces were being whittled down through death and injury. Moreover, they were near physical exhaustion and their ammunition and other military supplies were not going to last for much longer.

The revolutionaries now found their options severely limited, but not so for the colonialists. They had long reached the point of desperation, and the 'do or die' hour had arrived. From their hideout a despairingly worded P.D.L.U.D – PLEASE DON'T LET US DIE, more urgent than an SOS was dispatched. In quick time reinforcements by ships, of thousands of British soldiers and enough arms and ammunition to quell a modern day Red Army, were brought in. General Abercromby, who was based in Trinidad and reputed to be militarily astute, led these forces.

While Abercromby's astuteness was reputed, Fedon's own was well known to the British and he was not about to lose sight of their revolutionary objectives or his exhortation "Freedom or Death." He immediately ordered his troops to fall back five hundred yards to areas which would permit them to dig in and thereby provide greater protection. In doing so, the British would be required to extend their forces more and therefore be more vulnerable to attacks. And that suited Fedon just fine.

Over the next month or so British forces were tormented and harassed, not always able to anticipate when or where the next bullet would come from. But there were deaths on both sides and eventually the superior battlefield strength of the British began to tell. Fedon's forces were now only able to launch 'hit and retreat' attacks, scoring no major success. Soon, the 'hit and retreat' became more retreat than hit as they were pushed further and further away from St. George's. By then well over seven thousand former slaves had been killed and many of Fedon's fighters were either killed in battle or were captured and executed. For the first time, they experienced a death-ratio that was pointedly unfavourable.

Fedon was therefore forced to withdraw his forces closer to base at Belvedere where they held their ground for the next two months. But war is one of the fastest killers and there is hardly anything that saps one's energy quicker. War is debilitating, it is destructive, and it is callous.

In their weakened state, nevertheless, it became evident to the 'Fedonists' that their defenses were about to be breached and that Belvedere would be taken. In the face of that, they vowed to die rather than surrender or be captured by the colonialists. Many of the revolutionaries simply melted away but not Fedon and some of his seasoned fighters, unlike what the colonialists were left to believe.

Fedon and a few of his closest buddies retreated to his hideout. It was located above Belvedere and accessed through treacherous paths. A densely vegetated area that stood 2,509 feet above sea level; A place that later became known as Fedon's Camp.

It was June 19th, 1796, a date that was to have added significance in Grenada's revolutionary history almost two centuries later. It was much more than the typical English day. Outside was devilishly gloomy and dark, with thick fog erecting a temporary screen across the face of lush mountains. Thunder rolled in a manner that only it can, thunderously, and tree-patterned lightning flashed its occasional display across a sky that was heavily overcast and becoming increasingly dark.

My Mother and I

For the past hour savage rain pelted the earth with its unique makeup of H2O, soaking up everything in its way. The gods were definitely weeping, but they were not the Carib Gods Atabeyra, Yocahu or Obiyel Wa' obiran. They had ceased weeping a long time ago, though I sensed they had something to do with the day's events. It could not have been the Yoruban God, Shango, either since his hands were too full at the moment to meddle in the affairs of other gods.

But there was definite weeping by Mother's god and the god of the British, though they were both weeping for different reasons. Mother's god moaned Mother's loss and regretted the handing over of La Grenade to the British, and the god of the British moaned the losses suffered by the British and regretted the British acceptance of Mother's gift. As its name indicates, Grenada is trouble, it is explosive and comes at an extremely high price, a truth that successive generations of those who wished to claim Grenada as their own was destined to discover.

Fedon and his chief lieutenants were instrumental in passing on this lesson to the British, a responsibility they took on with pride, honour, enthusiasm and dignity. They knew that their mission was just and were confident that others would take up the cause for which they were prepared to die. As they stood now on the verge of defeat, not too far from a precipice, they felt no regrets over their taking up arms, freeing the slaves, and seeking to kick the British Colonialists out of Grenada.

The rain weighed heavily on their shoulders however, and they felt no need to delay the inevitable any longer. Without any warning to the singing, gray and brown Finch birds overhead, the only witnesses to this dramatic scene, Fedon and four of his co-revolutionaries flung themselves bodily and with an air of triumph, to their instant deaths at the bottom of a hundred-feet precipice.

I did hear indistinct sounds coming from the Carib gods and though they sounded somewhat alarmed, no one knew exactly what they were saying. Yet Fedon's jump into history linked forever the struggles of peoples generations apart.

Less than fourteen hours later, a landslide, caused by the persistent and drenching rain, buried Fedon and his revolutionaries. Their broken bodies were never found, but the British wanted Fedon badly, dead or alive, preferably dead since they did not trust a Fedon who was alive. Anyway, they were willing to pay five hundred pounds sterling for either to any bounty hunter.

Weeks later, one of Fedon's sympathizers, thinking Fedon was in hiding and wanting to be of help, concocted and peddled the story that Fedon had drowned in an attempt to get to his brother in Trinidad by boat.

The British, wanting to put an end to the spectre of an elusive Fedon haunting them forever, bought the story without even adding a bit of salt then turned around and began selling it themselves more cheaply.

Jacques Chadeau, one of Fedon's lieutenants, was sold out just as cheaply and it was not something that was worth losing his life over. For twelve years he eluded the British, not giving them even the merest sighting of his shadow.

Other persons had a far more intimate view of much more than that and that was where Chadeau's problems began. Chadeau had the reputation of banging anything which wore anything that looked like a skirt. Thank Papa God no kilt-wearing Scots-men resided here. But many women were drawn to Chadeau and many were prepared to help him, not only because of the universal sympathy which existed for the 'Fedonists,' but he was handsome and exuded enormous magnetism.

Chadeau, then, had no difficulty finding hiding places, under skirts included. Women were happy for the opportunity to do their revolutionary duty, as they saw it, by protecting him and at the same time looked eagerly to the chance to be his lover. On this occasion, however, Chadeau followed his reputation and banged one woman too many.

There is no greater wrath than a woman who has been jilted, so it is said. Moreover, I have overheard stories from women who swore hell and damnation on the heads of men who, they believed, two-timed them. Chadeau's last mistress may well have sworn similar affliction upon his head and meant it.

Unfortunately for Chadeau, she took his lovemaking as an act of commitment and this was compounded when, in the throes of ecstasy, he declared his eternal love. But then one cannot blame Chadeau entirely. This is what knowledge of the Kama Sutra in the hands of a skilled woman can do.

When Chadeau left her small, wooden hut early one morning and did not return by the end of the day, she became very worried. But when she later learnt that he was with another woman who lived not too far from her, she became extremely upset.

She was seething with anger and vowed that if she were not good enough for him, then no other woman would be. She wasted no time in contacting a British soldier who then informed his superiors. Thus betrayed, the elusive Chadeau was captured, hung and left strung up on a lamppost in Cherry Hill, just north of the capital city. He was left there for one week so that all those who may think the actions of the 'Fedonists' worth emulating would be duly warned.

Other revolutionaries were also captured, and similarly hanged and strung up on lampposts in different parts of the island, or were summarily executed. Their properties were seized as well. For the next five years the British instituted a reign of terror that would have been the envy of any latter-day police state. Intimidation and harassment became a daily practice. Anyone found to be, or thought to be, harbouring insurrectionist ideas, or of having latent sympathies for the 'Fedonists,' was promptly shackled and shipped off to Santo Domingo.

Fedon had aimed to ship them off to a destination much further than that, but the ships, perhaps, may have been too slow for the British. The 'Fedonists' did not succeed at their mission, but it was to the benefit of Grenada and of revolutionaries many, many generations later that descendants of both sides of the Fedon Revolution – Fedon, Ventour, Phillip, La Grenade, Gahagan and Parke – found themselves on the same side in the making of a revolution that Fedon helped to inspire.

Chapter 19

The interregnum between Fedon's abolition of slavery and its reinstating by the British following Fedon's defeat, did not affect my hospitality in any negative way. Many a praise were heaped upon my head for unfailing and indiscriminatory ministration to all. None were unable to cite examples of my meritorious conduct, and all agreed that quality service was the better part of me. What a difference it would have made if, after periods of hospitalization, my patients had seen the sly smile which preceded my tacit entreaty, "Please come again!"

Kinfolks nourished and stroked my exuberance with the dexterity of a masseur. They who solicited and whined for care and attention were among the nouveau riche: Big planters; some however, through the actions of the British, were no longer big or planter. They were also former members of the "Conseil Souverain," the Governor-General's advisory body who watched over Mother's interests with a hawk's eye, as well as members of the Court of Appeal who were themselves plantation and slave owners.

Judges, Lawyers and Justices of the Peace who were now disbarred, suffered more from the loss of power than from any physical illness or injury.

Officials of the Clergy, some of whom owned slaves, thick and thin with colonialism and now "dechurched," eagerly sought me out to vent the bitter outrage and indignity they suffered, rather than for emotional or spiritual salvation.

Speaking of which, the ex-army officers and soldiers would have opted for membership of the Salvation Army rather than accept their own disbandment. Instead, their only choice was to seek solace in my arms or face a life that was terrifying at the hands of the British. They chose the former and that had little to do with the fact that they were libertine.

The new colonial masters, too, either armed themselves or were forcibly armed with good reason to visit me. Diseases of one kind or another, including the mental disorder of always wanting to own and subjugate others, were efficiently cultured in their warm and unwashed bodily recesses.

But fumigating their bodies did not get rid of the diseases. It was only a necessary prerequisite for effecting unconventional treatments, the likes of which would have had Lothario awestruck.

No such amatory techniques were required to tend their numerous cuts and bruises. These were sustained when they unavoidably found themselves in the way of various missiles hurled from the launching pad of deprivation, anger and hatred of a colonized people.

The British, too, were among my prized clientele, as were all 'whites' and residents of the town of St. George. Surely, Townsmen could be used alternately with 'whites' without a scintilla of misrepresentation, since the slaves weren't even allowed a sniff of the air proffered by the goodly saint, without written permission. Nay, if the slaves were bold enough to contravene this edict, as they often did, and suffered the ill luck of discovery, they were made to keep fellowship with St. George's prison. Or they could be interned in one of the overrated pigsties built for that purpose throughout the Colony, whose surroundings were less elegant.

And as if to make their accursed lives more infernal than they already were, neither Mother nor the British permitted the slaves to tamper with my portiere much less to enter me. Nothing overrode this prohibition, not even if the reason for coming to me was to deliver a message.

There was something peculiar and disturbing about this, enough to have provoked a rare, though brief, tête-à-tête between my sister, Jeudy, and I.

"Say sister!" a highly accentuated voice called out; one that I wouldn't have recognized save and except for its condescension.

Jeudy thought it beneath her social standing to speak to me. To her I was not worth one cent more than a hussy, and twice times less the going price of a harlot. She told me these things to my face, and when she spoke to me it was usually to give tongue to one of her scathing homilies.

She lived towards the south of the Colony, about one and a half miles as the crow flies away from me. And to maintain the appearance of being sanctimonious, she kept her distance.

But Jeudy was bewitching even if a wee-bit bosomy. In her brick stockade overlooking the sea, she painted an imposing figure easily mistaken for a sea-nymph blessed with the charms of Aphrodite.

Nonetheless, as some who have paid lavishly to find out know, there was nothing charming about her when it came to the defense of Mother's interests. In this she stood unyielding at the breech and as fiery as a bitch giving protection to its young.

Snippets of such devotion and fierce loyalty never failed to bare itself in Jeudy's conversations. But so did her caustic humour:

"If there is a road to salvation for you, it is sure to pass through Hell!" she added, jolting me out of a momentary daze. Jeudy long concluded that I was beyond redemption, and there was little I could do to convince her otherwise.

"Why do you condemn me, sister?" I asked lugubriously.

"Because you're as perturbed as someone about to commit one of the seven deadly sins, what ails you sister?"

"I feel that the slaves are being treated unkindly."

"What!"

"I should be allowed to give them the care that they need……."

"Would you permit asses to enter you?"

"No."

"Well these slaves are no better than asses!"

"I don't agree with you, they have needs as we do."

"Their needs are already taken care of and you're taking care of yours good enough!" Jeudy responded derisively, not missing the mark with her jibe. Though a little ruffled, I persisted:

"It does not cost me anything to mend their broken bodies, and the better they will work for it."

"If you're not careful you would soon need to mend yours."

"What the ……..!"

"Mother stated quite explicitly that they are not to enter!"

"Have you ever stopped to consider the plight of these…..these…people?"

"People?"

"Yes, that their conditions and status always remain the same or get worse, while ours and the Brits often change, and change for the better?"

"I see I wasn't wrong about your vile intentions, but let us not forget the reasons why the slaves were brought here!" Jeudy angrily retorted just before she retreated to the shelter of her fortress.

The slaves weren't only brought here, they were dragged here, trussed-up hand and feet in the fashion of dangerous criminals. Unbeknownst to them they were sentenced to a life of hard labour on the plantations, in conditions which were utterly merciless and pitiful. It was to this regime that the Caribs justly refused to submit, and the colonizers were not about to volunteer their services.

Instead, the colonizers first cast their eyes in the direction of their own people. They tried the hands of persons "banished for political reasons," and those who may have insulted or shown disrespect to the monarchy. They tested the stamina and patience of Engagés (Indentured Servants) and placed on trial the work ethics of those who were "captured during periods of civil war." Similarly, convicts were transported to the colony; but the zenith of desperation was finally reached when their citizens were kidnapped on the streets in an effort to satisfy the demand for labour.

The supply, however, was insufficient, inefficient, unreliable and unable to stand up to the rigors of the growing plantations. The solution was to be found among the inhabitants of Africa, a land so vast that Mother could be subsumed within its borders fifty-seventy times.

Chapter 20

A relatively uninterrupted coastline made it all the more difficult for any one country to monopolize the slave trade.
 But traded they did in human cargo even if their progress was constantly in check by the absence of almost no natural harbours, deep bays or isthmuses.

Africa has been lavishly anointed with rivers, rapids, lakes and falls. Plateaus and mountains, some snow-capped, make a parody of Mutt and Jeff. At a thousand feet high or more, crowns of foliage played the game of "in-and-out-the-dusty-bluebells;" whilst vigorous plant life, dense forest, savannahs, plains, velds, deserts, jungle and swamps looked on with lively amusement.

Throughout this expanse of virgin land hordes of wild animals gambolled, spreed and scouted, making Africa the top-notch zoological garden that it was. This natural menagerie without cages included pests and insects of the most pernicious variety. Reptiles too, were considered part of the dangerous breed, and in some places it was still possible to see a parched earth stamped with the massive footprints of extinct dinosaurs.

A more erudite explanation for the demise of these behemoths would be that they evolved into even more dangerous species like the Hitlers, Stalins, Pol Pots and other contemporary 'ground-gods,' who stalk this earth. But no, scientists continue to bother their heads with the futile hope that they could come up with something better. Some believe that the dinosaurs were frozen out of existence by the effects of the Ice Age. Others hold that the radioactive fallout and the intense heat of meteoroids slamming into Africa were too hot for the dinosaurs to handle.

Whatever it was, heat was the one constant factor of Africa's climatic equation. Not only was it at times as hot as guinea pepper, but one was stirred by the need to empathize with the thermometer which must remain in place and absorb every Fahrenheit of it.

General weather conditions, though, were as diverse as Africa itself, especially with regard to its rainfall. When it poured it really poured and it was then one felt most inclined to believe that the rain-god did nothing else but piss all day. When the rainfall was moderate to little, was perhaps an indication of a partially blocked urinary track. Conditions of drought would therefore complete the whole story, but its occurrence sometimes had an even worse effect than a major pestilence.

No less a pestilence than the pestilence-to-be who were drifting in weather-beaten ships, eager to commence their vocation in slave-trafficking, along the shores of a land with a bountiful supply of natural resources.

The province of Kaffa, in Abyssinia, volunteered an English strain of its name to one of its tropical shrubs, coffee. A few stomach-warming cups of this drink would have done the first slave-traders well. It would have helped them to stay awake after weeks of sleepless anxiety to reach the African coast.

The second largest continent housed a patchwork of different African races that were further sundered by a mosaic of tribes. The people of this nation, filled with amour-propre, were held together by strong traditions, values, cultural practices and a common need to survive. Yet, jarring sounds of discord were often heard, especially when they flowed from the instruments of tribal animosity.

Nonetheless, the twirling baton of the drum-major also bespoke a great capacity for love, hospitality and an expansive spirit. They were far more than the popular notion which saw the African as black skin, thick – sometimes protruding – lips, kinky hair, broad noses and uncivilized. Indeed, a truer characterization may include full lips, full and well-rounded figures, in some cases seductive eyes, gentle, cheerful and cultured.

In South Africa one would find the Bushmen who were light-skinned, short and with curled hair. Their neighbours were the Hottentots who were said to be Bushmen with a dab of Bantu blood. They were nomadic and one of their women's chief identification marks was the ample backsides with which they were endowed. Truly, if the size of one's bottom was indicative of wealth, then the Hottentot women were billionaires. As racist as Mother is and as offended as she would be, I must confess that the first time I saw one of these women I harboured a secret naughty wish to be a beggar, as in 'if wishes were horses all beggars would ride.'

One may say, however, that it was these qualities, and the image of African women as superb lovers, which captured the fancy of Moses. He hastened down the church aisle with a nubile Abbyssinian beauty at his side, athirst for the delights of the African conjugal bed.

Of course, the familiar wrangle ensued. Like the mother who thinks a woman is too low-grade for her son and let it be known, family members drew verbal swords in readiness to do battle. In the community, persons were vituperative in their disapproval, but there was an equal amount of bad-mouthing.

In defense of this Abbyssinian belle, Solomon, the reputed connoisseur of women, proclaimed "I am black but comely, O ye daughters of Jerusalem!" For Moses' part he comforted himself with the thought that 'if Solomon say so, is so,' and got on with the job.

The cross-section of Africa's native people wasn't only typical of its infinite worth and richness in variety. It was also an unsettling realization of the demographic power waiting to fuel an European-provoked explosion of civil strife, interracial and intertribal rivalry and bitterness, and an unprecedented decline in wealth and living standards.

Sleeping-sickness of the Tsetse fly and malaria of the mosquito were only two of the several pitched-battles constantly fought for the preservation of health, well-being and happiness. These hostilities in turn released previously untouched supplies of verve and gave vent to the enormous creative and artistic talents of the African people.

They were the best weavers of cloth singular in its aesthetic beauty. Solicitous about their appearance, they dressed always to attract, and their garments did just that because of the explosive give-and-take of their colours. This may have helped make their loin-cloths sexy and gave Africans a dapper look when outfitted in flowing robes, wraps, dashikis, frocks, pants-suits, safaris or the Nehru-collared, long-sleeved, formal jackets worn on some ceremonial occasions.

The matching headscarves and turbans underscored the fact that they were full of dash. For tribal rites, however, elaborate headpieces, sometimes generously embellished with varicoloured plumes, were preferred. The number of plumes and their colour-pattern tended to indicate status. Gold and silver earrings, nose rings, bracelets, armlets, anklets, lower-liprings and necklaces made of gems or strung together with colourful beads and carved fetishes, completed the ensemble.

Africans were extraordinarily gifted carvers who made drums, fetishes and figures which abounded in diversity. Hardly an opportunity would pass without subjecting some object to fretwork, filigreeing, tooling and other decorative designs.

When caves were still the preferred place of abode for European Neanderthals, Africa's Homo Sapiens were living in huts that were pleasingly adorned. Generally, they sought to spruce up and ornamentalize almost everything and succeeded in appending aesthetic value to whatever they touched; whether they were calabashes, knives, doors, sandals, sticks, wooden plates, pots, spoons, buildings, textiles, metal work, ivory or tools.

Secret Societies, which were distinctly West African, also, bestowed social status on its membership. These groupings had their own internal rules, regulations and judicial system. Masks and ceremonies, which were impossible for the uninitiated to follow, were extensively used.

In many ways nothing went to waste. Full advantage was taken of all available resources, including some plants that had medicinal value and others whose fibre proved suitable in the weaving of silks.

But perhaps more tellingly, they excelled in the execution of three-dimensional art as they did in pottery – an old craft done mainly by the women and passed on through the ages, like genes, from Mother to daughter.

Speaking of things hereditary, music was the natural preserve of Africans who exercised a command over this art form that was complete. Complete in its freshness, exhaustive in its sublimity, impeccable in its rhythms and absolutely visceral in its out-reach.

These virtuosos were the standard-bearers for much of civilization as they were in other fields. They showed an aptitude for string, flute, piccolo, drum and a range of other percussion instruments that was unsurpassed; and lacked nothing in spirited musical accompaniment for their many dances and ceremonies.

The leitmotifs on such occasions were frequently sacred, as a devout people sought to establish contact with their Master Workmen. Judging from events, which immediately followed, success couldn't always be claimed. Ironically, it was easier to establish communication among their own people, than it was to attract the ears of gods whose form and character were sometimes fleetingly grasped.

Indeed, so developed were their means of mass communication that the telegraph was to be modelled after the intricate drum language, which enabled messages to be sent to any part of the Continent with speed and accuracy. It was the lingua franca that brought some order to the African Babel.

Nevertheless, few, if any, would have engaged themselves in actually building a tower to Heaven. The Animists were many and held sway despite the encroaching influence of Islam and Christianity. Their deities were to be found in trees and animals, in the moon, sun and stars. All animate objects were held inviolable, all things inviolable had souls and what was blessed with spirituality was venerated.

Fetishes and whatever magical powers they possessed also excited religious fervor, as did their belief in fairies, monsters and other chimerical beings.

The Africans had what would seem unusual methods for interceding with their gods. This included the practice of witchcraft, which wasn't altogether esoteric, yet labyrinthine and complex enough to require specialized training. Those who emerged successful were designated witch doctors.

Of the innumerable Gods who were invested with the responsibility for the Kismet of the African people, Shango, the Yoruban god of Thunder, was first, second and third among equals. His power and prestige was consummate while the fear he instilled was proportional to the love evoked.

Like two persons in one, he was both the god of boon and the god of bane. He lashed the earth with terror but smothered it with insouciance. Vexed thunderbolts caused the earth to buckle at its knees and fevered storms tore at its seams. But the torrential rainfall, which the parched land drank so avariciously, slaked its thirst and helped sustained the life of plants, animals and man.

Shango's devotees maintained a rather complex personal relationship with him. His many acts of compassion and malfeasance elicited interminable feelings of ambivalence. They prayed for his gifts yet dreaded that his ostensibly charitable deeds, like a Trojan Horse, masked sinister and destructive designs. When they were right they wallowed in pain, suffering and regret; when they were wrong choruses of the Africanized version of hallelujah perforated the air. But nothing could beat back the winning smiles which measured the full width of generous mouths, and for some this was no mean achievement.

Shango gave Africa its first royal ruler, oh yes! No doubt about that. Shango was well equipped with the basic requirements: a healthy libido, fertile wives and knowledge of the elementary gymnastics necessary to give His Majesty life. Ah well, so went the popular belief; and as persuasive as the tenet stubbornly held by many tribes that a woman, once married, lest she be cursed, must remain eternally faithful to her husband. Thus, should a husband be away for more than nine months and return to find his wife heavy with child, he was apt to believe that a Supernatural Being had done the honours.

Like all gods, Shango's name was glorified and revered, and often called upon in seeking approval for would-be kings ascending the throne.

Shango began his own ascension when he gushed forth from the womb of the All-Mother Yemaya, like a spent cartridge from a revolver. Except that he was very much a live-wire waiting to shock his domain with his incredible capacity for iniquity and kindliness.

He was a belligerent god, his might and power stupendous, and for his lowly petitioners, unfathomable. But he was a noble god, liberal in his magnanimity as he was with his terror. And yet gracious in his acceptance of the abundant hosannas with which he was diurnally bombarded.

The god of thunder wasn't without the means to reciprocate in his own way. He emitted startling bright lightening from the effulgent, bronze-plated palace, in which he lived, and found it necessary to supplement the volts in his bolts by exhaling balls of fire through the mouth. Such abracadabra was achieved by consuming magic medicine.

Still, Shango wasn't just his own pharmacologist. He successfully rebelled against parental restrictions decades before and became his own man long before becoming a god to millions.

Surrounded by his many wives and attendants, he was sometimes visualized as living in the midst of vast lakes and rivers, a symbolic reference to his purity and potency.

Indeed, the people's perception of Shango was nothing short of phantasmagoria. He was a giant of a man with several heads or with as many heads as it wasn't too difficult to imagine. Heads usurped the locations intended for hands, feet, genitals and other parts of the body. Then he adopted features akin to Cyclops, the Greeks one-eye giant, with his hands full of thunderbolts.

It had been widely conjectured that Shango went skinny-dipping regularly with his many wives. On those occasions He took on the attributes of a Merman, while his spouses were granted the properties of Mermaids. But try convincing his followers that he wasn't half man and half animal constantly riding a ram, and you may have to nurse a migraine for the rest of your life.

The experiences of Africans abducted into slavery were grossly more painful than headaches. Have you ever suffered the ordeal of being suddenly dragged away from your loved ones, not knowing when or if you'll see them again? Of being severely brutalized and otherwise manhandled in the process? Of discovering that your abductors are complete foreigners with the power, by sheer might, to do with you as they please? And, as if almost total confinement is not enough, they subject you daily to the most depraved acts of humiliation and degradation?

Chapter 21

More than two hundred years later the memory is still as bitter as Alcupa. Some of the most scenic views can only be obtained from my location, but on those days of wanton abduction, I wished I was blind as love. In fact, I would have been happy to have been aborted at birth.

But Mother, in my case, was a 'right to life' advocate; and being a grown adult at that time and with eyes nourished by many years of carotene, how could I not have seen?

They painted an overwhelmingly pitiful sight and my immediate response was, 'Why the hell did these slave traders have to escape the Bight of Benin? And why, damn it to hell, could they not have been swallowed up when they entered the mouth of the Senegal River?' But many of them survived to wallow in the filth of their human enterprise, and from what I saw they could not have been found guilty of having a social conscience.

The landed slaves, thousands of them, with shackled feet that appeared to be struggling to carry the load of their similarly shackled and battered bodies, were a sight not worth having. Gaping wounds on several of them, in some cases bleeding, in other cases already putrefied, the result of severe, merciless beatings, described in part the horrible, sub-human conditions under which they were transported. They obviously suffered the worst indignities imaginable. Human beings treated the worst, that were made to look their worst and by the way they carried themselves, to also feel their worst. Many of them crying, including women and children, wore drooped shoulders but were otherwise naked. Some, caught in the grips of terrible illnesses, were retching out their empty insides in an involuntary but futile effort to vomit.

Just looking at them made me feel sick. Perhaps emptying my own insides would have been an acceptable and natural reaction, but one that would not have been possible since my insides were filled with the sick bodies of my own clientele. Further, I made a commitment to keep them there until they felt whole again. Yet I prayed for the attributes of the whale that delivered Jonah unharmed from its belly, anything to make me feel better.

I "weep with them that weep" as the Bible text says, but that did not help, and with a bleeding heart, feeling better was hardly possible in the circumstances. Though they came from a land that was different from my own and though their ethnicity was far removed from my own, I felt profound empathy for them.

Made to survive on biltong, corned fish and breadfruit, their treatment on the plantations was no less gruesome and I went out of my way, as immovable as I may have been, and against Mother's explicit orders, to treat them as compassionately as I was capable of. Except for the few 'trusted' ones that were allowed to work within my confines, slaves were not permitted anywhere close to me. But I found illicit ways to extend the hand of humanity to them, and I did not discourage them either when I overheard whispered conversations of sabotage and revolt. After all, man cannot live by biltong, corned fish and breadfruit alone, especially the corned fish!

Many of the slaves were physically broken when they arrived but mentally they were as tough as wall-nails. If the slave owners were sufficiently discerning when the slaves limped off the ships, they would have seen the proud look in eyes that were unblinking in most of the men for what they were, a stubborn refusal to submit.

They escaped from the plantations regularly, though they knew that if they were caught they would be made to pay with their lives. Yet the possibility of death or of being beaten to within an inch thereof, did not deter them in anyway. They set fire to the plantations and the out-houses at the risk of being strung-up on a post and whipped until the skin was torn off their bodies. Sometimes they worked much slower than the overseers demanded and when the overseers insisted on demanding more, they would take the whip away and administer a warm licking.

The slave owners and overseers may have done some licking in another regard, but regularly they screwed the wives and daughters of the slaves and they did nothing to pretend otherwise. But when the opportunity presented itself the slave men quietly did the same to the wives and daughters of the slave owners and overseers. Indeed, going to bed with the slave men was a common fantasy of these wives and daughters, and once they did they became addicted. The slave men, then, were not infrequent recipients of invitations of sexual congress. Sometimes, these acts of copulation took place on the slave-master's bed. This gave the slaves unbelievable satisfaction and they would laugh behind his back when he came riding in on his horse and thumbing his nose in his high-and-mighty manner.

Nonetheless, it was the revolts that the slave owners and plantocrats feared the most. At least these they knew of, albeit after they had already begun. In any event, the revolts went to the heart of the system of slavery itself. From day one the slaves never accepted slavery and were prepared to demonstrate this en masse, and sometimes in the most violent of ways.

Once they had sampled the sweetness of freedom which Fedon engineered for fifteen months, they were not prepared to meekly accept the status quo ante. Fedon's revolution dramatically lifted their horizon of possibilities, and try as they did, there was nothing the plantocrats could have done to stop Big Ben.

Slave protests erupted on plantations all over the island like sores on the skin of someone chronically ill with leprosy. Antibiotic treatment may have helped but you were almost certain to have died. This would not have been good news for the colonialists who were doing everything to preserve and maintain the system of slavery. Clearly however, they did not do enough when, in the 1830's, two major slave revolts on West Coast plantations shook the foundation of the colony and sent the colonialists scurrying for ideas to halt actions which were threatening to derail their very livelihood.

The West Coast of Grenada was still Fedon's strongest sphere of influence and though he may have long gone, his spirit continued to spook the British. Sure, they could not be certain that he was dead but regardless, they saw Fedon's rebellious hands in anything which appeared menacing.

Obviously, the British, all the way in England, were of the opinion that it was Fedon's revolution and its consequences, as well as similar actions throughout the Caribbean that made the situation untenable. They came to the unavoidable conclusion that slavery, in its present form, could no longer bring them the required returns and sustain the quality of life they wished for themselves.

Around a long, expensive, highly polished mahogany dining-table in the upstairs of a fancifully built manor house, opulently decked-out with chandeliers, sat the colonial decision-makers on chairs that matched the grandeur of the room. Some were jacketed, others wore fine coats but all had a laugh that was equally high-priced.

The house, which boasted a mixture of Gothic and Tudor architecture made popular in the Victorian Era, was located in Liverpool, in Northwest England, an ideal and very profitable slave port. The estuary called Mersey ran close by and

Merseyside, with its not altogether rustic atmosphere, was the home of many of the traders in slaves.

The colonialists, sipping coffee, the product of labour derived from treating others no better than animals, had gathered to contemplate first, their future, then secondly the future of the slaves. After much discussion and mutual back-patting for the successes they had scored, they determined that it was feasible to grant the slaves the illusion of freedom while keeping them tied to the land and slaving for slave wages.

"After all, what choice would the slaves have?" asked one.

"Freedom exists when one has choices and if one has no choices then one has no freedom," philosophized another.

"We own the lands and all the possible means of survival, so unless the slaves want to die of starvation, which I doubt very much, then they have no choice but to work for us at the barest wage we would set," interjected a third.

Thus decided, the colonialists knocked glasses in repeated toasts, laughed the haughty laugh of the grossly rich, bragged about how easy it was to dupe the slaves, then appointed August 1st, 1838 the date on which the slaves would be granted their 'freedom'.

When the news, emanating from a fully furnished, luxurious dining-room in Liverpool in the form of a proclamation signed by King William IV, reached the slaves, there was an immediate work stoppage that was not the result of sabotage or revolt. The slaves spontaneously burst into applause and that heralded the start of celebrations that were to last long after August 1st, 1838 came and went. They danced, frolicked, made music with whatever they laid their hands on and beat drums that were speedily made. They sang the songs of their African origin which they were previously forbidden to sing, but which they secretly preserved through the ages. So unbridled was their joy that they drank themselves to a stupor from plantation-brewed alcohol which they kept hidden for use on special occasions.

My Mother and I

It did not take much for the plantocrats and slave owners to make the slaves believe that this was indeed a special occasion and that they shared in their joy. They made certain allowances, permitting the slaves a little time-off and not doing anything to restrict their merry-making once the day's work was completed.

But it was not long after emancipation day would have come and gone, that the former slaves discovered that nothing much had changed. They were not only still tied to the land, they were tied to the plantation owners as well and at their mercy. They had no land of their own, so they were still compelled to toil the Planters' land under slavish conditions. They had no houses of their own so they were forced to continue living in the run-down, foul-smelling, termite-ridden, thatched huts on the plantations; and now, God forbid, the planters took out from the meagre wage they were paying them for something called rent.

Soon, though, the Planters had grave difficulty in paying wages in cash. Sugar as the primary cash-cow was no longer earning them as much as it once did and many of the former slaves had drifted away from the plantations. This sent most of the plantations into an economic tailspin and forced the introduction of the Metayage, a semi-feudal system of crop-sharing.

The former slaves, hoping that things would improve, were not yet ready to yell 'bloody murder.' Their entire daily bread was dependent on the plantation. Accordingly, they spent several years trying to scrape along but inevitably this new arrangement became too much to bear. It was not what they expected from their granted freedom, which was so unlike the joyous though difficult months of liberation which Fedon claimed for them.

Sadly for the plantocrats, their former slaves were not prepared to settle for any less. On repeated occasions in 1864 and 1874, former slaves on plantations on the West Coast and in St. Patrick's screamed 'murder, murder police' by laying down their work-tools in strike action and engaging in other forms of militant protests. They were determined to get betterment for themselves, their children and their children's children.

Moreover, in their guts they were still driven by the cause of genuine freedom, Fedon's cause, a cause that was to unleash the revolutionary ardour of many yet unborn.

Chapter 22

When Fedon and the 'Fedonists' swept through the island capturing all of it except St. George's, he stretched tautly my capacity to care for the sick and injured. That was a long time ago but I am still feeling the effects of the necessary workload which he created. In any event, old, arthritic joints tire quickly.

Furthermore, all of that came on top of my normal and daily workload, and though I have never shirked my responsibility, the weight of it all was beginning to feel like a thousand sandbags upon my shoulders.

I began to question my own ability to cope when, in June 1854, I was pushed to the furthest limit of all that I was capable of. A cholera epidemic untethered its biological nuke among the hundreds of soldiers who were encamped at Fort Frederick and Fort George.

If I were less learned, it would have been easy for me to believe that Mother's God was revengeful and that this epidemic was His way of continuing what Fedon had set out to do. Surely, though, Mother was not complaining and had it not been for the added grunt and grind involved in caring for the diseased, I would not have complained either. But the work had become too much and in those days there was nothing like overtime pay. Even my own brothers and sisters showed me little gratitude and scant regard.

By September 1854, someone did a number on me. It may have been someone who had been overly sympathetic and was eager to put me out of my apparent misery. Or it could have been somebody who hated me to such an extent that my presence was no longer bearable. Probably though, the person may have only wanted to rid the colony of any trace of the cholera.

Whatever the mens rea of this quite likely good-for-nothing scoundrel however, a fire, ostensibly a bush-fire, was set a little away from me, indeed, not a great deal further than I would have been able to piss in my healthier and younger days.

Given the very dry conditions that were being experienced throughout the colony, it did not take long for the fire to spread and engulf me like a blazing inferno depicted in a typical Hollywood movie. By the time two water-tanks on carriages arrived, carriages that were drawn by tired-looking, demonstrably thirsty horses that were twitching their heads back as if wanting to bite the tanks, not much more than the memory of me was left.

I could not imagine a more horrible and excruciatingly painful death for myself. I twisted and writhed in agony but I could not go anywhere since my feet were stuck in concrete. I cried a river that day and screamed the full width that my lungs allowed, but no one appeared to have heard me.

My death then could not have been a lonelier one. Those who put me together under Mother's strict supervision, came later and determined that the cause of my death was fire, something I and the rest of the world had already known. I was also killed by asphyxiation which they did not mention. However, when they finally declared me dead, I already knew that I was dead for more than twenty-four hours.

My Mother bemoaned my passing and there was a great sense of loss among my siblings except for my sister, Jeudy. What Jeudy felt was elation, and though well aware that I was female, she was heard to say, "That is sure good for that son-of-a-bitch!"

By force majeure, my 'son-of-a-bitch' services as a hospital were no longer in demand and if my death were not required for that, I would have raised no objection. In the mid 1860's, quickly abandoned attempts were made to bring me back as a lunatic asylum. It was only then that I was struck forcefully by the idea that it must have been some crazy lunatic who burnt me down to the ground. And no, I am not suggesting that the British may have needed such a facility to house themselves.

In any case, the British could not do without me for too long and in whatever form my resurrected being would take. My eventual born-again experience occurred at the end of 1879 and it was a new and different me, yet I remained my Mother's child. For one thing the ribs in me were inherited from her. And though the British got a chance to sire a male child and took to it with the delight and ardour of a teenage lover, they could not replace my Mother.

When Edward Prince of Wales, who later became King Edward Vll, visited Grenada, he did not delude himself by believing otherwise. Instead, on January 26th, 1880, he hurriedly reclaimed me as their own and proudly proclaimed me as Grenada's Prisons. First, I thought that was one of the usual tasteless British attempts at humour, but when I realized that the Prince was serious, a pall of death washed over me and I said a quick prayer for the return of the arsonist. Sometime later it occurred to me that I could have done far worse by being a lunatic asylum and I felt immensely consoled.

Still, I found my new responsibility distinctly unattractive. I went along with this ridiculous assignment because I had no choice. I simply could not have done as I wanted to, so I did what I was instructed to. Further, I supported my brothers, despite my Mother's angry protest, when they stormed the Bastille in 1789 and now I feared that one day others would do the same to me.

The unenthusiasm with which I pursued my new responsibility soon gave way to lethargy. The same tiredness I felt before my demise by fire came back to me with the force of a grudge carried over from one generation to the next.

It was not only physical exhaustion, it was mental fatigue. Maybe I had seen too much and I had heard too much, though no one ever accused me of having peeped too much. With war-inflicted head wounds which I suffered both in my old life and my new, my information-processing capacity had been greatly reduced. Perhaps, too, the arthritis that had finally begun to attack my joints had somehow seeped into my brains through some kind of biological mishap that medical scientists are yet to put their hands on.

Whatever this brain-chewing malady, I had not become dim-witted though my ability to recall was also affected. But for as long as I remain my Mothers' child, no matter how many times I may be declared dead, there are some things that I could never forget.

Chapter 23

The world then was not as small as it is now. It was still relatively close to what, according to Genesis, God had made some fourteen billion years ago. Rising sea levels had not yet swallowed up great chunks of the land. Not much of it had been lost through soil erosion caused by the systematic destruction of the rain forest. Floods and rivers overflowing their banks were not gobbling the best lands. The world was still pretty much intact and pristine.

Notwithstanding the claim by some that comets got life started on earth, the problem was that man, whom God created to inherit all of it, had grown egos to match the size of the world as big as it was then. And, unfortunately, clashed egos that large can sometimes have unforeseen results.

No one expected that when, in 1914, Austria's Archduke Francis Ferdinand and his wife Queen Sofia, paid a visit to Serbia and were assassinated by a Serbian Nationalist, that that would have precipitated the start of the First World War.

Ethnic conflict and other forms of rivalry were as common in Europe as tribal conflicts were in Africa. There were constant alliances formed, alliances that were forever shifting and changing as various Empires sought dominance.

Any excuse, then, to change the balance was exploited to its fullest potential.

The assassination of the Archduke and his wife was just such an excuse for the Austria-Hungary Confederation which, in concert with their ally, Germany, did not waste much time in going to war with their archenemy, Serbia, and its ally Russia.

It was arguably the bloodier of the two world wars. In fact, it was extremely messy, and when Napoleon described war as "the business of barbarians," that war proved him right. Whereas today weapons of war, (including multiple independently targeted reentry vehicles, other long-range missiles and precision bombers), are committed to the battlefield, then it was the foot soldiers in trenches with Lee Enfield .30 caliber bolt-action, repeating rifles. And when those ran out of ammunition one had to face the enemy with a bayonet, bare hands or mustard gas.

Although mustard gas was introduced into the war by the jack-booted Germans, all of the major warring parties used chemical agents. The British did when England, together with other Western allies, entered the war that same year on the side of Serbia.

The British army included hundreds of conscripts and thousands of volunteers that were to come from its vast empire – its many colonies around the world. Despite its still prevalent anti-colonial sentiments, Grenada was one such colony that provided cannon fodder for the army of King George V.

Thousands of family members, friends, well-wishers and other curious onlookers gathered at the St. George's port one bright and sunny afternoon, to bid a hundred volunteers farewell and Godspeed. It was a typical day in the sun and the mood of the thousands matched its radiance. It was a buoyant gathering.

There was no flourish of trumpets but if one listened intently it was possible to imagine it, such was the extraordinarily warm send-off that was being staged by the colonialists.

Those parents who felt saddened to see their sons depart to an uncertain future, not knowing whether they would ever return, soon had their misgivings drowned out by the oft repeated 'hip hip hooray' of almost a thousand voices saluting Grenada's brave sons.

Yet a few sniffles could be heard as the young recruits, militarily dressed, climbed the gangway and boarded the ship. When the ship's moorings were removed and the ship began to plod its way out of the harbour, the vast crowd joined in together, following the lead of a small number who began singing:

> "Off to war our brave sons gone
> To join the King's army,
> Off to war our brave sons gone
> To bring us back the glory."

They continued singing well into dusk when moonlight shadows were evident and before the crowd straggled away from the port, but even the next day and the next, small gatherings could be heard singing:

> "So off to war our brave sons went
> To fight for King and country,
> They did not have to be paid a cent
> Their loyalty know no boundary."

The brave Grenadian soldiers served with distinction, discharging their duties both on the battlefield and in support services.

Twenty million deaths later, the war ended with the defeat of Germany and its allies in 1918 and soon it became time for the war-weary Grenadian soldiers, less their unlucky compatriots, to return home. Some of them still wore bloody bandages intended to conceal and protect the wounds of war. It was not possible to conceal the stumps which gave more than a hint of missing limbs, however. Many walked with obvious limps, others had shoulders that were slightly stooped almost as if they were still carrying heavy backpacks. Some had far-away looks, looks that could have indicated experiences that were deeply traumatizing. They appeared much older than their years. And yet, when they landed, they were greeted with remarkably little fanfare by the local colonialists.

Ordinary Grenadians who were sent off to war and possibly to die as heroes and patriots, whose virtues were personally extolled by the Governor, were given such a tepid welcome that they could have been sympathizers of Fedon returning from enforced exile in Santo Domingo.

The ex-Servicemen, veterans of war, were left to fend for themselves, depending on the assistance of their families and the benevolence of friends. They found themselves unable to get jobs and, because of their skin colour, found themselves discriminated against in their own country by the colonialists and local 'whites.' After fighting for King and country with honour and courage, the colonialists could not have cared whether they lived or died. But the ex-Servicemen were determined to stay alive and soon they were chanting their own refrain:

> "Off to war we went, fought brave and hard
> For King and country,
> Only to return, treated with scant regard
> Our pockets notoriously empty."

This was one of the chants heard regularly in 1920, during their many street demonstrations held over several weeks in St. George's. Their demands were simple and manifestly reasonable: Treat us with respect, give us jobs and cease the discrimination. But they didn't only chant, they decided to take the fight to the British.

Adopting as their own the tactics of the British which they may have learnt during their overseas tour of duty, they engaged in several acts of civil disobedience, and at times engaged the colonial police in pitched-battles. And when the colonialists did not heed their cries for help, the ex-Servicemen burnt down almost one-third of the Town. This was at the height of their struggle which became known as The Ex-Servicemen's Revolt.

The burning of the town was worse than lighting a fire under the behinds of the British, but the effect was not dissimilar. The British hurriedly summoned the ex-Servicemen and unconditionally agreed to their demands. The war veterans, after all, were determined to ensure that the honour with which Sgt. O. Ferguson, Sgt. C. Rennie, Cpl. G.P. Depradine, L/Cpl. O. Bertrand, Pte. G. Bartholomew, Pte. B. Cox, Pte. C. Philbert, Pte. C. Parkes, Pte. A. Grant, Pte. J. Pascal, Pte. E. James and twenty-two more of their comrades served and sacrificed, were accorded the respect it deserved.

Consequently, fires lighted somewhere were to become one of the hallmarks of subsequent struggles of the Grenadian people. But the treatment of veterans of two ensuing wars, including Elaine Archibald, Eileen Moore and John Parkes of World War II, became pointedly worse.

Chapter 24

If the Carib Chief, Kaierouanne, were to be given a new lease on life by the Carib god, Atabeyra, the earth Mother and guardian of moving waters and childbirth, he would have had little difficulty finding his way around Grenada in 1951.

Much had changed in the intervening three centuries, yet a great deal had remained the same. Still refreshingly and relatively unspoilt, Grenada was largely a rural society. Most of its population, including the majority of its workforce, lived in rural communities. And for the hundreds who worked on the nearly one hundred estates from which Grenada derived much of its earnings, their wages remained the same between 1838 and 1938, with only an incremental, hardly perceptible, upward shift between 1938 and 1951.

Others who had the good fortune of finding jobs in Government offices were paid wages only slightly better, but many had to make do with the menial jobs as road workers, street cleaners and domestic servants, and paid menially as well. Being a domestic servant meant doing the washing, caring for the children, cleaning, cooking and generally being at someone else's beck and call in the homes of the colonialists, planters and middle class. It meant enduring the sexual abuse that was not uncommon. It also meant suffering racial abuses that were quite prevalent throughout the society.

Grenadians were bled white while Grenada remained an impoverished island held in the firm, racist, exploitative colonial vice of underdevelopment. Poverty, not cloaked in a modicum of human decency, was at its best. The majority of homes had no electricity and had to get by from the light of the 'Masantoe' – a bottle filled with kerosene with a lighted cloth wick at its mouth. It was the same light households had to depend on when, in the middle of the night, nature's call led them to a pit dug some distance from the house, or for the less poor, to a latrine that shielded itself from inquisitive eyes with discarded, rusty corrugated sheets or mite-infested pieces of wood.

These homes had no running water and no amenities like refrigerators, phones or stoves, but even if they had, many may not have known how to use them. One-third of the population could neither read nor write and another one-third were barely able to spell, write and identify their own names. Without that knowledge they were nonetheless able to carry trays of stones on their heads when repairing the roads, and to use the cutlass, fork and hoe, the main agricultural tools. They did not require special education for the making of a fireside or for the cutting of firewood with which to feed the fire. Education, then, was not a necessary prerequisite in the daily grind of eking out a living. In any event, the colonial stranglehold on improved quality of life and personal development remained firmly rooted in the system of colonialism itself.

Chapter 25

Since water, in acceptable quantities, is often associated with special blessings, for the downtrodden people, Gairy must have returned to Grenada on a very rainy day. In fact, that day in 1950 was unusually rainy for that time of the year. It was unseasonal rain that appeared to have had its origin in an insufferable heat wave of the previous two weeks. That, too, was perhaps the result of a sun-storm, but the torrid weather was too much for the several animals which perished. The people did not have their wish that the colonialists would have come to a similar end, but nevertheless, they had good reasons to be thankful for the rain.

Yet if there were no rain that day, the many people who staunchly supported Gairy were likely to believe that he emerged from a womb containing more amniotic fluid than normal.

Eric Mathew Gairy, who came from humble beginnings, was born February 18th, 1922 on the eastern side of Grenada. But whether he was born in Moyah or Dunfermline, in the Parish of St. Andrew's, remains almost, grounds for war between those two rural communities; such was the increased intensity of this debate the more popular Gairy became. With neither God nor his mother available for comment, this issue may remain an unresolved bone of contention.

Gairy's antecedents went as far back as slavery. This being so, he may have nurtured from his forebears a terminal dislike for the colonialists, or it may have been passed on to him in the genes he inherited.

Since he grew up in abject poverty, however, there was not much to inherit except perhaps an abiding hatred for the living conditions to which he, his family and the ordinary people were life-sentenced. His parents worked on an estate as most parents in his community did, and as a boy he had an early taste of estate life, including running errands for the overseers. He did whatever was necessary to help his family scrape together a living.

Life for him and his family, then, was a daily attempt at the impossible – making two ends meet, as impossible as it would have been for Fidel Castro to have found love in the White House. Despite the Gairys' best efforts, poverty held on rigidly.

Consequently, much of his elementary and primary education came from home and the community, and as bright-eyed as he was, he never saw the door of a secondary school. Since secondary education was not accessible to the poor, he was largely self-taught.

Gairy inculcated the finest qualities as a young man. He was handsome and he was black but the way he carried himself left no one in any doubt that he also thought himself comely. The giggling young ladies who sought out his friendship were for him positive reinforcement. He was proud of his blackness. His clothing, though, was never as fine as his qualities were. More often than not it was either borrowed or hand-me-downs, and although they were never a far cry from being classified as rags, he wore them with an immaculateness which bespoke the most expensive finery found on Saville Row.

From an early age he vowed to find a way out of the life-sentence of poverty. In his teens he was able to secure a job as a primary school teacher in his community, and just at the time when Hitler was asking the rest of the world to wake up and smell his brand of coffee, Gairy made his way to Aruba with the help of friends.

For sure, several, including Gascoigne Blaize, and the brothers Rupert, John and Roy Bishop, also travelled to Aruba while others went to Curacao as well as other countries in an effort to stay afloat. And to Gairy that was the more sensible thing to do, rather than going off, as many Grenadians did, to serve and die for ungrateful, racist and exploitative colonialists in yet another World War. So while Hitler was marketing his coffee across Europe, Gairy was seeking to have his bread buttered in Aruba.

Aruba, part of the ABC islands that include Bonaire and Curacao, is a small Caribbean island of the Netherlands Antilles. It is sixty-nine square miles and located Northwest of Venezuela. Like most Caribbean islands it has its own natural and irresistible beauty, and although in later years much was done to attract the tourist dollar, it was best known for its oil refineries.

The refinery with which Gairy was employed was the American-owned *Largo Oil Refinery*. It occupied many acres of land, almost a State of its own that was hemmed in and protected by miles of barbed-wire which went several feet into the air, iron gates, guard dogs and armed guards.

Gairy was such a charmer that even the guard dogs fell under his spell. Don't talk then about the armed guards, his co-workers and especially the ladies. In fact, his disarming personality drew people to him and made him the centre of attention much more than he could have bargained for. He knew not then that he would soon be doing other bargaining as well, but in the meantime he felt quite at home although he lived a few miles away from the refinery.

Resolved as he was to lift himself out of poverty, he used whatever little spare time he had reading and learning all he could about the oil industry. He was not thinking of starting any oil exploration of his own, but he wanted to ensure that he was well placed to take the fullest advantage of the opportunity that Largo presented.

Gairy worked hard. There was much work at the refinery since its oil was in great demand. The robust war machinery that was necessary to sustain World War ll required massive amounts of oil on a daily basis. Its war factories and the whole range of deadly weapons which they produced, were being fed like camels with bottomless stomachs.

But Gairy had himself to feed and clothe and the outward vestiges of his indigent past to erase. He soon took to wearing fancy, high-priced zoot suits and cultivated an accent to match.

Because the passage through which his brain transmitted its message to his mouth commanding it to stay shut was temporarily blocked, Gairy spoke often but he spoke well, he spoke impressively.

It was not long before he saw things at Largo that needed speaking about. The refinery's wages were a prettier sight than the wages paid to estate workers but not that prettier, and neither was its working conditions that dissimilar from the estates. Largo's operating policy clearly was not driven by humanitarian concerns. Sap the worker for all he was worth did not mean paying him for what he was worth.

'Take what you get or leave' could easily have been emblazoned across the tall iron gates at its entrance, and Largo's attitude would not have been misrepresented in anyway. The workers were paid a minimum wage and in the refinery's language that meant the equivalent of two meal tickets daily and the cost of transportation to get to work.

One could have had his wage docked by arriving late or by being absent from work for whatever reason. Further, reasoning was not a particularly strong point of Largo's employers. The workers were regularly subjected to racist and sexual abuse for the most contrived of excuses. And it was not uncommon for workers to be physically beaten by the armed guards or for the flesh on their legs or arms to be torn by the intimidating fangs of the ferocious guard dogs. By the way the employers responded on such occasions made it clear that they considered that to be normal and acceptable treatment for their employees.

What Largo Oil Refinery instituted was not apartheid but 'largothied.' The bathrooms, toilets and water-coolers for blacks were separate and apart from those provided for the whites, reminiscent of Botha's South Africa and pre-civil rights U.S.A. This racist policy was so strictly enforced that the black workers preferred to comply rather than risk the consequences of flaunting it. Moreover, there was no one to turn to and they could not resort to trade union representation because none was allowed.

Largo's employers could not have known, then, of Gairy's visceral hatred of racism and exploitation, and of his swearing to God to resist its manifestations wherever. Nor of his determination never to return to the crushing poverty which he left behind. They would not have known, too, of his acute stubbornness and stick-no-nonsense attitude which he imbibed through the nipples of his mother's breasts.

Gairy's mother and mine were both of the conviction that breasts were always best long before that notion was made popular in health and erotic journals. Gairy, then, was well fed, as so was I. But he was not only strong-minded, he was strong-willed as well, something Largo's employers were to discover to their own chagrin.

Since the passage carrying shut-your-mouth messages from his brain to his mouth remained blocked, there was nothing to prevent Gairy from speaking as far as he was concerned. He was listened to. He was also admired and that may not have had everything to do with his self-proclaimed comeliness. Gairy had a way with words and he sure had a way with people. Although he never played even a toy guitar in his life he knew how to strike the right chord. His co-workers were made to feel that he cared about them and that he shared in their suffering, which in fact he did.

It was not long before Gairy took up the cause of individual workers and soon he was speaking on behalf of almost all of Largo's employees. He wrote letters and made representations to the management. He protested the extremely low and unfair wages. He complained about the docking of workers' wages when they were absent from work because of illness and had a doctor's certificate to prove it. He objected to the sexual, physical and racial abuses and the 'largothied' of separate facilities for employees based on race. He recommended days off for workers who had to attend to urgent family matters and paid holidays for all workers. He demanded that all workers be given overtime pay and protective gear while at work.

Largo's employers tried to cajole Gairy into giving up this new role that he had acquired for himself, but that did not work. They tried soft-soaking him with promises of improvement here and there, but that got nowhere. Attempts to buy his mouth with the offer of large sums of money met with utter scorn, and to the employers' dismay, threats to break the more than two hundred bones in his body only added to Gairy's excitement, as perverse as that may seem.

It became clear to the employers at *Largo Oil Refinery* as clear as a properly washed champagne glass ought to be, that Gairy was not going to be bought, intimidated or dissuaded; but when Gairy began taking active steps to establish a trade union, the employers had had enough. He and his two lieutenants, Gascoigne Blaize and Roy Bishop, were summarily dismissed. Within forty-eight hours they were declared persona non grata, unceremoniously placed on a plane and deported from Aruba.

Chapter 26

"These damn Dutchmen! How could they be such muttonheads?" The Dutch Authorities would not have been aware of how much they were being cursed by the British for sending this agitator, rabble-rouser and mischief-maker back to Grenada. The British had already received reports of Gairy's activities prior to his return from Aruba, and was hoping that the Dutch would have discreetly dropped him off on an uninhabited island far from Grenada. They did not. Uninhabited the island may have been, but they had good reason to fear that Gairy, given the chance, may even have mobilized the wild animals into a trade union and come back to cause them trouble. They were not going to have any of it.

"The British created him so they must have him and the easier it would be to keep an eye on him," the Dutch colonialists concluded. So off to Grenada this smouldering volcano of trouble was sent packing.

But the British colony of Grenada, with the colonialists riding roughshod, was familiar territory for Gairy and he was not unhappy to be back. Regardless of its proffered quality of life, there can be no place as sugared as home, and yet Gairy felt refreshingly challenged to make it more livable.

My Mother and I

Not good news for the British colonial government and the planters who were hoping with the hope of someone with no other option, that Gairy's expulsion from Aruba would have deflated him sufficiently so as to transform him from firebrand to water-hydrant of docility and submissiveness.

"The anger of these wretched people, in particular the estate and road workers, is almost palpable and needs to be urgently cooled," said the colonialists who were becoming apprehensive.

But Gairy was not about to comply with the futile hopes of those whom he detested so much and who not only created him but also, through their ruthless, racist and exploitatively based policies provided a nurturing atmosphere and the right environment for him to breathe and grow.

And grow he did. Gairy got off the plane running, or so it may have seemed, given the speed with which he began making waves. Almost immediately Gairy started petitioning the colonial government and the planters for increased wages and better working conditions for estate, road and domestic workers, and for the peasants. He held public meetings and made bold his demands.

As word of Gairy's actions grew, commensurate with his popularity, more and more workers began identifying with him and many more attended his public meetings. It was not long, then, before Gairy established his trade union, the Grenada Manual, Mental & Intellectual Workers Union with himself as President General. Together with his lieutenants Gascoigne Blaize, Roy Bishop, Lowe, Williams and McKie they went to every nook of the island mobilizing the workers, and within three months more than two thousand had signed up as members of the GMMIWU.

The colonial government and the planters grew increasingly uneasy. They were not just seeing the waves which Gairy had set in motion; in their mind's eye they saw out on the horizon and advancing rapidly, a destructive tsunami of bad-tempered workers who had forgotten their place.

"There is no more dangerous a people than those who have forgotten their place," the colonialists pontificated, not remembering theirs either. They blamed Gairy for the workers apparent memory failure and for everything else. The colonialists and the planters like DeGale, Noble-Smith and Denis Henry began organizing themselves in response. They held several meetings and vowed never to give an inch to these good-for-nothings led by a no-good instigator.

Despite the several attempts to divide the workers, the dismissal without cause of many of them, other acts of intimidation and the violent threats made against them and their leaders, the 'no-good instigator' and his 'good-for-nothings' decided that an inch was not going to do, they demanded a yard.

By then thousands more had joined the GMMIWU and the workers were bristling with militancy. Successful strikes on several estates occurred and workers on other estates put down their forks, spades, cutlasses and hoes in solidarity without being asked to. This went on for an entire month but the planters and colonialists held fast.

There was nothing that could have fueled the wrath of the workers faster than the intransigence of these neo-slave masters, as the workers saw them. They became furious and were on the verge of marching on the Governor's residence, when the leaders of GMMIWU were summoned to a meeting. After lengthy and heated discussions and with the personal intervention of Governor Robert Arundell, the colonialists and planters gave more than an inch and the GMMIWU accepted less than a yard. Albeit, a temporary agreement.

This significant victory for the union, however, fed its ranks with thousands more workers and in a jiffy saw it mushroomed into, and easily became by far, the largest trade union in Grenada.

The union then began to feel its weight in numbers and dynamism while the planters measured theirs in pounds sterling. Gairy, once poor and moneyless, had now become the incontestable, popular and proud leader of all the ordinary people. In fact, he was not just their leader but their God-sent hero, God-fearing, full of charm, well-spoken, always nattily dressed and giving the planters and the colonialists real hell. He was held on a pedestal and many were in awe of him though he was revered by all.

Gairy's acclaim went beyond Grenada's borders. Respect and admiration for this remarkable leader became too much to be confined within one hundred and twenty square miles. Other trade union leaders like Grenadian-born, Tubal Uriah 'Buzz' Butler, based in Trinidad, Ebenezer Joshua of St. Vincent, Vere Bird of Antigua, Robert Bradshaw of St. Kitts and Alexander Bustamante of Jamaica established contact and a warm friendship with Gairy. They shared with him ideas coming out of their own experiences and pledged their unwavering support and solidarity.

So when the planters in collaboration with the colonialists began dismembering their earlier agreement with the GMMIWU, like a surgeon eager to get his first bite at amputation, Gairy was concerned but not unduly perturbed. Increased wages, improved working conditions, including annual holidays and sick leave with pay, the use of mules and donkeys to carry the heavy produce from the fields to the estate yard, instead of the use of women and the provision of pipe-borne water in places that would allow for drinking and domestic use, were all patently reasonable demands. Trade unions in other islands had already won those conditions for their workers. They were conditions which one human being should never deny another, and for which Gairy was prepared to throw down the gauntlet and serve on the British his own sanitized version of the bombing of Coventry.

Chapter 27

When in January 1951 the planters again failed to respond adequately to a letter from the GMMIWU setting out its renewed demands, they had no idea what they were getting into. It would have been to their benefit if the blackbirds, which were frisking in and out the top of the trees, were mindful to bring them the message. Yet, given their dour mood and the risk which the messenger incurs, they were likely to have shot the birds.

The only shooting that day, however, came from the sun's solar gun. It sprayed its ultra-violet rays all across clear, blue skies and parched earth and shrivelled up everything that was not sufficiently armoured to withstand its intense heat.

The workers on most of the one hundred estates and their union were also feeling the heat. Moreover, they felt exasperated by the obstinacy of the 'White man.' Strikes were already taking place on some estates and in a few cases on the initiative of the workers themselves. It was as if they were determined to pass on as much of the heat to the planters and colonialists as was possible. They were ready to take the fight where needed.

In a public meeting summoned by his union, Gairy declared:

My Mother and I

"Enough is enough and if you ask me, I think we have had enough of these upper class people, these white people who care nothing about the conditions under which you work and live. What they do not understand is that we are not prepared to accept that any longer. They have jooked a "mibone" nest and they are going to get bite."

Amidst rapturous and seemingly unending applause and shouts of "You are our leader, we are with you," Gairy called for a general strike to begin on February 19th, one day after his 29th birthday. That call was like taking a lighted matchstick to a clearly labelled combustible fuel tank. The strikes which were already taking place on some of the estates received added momentum and soon strikes were taking place on almost all estates. The road workers had also joined in. In no time the rest of the island was engulfed in protest activities that went way beyond Gairy's initial call to lay down tools. The workers were in a riotous, no-nonsense mood.

The workers abandoned the estates and other areas of commercial activity. Some estates were seized and in other cases crops were destroyed. The planters and colonialists began to feel qualmish in their stomachs and became red in the face, a sure sign that the actions of the workers had gotten under their skin. Perhaps, then, it was time to save their skin. Immediately they SOS'd police reinforcements from St. Lucia and other Caribbean islands and asked the British warship, HMS Devonshire, to use all of its possible knots to get to Grenada as rapidly as it could.

But there was nothing to slow down the actions of workers whose anger was fueled by the naked injustices to which they and their forebears had been subjected for over a century. Thousands took to the streets, in particular, estate and road workers, in mass demonstrations. They were extremely agitated. Week after week there was no sign that there would be any let-up in their combativeness. I had no direct involvement, yet, where I stood, unmovable in a concrete base, I felt the fear of God seeping through my boots. If the British were quaking in theirs then they had a right to be.

The workers led by Gairy were chanting and singing loudly and confidently, in a 'no-one-can-stop-us' sort of way. They sounded like Napoleon's conquering army on the march and could be heard within a radius of several miles. With the intermittent blowing of the wind, however, only snippets of their words reached me where I stood on a hill overlooking with interest, the southern end of the city. What I heard nonetheless, was enough to underscore Gairy's overwhelming support from the workers and his almost complete influence over them.

> "We will never let our leader fall
> 'Cause we love him the best of all
> --------------And when we fight
> We will fight, fight, fight."

They sang and chanted over and over with the enthusiasm and energy one would associate with persons who had been eating balanced meals each day, and accustomed to a much higher standard of living than the lives of misery with which they were intimate. They sang and chanted as if they meant every word of it, and the British were not in any doubt that their word was as good as the pound sterling.

That thought reminded the British that they had too much to lose. The cocky colonialists unleashed on the ordinary poor people the full benefit of their centuries-hardened contempt and hatred, as if to say 'how dare you!' As far as they were concerned, people who had been living improvised lives, the direct result of their racist policies, had no right asking for better wages, proper housing and drinking water.

Helmeted, khaki-garbed police from the other islands, armed with pistols and riot staffs were dispatched to clean up the streets and guard the estates and the homes of the plantocrats and colonialists. They were supported by British troops who were more intimidatingly attired.

The demonstrators were indiscriminately and mercilessly beaten, a few were shot and killed and many were arrested. The colonialists took their attacks to the estates where more were shot and killed and others arrested. It was on March 13th, the day three workers, John Duncan, Agatha and Nell Fraser, were brutally shot down in La Tante, St. David's, that the workers, in their bid to quench their thirst for justice and the nefarious response of the colonialists, unwittingly set the stage for what was to come decades later and with far more profound consequences. But none of Massa's inhumanity daunted the fighting spirit of the workers led by their charismatic leader. It was like a raging fire that was intent on destroying a city despite repeated efforts to dissuade it with considerable gallons of water.

Nothing, it seemed, was going to halt the workers in their quest. That much was made clear by the demeanour and conversations of those that were arrested and thrown into cells. After all, it was I who was ordered to provide safekeeping for those arrested, so there was much to hear and observe.

If the colonialists and the planters who had now armed themselves with guns believed that the workers were weakening and that they had run out of ideas, then they were failing to understand the resourcefulness of the workers, the same resourcefulness that had kept them alive in conditions of abject poverty.

Gairy and the GMMIWU defied the British and summoned a public meeting in the Market Square in St. George's. There was simply no space for the many thousands who attended, and in the face of this massive show of strength, all that the hundreds of armed policemen could do was stay at a discreet distance and listen with scowled faces.

At sharp variance, the faces of the workers showed an ethereal joy in what they were doing. Determination and the certainty that their just actions would bring them victory, were etched in faces that were of different sizes, shapes and attractiveness but unified in their blackness. Their mood was buoyant and their eyes remained acutely focused on their goals and on the platform where some of the leaders of GMMIWU sat.

Gairy looked his best, conspicuously dressed as he was in a white suit, the significance of which was not lost on the large crowd in attendance. That had the effect of sending them into a near frenzy. The white suit shrouded him from danger and imbued him with a spirituality that placed him next to God. Another sure sign that he was God-sent and especially blessed, and with God's personal imprimatur stamped on their struggle, they were sure to win.

Gairy was also at his best and it was not long before he got into his usual eloquent stride:

"...These mindless people, these uncaring people, these boldfaced people, these upper class people have taken us further than we expected to go, but not as far as we are prepared to go. My dear people, all we are asking for is a decent wage and a decent house but they find that too much for us. These white upper class people feel they better than us but we want them to know that massa days done, it done, it done, it done. Because we black and poor they feel they could do us what they like. But they must know that if they keep on jooking the mibone nest, they would keep on getting bite. Victory is ours because God is with us! So my dear people, we must keep the fight on! I am not saying to burn, I am not saying not to burn but is sky-red tonight! ... "

The crowd broke out in a spontaneous though uproarious rendition of what had become their theme song:

> "We will never let our leader fall
> 'Cause we love him the best of all
> We know how to fight
> With all our might
> And when we fight
> We will fight, fight, fight."

They sang their way to the board buses, some belonging to the **Penny Bus Company**, or whatever transportation was available to take them back to their communities. Many walked but all left with a common understanding of what their struggle required of them.

That night was pretty dark. Streetlights adorned the fronts of most Government buildings and the homes of the colonialists and planters. But otherwise they were completely nonexistent, especially in the rural communities and villages where the poor black people had to use all their wits to be able to see the light of day.

For those people the moon performed an act of mercy, as if a lunar Samaritan directed its radiance where it was most needed. It shone brightly across vacant fields and densely bushed areas that habitually rustled with eeriness. If local folklore were to be believed, departed spirits and jumbies resided there, and if you were travelling alone you did not walk, you ran and tried your best not to look back. If you did it may have been your misfortune to fall into the hands of a Mamamaladie or a La Diablesse. It was Soukooyah I feared the most, however, and the mere mention of her name made me cringe. I was even more determined, then, to stay where I was put.

No such spirits were on the prowl that night, or so one would have thought. But when the skies mysteriously turned red from fires towering with rage that night, the blame was laid squarely at their feet.

"Fire, fire, fire" was the news that was whispered through the villages, but no one knew how they might have started, nor seemed particularly interested in finding out. They were being paid indecently as workers and yet they felt not the least bit motivated to become police officers who were being paid much better wages.

Government buildings were burnt to the ground as flames of fury avariciously leapt skyward. No timber or wall was too thick or too tall for the fires which consumed everything. Estate buildings were not spared either. The speed with which the sea of flames seemed to be spreading everywhere, was as if the jumbies had a time-table to meet and a contract to fulfil.

The British had their own obligations. They moved swiftly to have the matter investigated and before you knew it, the remaining Government and estate buildings were given such armed protection as to suggest that their façade consisted of all of El Dorado's gold.

But Mamamaladie and her attending spirits were after something more precious – the soul of the 'white-man.' The following night the conflagration continued as more buildings disappeared from the landscape, despite the heavy, armed presence of police and soldiers. And when it seemed as if Grenada was threatening to become one massive bonfire, the British lost first their soul and then their mind.

They did not know at whom to point their fingers until they finally settled on Gairy because someone had to be blamed. No chimerical being was made to account and since the British were not able to put their hands on any of the departed spirits, the leader of GMMIWU was held accountable.

Both Gairy and Gascoigne Blaize were held without charge and without trial. The British considered detaining them within my confines but thought that would have been too risky, given Gairy's popularity and the violent mood of the workers. I did not mind since I did not want anyone breaching my walls the same way my brothers stormed the Bastille. The next stop for the detainees, then, was Carriacou.

Carriacou is a twelve square mile island and located northwest of Grenada, thirty miles from its closest point. Together with Petite Martinique that was renamed by Mother and means 'Little Martinique,' they are dependencies of Grenada. Carriacou, meaning 'Land of many reefs,' retained its Carib name and identity.

The Caribs bequeathed to its people as well the spirit of resistance, something the British did not take long to find out. The Carriacouians were extremely angry when they learnt that Gairy had been detained and was being taken to their small and peaceful island. Peaceful yes, but not that they were not experiencing the rumblings of the anti-colonial struggle, but their 'Land of many reefs' was high tide compared to the ten-foot waves that were Camerhogne, the 'Spiritual Home' of the Caribs.

Loupgaroo and La Diablesse lived in Carriacou too, and the spirits of the departed roamed freely there. The spirits of their African ancestors who brought the Big Drum to Carriacou were also still alive. In fact, it had been a long cultural practice of the Carriacouians to hold 'Stone-feasts' in order to appease the spirits of the dead. Success though had been very rare and that meant that the dead were alive, active and revengeful in spirit for most of any one night. Carriacouians then, spent little time differentiating between the spirits and their varying capacity to inflict harm. All spirits were jumbies which you gave no opportunity to get close to you.

Their closeness to the dead, however, endowed them with the ability to invoke the departed spirits for their own designs that were seldom of the nature to be made public. The British, though, were left in no doubt of the disposition of the people of Carriacou, who made clear their vigorous objection to the detention of Gairy and Gascoigne Blaize, and even more vehemently the use of Carriacou as a bullpen.

But when they threatened to march on the detention center and physically free Gairy and Blaize from the pen, and more petrifyingly, to turn loose all of the jumbies of Carriacou, the British did not wait to hear another word. Just before dawn one morning, the detainees were spirited out of Carriacou and locked up on the **HMS Devonshire** which was at anchor a few miles off Grenada. The only reason why this was not done in the middle of the night was because the British too came to believe that that was the time when the spirits of the departed were at their busiest.

For their own well-being and safety, they wanted at all cost to avoid any encounter with the walking dead. And since the freedom of wandering spirits could not be legislated against, that was their best bet.

But the colonialists and the planters were able to pass laws to suppress the struggles of the workers, and they did. Moreover, they declared a State of Emergency. Yet the protest actions continued, including incidents of burning, and the British kept on blaming Gairy. And when they became completely overwhelmed by trepidation, to the point of hallucination, they began to have double vision. Sometimes they saw Gairy, sometimes they saw Fedon, and at other times Gairy became the regenesis of Fedon. The planters' vision was less obstructed, however. Gairy was simply a communist, an unreconstructed one at that.

The colonial government and the planters needed to construct a way out of their troubles, nevertheless. Gairy and the GMMIWU were steeled in their demands and were not going to budge by even one degree, that much was quite evident. The solution, then, was not to be found in further intransigence, but in the adoption of a posture of reconciliation which could only have meant the unconditional acceptance of GMMIWU's demands.

When, on March 19th 1951, the British reluctantly announced their capitulation and the freeing of Gairy and Blaize from battleship-arrest, they could not have worn longer faces. They were made sad by the fact that they had no other choice, and from their at times woebegone expression, I almost felt sorry for them.

Gairy, the leadership of GMMIWU and the thousands upon thousands of workers who were doing a victory dance through the streets, needed no such pity. What they needed was more space than the narrow streets allowed. They had much to be joyful about but not enough room to do justice to its manifestation. After all, significant pay increases, much better living and working conditions, a new found pride in their blackness and the lifting of a psychological barrier to what they were capable of achieving, were no mean feats. A sense of self-worth, self-respect and an appreciation of their strength as workers were seen in their sweating faces. And, as they moved and pranced, happiness in the form of perspiration oozed out of every pore of their sun-soaked bodies. But when the further announcement came that, in accordance with what was happening in the rest of the Caribbean, Grenada was being granted Universal Adult Suffrage, the dancing became wildly unchoreographed.

The politically astute Gairy was still dancing when, almost immediately, he formed and launched his political party, Grenada People's Party. He soon renamed it the Grenada United Labour Party in order to, more precisely, reflect its origins and his support base which he felt would have propelled him into office. With many thousands of poor, ordinary people now allowed to vote Gairy, not unexpectedly, swept the general elections which were held later that year. He rhumbaed his way into his new office as Chief Minister, and, while he was still dancing, the Dutch praised their foresight while the British cursed them and their own ill luck.

Their misfortune was Gairy's success, but he had more than ***Tyche***, the Greek god of Providence, to thank. Several persons, including William Galway Donavan and to a lesser extent, Theophillus Albert Marryshow, opposed Crown Colony government and agitated relentlessly to have it replaced by representative government. But where Donavan was willing to provide employment for a reincarnated Guy Fawkes, Marryshow was accommodating. Yet King George VI was duly warned.

The 1951 General Elections, then, was a flag of success which could have been legitimately waved by Donavan, Marryshow and others. By then, Donavan, himself a Federationist as well, had passed on and Marryshow, who had been his apprentice, had inherited his printery and some of his ideas.

T.A. Marryshow, who was born on November 7th 1887, sat on the Legislative Council since 1925 but became an elected member of the Legislature in 1951 and right up until his death. But he was not just a politician. The once carpenter and newspaper boy had learnt well at the feet of Donavan and soon established his own *'The West Indian'* newspaper. In it he promulgated his passion for education and justice and unceasingly advocated the federation of the British West Indian Colonies.

Marryshow, known throughout the Region and in the hallways of Whitehall and Buckingham Palace as the Father of Federation, served for a few months as Grenada's representative in the upper chamber of the Parliament of the Federated West Indies.

His death on October 19th 1958 preceded by mere months the death of the Federation itself, the establishment for which he vigorously campaigned. But notwithstanding the deaths of other Grenadian leaders on October 19th twenty-five years later, and the discord among Caribbean leaders which followed, Marryshow's bosom-deep vision of a united Caribbean remained alive and was to influence the actions of subsequent generations of Caribbean politicians.

Chapter 28

Grenada had been at its most tumultuous in the 1970's, since its 1951 awakening and social revolution led by the flamboyant Eric Mathew Gairy of the accented and well-modulated speech. In fact, I remember that, as a boy, he spoke so much that some of his friends teasingly joked that 'Eric' was a misnomer; he should have been called 'Ear-ache.'

For me, if pain meant tiredness, then I would have done well with an injection of a thousand doses of morphine. Or perhaps a stimulant of some sort like Bois Bandé. Indeed, I could have done with any good pick-me-up given that I felt so much like an old man who had done too much, heard too much and seen too much.

Yet I was still in control of my faculties, and one would have hoped that Gairy, who had by 1973 won five of the seven general elections, had not lost his. But even when, in 1961, Gairy could not get his hand out of the cookie-jar fast enough and was accused of misappropriating government funds in what became known as 'Sqandermania,' psychiatrists said that was a very bad sign. The British Governor concurred and said Gairy's conduct was unacceptable. They, with due haste, suspended the Constitution and promptly removed Gairy from office seven months after he was elected in 1961.

However, Gairy's support among the agricultural workers, the rural poor and sections of the middle class remained as impenetrable as the hymen of a Mermaid's vagina. In 1967 he was again sitting comfortably in the Chief Minister's chair, and soon thereafter was provided with more powers and better accommodation in the tastefully furnished office of the Premier. In an effort to cut down on their overseas obligations, the British granted Statehood to Grenada and other islands of the Caribbean. For the first time Grenada had its own flag and a State anthem.

But Premier Gairy did not only accept what was granted, he took for himself in very large amounts and it would not be too long before the psychiatrists were doing a study of him as a case of megalomania. While the economic status of his thousands of staunch supporters had not changed since 1951 and they were still so poor the poverty line did not even exist for them, by 1973 he had improved dramatically on his cookie-jar expertise and had amassed property that was worth millions of dollars.

No one knew how much Gairy's Secret Police (modelled after Haiti's Ton-Ton Macoute), and Mongoose Gang were paid, but they were a violent buffer to a growing resistance to his rule.

The Mongoose, a skittish mammal originally from India, was brought to Grenada from South America to kill-out the harmless snakes that were plaguing the canefields. Reputed to be quite sly, they soon out-snaked the snakes then quickly turned their attention to the cane itself. The mongoose made countless meals of the cane fields and routinely added birds, fowls and their eggs for good measure. The Mongoose Gang made their presence felt in the late 1960's when they were initially employed to entrap the mongoose that had become a greater pest than the pests they were brought in to get rid of.

Gairy's pests in the form of those who were in opposition to him had to be gotten rid of too. Once the Mongoose Gang proved their worth in terms of blind loyalty to Gairy and an enormous propensity for violence, in addition to specific instructions, they were given carte blanche license to intimidate, terrorize and destroy. So while the mongoose became a threat to health, livestock and agriculture, the Mongoose Gang became a danger to life and limb.

This ever present and deadly peril and sometimes loose cannon, was felt in 1970 when the wind of black consciousness began blowing through the Caribbean. The wind had its origin off the African coast and took a path right across the Atlantic Ocean and into the Caribbean Sea. It was not the bearer of the Sahara dust and neither was it an ill-wind, but it carried with it lasting effects.

The Black Power Movement when it came to Grenada had many young intellectuals and an army of unemployed youths from which to do its recruiting. It was a period of empowerment for them and a time to give vent to increasingly strong anti-establishment, anti-Gairy sentiments.

Dressed as they usually were in Afro hairstyles, jeans, jerseys that were often black and with a dab of red and green somewhere, or brightly coloured, loose-fitting Yoruban dashikis, sandals, silver bracelets that symbolized the breaking of the chains of slavery and oppression and with pendants of wooden, clenched fists or maps of Africa hung around their necks from black shoe-laces, they drew attention to themselves and their cries of "Black is beautiful."

That, as well as other slogans such as "Be black and proud," "Stand and fight, black is right," "You are black don't stay back" or the initials 'O.B.U' which meant Organization of Black Unity, appeared scrawled in charcoal or spray-painted on walls all across the island. A white statue of the Virgin Mary outside of the St. Joseph's Convent in St. George's, received a coating of black paint one night. No one knew if the Virgin would have been pleased.

The Black Power advocates were more than happy; Gairy, his Mongoose Gang and Secret Police were not. They watched with uneasiness as clenched-fisted youths held fora, picketed and took part in protest marches that were black consciousness-driven but essentially anti-Gairy. They rallied around cultural activities in which the African drums had a dominant role, drums which were often seized and destroyed by Gairy's forces – as they had been, in previous times, by the slave owners and colonialists. And they shared in the food that was part of the Africanized 'Harambee' celebrations.

But events took on an incendiary dimension. Publicly and privately owned buildings such as **Hollywood Fashion House, Mitchell's Pharmacy, George De Frietas** and **Frenchie's** were felled by wrathful flames during the course of several weeks. The fires, which took place only at nights, were as if the obliterators were allergic to daylight. The ravaging fires, nevertheless, drew very large crowds and were a reflection of black conscious, unemployed and harassed youths who were seething with explosive anger. It mattered not to Premier Gairy, his Mongoose Gang and Secret Police however, that many of the volunteer fire-fighters were themselves Black Power advocates or their sympathizers. They had stopped watching and there was at least one good reason why they did. They had been made blind by the need they felt to strike out at non-conformist youths who, by their actions, were undermining the legitimate right of the government to rule in their own likeness. Now it was time to start doing more than they had done before.

There was only one way to bring these 'miscreants' to heel and that was by force, or so Gairy believed. In a national address on Radio Grenada he stated in his customary classy cadence:

"I cannot close my ears to the ugly incidents alleged to have taken place recently, and it may be timely here to mention a few - three youngsters, clad in black, entered the 'Red Crab' Restaurant and ordered drinks and food, ate, and then shouted 'Black Power', and left without paying; another three demanded money and drinks from two foreigners at the Nutmeg Restaurant; others molested some other visitors by the Portofino Restaurant and at the 'China Town' Complex of Restaurants.

My Mother and I

"A stitch in time saves nine" is indeed a wise maxim. My Government will not sit by and allow individuals or groups of individuals to agitate or incite, to promulgate or to promote any racial disharmony in this peaceful 'Isle of Spice' - the Caribbean Garden of Eden."

"...I am the first Black Power advocate in Grenada. My dear people it was I who fought for and won great benefits from the white colonialists. Don't forget it was I, through my years of indomitable struggle, who pressured the bank owners into employing the first black-skinned worker in the banks. So no one can tell me about black power, and I will not allow the unruly and misled to bring instability to our dear land...My dear people, I have recruited the toughest of the roughest roughnecks in the land...It takes steel to cut steel..."

On cue, the Secret Police and Mongoose Gang, and the newly created Voluntary Intelligence Unit for the Protection of Property (VIUPP) and the Night Ambush Squad, brought their specially designed pieces of iron pipe, sticks, pieces of wood, whips and their truncheons to bear. Bodies and skulls were shattered right across the island as more and more youths were severely beaten. Students, who were preparing for exams and were on their way home from studying at school late at nights, could not escape a violent test of physical endurance. Unfortunately for them, they were unaware that the nightsticks were not inscribed with specific names. When they later succeeded at their exams, though, some masochists credited the pedagogical ability of the truncheons.

Later that year, when the Nurses and their hundreds of supporters took to the streets to protest the shocking and sickening conditions at the Colony Hospital, they were to discover that the set was still the same. They were manhandled, tear-gassed and water-cannoned with a pink mixture that irritated the skin, and many of the marchers were brought into contact with the wrong end of the policeman's baton. Shortly thereafter, several of the Nurses were summarily dismissed from their jobs and some of them, along with about twenty persons who marched in solidarity were arrested, charged with 'assembling for the purpose of inciting a riot' and brought to Court.

There were some that were not able to see a puisne judge but were instead given a quick dispatch to seek audience with their ultimate Judge. By 1973, persons, including Jeremiah Richardson, Lester Richardson and Alister Saunders were all cut-down by Gairy's steel. Others were also shot, though not fatally, some were chopped-up and many were otherwise brutalized. Clarence Ferguson was one of those who were savagely attacked by the Mongoose Gang, while his young daughter was publicly stripped naked. If it were a stripped-search and was not meant mainly to humiliate, then I am at a loss at figuring out what they could have been searching for.

But, together with the arbitrary searches to which many were subjected, all of that added to the further indignation and alienation of the young people. Students, too, were similarly disillusioned and took to the streets in large numbers protesting police brutality. Unlike their parents and those of their parents' generation, the young people had nothing to thank Gairy for, except perhaps their inability to find jobs. They knew Gairy best for his brutality and his exercise of total power that was very often arbitrarily used. They knew too, of his wanton corruption. Gairy and his government became increasingly irrelevant as many joined the eternal search for an alternative.

"But there are always alternatives," I said to no one in particular.
"Man at every stage of his development seeks an alternative," I murmured, drawing stares which suggested that an old man speaking to himself must be a candidate for the psychiatric hospital.

"Yet the alternative chosen may not always be in his best interest nor lead to his long-term happiness," I whispered, as I sought to avoid further attention.

"So what predetermines the rightness or wrongness of the alternative chosen?" I asked as I began to question my own sanity. Still, I felt inwardly pleased with myself and the barely restrained smile on my face would not have deceived those who continued to watch from the corner of their eyes. I thought I was well on the way to fashioning a thesis on alternatives and hoped for the stares of the Noble Prize Committee instead.

The minds of the young people were however occupied in finding solutions to their more urgent problems. They wanted them to be addressed and done so genuinely. They wanted the island's interests to be taken at heart. From their many discussions, though, doubts remained as to whether any of that was possible within the framework of what the establishment allowed. The young people were in search of agents of change.

Chapter 29

March 11th, 1973 was bang-on in the middle of the dry season, sunny and scorchingly hot. The atmosphere was bereft of any moisture, nothing remained of the cold-front from North America which seasonally drifts over the Caribbean as it did up to a few weeks before.

Although we had an unusually wet season with one to two inches of rain recorded just for December alone, the pipes which carried water to the homes and hotels, particularly in the south of the island, were already dry. In other parts of the island people could be seen toting buckets and lugging other containers to standpipes on the side of roads and to rivers.

Many looked to the skies in supplication, seeking the intervention perhaps of the Rain God. But the skies remained a silent blue without a hint of the clouds which would suggest that the Rain God was listening.

It was an otherwise beautiful day, but it was not the day itself which gave birth to the New Jewel Movement (NJM). It was more likely the unfolding of events which created the need for a new type of politics in Grenada, and yet it was on that day that the NJM was born, a child of necessity.

The Labour Room was not at the Colony Hospital but in a house in the rural community of Thebaide, St. David's.

Bleasdille was one of the witnesses to, and participants in, this birth. The room was not that large so fifteen young men, most of them bearded and a young woman, Esther Alexander, came close to making it overcrowded. Other persons present included Unison Whiteman, Maurice Bishop, Teddy Victor, Sebastian Thomas, Peter Hazzard, Witaker Jeremiah, Fitzroy Bain, Reginald Buckmire, George Brizan and Kenrick Radix. Though they represented two different political organizations, the St. George's based Movement for Assemblies of the People (MAP) led by Bishop and the St. David's based JEWEL – Joint Endeavour for Welfare, Education and Liberation led by Whiteman, they were united in their commitment to chart a new course for Grenada and Grenadians.

Bishop, Aruban born and the chief architect of MAP, had returned to Grenada from England in 1970. He was not an Episcopalian but a brilliant lawyer with a yearning for freedom who was keen on making his contribution. Since he was the son of Rupert Bishop and the nephew of Roy Bishop, one of Gairy's chief lieutenants in the 1951 revolution, both of whom travelled to Aruba at the same time Gairy did, one may argue that his revolutionary fervor was either genetic or nursed. This, notwithstanding the fact that Bishop was a descendant of Captain Louis La Grenade, a French coloured, who fought with the British against Fedon.

Whiteman, whom Gairy came to detest with almost equal venom as the 'white-man' of his anti-colonial struggles, had returned from the United States of America where he graduated as an economist. He soon went into teaching but could not resist the magnetic pull of politics. In the 1972 general elections which Gairy again won, he was one of the candidates of the then Opposition party, the Grenada National Party (GNP). Together with Selwyn Strachan, Fitzroy O'Neale and Keith Mitchell, they were the young turks; to Gairy, though, Strachan, who was his challenger for the seat of St. George's South, was a 'political mosquito.' But it was their defeat at the polls and the disillusionment with politics as it then was, which gave the impetus to the formation of JEWEL.

It was under the auspices of this organization that, in January of 1973, an Englishman, Lord Brownlow, was made an unwilling defendant in a People's Trial that he probably still remembers. It was not the first People's Trial to be held in Grenada. Fedon held a few of his own before the exigencies of war forced him to bypass the Trial and move straight to the execution of sentence.

But Lord Brownlow, who was charged with denying the people of St. David's access to La Sagesse beach, as if when he came to Grenada from England the beach were part of his luggage, fared much better. The many police officers who were present and whose intended role underwent a situational change, became passive officers of the 'Court.' They observed very orderly proceedings and at the end of which Lord Brownlow was found guilty. The people then proceeded to remove the barriers which had been erected and restored to themselves unhindered access to one of the more beautiful beaches in Grenada, access which they had enjoyed for over a hundred years.

Among those who participated in this exercise of people's power, and later asked to attend another Court to face charges of destruction of property and disorderly behaviour, were Unison Whiteman, Maurice Bishop, Teddy Victor, Hudson Austin and Sebastian Thomas. They were members of both JEWEL and MAP.

That was at the height of their mating call and it would not have been long before, having already fallen into love, the question was popped and Shakespeare's "world-without-end bargain" was entered into. They fell all-over each other onto the conjugal bed and the end result was a begotten son who all endearingly referred to as NJM.

All of that happened in a single day and one can easily imagine such hymeneal rites occurring in a place where man had never been and no earthly eyes had ever seen. A place that had no particular form or shape and was not easy to conceive. There was no distinct landscape with boundaries. Just infinite space with lots of blue and white clouds drifting around aimlessly. The place was airy and light. Yet there was time, there was location.

The church would not be suffocating with invited guests because there was no church. The streets would not be crammed with scores of uninvited guests seeking to get an inquisitive peep at the bride and groom, only to have the most unflattering comments to gossip about their appearance, because there were no streets. Indeed, only the chosen were allowed in but there was no confined area, just open space. Even so, there was a gate manned by someone. That person was difficult to get by, someone with character and form but no substance. On closer inspection one would have discovered that the person was made of a cloud, a gray, male cloud. His purpose was mainly to keep the gate-crashers out, but one stood a chance if one was able to answer any of his many questions, the difficulty of which depended on one's economic status. The wealthier you were, the more difficult the question. It was not uncommon to be asked questions like, "what are the names and ages of all the inhabitants of the earth since it came into being, and how many gallons of urine have they discharged collectively?" There was hardly any risk then to the chosen remaining the chosen no matter how many may have been called or gate-crashed.

There were numerous bridesmaids, bridesmen, flower girls, best men, ring-bearers, and ushers in attendance, all floating around on wings. With instruments such as trumpets, flutes, harps, lyres, harpsichords, mandolins, horns, kettledrums and tambourines, a band stationed aloft and enveloped in blue clouds played nuptial songs in chords that were previously unheard. Their bodies, like all those in attendance, had distinctive form and substance but were so phantomlike that they may have been hued from marshmallows. They were all gloriously naked. In that place nakedness did not arouse testosterone or progesterone or anything else. It was as natural as igloos were to Iceland or as the cool rays of the sun glowing away in the distance.

This gave a surreal appearance to the events, much like the facial appearance of the bride and groom and the one who administered the sacrament of matrimony. He sat with a quiet and warm smile. He was unassuming, yet there was no one with greater presence, and his bearing bespoke power that was impossible to fathom. They all sat on chairs made from gossamer and their wispy bodies were covered in flowing, cream robes.

After the vows were solemnly exchanged and the bride and groom flew off to the bride-chamber, the buzz of excitement became distinctly louder, though it was insignificantly above a whisper. There was in fact no chamber, just more open space but there was location. Those outside the location could not see what was happening on the connubial couch over which hovered the bridesmaids.

The procreation of another vapour-like being was not as a result of sex the way earthly beings knew it. The required configurations of the body were so complicated that they had to be boneless; and they were. It lasted no more than sixty seconds and there was no physical exertion. Penetration could have taken place in any part of either of their wispy bodies depending on the preferences of the couple. There was no obvious sign of enjoyment and it would have taken an extraordinarily keen, earthly ear to pick up the sounds which came from the couch just when ecstasy contained the most sugar. It was more like a toneless flutter just above a whimper. Nothing like the squeals, the 'Oh God' and the 'aaahhhhs' which come from earthly beings. Yet for the residents of that surreal place, the sounds were loud enough to easily have come from a gate-crasher who was attempting to get past the gray male cloud without answering one of his questions. The 'ah-ha' could have been the cloud's own expressed satisfaction after tanning the fanny of the would be intruder.

NJM's creation did not follow quite the same pattern but it quickly captured the imagination of almost all of Grenada, particularly its young people who rallied to its side like migrant ants which have fallen upon an accidentally dropped piece of bread. It was the answer to the alternative they sought. Even its detractors and Gairy himself were forced to take notice.

They could not have failed to observe that its leaders were youthful but mature. That they were intelligent, enthusiastic, dynamic, hard-working and of strong character. Their attention would have been drawn by the passion with which they spoke and their ability to connect with the people without much effort. They would have been alarmed by their publicly stated commitment to rid Grenada of Gairy and Gairyism, and felt threatened by this and the ideals which they professed. They would have cognized as well the name 'New Jewel Movement' and made uneasy by its meaning. They would have pondered long and hard on the 'L' in JEWEL, and the original coiner of this name, Sherwyn Lazarus, would have gotten much of the blame.

To the Gairy regime there was nothing about NJM that was not censurable, most of all its well-stated, though ominous, intentions which to Gairy could only have meant one thing – "engaging in subversive activities to remove a constitutionally elected government." Just as disconcerting to him would have been the speed with which "The Jewel Boys" spun their glitter over vast sections of the people.

Within a few days the NJM had a twelve-member Political Bureau in place which included Maurice Bishop and Unison Whiteman as Joint Co-ordinating Secretaries, Reginald Buckmire, Teddy Victor, Bernard Coard, George Brizan, and Sebastian Thomas. Buttressed by the indefatigable energies of several other party members, they took to the field with the vigor of stallions. Political meetings were held right across the island mobilizing the people around the issues of the day and the concerns which affected their daily bread. In one month the island could have been criss-crossed several times by squads of young political activists carrying the message of liberation. The farmers, fishermen, commercial workers, youth and women found in the NJM, leaders whom they could trust and who were willing to sacrifice on their behalf and spearhead their struggles for betterment.

NJM took its programmatic platform to Seamoon, in St. Andrew's, on May 6th, where it held its convention on Independence, a cause which was being championed by Gairy and which formed part of his electoral campaign in 1972. Thousands attended and showed their support for NJM, which said yes to Independence, albeit meaningful Independence, which they did not think possible under Gairy.

But Gairy had his own ideas about what was possible or was not possible. His government acquired, in several cases without compensation, the lands of some of his political opponents in a scheme which he dubbed 'Land for the Landless.' He seized control of the Nutmeg, Cocoa and Banana Boards which provoked street demonstrations and which he responded to violently. Other persons were beaten, some were killed. Professionally trained police officers were gotten rid of and specially chosen ruffians and men of questionable character were brought in to replace them. Public Workers too, were regularly victimized.

In plain sight to all, Gairy's back was up, and in the face of that a fickle and cowardly group would have packed their bags and gone home. But not the NJM, they got their backs up too. By then, though, its Political Bureau, for various reasons, had begun to change its make-up. Persons who included Selwyn Strachan and Hudson Austin replaced those who had left. Others like Lloyd Noel, George Louison, Jacqueline Creft, Chester Humphrey and Basil Gahagan were to join later. But whatever changes were taking place, NJM remained resolute in its determination to rid Grenada of Gairy and Gairyism.

Despite the large turnout of fully armed police officers, the roadblocks and arbitrary searches, close to ten thousand ordinary and enthusiastic Grenadians participated in the November 4th, People's Congress held at Seamoon. Its pavilion proved way inadequate and many persons had to stand on the field to the front of the gable-roofed, wall and wood structure. But Seamoon, like the Market Square in St.

George's, had quickly become the preferred rallying ground for resistance to Gairy. The police did not succeed in intimidating the people, but the people, by their huge numbers, may have intimidated the police as their voices resoundingly acclaimed Gairy's guilt in response to the twenty-seven charges which were read out against him. It was yet another People's Trial, and among other things, Premier Gairy and his GULP government were given until November 18th, 1973 to resign. Failing which, there would be a national strike until the government stepped-down.

Chapter 30

It was November 18th 1973, a Sunday, another day that the Lord had made. Although the tension in the air was perceptible and those who were politically attuned would have felt a deep foreboding, it was, by and large, a normal day.

Whether the sun inconsiderately showered its cancer-causing rays upon the earth unhindered or the earth was liberally soused with Adam's ale, it was still a normal day, it was still a beautiful day and it was still a day that the Lord had made.

That day though, the sun was out and exhausting its supply of brilliance. A good number of churchgoers, less an abundance of young persons who no longer saw the church as relevant, would have gone to church that morning. The church, as seen by many, had become a tomb of silence, living as it were, in their own cocoon. They largely abdicated their responsibility to provide the society with direction on moral, social and political issues, believing, it seemed, that only the souls of its followers needed to be looked after. The further the society drifted from Christian values, the more silent they, including many who claimed to be Christians, appeared to become. I myself, living within thick, stucco walls which were a part of me, came to the view that Grenada was not a Christian society but a society in which some Christians lived.

But for those who would have graced the insides of churches, some of which were a throwback to twelfth century, arch, vault and stained glass Gothic architecture, Papa God's presence would have been felt. They would have implored His blessings on whatever the endeavour or concern that was foremost in their minds at that moment. Without doubt, many would have been mindful of the political events in Grenada, and anxiety levels would have reached a near critical point.

NJM enjoyed uncritical support from a wide cross-section of Grenadians which embodied sizeable percentages of congregations. Its sphere of influence had grown substantially as it became more deeply rooted amongst the people. Its published manifesto as well as its popular, flagship newspaper, '***The New Jewel***,' which was produced weekly had immeasurable impact and sway over its rapidly increasing readership.

While Gairy's hard-core support remained as unendangered as politicians' ability to tell lies, NJM had begun to win over some well-known and longstanding Gairy supporters. That was unsettling news for Gairy, but NJM's move to force him out of office was bad tidings for the Duvalier in him. Gairy resolved to uproot the "upstarts" with the delicacy of a category two hurricane.

Unaware of Gairy's intentions, worshippers, home from attending church services, were not making preparations to go into hurricane shelters. They would have been sitting down to a Sunday lunch of rice, salad, vegetables, macaroni-pie and chicken or beef, a Sunday staple in ever so many homes, just when six NJM leaders set off from St. George's in three cars for a meeting in Grenville, St. Andrew's.

Grenville is the town of the largest of Grenada's six parishes. It is on the east and sits at the end of a half an hour journey by vehicle, assuming that one travels at a moderate speed along the hilly, mostly narrow and in some places treacherous, asphalt-paved, Grand Etang road which runs through the center of the island. And assuming too, that the driver avoids an accident. But otherwise it can be a relaxing and refreshing journey. The dense vegetation, which the road bisects, and the cool fresh air, provide a salutary connection with nature in its almost unsullied state, and it was difficult to escape the feeling that that was how Papa God intended the world to be. The scenic views, too, make it altogether a therapeutic experience.

The effect was just that on the six NJM leaders who were travelling along the same road. The first car was driven by Hudson Austin and had as its other occupant, Selwyn Strachan. At the wheel of the second car was Simon Daniel, and Maurice Bishop sat next to him. With Kenrick Radix driving the third car and Unison Whiteman occupying the front passenger seat, the small convoy made its way at a quick clip to the coastal town.

It was about 1 p.m. when the travelling party made their final preparations to leave the home of Bishop at Parade, in South East St. George's. Obviously, with the day's sunshine having reached its mark, they were in good spirits and joked among themselves.

"Sello, I have been trying to reach you on the phone for the whole night without success. Do you care to explain?" Bishop said to Strachan with a smile that revealed his suspicions.

"How you mean?" Strachan asked, feigning innocence. "Is the Telephone Company you need to ask."

"Come on man, you know what I mean; the telephone works perfectly," Bishop responded jokingly and unintentionally giving a plug to the Telephone Company. "Whatever else you spent the night on, it surely was not the phone," he quipped.

"Well... hear nah man..." The rest of Strachan's retort was lost in a gale of boisterous laughter, but his uncharacteristic stammering was a bad sign.

There were other bad signs that day. A few policemen were keeping watch on Bishop's home and relaying messages through walkie-talkies on the movements of the NJM leaders. Yet these men felt no undue worry. After all, their trip to Grenville was for the simple purpose of holding a perfectly legal meeting with businessmen to discuss the proposed general strike. Moreover, they felt buoyed by their mission and by the undoubted support which they had been given title to from far and wide.

By the time they left Bishop's home and turned left, radioed messages had already forewarned that they would be travelling along the eastern seaboard, through St. David's and not along the Grand Etang road as had been expected. That alert immediately set into motion a deployment of scores of Gairy's Secret Police. Those who were waiting on the Grand Etang road hurried pell-mell into Grenville, while others were sent along the St. David's route expecting to be in time to waylay the unsuspecting leaders.

But the convoy's left turn had been a deliberate ploy, hoping to confuse the surveillants. They quickly doubled back, went through Mt. Parnassus and were soon onto the Grand Etang road. It was an unhindered and untroubled though hurried trip through the lush, green, forested center of Grenada.

In twenty minutes the small convoy was entering Grenville from its northern end. There was no welcoming party and they did not expect any, yet there were seventy-five, fully armed Secret Police awaiting their arrival in front of the Deluxe Cinema where the meeting between the businessmen and NJM leaders was scheduled to be held. Mr. H.M. Bhola, one of the businessmen, was also there and spoke to the leaders who had prudently remained in their cars. He apprised them of the situation and advised that, in light of the presence of uninvited guests, the meeting be shifted to his home.

The convoy which had arrived early, as did the Secret Police, for a meeting set for two o'clock, drove along to the home of Mr. H.M. Bhola, two hundred and fifty feet away.

Although the Secret Police were in the business of naked brutality, with all respect to them, they were not considered businessmen and had not been invited. Moreover, it was a Sunday, a day on which commercial activity was restricted by law. But the Secret Police may have well thought that they had urgent business to conduct with the NJM leaders, business which could not wait for another day.

While Mr. Bhola went upstairs of his home to contact the other businessmen by phone, the NJM leaders, now out of their parked cars, stood on the outside of the downstairs which was not more than four feet adjoining the road. They stood talking and it was not idle talk, though they did share a little private chit-chat that evoked some quiet laughs. However, they reminded themselves about what was needed to be achieved from their meeting with the businessmen, and noted as well the presence of the Secret Police in front of the cinema.

No one knew when Simon Daniel had disappeared or where he went. He could have gone to see a friend, and equally possible, he could have gone to a shop which strictly did not observe the Sunday sale prohibition.

But they knew he had left and was making a rather quick return when the sight and sound of Daniel running towards them at full throttle halted their conversation. He was being chased by fifteen Secret Police armed with sticks, batons and bull-pestles of varying size.

Daniel was fit and strong and gasping. But he did not need to say anything to his colleagues who had surrounded him. It was easy to infer what had happened, and the hardened faces and bloodthirsty expressions of the Secret Police, who were now milling around, confirmed that the inference was more than reasonable.

The NJM leaders became increasingly apprehensive and alarmed as more and more menacing looking Secret Police gathered around, like vultures swooping down on a fresh carcass, brandishing the tools of their trade. Yet the leaders knew that they were on a totally peaceful and legal mission and as such felt no need to leave. That was until, with about seventy-five Secret Police thugs present, Inspector of Police, Innocent Belmar, announced his arrival as he screeched his car to a stop, jumped out and gave the order "Get dem dogs."

No one saw where Daniel passed; it was as if he had never stopped running after he was initially chased by the Secret Police. Radix followed close on his heels and his chubbiness, contrary to the laws of physics, made him move faster. But then it was the more powerful law of survival in operation. Austin was not that far behind as they sought safety in the upstairs of Mr. Bhola's house. They moved with due haste and they had a right to.

Bishop, Strachan and Whiteman could not make it to the entrance of the house in time. Without the power of levitation they could not have gone up into the air, and Atabeyra, the Caribs' Earth Mother, was not about to open up and provide them with protection within her rocky and muddy depths. Their only possibility of escape was around the back of the house and the required distance was not covered at a leisurely pace.

Yet they were not fast enough for the avenging thugs who descended on them from both directions. At that point their lives, more than ever, were in the hands of Papa God, as their deaths were hungered after with the craving of maniacs. Blows were rained all over them with such urgency and fury that they hardly had time to breathe. They were thrown to the ground and savagely beaten with sticks of varying thickness, axe-handles, batons and bull-pestles. They were repeatedly kicked, at times to the head, and stamped on. Blood flowed profusely and seemed to come from everywhere and yet there was no letup in the blows which were delivered with such ferocity that the surrounding walls cried and pleaded for mercy.

Just when it appeared that the men were drifting into unconsciousness, or death was getting the better of life, amazingly, despite the furor of the feeding vultures, the beating frenzy stopped. Perhaps they heard the weeping of the walls, felt Papa God's touch upon their anesthetized hearts, or their hands may have gotten tired.

Battered and bleeding, they were literally dragged away, thrown into the back of a van and carted off to the cold cells of the police station a few yards away. They were soon joined by those who had taken cover in Mr. Bhola's house, but on their way they could not escape an unappetizing dessert of licks for having missed the main meal.

With Whiteman, Bishop and Strachan slipping in and out of consciousness and moaning in pain, they were left unattended to feed on their own blood for the entire night. Also in pain and nursing their own wounds, Radix, Austin and Daniel attempted to provide whatever little succour they could have to their colleagues during the course of the night.

Next morning, still in agonizing pain and caked in blood, they were hauled before Magistrate I.I. Duncan to be read charges of possession of arms and ammunition and attempting to overthrow the government. Yes, they wanted to rid the island of Gairy and Gairyism but not with arms and ammunition. For one thing they had none. The Magistrate refused to grant them bail despite the pleas of lawyer, Lloyd Noel, and others. And, notwithstanding their bloodied and mauled appearances, Mr. I.I. Duncan did not even suggest that they be given urgent medical attention. The 'I.I.' in his name must have stood for iniquity and inhumanity.

The treatment of these six NJM leaders at the hands of a morally depraved regime shocked all Grenadians except the die-hard Gairyites. No wonder that what most felt was moral revulsion. Even as they were locked up in cells deep within me as they were ordered to be by the Magistrate, public abhorrence grew. Widespread concern, including those emanating from the Governor's Office, about the refusal to provide them with medical care, had its effect.

The day was several hours old when the six were seen and examined by Dr. Mahy who ordered the immediate hospitalization of Bishop, Strachan and Whiteman. Collectively they were found to have suffered cracked skulls, broken jaws, extracted teeth, cuts and a ruptured back among other injuries.

These injuries were so serious that medical treatment was sought overseas two weeks later.

In the meantime the government continued to play 'footsie' with the judicial system. Magistrate Lloyd St. Louis came up to me to deny a second application for bail within a matter of days. It was only when the matter was subsequently taken to a High Court Judge that bail was finally granted.

Yet weeks later the government was still playing games, a major preoccupation of politicians. I have been around long enough to know and as far as I could tell their favourite playthings were the Court, the Police, the Parliament and the Treasury. The politicians enjoyed kicking most, so to them these institutions and their personnel represented balls which were filled with air and nothing else. But if, indeed, they were not balls but human beings who lacked backbone, then they also lacked balls. They had no character and no mettle or intestinal fortitude so they allowed themselves to be kicked in the direction of the politicians' choice, and to be manipulated for their benefit.

There was once a Judge who was booted so hard that he zoomed through the air with the speed of an unidentified flying object, except that the sucker and the scamp, all one person, was well known. He bounced off my exterior with skin-abrasive impact and boomeranged onto the judge's bench, where he was met by an emissary promising a new posting and a hefty purse of perks to go with it. This brought on instantaneous amnesia that had nothing to do with any diagnosable medical condition. He promptly forgot his training and oath of office and was overheard singing sotto voce to himself in the privacy of the judge's chambers, "The more you pay the more you sway." His written judgement in favour of the Applicants was hastily dumped and a new one upholding the government's arguments was subsequently delivered.

One may feel the need to be skeptical but believe me when I tell you that some of these balls relished being kicked, the harder the better and once the politicians' boots landed squarely on their round backsides, they could not ask for more.

While, then, games like cricket, tennis, basketball, golf and even liar's poker and conman's crap remained popular among politicians, by far the game that found most favour with them was football which some called soccer. Still, in addition to be booted around, these balls would not have minded being pushed around like pawns on a chessboard.

Chapter 31

By next day there were early signs that people were not going to be as inanimate as balls or chess-pieces, nor as unresponsive to the spate of governmental abuses. Anywhere you turned people were gathered in cells and from their intense looks and the movement of their facial muscles and hands, it was clear they were not discussing the weather or the recent showing in Regal Cinema of ***Sounder***, starring the Kittitian, Cicely Tyson. Some claimed that she had Carriacouian roots but that was not an item of conversation either.

Grenadians have very expressive faces and their concern could not have been masked. Nay, their faces spelt danger for Gairy which he would have seen if he were able to see past his Jewel-phobia. And if he were able to lay a finger on the pulse of the people, he would have been able to feel the danger as well. But Gairy was smart enough not to risk, unnecessarily, his life and his continued reign by getting physically close to the people. That would have been the wrong time to do so. He may have caused skulls to be cracked, but that did not say he wanted a scratch on his.

The law of survival existed for him as much as it did for the NJM six, on whom such savagery was inflicted, as to provoke the mass demonstrations and national strike that it was intended to forestall. An 'unpolled' consensus had taken definite shape among the people. Thousands of persons took to the streets, week after week, with the sheer determination to uninstall Gairy from office.

It was the twenty-first day of January 1974, a Monday that was unlike all previous Mondays, as if Papa God had set aside that particular day for man's worst defilement. That was not recorded in Genesis, but biblical scrolls made of papyrus that are yet to be discovered in caves along the shores of the Red Sea may well reveal this.

The day gave no prior announcement of its intentions and no one knew exactly what it held in store, but tension gripped the island as tight as an underwear several sizes too small. Though warm fronts and low pressure areas were furthest from the thoughts of Grenadians, it was a sunny day and not unbearably hot. A light intermittent breeze tiptoed through the paved streets, through cobbled-stone alleys, over and around concrete buildings, providing just enough encouragement for the thermophobics.

There was no other fear, however, as thousands of people coming from all parts of the island flooded the Carenage in St. George's, extending from Otway's House, the headquarters of the Seamen and Waterfront Workers Union. Those within the confines of the city walked but many would have travelled on the Japanese-made "One More" buses, as they were indigenously called, or the local wooden buses such as "*Comfort*," "*Largo Pride*," "*Sweet Roses*," "*Content*" and "*Mayfair*."

The multitude which gathered on that morning brought with them a spirit of resistance, and from their graves Kaierouanne and Fedon sang their praises. The people made their countless ancestors and their many revered deities extremely proud. It was a spirit which was reflected across the island. The atmosphere was rife with optimism. Gairy had to go: and if he had not gone by the end of the day, it would not be too long, as was the popular view, before he skedaddled out of Mt. Royal, the official residence of the Premier.

No one, it seemed, wanted him in office. He may have gotten away with his cookie-jar expertise but the people were not prepared to put up with his dictatorial actions and his proven capacity for violence. More than that, because everyone knew what he was capable of, no one wanted to find out what he would have done with the increased powers of a new Independence constitution.

Otway House became the assembling point for the anti-Gairy, massive street demonstrations which took place every day except on Sundays. January 21st was one of the highest points of such demonstrations, and there were at least twenty-five thousand high-spirited people present. Two days before, twenty-seven thousand took over the streets of St. George's, one thousand for each of the twenty-seven charges in NJM's indictment of Gairy.

But there were not that many people when the street demonstrations began on November 21st, 1973, three days after Bloody Sunday. Only the exceptionally stout-hearted were willing to take to the streets so quickly after Gairy's bloody onslaught. This time it was the law of preservation at work, not nearly as safety-seeking as the law of survival. People were being cautious and they had a right to be. Many persons then, I guess, would have required more time to harness their courage. I myself did not feel the need to throw caution to the wind, and preferred to stay where I had been put on top of a hill peering down on the southern end of the city. With Gairy sharing jaw-breaking licks, it was better for me to observe the proceedings from a safe distance.

The twenty placard-bearing, young stalwarts who began the street marches showed remarkable ballsiness. There were also young women among that small group of protestors who congregated outside the Law Chambers of Maurice Bishop and Kenrick Radix on Lucas Street. They then proceeded down cobbled-stone Market Hill and into the heart of the city.

That show of quiet courage and the revulsion felt to the brutal acts of the Gairy regime, fed on a reservoir of sympathy and universal repugnance waiting to be tapped. The ranks of the marchers doubled and tripled faster than it took for the news to be telephoned to Mt. Royal. And while the developments were being communicated the people chanted:

> "G-O go Gairy must go
> G-O go Gairy must go
> G-O go Gairy must go…"

Gairy watched and listened with mortal horror but felt he could do nothing. His natural instincts were tempered by the many, including those in high places locally and regionally, who took exception in the strongest terms to his Bloody Sunday exploits. While he watched with misgivings and did nothing, people were emboldened by his inaction and thought they were witnessing the cowering of a defanged and grievously hurt, though otherwise dangerous beast of the wild. Yet it would be almost two months before they realized just how bloody dangerous a bloodied beast could be.

It was specific foreknowledge which they did not have and had not perceived. In the bliss and comfort which this provided, they laid claim to the streets of St. George's in their thousands, as each day more and more people added numbers to the legions of demonstrators ready to do battle for the cause of freedom:

> "We fighting for our freedom
> We shall not be moved,
> We fighting for our freedom
> We shall not be moved
> Just like the tree that's planted by the water
> We shall not be moved.
> We shall not be, we shall not be moved
> We shall not be, we shall not be moved
> Just like the tree that's planted by the water
> We shall not be moved…"

My Mother and I

Voices covering the full range of the octave scale, some a great deal more melodious than others, and cushioned by bass tones struggling to stay alive, sang out their commitment to continue the fight no matter how long it took. Soles of shoes on tired feet were worn out to the delight of **Bata Shoe Store.** The overly supportive sun baked the epidermis with the efficiency of a technologically advanced, 51st century, world-sized solar oven. The Grenadian white turned red, light brown skin became dark brown, dark brown became black and black became toasted bread that had been left in the toaster one minute too long. And yet the people showed no sign of fatigue. It was as if they were being driven by a collective will or powered by a well-oiled D10 engine hidden somewhere in their midst.

Gairy saw and heard, and every time he stole a covert glance out of his window, he felt less restrained by the censure of important persons in and out of the island. He was convinced that the people were coming for him where he was holed up in his official residence.

> Gairy in Mt. Royal hiding, hiding, hiding,
> Gairy in Mt. Royal hiding
> Hiding from the crowd,
> Gairy where are thou?
> Gairy where are thou?
> Gairy where are thou?
> He hiding from the crowd…"

They left no doubt in song at whom their protests were targeted, and many demonstrators, who made bold their intentions one Saturday to physically remove Gairy from his sanctum, had to be discouraged by others. There were visibly armed policemen at intervals from the end of Sans Souci which led to his residence. On the other hand, Gairy was neither a homebody, a hermit nor a cloistered monk as he had pretended to be for the previous few weeks, and as angered as the people were, no one wished for him such a horrible death as can be caused by solitude.

Alas, with the two and a half weeks break which the protestors took for the Christmas season, Gairy was able to look out his window without first peeping over its sill furtively. He breathed lungfuls of fresh, clean air. But in early January of 1974, the demonstrators were back out on the streets en masse and the air, which Gairy breathed then, was not as refreshing as he would have hoped. It smelt of more trouble for him.

The militant dockworkers of the Seaman and Waterfront Workers Union had by then taken strike action, completely shutting down Grenada's main seaport in St. George's. With an economy based on imports and exports, this critical act of solidarity meant that, without an international airport, an economic stranglehold had been placed around its neck. And as far as Gairy was concerned, he was already choking.

But he was entering the "valley of the shadow of death" when NJM, in collaboration with the **Committee of 22**, comprising of twenty-two employers, Trade Unions, church and civic organizations, decided to apply an airlock squeeze. News of their decision to immediately begin a national strike, thereby shutting down the entire island and hopefully forcing Gairy out of office, were Gairy's last rites as he saw it. Premier Gairy considered his options, including yielding to the popular demands of the people by stepping down, and pushing out a white flag through his window if he could have so managed. He rejected all, except one. He was chomping at the bit to once again play the card which he had always relied upon.

For the thousands who thronged the streets, a national strike was Gairy's cul-de-sac. They took to the bitumen-paved roads with an avenging spirit, confident that he was on his last legs, and they were certain that if his legs were still able to carry him, he was going if he had not yet gone.

When the protestors reached upper Lucas Street, which the Georgian-Edwardian architectured Government House overlooked, twenty thousand voices were chanting in unison,

My Mother and I

"G-O go Gairy must go, G-O go Gairy must go" as if directed by an unseen, baton-wielding hand of a chant-master.

Government House was the official digs of the Governor, and its resident, the widely admired and respected Grenadian born and nurtured Governor, Dame Hilda Bynoe, needed no one to direct her thoughts. She looked upon the crowd soberly and not the least bit bemused. A few days later, however, everyone knew what she had been thinking. She submitted her resignation with almost immediate effect, and may have considered it an affront by Gairy to have committed his Bloody Sunday atrocities on the same day as her 52nd birthday. So although it was clear that it was not her that the people wanted to go, there were ample reasons why she was no longer willing to be associated with the Gairy regime. Dame Hilda's equation was quite simple: she was not prepared to stay if Gairy was not prepared to go.

The peoples' own equation was just as straightforward: they were prepared to live on the streets for as long as Gairy continued to live at Mt. Royal. Gairy's refusal to budge, then, handed to the protestors tenancy of the streets, while the Governor's resignation was a powerful indication that victory was much closer than Grenadians' well-known understated 'just around the corner.'

>"We shall overcome
>We shall overcome
>We shall overcome some dayaaaay,
>For deep in our hearts
>We do believe,
>We shall overcome some day…"

It was with this steadfast faith that, on January twenty-first, 1974, the widest cross-section of Grenadian people, numbering about twenty-five thousand, boarded their buses early in the morning and headed, yet again, for the gathering point on the Carenage in St. George's.

Energy, enthusiasm and optimism filled their veins and went into feet which took them clamourously along well-beaten paths. They chanted intimidatingly, sang with élan and carried themselves with an air of invincibility.

In the face of that Gairy was not feeling particularly gung-ho. Indeed, he began to question his own mortality, and as determined as he was not to answer the summons of the people, unbidden thoughts of answering the summons of death filled his head. Those thoughts were similar to that of a bloodied beast, and depending on the circumstances they both respond by striking out.

Unknown to the demonstrators and while they were renaming the streets after the Caribs, the Fedonists, the former Slaves, Ex-Servicemen and countless of their other ancestors, one hundred of the roughest and toughest of Gairy's Secret Police and Mongoose Gang members were answering his call to a meeting at Mt. Royal that Monday morning.

In mood they were at their most homicidal, in character they were thugs of the worst possible vintage. They listened fanatically as their leader gave one of his typical 1951 exhortations:

"…I am not telling you what to do, I am not telling you what not to do, but these demonstrations must end once and for all. You must do what is necessary. These Jewel Boys have been asking for trouble and you must show them what trouble looks like. They want to overthrow your constitutionally elected government and we cannot have that…."

Properly soused with 'Babash,' locally fermented spirits, and perhaps some other mind-altering substance given their maniacal behaviour, these hired hell-raisers were sent on their way.

Meanwhile the demonstrators had returned to the Carenage, in front of Otway's House which sat on one side of the street. The other side was hemmed in by a sea that was usually at peace with itself. It provided moorings for the many inter-island schooners and water-taxis such as **Polar Bear** which, for a few cents, rowed you across one side of the

Carenage to the other. And with its inviting blue, the sea lapped entreatingly at the narrow sidewalk which ran the full length of the Carenage. The sidewalk too, was crammed with protestors who went there at the end of every march to listen to fighting speeches from various speakers. That morning, Finbar Johnson, a young student of Presentation Boys College, was at the podium waxing his best and at his most eloquent:

"Gairy's time and political life have already expired and he does not know it. Indeed, when he chose to unleash his animalistic cruelty on the NJM members, the expiry date on his government said 'immediate.' His days are no longer numbered, they are finished and this is our final warning to him, get out or we will push you out! You have ruined this country and you are not a fit and proper person to lead us into Independence. We will remain here..."

Johnson's fine oratory was interrupted first by distant sounds which could have been the growling of dogs. Then, as the sounds became closer, they assumed distinct form. They were the voices of men, guttural and ominous. The voices, still inaudible, crescendoed as they moved along Tyrrel Street, one street above the Carenage. The pounding of feet against the asphalt road could be heard as the men sought to hammer their anger into the ground, a forewarning of their maddening intent.

There was disquiet among the thousands as they turned apprehensively to face one hundred approaching Secret Police and Mongoose Gang elements entering the Carenage from their right, next to the Telephone Company. With whooping actions and distorted faces, they stomped into the road and sing-chanted threateningly in deep, rusty-sounding, untutored voices:

> "Jewel behave youself they go try us for murder
> Jewel behave youself they go try us for murder
> Jewel behave youself they go try us for murder..."

As this band of rowdy thugs approached, the large crowd needed no tutoring in expedient conduct and parted, like the Red Sea at the behest of Moses, in order to allow the thugs unhindered passage. The crowd was humongous but peaceful and avoided any violent incident.

But if the demonstrators were not going to be baited, the Secret Police and Mongoose Gang were overly eager to push the bait down their throats. A few minutes prior to their arrival, a truck loaded with empty bottles belonging to one of the soft drink companies, made its way through the gathering and parked no more than a hundred feet to their left. If that was not by design then it was as accidental as rain falling in the wet season.

Unquestionably though, it was convenient, as convenient as a policeman's baton. The hoodlums went to the truck the way disaster-stricken people will go after relief supplies. Bottles were hurled willy-nilly into the crowd and as rapidly as if propelled by the firing mechanism of an automatic pistol. People scampered to safety. Many ran like two Asafa Powells in one and were able to escape from the Carenage with a few cuts and bruises. Some, including Finbar Johnson, who a few minutes earlier had proclaimed his immovability, could have been one of those who ran so fast that only the strong wind left in their wake told of their flight. The several uniformed Police Officers who were present also ran away just as fast, leaving the people to fend for themselves and the Secret Police to reinvent the days of America's Wild West. A few young men jumped into the sea hoping to be shielded by a sea nymph and in a last-ditch effort to attract its irresistible charms.

Dozens of school children were hustled into the confines of Otway House and told to lie low. Together with the adults who were present, they pleaded to Papa God in prayer, mumbled prayers which rose up to Him so quickly that He needed the help of an electronic device to decipher what He was being asked. But He knew and He understood.

By then the truck had been emptied and for the Secret Police and Mongoose Gang elements in any case, the bottles had become outdated weapons of mass destruction. Concealed pistols emerged from nowhere it seemed, and caused a terrifying echo of pah-pah-paaahh as bullets ricocheted off the painted, concrete walls of Otway House, bringing back memories of the War of Jenkins' Ear. Some bullets found their way into the building and luckily no one inside was hurt.

Rupert Bishop, the father of Maurice Bishop and the brother of Roy Bishop who stood at the ramparts with Gairy in 1951, was not so fortunate. Yet he was conscious of the risk he was taking and the sacrifice he was making. Rupert, who was close to the door, heard the attempts of the thugs to enter the building. Knowing that school children were in there and would be at the mercy of these crazed fanatics, he decided to block the entrance with his body. This was too big an affront to be swallowed by the Secret Police. One of their numbers aimed his gun directly at Rupert and shot him.

There was nothing like gunfire to have an area quickly cleared or to get persons to beat a hasty retreat. Yet, although the Carenage was now completely in the hands of the Secret Police and the other thugs, two or three of the more resourceful demonstrators were returning gunfire from the back of buildings.

Shooting was one thing but being shot at was quite another. Suitably discouraged, the Secret Police hastily turned their attention to other pursuits. Starting from the Carenage and ending up in the center of the city, they went on an orgy of shop breaking and looting. Some places were targeted, especially those held to be closely linked to efforts to unseat Gairy. When they were through, such places as **Pressey's Cold Store**, **James Milne** and **Everybody's** supermarket were almost empty shelves of their former selves. Moreover, at the end of the day, Rupert Bishop was dead, many were injured and the Carenage and city center could have been spoils left behind by a marauding army. 'Bloody Sunday' had to have a 'Bloody Monday!'

Chapter 32

A group of young men left St. George's on a mission on the night of January twenty-first, 1974. It was the kind of night that Soukoyahs loved the most, eerily quiet, as quiet as a cemetery at midnight. It was as if Grenadians were bemoaning what had transpired that day while at the same time doubting themselves that it actually happened.

The neighbourhood dogs were not even barking at the moon. There was no evidence of a moon to bark at anyway. The absence of any moonlight meant then that the night was as dark as the inside of a black cat. This pitch-darkness which devoured the night became pitch-blackness because the streetlights had been turned off, reminding all of the general strike which began a few weeks before and which still continued.

By dusk all were indoors. No one trusted to be outside after dark especially on a night like that night. It was not just that people feared the unknown which comes with darkness, but people were wary of the political demons that were surely to be about.

Once inside their de-electrified, strike-affected homes with windows and doors tightly shut, blinds were drawn before flashlights were turned on or candles and 'masantoes' lit. No one wished to attract the attention of anyone outside at that hour. They could only have been evil spirits or the very demons with whom they had no business.

When Grenadians turned into their beds that night they took care of their business with Papa God first. But they had not waited a second longer before they heaped a bushel of curses upon Gairy's head. The worst imaginable troubles were called down on him, too much for him alone to bear. I feared then that Grenada was slated to share the burden of woes that were directed Gairy's way.

Eager to free Grenada from its dire straits, a group of nine young men filled with noble ideals and youthful zeal, gathered on the compound of the Presentation Boys College that night. In fact, they ran into each other moments after the Secret Police struck, and were together since then. Apart from a sound friendship, they were some of the early believers of the notion that violent, oppressive governments could only be removed violently, and January twenty-first did nothing to disabuse them of that belief.

Buoyed by their commitment and the bold, if not foolhardy, actions which they contemplated, they left their concentration point at 8.p.m. that evening travelling up the eastern main road. In their possession were rifles and pistols and that kept the fear of evil at a safe distance as they headed for the parish of St. David's in two cars.

Though no one could vouch for the whereabouts of chimerical beings at any given time, the road was clear of life souls as was anticipated. People were nursing their undisguised terrors and took to their homes before the island was awash in darkness. But the Secret Police and Mongoose Gang had their own anxieties, too, and once night befell the earth, they bolted for the safest corner in which to lay their heads. They expected 'Jewel' to respond and knew not what they were capable of. They feared the worst.

Yet neither they nor the police could have foreseen what was coming their way along the eastern coast. When the unit of nine men arrived in St. David's, it was no less a ghost town than the one they had left behind. The life souls which were evident belonged to some of the men with whom the St. George's unit were to join forces.

Together the men numbered twenty-one. The H hour was twelve midnight. For the next three and a half hours or so, the would-be combatants rested in the home of one of their comrades, while the leaders of both units made the final arrangements for the joint operations.

At about 11.55 p.m. the platoon left the house quietly, if not stealthily, although there was no one around to be aroused by a little bit of noise. Still, it was natural for militant youths on such a mission to assume the poise of professional soldiers, and by the look of things they were enjoying their moment in the dark.

There was no moonlight to direct the feet of men who were making every effort to move lightly, and there were not that many stars studding the night sky with its brilliance. In some respects, though, it could have been a celestial scene from a movie about religious devotees on a nighttime pilgrimage.

But these young men who had embarked on a military crusade, were not carrying pastoral staffs. In their hands were rifles and pistols, not that far a cry from World War II armaments. As they trudged through the interior, through densely forested areas, hills and gullies, there was anticipatory excitement communicated by the almost audible, accelerated beating of hearts.

Yet, although they were carrying no backpacks, this heightened biological rhythm could simply have been the result of exertion. Rain had not fallen elsewhere for several days but that had not been the case in the hills at the foot of Grand Etang. The ground in many places was wet, muddy and slippery and some gullies were flowing with water as lively as if they were recently restocked and promised a new shipment within hours.

At least one of the fledgling combatants was a tenderfoot and had difficulty staying on his feet, slipping and sliding as if the ground had been waxed. He was helped along and the platoon made its way safely and, despite the challenges of the terrain, energized.

They exited the dense undergrowth no more than twenty-five feet from a concrete building which, from its appearance, gave nothing away about its identity. Its windows and doors were shut, though the combatants were to shortly discover just how tightly. One had to have had twenty-twenty vision to discern a single flicker of light on the inside which could have suggested that it was inhabited.

But inhabited or not, the high-spirited young men had a plan to execute. While nineteen of them retained the cover offered by the foliage just at the top of the escarpment, two of the platoon leaders made it to the door of the building doing a convincing take on cloak-and-dagger actions. The two had prominent muscles and broad shoulders, which did not distinguish them greatly from most of their comrades. Strength was therefore not in short supply.

Together they went at the wooden door, hammer and tongs. Using their shoulders and upper bodies as battering rams, they heaved repeatedly into the locked door with the force of three hundred and fifty pounds, and made enough noise to wake up an entire village. Yet the door would not budge and neither did anyone come to answer it. The doors and windows of the building were not only locked, they were reinforced with battens as if its occupiers were expecting an unwanted visit from extraterrestrial beings or an invasion of immense proportions.

It was a Police Station, and crouching low and quavering on the inside, were police officers who had been stationed there. They too, had no business outside or with anyone. The 'Jewel' was a dangerous bunch and could not be trusted.

While people sought the safety of their homes at dusk, the police were battening-down inside the station. They were closed for the rest of the evening and the night. Any legitimate business would have to wait until the next day.

My Mother and I

As far as everyone knew, the police had not joined the general strike, so this unexpected withdrawal of their services and the barricading of the station placed a spoke in the operations wheel of the yet untested combatants.

The military plan as had been elaborated, envisaged the seizure of all the munitions held at the station with minimal collateral cost. The nabbed weapons would in turn be used in similar missions with not dissimilar targets. Once their arsenal was judged to be adequate, then a major assault would have been launched on the nerve center of Gairy's police, Fort George in St. George's.

When the platoon retreated into their guerrilla-friendly environment they left behind no evidence of their brief foray. At least nothing that could have been had without forensic testing. Any examination of their hardihood and will, however, would have placed them in good stead, ready to take on the next leg of their crusade.

Nevertheless, the platoon was soon to return to its original state of two separate entities when disagreements about strategy and tactics arose between the leaders of both units. The St. David's unit headed back from whence they came, while the St. George's unit continued the march through the thick vegetation which shrouded the hills at the base of Grand Etang.

The cool atmosphere which it generated, made relatively light work, even for 'Tenderfoot', of their return journey and soon they were in Willis, northeast St. George's. A scout was able to make contact with a friend who owned a "One More" bus and not long thereafter they were able to get to their individual homes with Gairy none the wiser. Well, if the police still under their beds in the police station had not informed him, then he was not aware of how close his bottom came to being microcooked. The combatants were still brushing up on their culinary skills so the option of having his 'boomsie' sautéed or done medium-rare was still available to him.

Chapter 33

"This is 6.10 Radio broadcasting from Abercromby Street in Port-of-Spain, Trinidad. Here is the latest news bulletin. News reaching our news desk states that one person was killed yesterday and many injured when Premier Gairy's Secret Police moved in to break up the street demonstrations which have been taking place for the past several weeks. The police reportedly attacked the demonstrators with glass bottles and opened fire on a building where school children had sought refuge. There are also reports of looting and of the police being shot at as well. As soon as we have more details we will bring these to you."

By force of circumstances, **6.10 Radio** was not only a window into Grenada for the rest of the world. It had become Grenadians' main source of information about what was happening inside Grenada. **Radio Grenada**, owned and operated by the Gairy Regime, was one of the many strike-affected casualties. In any event, it had long since become, by its outright lies and half-truths, a victim of self-immolation. Not many would have staked a five-cent coin on its veracity, and when it unashamedly won for itself the epithets 'Radio Lionel' and 'Radio Lie-Like-Hell,' most would not have gone beyond a penny.

My Mother and I

However, with persons like Alva Clarke, A.O. Palmer, Leslie 'Horse-mouth' Seon, Margaret Roberts, Rawle Howard, Ray Smith and Dalton Lashley in the **WIBS** of the 1950's and 60's, Radio Grenada came from noble stock. It would have remained that way if the British had not begun the practice of political interference. They fired Leslie Seon when he gave a report favourable to Gairy in the 1961 Elections. Subsequent generations of manipulative politicians, then, were to discover how easy it was to divest Radio Grenada of its testes and ovaries. Moreover, the Radio Grenada which preceded WIBS, remained a long-forgotten grandparent who had gone to the great beyond, an unlighted, unremembered beacon of the standards that broadcasting should require.

So with Grenada's single radio station bereft of complimentary standards and off the air, all turned to *6.10* with whom Grenadians had for donkey's years established a good and warm relationship. Leo DeLeon was loved as was Larry Haywood's *"The Voice of One"* programme which was as popular as **Radio Trinidad's** Auntie Kay and Uncle Bob who were lived and loved radio personalities and were welcomed as weekly guests in the homes of most.

No wonder then, Grenadians, who felt as if they were barely able to keep their heads above the rough waters of a tempestuous ocean, clung to *6.10* like a life-saving piece of log floating close by providentially.

There was not much else to depend on except the prayers which were sent upwards on a shuttle of invocation to Papa God. Manna was not about to drop from Heaven. Grenadians were journeying through the wilderness but they were not Israelites, so they had to make do with what they had.

'Open-bat' as banana or fig came to be called, was the new staple diet. Banana-pie, banana-rice, banana-soup, banana-bread and banana-tea nourishingly prepared, would have won for Grenada a golden award in any internationally held culinary display. Grenada had bananas in abundance since none could be exported through the St. George's seaport which was shut down as a result of the strike action. Everyday then, it was bananas for all meals and in all forms, some of which, by their taste, including banana-roti, went beyond the acceptable bounds of inventiveness. Moreover, despite all the suffering, it would have been hilarious if Grenadians had gone bananas because of bananas.

They almost did but they kept their sense of humour. Because of Mr. Courtney Renwick's rambunctious, high-pitched laughter he was often heard before he was seen. And when he was seen he could not be missed. One's first impression of 'Grubay' as he was popularly known, would have been, "here's a man who carried more stones than any quarry."

'Grubay,' in fact, weighed about three hundred and fifty pounds, only twenty-five stones, but at six and a half feet in height, he may have been the closest one may have gotten to Grenada's own homegrown giant. 'Grubay' ate as much as any giant needed to eat but he carried himself with an agility that belied his size.

In the sea he could not be matched. He swam like a merman, with the same speed and gracefulness, so much so the Olympic swimming pool would not have held a contender worthy of 'Grubay's' participation. When Hurricane Janet devastated Grenada on September 22nd 1955, its jetty at the St. George's port was destroyed and its warehouses sunk to the bottom of the sea. Without oxygen tanks, 'Grubay' dived to the sea floor and brought back to the surface bags of goods on his shoulders. Later he became a senior Customs Officer, and if he was not the Harbour-Master then he should have been. It was only natural that his sea-ability should have given him a position of command.

When the young men of the Carenage gathered around him, he held sway chiefly because of his humour and size and he had presence. The Carenage was where he lived in one of the low-pitched roofed, one-storied bungalows on the opposite side to the sea.

'Grubay' lived for everybody by his infectious laughter. If one looked at his face closely enough, one would have seen that a laugh was never far away. And it was a laugh that rang out across the sea from one side of the Carenage to the next and echoed upwards to Tyrrel Street, Cooper Hill and the surrounding areas. A laugh which invited all within earshot to laugh with him and they did.

That is what fourteen young men from the area, sitting on either side of 'Grubay' were doing one night. It was one of the dark nights of strike-stricken Grenada and there was hardly a better way to make light of the darkness than by listening to 'Grubay' rib his audience with humour bordering on the ribald.

They were all sitting on the narrow concrete sidewalk opposite the ***Empire Cinema***, which was next to the bungalows; the same bungalows which once housed the mentally sick. It was cheaper and more convenient to sit there, at least for 'Grubay' who would have required two chairs to hold his large rump and significant girth, and even so it would have been a tight fit. But that night he was sitting comfortably and if he were a book, then he was a definite bestseller.

"Hear me, tell me if you ever hear that one," 'Grubay' said with the upper end of laughter already crackling in his throat.

The fourteen young men were barely able to hold back their anticipatory snickers as 'Grubay' continued, "All yuh know 'Screw-mouth' in town, right? 'Screw-mouth' for Miss Rosie. Well one day he went by the doctor and he tell the doctor that he have a problem but he must promise not to laugh." And as if that was a signal for 'Grubay's' audience, they were already breaking out in difficult-to-suppress peals of laughter.

"Well boy, the doctor tell 'Screw-mouth' that he is a professional so he won't laugh. That how he doing this work for twenty-something years now and he never laugh at a patient yet. So stupid, ugly-face 'Screw-mouth' go and pull down he pants for the doctor. Boy...," 'Grubay' allowed his voice to linger an octave longer in suspense, "When the doctor see the teeny-weeny thing 'Screw-mouth' have dey for a prick, the doctor hold he belly, he roll on the ground and he laugh, he laugh, he laugh. Up to now he must be still laughing. Look, I sure he never see anything so small in he life yet."

'Grubay's' own contagious laughter had the young men holding on to their tummies too, anticipating the punch line that was yet to come.

"Anyway boy, after about ten minutes the doctor get off the ground, dust off he pants, smooth-out he shirt and straighten he tie. Then he tell 'Screw-mouth' how he sorry for laughing but to please tell him what the problem is. Yuh en know wha' 'Screw-mouth' tell the doctor?...that how he penis swell!"

With that, boisterous laughter rocked the Carenage and sent people in the neighbourhood scurrying to their windows hoping to somehow pick up the tail-end of the joke. Yet just hearing 'Grubay's' signature laughter accompanied by other healthy squeals riding briskly on the night breeze, made them laugh as well.

No one seemed able to stop. Everyone was just completely cracked up. Laughter had a way of making a sitting 'Grubay' sway to his left and then to his right. When he moved to his left his three hundred and fifty pounds carried all fourteen with him, and when he moved to his right the effect was the same. This swaying motion was always a sure sign that 'Grubay' was in full flight, and this tickled his audience even more. Some of the young men wanted to stop because their jaws and their sides were hurting them but they just could not. It was only when some of them held their tummies and walked away in search of relief did the laughter slowly subside.

But they did not have to go anywhere on the night of February 6th 1974 because it was right before them that a contingent of Royal Marines passed "left-right, left-right, left-right, left," on their way to Fort George.

The contingent had arrived earlier on a British battleship painted in its monotonous gray. They had come to take part in the activities to mark Grenada's coming of independent age that very night.

Although the street demonstrations had a premature end on January 21st, the victim of an invasive, brutal and botched abortion in the hands of Gairy's quacks, the general strike continued. As a result the whole island was in darkness, as did the stone-walled Fort George. It could not have been a good omen, then, that Grenada's formal ascendancy into its new state took place in darkness, other than for the powerful beams of car lights which were switched on.

Premier Gairy, decked out in his characteristic white zoot suit, endeavoured to beam as brightly as the car lights but did not quite manage it. It was the moment he was willing to risk anything for, yet he had not felt completely fulfilled. He must have been thinking to himself that that was his political mid-life crisis. Where were all the thousands of people he envisaged crowding the Tudor architectured pavilion at the Queen's Park, overwhelmed with excitement and shouting in naked idolization, 'Uncle Gairy, Uncle Gairy, Uncle Gairy!' Where was the unsurpassed pomp and grandeur of elaborate activities in the presence of world leaders and dignitaries which he dreamt of?

Instead, Gairy's grand speech as the first Prime Minister, the singing of the National Anthem for the first time, the midnight official lowering of the Union Jack and the hoisting of Grenada's National Flag were witnessed by relatively few and was pointedly subdued. Mr. Leo DeGale, the son of H. DeGale, one of the big planters whom Gairy fought against during the 1951 social revolution, was there. Leo DeGale was Grenada's first Governor General, having taken over from Dame Hilda as Governor.

One of those whose presence was conscripted however, was that of Maurice Bishop, one of the NJM leaders. At least, he was made to listen but not be seen. NJM represented to Gairy a major threat to his big night and day, and having Bishop within easy reach was added insurance and a possible bargaining chip, not unlike a hostage-taker. In any event, Bishop on the loose was not a gamble Gairy was willing to take. Twenty-four hours earlier Bishop was detained and locked-up in a cold, damp police cell on Fort George, not many feet away from where the ceremony was being held.

While Gairy was dressed resplendently, Bishop was divested of his clothing and left only in his underwear.

That was the condition in which he spent the night and watched, through cell-bars, the dawning of the day which marked Grenada's birth as an independent country on February 7th 1974. If Bishop's almost complete divestiture were meant to expose Prime Minister Gairy's intentions, then Grenadians could have expected to be stripped of their rights and freedoms, and for those who continued to oppose him, their livelihood.

It was in opposition to that kind of independent Grenada that thousands of people were drawn to the streets in protest and a cause for which they were willing to bear the sacrifices which a general strike required. The British saw, observed and empathized, but in the grander scheme of things did not feel able to do anything else. They remembered 1951 and decided that it was better to leave Gairy alone. But more than that, their colonies had become an economic burden and, like in the case of Grenada, a political embarrassment as well. That was the time to begin the off-loading process, and after Constitution Talks in England at which the Grenada National Party (GNP) led by Herbert A. Blaize was represented, Grenada was granted its independence.

H.A. Blaize, a cousin of Gascoigne Blaize who fought alongside Gairy in the trenches of 1951, also had on his delegation to England, Bernard Coard, one of the NJM leaders.

Eric Pierre, however, was an executive member of the GNP and the General Secretary of the Seamen and Waterfront Workers Union, the same union which played a pivotal and exemplary role in the general strike. The strike eventually fizzled out shortly after independence when it became evident that it was not going to succeed in removing Gairy from office. Moreover, the dockworkers were ordered back to work by their union and soon after, it was announced that Eric Pierre, a stalwart trade unionist, had been made a Senator by Gairy, granting him entry into the Upper House of Parliament.

My Mother and I

The peoples' parliament was taking place on the lowly streets of Grenada and I overheard many conversations, none of which were contemplating taking Gairy into their bed, as undoubtedly handsome as he was. That did not say that there were not a few beautiful young ladies who had a private itch to get into his. Some women were generally attracted to power, money and status and Gairy had all three, but there was one thing that Gairy did not have: the support of Grenadians in their vast numbers. They remained as combative as ever and steeped in the view that he had to go.

Chapter 34

I had no power and no money but being the proud child of a very powerful woman I had a little status. Very few women then looked in my direction and fewer still came to me. And those who brought warmth and life to my bed were manifestly the hard-pressed. It did not take much to lure them, but by the time they were sufficiently enchanted, testosterone was literally bursting out of my loins. As a result the lovemaking became so ardent that invariably the bed would breakdown.

In matters of the bed, my sister Jeudy kept a schedule that would have made **Le Pigalle**, Mother's red-light district, look tame. It was a schedule I could only have fantasized about. She was not exactly promiscuous, but she had an overactive libido. She simply could not imagine going two days without it, and because she was always so spent her ardency was far less than mine. She therefore had no bed-breaking episodes, yet one needed those to know just how exciting a noogle in the doogle could be.

For me that was a necessary distraction, but I had been longing to see my Mother who I had not seen in almost two hundred years. I had not heard from her in ages either, but I took consolation from the fact that my brothers and sisters were faring no better.

My Mother and I

Mother understandably was preoccupied by developments at home and spent a great deal of her time attempting to preserve the integrity of the family. The death four years earlier of her son and my brother, General Charles de Gaulle, had hit her particularly hard. Charles, who had risen to become the patrimonial head of the household, could not have been held in higher esteem.

Mother was not feeling quite the same way about my other brothers and sisters at home who, in 1968, had taken to the streets in open disobedience and defiance of her authority. For weeks my sisters and brothers who were students shut the schools down, including the universities, as they engaged in anti-establishment protests. They flocked the streets and were joined by my sisters and brothers who were workers. Offices and factories were closed down, bringing our home into a state of upheaval. Everything stood at a standstill and the risk of our family falling apart was very real.

The concerns of my sisters and brothers had Mother's sympathetic ear, but there was nothing more important to her than the preservation of her family and she was desperate. She pleaded, she exerted her immense charm to the fullest and used mild threats to bring them to heel. Eventually it was good sense which triumphed and a semblance of normalcy was restored to our home.

But the damage had been done. That near dismembering brought economic and political turmoil which required all of Mother's time. Since then she has been attempting to use her enormous resources to bring about healing and recovery, and with Charles's passing coming on top of that, no wonder Mother had no time for any of her progenies living away from home.

Yet, through regular reports, which she somehow had funnelled to her, Mother kept in touch with what was happening in Grenada. She knew of the Duffus Commission which inquired into the events of 1973 and 1974. After listening to weeks of evidence given by dozens of people, including political parties, the Prime Minister and members of his government, the Commission held, ***inter alia***, that there was a break-down of law and order and that the actions of the government and its agencies were aimed solely at suppressing the Political Opposition. Among its recommendations were the dismissal of A.S.P. Belmar from the Police Force, and his preclusion from holding any public office, as well as the removal of I.I. Duncan as a magistrate.

Mother became uneasy when she learnt of the formation of Gairy's two hundred-strong Defense Force shortly after Independence. They were largely a scruffy-looking bunch with few aspiring professionals among them. Members of that Force were christened "Green Beasts" by the people and subsequent events were to prove their singular expertise in giving appropriate names. Be that as it may, Gairy established ties with the repressive Chilean Regime of Augusto Ugarte Pinochet in 1975 and secured military assistance for his Defense Force.

Around that time the young would-be combatants who had set out on their mission to St. David's on the night of January 21st 1974, were still of the view that Gairy should be removed by force and were meeting and planning. While a few of the original recruits were no longer involved, its ranks had grown appreciably.

One of the new intakes was a former member of a regional regiment. He was a soldier and carried himself with a soldierly bearing. He was fanatically religious and walked around bare-footed almost like a messiah. He was tall and slim and spoke in a manner that befitted that image. Some thought, however, that he was taking his conviction too far when he indicated that on the planned attack of Fort George, the headquarters of Gairy's police, in addition to being bare-footed he would be armed, not with a rifle or some such weapon, but with his Bible. His comrades could not believe it and asked repeatedly for clarification, but his answer was always the same, "my Bible but no gun."

Strong faith is laudable but too strong a faith could be suicidal. Anyway, the attack never did take place so it could not be established empirically whether he and his Bible were mystically coated with high-grade armour. He may even have had a gun hidden in the Bible like Sancho in one of the old Western movies, or the Bible may have been capable of discharging bullets or something more lethal, but no one was able to find out. Mother heard and she was amused.

She was not smiling, though, when Gairy passed his Newspaper Amendment Act of 1975. This new measure required that $20,000 Eastern Caribbean dollars, up from $900, be deposited before any newspaper could be published. It was aimed directly at the **New Jewel** which had become the newspaper with the largest circulation and which stuck like a limpet on the hull of Gairy's tottering ship. It became an underground newspaper which was sold clandestinely. Its printing press, a **Gestetner** machine, was constantly moved around and the name of its weekly publication changed in order to avoid detection by Gairy's forces and the clutches of his law, a law that was vehemently opposed.

Soon after Gairy passed his law, a defiant Kenrick Radix, one of the NJM leaders, took to the streets of downtown St. George's one morning expecting to do a brisk sale of copies of the latest edition of **Jewel**. He would have, if members of Gairy's Defense Force did not move faster than Radix's would-be customers. On hand for such an eventuality, dressed in green and acting like beasts, the Defense Force members pounced on Radix like fowl-eating dogs. Radix had no time to cry foul himself. He was not exactly beaten to a pulp but it was close enough for him to seek medical attention immediately after. Later, when Radix promised to return like Mexico's Montezuma, a fleeting, rueful look crossed Mother's face but she could not help smiling again.

None of the contending parties approached the General Elections of December 7th, 1976 with anything less than absolute seriousness and Mother looked on with quiet expectancy. Street demonstrations and general strike did not remove Gairy from office but many were hoping that that Elections would.

Apart from Gairy's G.U.L.P. there were three other parties contesting the Elections. There was the NJM, the G.N.P. and the Winston Whyte led United Peoples' Party (U.P.P.). As a result of popular pressure and universal demand, and notwithstanding G.N.P.'s attempts to claim more than what they seemingly deserved, the three parties entered into an alliance, the ***Peoples' Alliance***. Since Gairy's core support was still sizeable and was not going to be easily influenced by the popular cry "Time For A Change," the opposition parties were forced to find ways to maximize their chances.

Gairy himself was not taking any chances. Police permission for use of a public address system was often withheld and when granted, its use was quite often so restricted in terms of time that the political leaders had to speak to large crowds with unamplified voices. And yet the people turned out to meetings in impressive numbers.

In the face of that, the propaganda war against the Opposition and NJM in particular was stepped up. **Radio Grenada** became Gairy's personal mouthpiece. It claimed, among other things, that the NJM was going to turn the churches into discotheques. And yet churchgoers were part of the growing ranks of the Opposition support.

Some of the public meetings of the Opposition were stoned-out and glass bottled-out and on the day of the Elections, despite the pre-election work done by the Opposition's morticians on the lists of voters, a significant number of dead persons were still able to vote. The Opposition asked for the dead to be interred and new elections held. Gairy refused, stating that neither his own hired Undertakers nor himself should be held to account for the actions of the dead. And further, if the truth be known, his plan was to bury the NJM.

Six elected members of the Opposition who were very much alive and which included its leader, Maurice Bishop, Herbert Blaize, Unison Whiteman, Bernard Coard, Winston Whyte and Norris Bain, entered Parliament to face the Government's nine. The Opposition could not prevent the passage of any bill so desired by the government, like The Essential Services Act which was passed two years later. Gairy saw the increasing influence and involvement of the NJM in the trade union movement and was not going to allow a repeat of 1974. Workplaces that were deemed essential were prohibited to strike. Anyway, the six opposition parliamentarians did a lot to expose the Parliament for the farce it was. The NJM held true to its commitment to struggle both from below and above, so when they became tired of the Speaker of the House, the unreasonable Mr. Reason, and his biased, injudicious conduct, they walked out and went down to the Market Square and elsewhere to speak with the people.

Ultimately it was the ordinary people who held the power and not the nine "elected" government representatives. The nine included Prime Minister Gairy and his wife Cynthia, George Hosten, Herbert Preudhomme, Albert Forsythe and Innocent Belmar who won the St. Andrew's northwest seat. In the case of the latter, Gairy was saying to the Duffus Commission, "I have an army, you don't."

In one sense, speaking was Gairy's forte but in another it was not, like on June 19th 1977. Hundreds of persons had gathered in the Market Square that Sunday afternoon for another of NJM's rallies. It was a bright sunny afternoon and because the sun was on the last leg of its daily westward journey, it was not too hot. Any strength that was left in its rays, were weakened by the many walled-buildings which perimetered the Square on all sides.

Being walled-in provided no one with any false sense of security, yet no one could have expected what happened that day. It was the day on which most Grenadians worshipped and traditionally therefore, respect was accorded to that day. One did anything on any other day but never on a Sunday. Moreover, scores of representatives from the OAS were in Grenada for one of its meetings. Indeed, a few of them were in the Market Square with their cameras.

Grenada is a photographer's dream, and its people peacefully gathered for a public meeting, chit-chatting in the shade of a sunny afternoon, were no less so. But it was a sight that Gairy could not stomach.

The meeting had just gotten into gear and the early amplified speeches were heard far and wide. Permission had not been granted for the use of a public address system but the NJM leaders decided to use one anyway. It was not long before police officers approached the platform and attempted to take the microphone away. The NJM leaders decided that the microphone was not going to be taken away and the meeting was not going to be broken up.

It did when Gairy's 'Green Beasts,' who had arrived earlier, began firing off SLR and .303 rifles into the air. Several persons remained put and had to be physically and threateningly driven away with guns pointed at their heads. Others, led by NJM leaders, took to the streets in protest but that was soon broken up by the 'Green Beasts.' They were chased off the streets, out of the Market Square, and for those who lived in the city, into their homes. Several were beaten and the cameras of the visitors were seized and the films destroyed. One young man, Alister Strachan, had to jump into the sea to try and save his life. The further he swam out, the more he was fired upon. His body was washed up on the shore the next day. Where he went to save his life he met his death. Mother watched and moaned.

By then very many people had not only lost their faith in elections but in Gairy's ability to mend his ways. Several persons were beaten post-independence. The peoples' own fears of what Gairy was likely to do next became worse when, in January 1978, Innocent Belmar was shot and killed. Three young men were arrested, charged and tried but later freed. Mother wept for Grenada.

But Gairy was not about to do any crying. He had long discovered that the chemical make-up of tears of joy and tears of sorrow were quite different, and he had none of the latter to waste.

The Prime Minister did not tarry longer than was thought necessary in pursuing his policy of victimization following the attainment of Independence. Several Public Workers and a few decent police officers who refused to allow themselves to be used as henchmen, were either dismissed or transferred, often to Grenada's Siberia, Carriacou. All authority was taken away from the Public Service Commission which was left emaciated. Gairy took unto himself the power to hire and fire, from janitor to cook to Permanent Secretary.

He had long since bestowed upon himself the power of life and death and when, in January of 1978, a dispute arose between the Government and the Public Services Association over salary increases, this became more evident. On January 28th Gairy held a rally in the Market Square and to the cheers of hundreds of his supporters bussed in from around the island, violence was threatened. More than that, prior to that rally, Union leaders and senior public servants received through the Post, scrawled warnings written in red which said, "If you strike you dead!" They were not quite ready to die yet so they did not strike.

The NJM leaders, too, needed more time to prepare their wills. Moreover, they were not going to expose the people to any unnecessary risk, so when Gairy responded to their planned November 19th rally in St. Andrew's by amassing in large numbers his armed military and quasi-military forces up there, the rally was called off. Gairy moved his forces by land and sea. He had no airplane but if one of his oft spoken about UFOs were available, they would have been transported by air as well.

The people by then had become totally fed up. Prime Minister Gairy was irredeemable, they agreed, and felt that by blocking the path to his peaceful removal from office and his resorting to force and the use of guns with maniacal regularity, he had left them with only one option. With NJM at the helm, they were ready, yet did not expect, to answer the call of history in a way that was going to stun the rest of the world. But not Mother. From her own experience she knew that revolutions were sometimes historical necessities.

Chapter 35

"The criminal dictatorship of Eric Gairy has been overthrown!" It was not the voice of Montezuma whose promised return had been looked forward to, but close enough. At 6 a.m. on the morning of Tuesday March 13th, 1979, Grenadians awakened to the sound of an unusual voice on Radio Grenada.

The voice was immediately recognized and incredulity took hold of faces that had only just declawed the hands of sleep. But when the full import of what was being said sunk in, they stared open-mouthed, popeyed and unable to move as if the temperature had made a sudden and precipitous drop to 0^0 degrees Celsius, freezing many in place.

It was not just the unexpected shock but the magnitude of the shock itself. It was a reluctance to believe that something, which they could only have dreamt of before had, through some sort of strange and as yet little understood occurrence, finally become reality.

When the shock-induced stupor wore out sufficiently, neighbour began calling out the news to neighbour. Friend got on the phone to friends and family, locally and abroad, shouting out the happenings through analogue lines and stunning others in the process. Many stayed at home that day moving about zombie-like but not going anywhere and not doing anything in particular. Yet many more flocked to the streets, quickly joining the ranks of the revolutionaries and giving whatever assistance they thought was required.

Three days before, on the afternoon of Saturday March 10th, NJM was in session. The members-only meeting was taking place on the uppermost floor of a three-storied brick-walled building in St. George's. It was at the back of the Police Traffic-Point from which traffic, flowing along Scott Street, Tyrrel Street and Lucas Street, was directed.

Like all other days, it was a day that was in the all-powerful hands of Papa God, seeing and directing as He saw fit. That day He said 'Let there be sunshine' and there was plenty of it, which was not unusual for that time of year. Yet it was special because the eve of the sixth anniversary of NJM's birth could only have occurred once.

That fact was noted as the meeting got going. There were forty persons present including Maurice Bishop, Bernard Coard, Unison Whiteman, Hudson Austin and George Louison of the party's Political Bureau, as its leadership was called. Both Kenrick Radix and Selwyn Strachan, other members of the Bureau, had been sent abroad on party matters.

Central on the meeting's agenda, was the registration of new voters, especially the young voters, which was being discussed. There was talk in the air, then, of a possible snap-general election being called by Gairy and NJM did not wish to be caught napping.

The forty party members, however, received an unexpected jolt when, in the midst of their discussion, there was loud, urgent pounding on the door leading to the room in which the meeting was being held.

"Who is it?" several voices asked simultaneously and with concern.

"Is me, Conqueror," a male voice that was not choir-trained answered. "Open-up!" he implored, in almost one continuous breath.

William St. Louis was well known to all as 'Conqueror.' He was a dockworker and a strong supporter of NJM. When the door was opened he rattled-off startling information: "The police just grab Vince at he home and Owusu up by Bish and dey gone with them. Dey looking for Bish and all the Bureau members, and dey surround their house too." 'Conqueror' was not taking this development lightly and his facial expression appealed to all to do the same.

Vincent 'Vince' Noel, a Political Bureau member, had returned to his home to collect a document and Liam 'Owusu' James, a member of NJM, had gone up to Bishop's home on Parade in St. George's, to collect copies of the latest edition of *Jewel*. Liam's car was searched and a box containing books about Che Guevera and Fidel Castro, among others, was seized. They were arrested and charged with the offence of being in possession of prohibited literature.

While it was clear that Gairy's latest thrust had nothing to do with any printed matter, none were willing to wait to be booked. The meeting broke up immediately and persons made their departure from the building as inconspicuously as the circumstances allowed. Bishop, Whiteman and Coard left together and drove off in a car which they had never used before. Austin and Louison left separately, but all the Political Bureau members promptly went underground, making it near impossible for their location to have been known by Gairy's forces who continued to keep their homes under close watch. Indeed, Bishop, Coard and Whiteman were where the police was least likely to look: in a house not more than a good two hundred yards from Gairy's residence in Sans Souci, St. George's.

The NJM leaders were underground but they did not find attractive the prospect of spending untold years in underground cells, deep within my bowels, which were apparently prepared for them. Prime Minister Gairy himself had left Grenada the day before on a visit to the United States of America, accompanied by a small delegation. Word was that he felt the "hot and sweaty Jewel boys," as he called them, were due for a lot more than a cold bath, one that would burden their memory for ages to come.

Information relayed to the NJM leaders, by sympathetic police officers, indicated that Gairy made clear before leaving that his cold bath was really a bloody bath. In any case, when Gairy thought or spoke in imprecise terms, only a fool would not have prepared for the worst. "The Jewel Boys" were no babes in the woods so they made the necessary preparations.

During the evening and early hours of the night of March 11th, fourteen public meetings were held, although sixteen were scheduled, throughout the island. The meetings were organized and carried out by the sub-leadership of NJM, since five of its Political Bureau members were in hiding, two were abroad and one was locked-up in a police cell on Fort George.

Despite the short notice, people responded in impressive numbers. The police, too, were well represented. It was the sixth anniversary of NJM and young, vibrant speakers attacked the Gairy regime with biting, uncompromising, combative words, and promised the people a new and bright future. The people were receptive but the police were unsure of what to make of what was being said. For the first time NJM was speaking in imprecise terms which gave NJM two good reasons to prepare, and they did. NJM gave the police and the Gairy regime, by their unusual obscure language, one good reason to prepare, and they did not.

Many months before, NJM came to the view that resorting to armed struggle with the hope of creating the conditions for a new day in Grenada, could become a requirement of the future, and marshaled its resources for such an eventuality. Barrels of grease were imported and in them were hidden twenty-five, American made, M1 rifles. And in America two Grenadians, Chester Humphrey and Jim Wardally, were arrested and charged with the offence of exporting arms and ammunition.

The shipment of weapons bolstered the training and military preparation of dozens of young men who, for the previous several months were engaged, in hilly and unpopulated locations, in mastering the craft of revolutionary warfare. They were committed fighters who did not think twice about making the ultimate sacrifice.

'H.A.', as Austin was more popularly known, pronounced his troops ready to answer the call to battle. It was Monday, March 12th and Austin and Louison had been summoned to join Bishop, Whiteman and Coard in the making of the most far-reaching decision ever confronting the party. The fate of Gairy and his Government had been deliberated on a long time before, but now they were to participate in a decision that was to shape Grenada's destiny forever and have enormous repercussions for its entire people.

From the position of the sun overhead that was drifting further away to my left, it must have been about 4:30 pm. that afternoon. At that time, by a vote of three to two, members of NJM's Political Bureau took the decision to remove the Gairy Government from office by force of arms, and set into motion an unprecedented revolutionary process in the English-speaking Caribbean.

James, who, along with Vincent Noel, had been released on bail later that afternoon, was able to say to persons in his community by six o'clock the next morning that Gairy had been overthrown and that a revolution was taking place. But the identical response of those persons who looked at James with a mixture of disbelief and empathy was, "Wait nuh, this little time yuh spend in ah cell, yuh start to go mad aready?"

Chapter 36

The night was as dark as one could have expected it to be at four o'clock in the morning of Tuesday, March 13th 1979. The pre-dawn was as dark as the other side of the moon and as quiet as if it had been struck dumb by a passing angel. Except for the frogs which were carrying on a chorus of potentially sleep-disturbing croaks, the land was entombed in the silence of the grave.

The True Blue base of Gairy's army, the 'Green Beasts,' in St. George's south, was formerly the site of **Expo '69** where, during a period of three weeks, regional and extra-regional countries had their goods, services, talent and culture on spectacular display. It attracted large crowds every day nd every night, and was a definite high point for the Gairy regime. It was far more successful than its **Easter Water Parades** on the Carenage or its quasi-economic **Bootstring** programme.

That night, however, the army's base could have been a cemetery. Nothing moved, not even the armed guards at the entrance to the base. Sleep, like an extraordinarily beautiful woman expert in the wiles of conquest, cannot be denied when it comes. At that hour of the morning one is least alert and, too, it is the time that is regarded as the most sleep-inducing even for the hardiest of soldiers. Unless one has been fortified by several cups of the most potent of Brazilian coffee, sleep is often irresistible.

It was by no accident that that was the hour chosen to launch the attack on the army's barracks. Four hours before, in the dead of night, forty-six combatants, among them Rudolph Ogilvie, Crispin "Bugman" Hypolite, Keith "Pumphead" Hayling, Victor Husbands, Strachan Phillip, David Lambert, Paulin 'Lordie' Lord and Keith St. Bernard and the five members of NJM's Political Bureau neither overseas nor in police custody, gathered at the top of 'Freedom Hill' after stealthily making their way there in small units.

'Freedom Hill', in St. George's south, was three hundred and fifty meters, as the crow flies and five minutes by road, from the army's barracks. It was densely bushed, with Mapoe trees which remained thick and green even during the dry season. The closest house was at the entrance of the road leading up to the hill, and with an elevation of one hundred and fifty feet above sea level, it provided enough of a safe haven for ripe candidates of treason and sedition if they failed in their mission and if they did not get killed in the process. One of the combatants had left at home his seven months pregnant wife, but they were not thinking about the possibility of failing or of getting killed.

"…Comrades, you are about to embark on a most important mission on behalf of the party and the freedom-loving people of Grenada. There is no greater sacrifice you would be called upon to make than the one you are now making. But the party is confident that you would do so with the discipline and commitment you have displayed this past many months, and the training you have received would guarantee our victory. So remember, comrades, the idea is to move with speed and the goal is to shock and instill fear so as to render the enemy's resistance as ineffective as it can be. Capture as many as you can but only direct your fire at the enemy if it is necessary to protect your own life. Onwards to victory, comrades! Long live our party and long live the people of Grenada…" H.A. exhorted his troops. In the Old

Testament, the feet of four men were made to sound like a mighty army and had their enemy, thousands of well-armed troops, scampering for their lives, thinking that they were being pursued, not by four men but by a mighty company of marauding commandoes. H.A.'s training was not only military but Biblical!

Hudson 'H.A.' Austin was born one hundred years after slavery and was the descendant of Caribs who came to Grenada from St. Vincent. In there may lie the origin of his indomitable spirit. H.A. headed his own road construction company and for the previous two years had been engaged in building access roads and creating house-spots on Freedom Hill. He had been contracted to do so by its owners. However, that provided him with intimate knowledge of the area and while road construction was taking place on one side of the hill, on the other side the would-be combatants were often engaged in military training away from peering eyes.

H.A.'s political history went back to Hubert Blaize's **Grenada National Party** (G.N.P.) of which he was a member, prior to his enrollment in the NJM. That night he was to disavow G.N.P.'s conservatism in a way that was to send many, with microscope in hand, scurrying to their world map to locate the hard-to-find Grenada.

The battle plan had been drawn up a long time before that night and rehearsed so often that the combatants knew every detail of what was required of them. Forty-six young men with H.A. in command were about to catapult Grenada into Caribbean and world history. It would have been forty-seven, but an otherwise stout young man of St. George's who spoke big and promised big, began having rear-end emissions when he was checked the evening before to fulfil on his promise. With a "Who? Me?" he disappeared into his washroom or under his bed. Hiding below one's bed for whatever reason, had long become a cultural norm for Grenadians.

The troops, however, were not hiding but well camouflaged as they moved as silently as they could across plateaus, slopes and a few lesser hills until they were practically able to look down onto the wooden barracks of the 'Green Beasts,' which were adjacent to where they stood primed for action.

After ensuring that all were okay and in formation, H.A. silently gave the command to advance and attack, pantomiming the words even as he spoke. Armed with M1 rifles, Enfield bolt-action .303 repeating rifles and a scattering of pistols, handguns and crude hand grenades of Molotov cocktails, the combatants raced down the slope, making more noise than Chief Sitting Bull and the Sioux Indians of America on a retaliatory raid on the 'White-man' settlement.

The intention was to use the element of surprise to maximum effect and to stun the 'Green Beasts' into inactivity other than to flee for their lives. The fighters then created a tremendous racket as they approached the barracks, by firing their weapons into the air as if it were not possible to run out of ammunition. Molotov cocktails too, were hurled at the barracks and other out-buildings. In the still of the morning it sounded far worse than it really was. To Gairy's soldiers who leapt out of their bunks terror-stricken, and with their minds befuddled by sleep, it could have been two thousand fire-spitting dragons, a troop of hell-raising elephants or a thousand-strong army equipped with the most lethal of weapons.

They did not wait to find out which it was. Now it was their turn to discover what the law of survival and self-preservation were all about. When one is running for one's life, no dress code is required. Clad, then, in only their underwear in the case of some, and stark naked in the case of others, they scampered out of their barracks like cheetahs being chased by lions and just as fast. For them, in a violent storm one headed for the nearest port, which meant dashing into the thick undergrowth which was close to the side of the barracks.

Though a few were captured, most were allowed to continue, unhindered, their mad rush to safety which took them deeper and deeper into the bushes. Some of them stayed there for two days. That was as long as it took to assure themselves that the fire-spitting dragons were not waiting in ambush. Thus assured, they made their way furtively to their homes and villages.

But the victorious combatants had secured the camp and gathered up whatever arms and ammunition that were left behind. The army's commander, Captain Hyacinth Brizan, who was not in camp at the time of the assault on the barracks, came speeding headlong towards its entrance when he learnt that something untoward was happening there. He was stopped, his vehicle surrounded and ordered to come out with his hands in the air. For a second he seemed about to comply then made the sudden move which would suggest that he was attempting to draw his weapon. This is what the revolutionary soldiers concluded and opened fire, killing the Captain.

His was not the only death that morning. Godwin Pysadee, a soldier of the Defense Force, was another of the three unfortunate deaths that day. The third, a revolutionary fighter, was accidentally shot during the night. Evidently, the intention was to preserve life as far as was possible. When a bus transporting members of the Grenada Voluntary Constabulary (G.V.C.), an adjunct to the Police Force, came seeking to outstrip the wind on True Blue Stretch, they were not stopped by a fusillade of bullets. The G.V.C., an inheritance of the colonial past, had been told by their superiors that there was a fire at the camp and had been sent from St. David's to assist. When the bus slowed by the **Carib Factory** to negotiate a ditch in the road, a combatant emerged out of nowhere and with pistol in hand, stopped the bus, went on board and redirected it to the Radio Station. It was only when the bus arrived at the radio station did the combatant realized that his pistol had neither magazine nor bullets. He was lucky, too, that the G.V.C. did not realize that either.

Earlier on a unit had been dispatched to seize Radio Grenada. When they got there it became immediately clear that more 'taking' than 'seizing' would be required. There was a single night watchman on duty and he was not watching, he was sleeping. Aroused, he appeared well past his prime, not that far from being described as old, and tired more from the boredom of his job than from his years of service. He was more than happy to be sent home than to be around these armed men who were courting more trouble than he wanted to witness.

But the revolutionaries, having already dispersed Gairy's 'Green Beasts,' were not expecting any more trouble than they did not think themselves able to dispose of. As if to indicate that the Gairy regime had been successfully vanquished, a hyped-up revolutionary smashed a prominently displayed glass-framed photo of Gairy, in the lobby of the radio station, with his bare hands. The splintered glass caused injury to his hand that necessitated a hurried trip to the hospital.

Other injuries were to come later. In the meantime a technician employed at the station was summoned to assist in getting the station on air, and soon the NJM leaders were issuing bulletins. The first voice heard was that of H.A. at six o'clock in the morning announcing the overthrow of the Gairy Government. There were to be about sixteen bulletins that day, each appraising Grenadians of what was happening and seeking their assistance. Bulletin No.10 was one of those. It was the voice of Bernard Coard calling on Grenadians to deal with the Secret Police and 'Mongoose Gang' who were reportedly attempting to escape up the West Coast. But not much seeking was needed as thousands poured out onto the streets, setting up roadblocks and arresting persons closely associated with the regime.

It was through one such roadblock in Tanteen, St. George's however, that Derek Knight, a Senator and longstanding senior member of Gairy's Cabinet, made his escape. Knight was saved many months in prison by the charitableness or the indecisiveness of the person controlling the roadblock who was unsure about what to do. Knight was allowed to turn around his car and with that he headed speedily up the northwest road. Along the way, he boarded a small boat

My Mother and I

in one of the many bays and made good on the opportunity that was unexpectedly given to him. Not a veteran of any war, he nevertheless signed himself numerous times since that morning and thanked the Unknown Soldier.

Had Knight been captured he would have been brought to the radio station which was also serving as a temporary detention center. Other members of Gairy's inner circle were there as well as senior police officers and members of his Secret Police and 'Green Beasts.' The radio station was not just a radio station. It had become the headquarters of the Revolution. Radio Grenada then quickly became **Radio Free Grenada** (RFG), *'The Voice of the Revolution,'* and from a flagpole on its concrete roof fluttered the red and white flag of the Revolution. The red circular patch on a white background signified the blood and the struggle of the people for meaningful change.

As if beckoned by the flag, scores of people gravitated to RFG bearing gifts in the form of food. No one requested them to but they knew the requirements of their fighting men. The revolutionary soldiers were well fed.

Sustained by food, love, commitment, revolutionary zeal and the enthusiasm of the young, units of soldiers set out to accomplish various tasks. They could be seen going hither and thither on trucks, vans, in cars or whatever, dressed in camouflaged uniforms with small replicas of the revolution's flag pinned on their proud shoulders and with rifles in the air proclaiming the peoples' victory.

All around the island people formed themselves into platoons and armed themselves with whatever could have been used as weapons. Yet many were armed with just their enthusiastic support for what was happening. Where necessary, however, they provided the motivation for Gairy's eight hundred police and 'auxiliary services' in thirty-six police stations to raise the white flag of surrender. In the case of Fort George, the headquarters of the police, the white flag rose so fast it could have done so on its own volition. Not even the kind request of a Bible-bearing would-be combatant was needed.

For me, my worst fears were about to come to pass. I felt so unsteady in the feet and for such a long time it was as if an earth tremor once started did not know how to finish. And it all began when my status was changed from what I once was to what I had been turned into. For years I have had nightmares and premonitions and saw myself being ravished by conquering soldiers. I felt myself being raped by soldiers who pillaged the land and everything in it. I squirmed from the anticipatory horror and pain of feeling myself being breached the same way my brother, the Bastille, was stormed by my revolutionary brothers in 1789.

Yet it was not as bad as I dreamt it would have been. When they came that very morning, the gates were opened for them without their having to shoot their way through, so I suffered no physical damage or injury to any part of me. For that reason and despite the one hundred and ninety years that had elapsed, I felt greater sympathy for my brother.

The revolutionary soldiers were firm if a little disrespectful on occasions, which I put down to the heat of the moment and their overzealousness. Undeniably, they meant well and they did what they had to do, including taking away the Superintendent without creating too many unnecessary ripples. Further, they had arrived in time to put a halt to the process that would have led, within a few days, to the hanging of death-row inmate, George Joseph, who was already in a Holding Cell for that purpose.

Nevertheless, nothing could have taken away from the enormity of what had happened in the early morn of that day, its tremendous positive impact on Grenadians and Caribbean people and the historic significance of the Grenada Revolution. One big celebration was taking place in Grenada and throughout the Caribbean.

While the overwhelming majority of the people of Grenada were simply ecstatic and finding it difficult to contain their sheer exuberance, West Indies was playing Australia in a cricket test match at the Kensington Oval in Barbados. It was the **Kerry Parker Series** and for most Caribbean people, cricket is right next to God and for some God is right next to cricket. It was an exciting match, but there was no greater excitement than when the Caribbean radio stations interrupted the commentary to bring reports on this remarkable development in Grenada. People all over the Caribbean erupted in spontaneous applause and backslapping and did a dancing step or two. Even at the Oval the cricket was temporarily forgotten. Unplanned parties broke out right there in the Stands.

But the NJM had no time for parties just yet. Maurice Bishop was sitting at the manager's desk in RFG with a stack of phones before him. He was making every effort to speak with the Caribbean leaders, seeking their support. Countries like Michael Manley's Jamaica and Forbes Bunharm's Guyana were among the first to recognize the new government of Grenada. Cuba's recognition came a few days later as did the British. The Americans did so ten days later after considering their options, including a military blockade.

It was the height of the Cold War. The world was severely polarized into East and West blocs, represented by the Soviet Union and the United States of America, each seeking political, military and ideological hegemony; and zealously guarding what they saw as their own turf. The Grenada Revolution, then, would have been seen as the product of growing Soviet influence in the Caribbean and as an affront to America. However, the nuclear capabilities of both blocs and the threat of nuclear war at the touch of a button encouraged restraint and kept the world in an uneasy balance.

It was also a period of decolonization, and Liberation Movements, particularly in the Third World, were on the move. Guinea Bissau, Angola, Mozambique, Sao Tome and Principe, and the Cape Verde Islands had all won their independence from Portugal. Vietnam had kicked out the Americans humiliatingly and Pol Pot's brutal reign in Cambodia was brought to an end. The Shah of Iran was overthrown, Samoza of Nicaragua suffered a similar fate and Idi Amin of Uganda had to beat a hasty exit.

All of these geo-political factors, regional and international, influenced the NJM and made March 13th, 1979 possible. The objectives of the Revolution were well articulated when Bishop addressed Grenadians on radio at 10 o'clock that morning.

> "Sisters and brothers, comrades, Grenadians all....this Revolution is for food, for health and for housing. It is for bread and justice...it is for jobs...it is for peoples' participation. It is for a return to constitutionality.... Preparations will be made for the holding of free and fair elections...Long live the free people of Grenada! Long live the Revolution!"

Chapter 37

Maurice Bishop was an only son and therefore may have been considered a jewel from birth. Born on May 29th, 1944, he was one of three children of Rupert and Alimenta Bishop. His parents were strong Roman Catholics and Maurice was therefore brought up accordingly.

He attended the Presentation Boys College (PBC) in St. George's. Although he was not then an activist and only peripherally involved in some of the school's activities, he was a powerful influence among his peers.

When, in 1962, the Manager of Empire Cinema accused the boys of PBC and the girls of St. Joseph's Convent in St. George's, of going there to smooch and for a bit of billing and cooing, Maurice, like the rest of the Catholic Community, took strong objection. The accusation which was printed in one of the local newspapers was denounced by the Catholic Church, parents, civil society and prominent persons like Walter Coard and his wife.

A boycott of the cinema was launched and despite the fact that ecumenism was still unknown in Grenada, a cross-section of the religious community participated. It was therefore a successful boycott which lasted two to three months. The Manager of the cinema was forced to apologize and to admit as false what was in fact true.

In those days, and for the many decades before, the rivalry among the five secondary schools in Grenada was especially poignant. The boys of the Grenada Boys Secondary School (G.B.S.S.) and the girls of the Anglican High School, did not speak to the PBC boys and the girls of the Convent. Maurice saw that as ridiculous and did everything to break the barrier. When the G.B.S.S. boys led by Bernard Coard and Ashley Bernadine sought the support of the PBC boys, led by Maurice, and the Convent girls in seeking the resolution of a Technical and Allied Workers Union (TAWU) strike, Maurice delivered willingly. The students were hit hard by that strike, led by TAWU's founder, Derek Knight, since they were affected by the resultant lack of electricity to prepare for their December exams.

Maurice loved life and was full of life. He played tennis and liked his parties. From an early age it was obvious that he would have been a six-footer plus. And with his natural handsomeness and immense charm, he would have been a preponderant female choice for smooching, billing and cooing in the Empire cinema. Maurice liked the ladies and the ladies were crazy about him. It was as simple as that then, but it became more complicated later in his life.

When Maurice left school he became a member of the 'Grenada Assembly of Youth after Truth.' It had a membership of sixty, both former and current students. But it was not long after that, in 1963, that he migrated to England to pursue studies in law.

While in England he lived in Tulse Hill, South London, where his wife, Angela, and himself shared a house with the Evans brothers and Kenrick Radix. To help finance his studies he worked in the Inland Revenue of the British Civil Service. But it was not all work. During vacations he journeyed across the North Atlantic to visit friends in America, where he fraternized socially with Bernard Coard who was pursuing studies there.

My Mother and I

Maurice was successful in his own legal training, obtaining an LLB. He subsequently enrolled to do a Masters Degree and spent many hours doing research for his thesis on Julien Fedon. But that was not to be. The pull to return home to serve and to contribute was too powerful to resist. In 1970, he abandoned his pursuit of a Masters Degree, packed up his belongings and, together with his wife, returned to Grenada.

His interest was always law, politics and issues of human rights. He promptly set up adjoining offices with Kenrick Radix from which he began a successful legal practice, representing ordinary Grenadians. His legal fees for such persons ranged from ***pro bono*** to minimal.

He may have abandoned the pursuit of a Masters Degree but he was a masterful orator. Moreover, Maurice's grasp of the law and his advocacy skills were far superior to most of his peers, and soon his reputation as a brilliant lawyer went beyond Grenada's borders. His services were in great demand and he represented clients throughout the Caribbean.

His legal prowess was not confined to the Courtroom, however. Maurice was the central figure in the formation of the Movement for Assemblies of the People (MAP) and became a founding member of the New Jewel Movement (NJM). He challenged Gairy in the courthouse, on the streets and eventually in the Parliament. Together with the NJM, he became Gairy's nemesis.

He took up the issue of human rights violations of which Gairy was habitually guilty. Working conjointly with other Caribbean personalities, he was a founding director of the **Caribbean Human Rights and Legal Aid Company** headquartered in Suriname. Through regional offices, including here in Grenada, human rights issues were highlighted and persons who complained about the violations of their rights received assistance.

Unlike his uncle, Roy Bishop, Maurice had no interest in becoming a trade union activist, though he was always concerned about the plight of workers. And unlike his father, Rupert, who was the first to introduce Duke Boxes and Pool

Tables to Grenada and owned the **Beverly Flats**, a chicken farm and a shipping agency, Maurice had no interest in becoming involved in business activity. Yet his father was a very humble and simple man who had a feel for people, carried no false airs and graces and was compassionate and caring. Maurice may well have inherited his common touch from him.

Maurice liked to laugh and had an almighty sense of humour. His genes in that respect must have been passed on to him directly from his father, with his mother, incredibly strong and stoic, being a quiet bystander. Rupert was sharp-witted and his own sense of humour was killingly funny. He would regale his customers and anyone who had a moment to listen, with light-hearted banter and belly-busting jokes that left them reeling with laughter.

"But look nah man, that big belly you carrying in front of you there, you need to do something about it, you need to look at it," one man said to another.

"Well, why you think ah have it in front ah me, so I could look at it," the man briskly replied.

There was a popular shop proprietor who erected a bold sign on the outside of his shop which read, 'FRESH FISH SOLD HERE.'

The first friend of the proprietor came along, read the sign and pondered. "How you mean 'sold here?' This is your shop so it must be here that the fish is sold." He then took out the ladder, climbed up to the sign and painted out the word 'HERE.'

The second friend who was passing by shortly after, read the corrected sign which said, 'FRESH FISH SOLD.' "How you mean 'fresh fish sold?' You not giving it away, so it must be sell you selling it." He too got out the ladder, climbed up to the sign and painted out the word 'SOLD.'

By then the proprietor was becoming wary of his friends, especially when he saw his friend who thought himself an intellectual, approaching. The friend looked at the sign askance and exclaimed aloud, "FRESH FISH! Fresh fish? I would hate to think that you are selling us stale fish. It must be fresh fish that you have here, unless you wish to give your customers wrong ideas. "The word 'fresh' is superfluous," he said, stepped onto the ladder and erased the word 'FRESH.'

The fourth person to come by regarded himself as a friend but the proprietor had other ideas, which may have included the use of violence after listening to him. The would-be friend laughed aloud when he saw the sign which simply said 'FISH.' "Ff-iii-ss-hh," he dragged out as best as he could manage in the midst of his uncontrollable derision. "We know is fish, we smelling that from all down the road."

There was another shop owner who stocked all sorts of goods, including foodstuffs, hardware items, products for home use, clothing and textiles. The shop owner, wishing to make shopping more convenient for his customers, posted a sign which read, 'Everything Sold By The Yard,' referring only to the textiles, of course.

Mr. Sam, a witty, middle-aged man, pompous but not excessively so, walked into the shop one day. "Eh-hem," he cleared his throat, both to get the shop owner's attention and to indicate that an important customer had arrived. "Everything sold by the yard, I see, I see," he said softly, but loud enough for the shop owner to hear and nodding his head as he said so, as if contemplating the meaning of the words. "Mr. Smith, could I have a yard of Condensed milk please? He asked of the shop owner with feigned seriousness and pretended respect.

"Sure, coming up in just a minute," Mr. Smith answered unfazed. He then went to the shelf, took down a tin of Condensed milk, opened it and poured a yard of its contents along the measuring rod that was nailed onto the counter. "Right, here you are," he said, as if he felt no greater honour serving Mr. Sam, and spreading his hands and smiling broadly to suggest that he had accomplished the unexpected.

"Oh, thank you very much," Mr. Sam said in a way which acknowledged Mr. Smith's resourcefulness though not mentioning it. The expression on his face, too, said how happy he was for such prompt service.

"Um, Mr. Smith, can you kindly wrap it up for me please?" Mr. Sam added airily and with a note of triumph in his voice.

The expression on Mr. Smith's face fell and he could only stand there shaking his balding head. He was a man who knew when he had been beaten.

That was Rupert Bishop at his jocular best. Though Maurice was serious whenever he needed to be, he had a similarly jovial personality.

None of the fruits which Maurice loved so much fell far from their trees. Indeed, he spared neither fruit nor hardly anything that could be eaten. He loved food and he had a healthy appetite. As healthy as his passion for life and his concupiscence.

Maurice had three children, two boys and a girl and now, collectively with the NJM, he had taken on the care of one hundred thousand people.

Chapter 38

One of the early visitors to Radio Free Grenada, from where the Caretakers were managing the initial affairs of State, was Sir Paul Scoon, who succeeded Sir Leo DeGale as Governor-General of Grenada in 1978. If only in terms of his speech, speaking as he did with a locally cultivated Eton accent and as if he had swallowed the queen's canary, Gairy could not have found a better representative of the British Monarch in Grenada. He wanted assurance that he was not out of a job and that the perks and privileges associated with the governor-generalship would still be at his disposal.

The British Government of Margaret Thatcher was itself reassured when it became clear that the Monarch was not going to be replaced as Head of State, nor would the historical relationship between Britain and her former colony be altered in anyway.

Perhaps if Gairy had declared himself King the chances of his own survival would have ranked higher than the Devil's chances of ascending the heavenly throne. But he did not and neither he nor his government could have cheated the logical advance of history, and now the Caretakers required a governmental framework within which to adequately respond to the needs of the people.

With Bernard Coard as his deputy, Maurice Bishop was announced as Prime Minister and the head of a Provisional Revolutionary Government (PRG) that came into being a few days later when members of the NJM met in the Recording Studio of RFG. A twenty-two-member government, including Lyden Ramdhanny, Pamela Buxo, Lloyd Noel, Sydney Ambrose, Dr. Bernard Gittens, Norris Bain and Simon Charles along with eight party members elected by secret ballot, was decided on.

However, the government's high-powered engine, its seven-member Cabinet, was named by NJM's Political Bureau and comprised of Maurice Bishop, Bernard Coard, Unison Whiteman, Selwyn Strachan, George Louison, Norris Bain and Lloyd Noel who was sitting in for Kenrick Radix.

Noel served briefly as the Acting Minister of Legal Affairs and Attorney General and would have assisted in strengthening the legal teeth of the new government. Peoples' Laws, which were passed by proclamation, subsequently and retroactively established the Peoples' Revolutionary Government (PRG) and the Peoples' Revolutionary Army (PRA). In the ensuing weeks, months and years the Cabinet went through its own regenerative process and by 1983, Noel was out and Hudson Austin, Jacqueline Creft, Christopher De Riggs and Lyden Ramdhanny were in.

But the Revolution was not about generating wealth for the revolutionaries, unlike the Gairy Government, which exempted its Prime Minister, its Deputy Prime Minister, and Minister of Finance from paying taxes on their income. The Revolution was about creating betterment for the entire country and all its people. A process that called for selflessness and great sacrifice, and the revolutionaries were prepared to lead the way.

One of the first acts of the Cabinet, then, was to cut the salaries of all Government Ministers by **30%** and remove most of the allowances. The salary of the Finance Minister, for example, after taxes were paid and the compulsory NIS deductions were later made, to which all Ministers were subjected, was EC$1,050 per month. All of this was inimical to Gairy whose vast holdings such as **Rock Gardens**, **Tropical Inn**, **Evening Palace**, **Portofino**, **Apple Inn** and several acres of the Golf Coast, were seized by the PRG.

Nonetheless, there were countries, individuals and regional institutions that were not going to allow the PRG's efforts to uplift the quality of its peoples' lives, to be an evening stroll down Tanteen.

The Supreme Court of the West Indies Associated States, to which Grenada was constitutionally bound, was peremptorily withdrawn from Grenada. It was a decision of the Prime Ministers of the other small island States, which left Grenada with no alternative than to create its own Court, which it did. Judge Archibald Nedd chose to remain in Grenada and to continue serving as its High Court Judge and with Justices Telford Georges, J.O.F Haynes and Nick Liverpool sitting on the Appeal Court bench, Grenada's judiciary was in good stead and of regional and international repute.

To this end, however, the PRG was forced to suspend the Grenada Constitution, though to a large extent constitutional rights were upheld. But it was not the first time that the Constitution was being suspended. In 1961, during 'Squandermania,' the British did so in order to kick Gairy out of the Chief Minister's office.

The Prime Ministers of the Eastern Caribbean States also had their own kicking out to do. They made efforts to expel Grenada from the Eastern Caribbean Currency Authority, which meant that Grenada would have had to create its own currency and suffer all the attendant economic problems that would have gone with it.

The aim from the outside was to nip the revolutionary bud before it had time to bloom. On the inside the promise of a rare and exotic flower turned Grenadians into mulchers and weeders.

Chapter 39

The Revolutionaries spent the early days and nights consolidating their hold on power. Squads of revolutionary soldiers could be seen moving about to the pulsating music of RFG, like Valentino's *Stay Up Zimbabwe*. They went to and fro in vehicles of various types during the day, and at night their very presence and the sound of intermittent gunfire, was enough to enforce the dusk to dawn curfew.

The two weeks of the curfew, was the best time for many wives. There could not have been a better way to keep their husbands at home. However, it was not oppressively and unwaveringly enforced. Celebratory house-parties were held and when a group of soldiers on night patrol came upon a parked car on the Lagoon Road, they would have thought nothing of it except that it was rocking. Although music coming from one of the houses could be heard, cars do not normally dance so the soldiers decided to have themselves a closer look. In the car were a young couple, *flagrante delicto* and feet in the air and all, having a time of their love. They were so engrossed and entangled in what they were doing, they were unaware of the soldiers' presence and, by the look of things, could not care less. The soldiers smiled, drove away then burst out laughing. "By de morning da car go need new springs," one said amusingly.

By then, the process of establishing military camps around the island was on the way. There was already **Camp Villa** in Sauteurs, one in Grand Etang and another in St. David's, **Camp Alister**, named after the martyred Alister Richardson. Yet another was on the Morne Rouge stretch in Grand Anse, St. George's and occupied the premises which was formerly **Knights Inn**, a small defunct hotel. **Camp Butler**, as it was called, was named in honour of Tubal Uriah 'Buzz' Butler, the Grenadian Trade Unionist who was based in Trinidad but fought struggles which benefited workers throughout the region.

It was to that camp that many young men who wished to enlist in Grenada's new army, the Peoples' Revolutionary Army, came. They were from all creeds including Rastafarianism and they came by the scores each day. True, unemployment was insufferably high at 49% but with the pay at E.C. $200 monthly with no prospect of an increase anytime in a hurry, it must have been that they came, in the main, out of a sense of patriotism and an eagerness to serve.

So eager were they that, without the knowledge of their superiors, a group of soldiers under Commander Wells left Camp Butler one night, commandeered the Coast Guard boat and headed out to sea. The rumour that Gairy was hiding out in St.Vincent was hot on the streets and many believed it, including the gung-ho Commander who was determined to seek him out.

The sea that night, given its placidity, must have been in on the hunt. It gave off only slight swells for Commander Wells and cooperated in every possible way. The boat, sensing the urgency of the Commander to get to his destination, went full speed ahead. It made quick time and within a few hours the boat made its first docking in Union Island, one of the small islands belonging to St. Vincent.

Commander Wells had no money to pay the required docking fees; neither had he secured prior permission to dock.

But docked he did and disembark he did. Clad in military green as he was and armed with a side-pistol and what appeared to be an especially dangerous looking rifle, he seemed threatening to those who immediately gathered around. His stern expression would not have helped either.

The officials on the island may have thought it prudent to keep a safe distance, so the curious onlookers were boldly informed "Commander Wells is here" and of them he demanded to be told where Gairy was hiding and that he be handed over without delay. The people stammered a hurried, frightened though sincere response "No-no-no sir he-he ain't here."

Satisfied, Commander Wells re-embarked, convinced that if Gairy was not in Union Island then he must be in St. Vincent proper. The boat hardly waited for directions and set a course unerringly for the Commander's next destination, exhausting all of its knots to get there as quickly as the sea was willing it to.

Within half an hour the boat was sideling up to the port at Kingstown and throwing out its ropes to be fastened. Commander Wells moved with speed, certain that he was closing in on his target and in no time he would have Gairy bundled-up and back in Grenada.

And that is what the port officials wanted to do with the Commander when he disembarked. At least, unlike their compatriots over on Union Island, they held a brave face when they approached him.

"May I ask who are you?" One hesitatingly directed at the unwelcomed soldier.

"I-I am Co-Commander Wells from Grenada," answered Wells who had a pronounced stammer.

"And why are you here?" Piped in another.

"Ah-ah come…"

"By the way man, who give you permission to come here?" An officious third interjected before Wells could finish what he was saying.

"Gre-Grenada just had a revolution," he informed them as if they had not been listening to the news. "Listen nah man," the Commander continued, "we ununderstand Gai-Gairy here and-and we come for him, that-that is all."

"You have no right to be here and I am afraid you will have to leave," Mr. Officious stated.

Commander Wells looked at him menacingly then allowed his stare to slowly drift over the rest of the officials contemptuously, as if he was considering some other option other than leaving. Indeed, fleeting thoughts about the jawbone of an ass passed through his mind and when he glared at them anew and smiled an ominous smile, they knew exactly what he was thinking. Commander Wells turned, boarded the Coast Guard boat and returned to Grenada, unsure whether Gairy was in St. Vincent hiding.

Months later, providing all of the relevant documents, including the report of the Duffus Commission, the Government requested Gairy's extradition from America but the Americans refused. However, Commander Wells' incursion into St. Vincent's territorial waters, was the Revolution's first 'diplomatic incident' outside of Grenada's borders, but there were to be other incidents of other kinds.

The back of Camp Butler extended right on to the world-famous Grand Anse beach where some soldiers were relaxing one afternoon. Although it was a cool and bright afternoon, not many beachgoers were in evidence. Yet it was an ideal time for dropping one's shoulders, kicking off one's shoes and taking off one's clothing if one believed in skinny-dipping or were willing to risk the attention of the few beach-studs hanging around.

There was a gentle breeze with wind speed measuring between eight to twelve miles per hour on the Beaufort Scale. A good time for sightseeing either by land, sea or air. But that was not in the soldiers thoughts when a small four-seater Piper plane flew overheard, drawing concentric circles in the sky that became smaller and smaller. The soldiers, looking at the plane intently, painted the same concentric circles with their eyes as they followed the movements of the craft. As the plane drew closer the soldiers began shouting at it but neither the pilot nor its other occupants answered them or responded to their desperate hand signals driving the plane away.

There was obvious concern and when the plane appeared to be buzzing and hedge-hopping the camp, the feeling of concern became one of dread. The fears of the soldiers were expressed aloud as they dashed into the makeshift barracks to collect .303 rifles and then dashed back out.

Two simultaneous fires in the tourist sector had already taken place and an American student, who claimed insanity, was held responsible. Further, with the threat of an American invasion or a possible mercenary landing already looming large and playing heavily on the soldiers' frame of mind, they thought the worst. As they loaded their bolt-action weapons it occurred to them that it was not too early either to get in some needed target practice.

The plane, with every low pass over the camp, appeared to be taunting the soldiers in much the same way as a flirtatious woman would tease a horny man released from prison after ten years. His resistance would not be any better than that of the soldiers that afternoon.

There was no order other than that dictated by expediency. The soldiers, six of them, opened fire at the plane creating a din which shattered the quiet of the afternoon. After about thirty seconds the pilot seemed to get the message loud and clear. Echoing Maurice Bishop's solemn advisory "We are in nobody's backyard," the soldiers were saying to the pilot "the back of the camp is our backyard." The plane flew away and disappeared into the distant blue sky.

Before the barrels of the weapons could cool, one of the officers of the camp received telephone calls from Pearls Airport and from a government official. Belatedly, he was being told that the plane had authorization to fly over and take photos for a tourism-related project. Instead of taking photos however, it received bullets on its fuselage just above its gas tank, and it must have been a miracle that it landed safely at the airport.

A soldier from the Pearls Airport camp, Kenny Budhlall, was also on board the plane so understandably the other soldiers at that camp were quite angry. A vanload of them, well armed, appeared at Camp Butler not too long after and did nothing to camouflage their anger. Indeed, their demeanor indicated that they did not come to talk. But good sense prevailed and once it became clear that there was no malicious intent, they left, less angry than when they came.

There would be occasions however, when rotten tempers were not involved and the consequences were far more tragic. Weapons can go off accidentally, sometimes through negligence or by failing to observe the basic safety measures. Several soldiers were killed that way or injured or were left permanently maimed or crippled, as was the case of Sheila Joseph now confined to a wheelchair.

Chapter 40

I was dreaming. It must have been a dream because where else than in my fertile mind could so much be done with so little for so many and in such a short space of time. I was in this place, it was not a strange place but it was so much more beautiful than any seen before.

Its hills and valleys, lushly covered in the greenest green of vegetation with the correct blend of flora of various colours appearing at just the right moments, locked gracefully into each other. It was a scene of hallucinatory peace where only angels should reside. But I was living it, experiencing it, tasting it right there in my mind. I was not an angel so it must have been a dream.

Yes, there was definitely a revolution, I remember now. There was a lot taking place, a bustle of activity yet there was harmony, there was tranquillity, there was fulfilment. The people were happy and proudly proclaimed their nationality wherever they went. They felt a part of the events, they were involved and were now able to measure their true worth. But things were happening so fast that it was as if the revolutionaries were attempting to outrun time.

Perhaps clairvoyantly they knew without actually realizing it, that they only had available to them four and a half

My Mother and I

years to accomplish what otherwise would have taken twenty years. In my dream it was extremely bright as if a thousand floodlights had been switched on all at the same time. The actions of the revolutionaries were being measured by a flash of light, revolutions per minute and a jet aircraft zooming from the visual cortex to the hippocampus of my mind and back again. All three were utilized by a record-keeping hand of indistinct form as if it knew that the memory chip in my dreaming mind provided limited storage capacity.

One minute I wanted to wake up and the next second I did not want to. It was not time to, anyway. Who would want to wake up when Miss Universe was about to remove her last item of clothing? Well no, probably a eunuch, but even in my dream the family jewels remained intact. It was a seductive unfolding of events, it was unworldly wisdom that I had to have.

The hand of no particular form was tapping me on the shoulder and asking, "Do you remember? Do you remember?" But I could not remember a single thing. This strange-looking hand was right, my memory chip may have once belonged to a prehistoric man with a pea-sized brain which somehow got passed on to me through some unexplainable phenomenon. But I wanted to remember, and the indescribable hand had found an avid listener.

"Then let me remind you..." it began, and rattled off for me remarkable events and accomplishments which took place over a short period, events which were spearheaded by men of unusual dedication and which were aimed at transforming Grenada and its people economically, politically and socially.

"...That one in every six Grenadians had their homes repaired under the House Repair programme. That many in St. George's, St. Mark's and St. Andrew's benefited from new low-income houses which were built, and many more would have lived in one of the five hundred, two and three bedroom houses that would have been built by the ***Sandino Plant*** each year.

Several hundred university and tertiary scholarships in over thirty countries worldwide were provided to the children of the ordinary people, and today many are serving Grenada in the medical and other fields. Free secondary education along with school books and uniforms were to be had. All sixty-seven primary schools were repaired and school meals served. The National In-Service Teacher Education Programme (NISTEP) would have meant that all primary school teachers would have been professionally trained in two years. While the Center for Popular Education (CPE) adult literacy programme mobilized thousands as teachers and students in a massive drive to create a completely literate society.

'The Revo Milk' through the milk-feeding programme, milk the PRG obtained from the European Union, was quite popular. The health of its citizens was a major concern of the new government. As a result of assistance sought from the Cuban Government, scores of Cuban medical doctors worked selflessly throughout the island, including Carriacou and Petite Martinique, looking after the health of the people. Medical clinics were built, and the granting of Maternity Leave with pay to women who became pregnant, became law.

Community centers, sea defense walls and bridges were also built. Phase one of the Port Expansion was completed, as were jetties in Carriacou and Petite Martinique. The first part of the Eastern Main Road had been done, and funding for work on the Western Main Road had been obtained. Over fifty miles of Farm and Feeder roads were also constructed. But the flagship construction project of the PRG was undoubtedly the building of its US$70 million International Airport at Point Salines, with the pivotal support of the Cuban Government. The funding for the airport was obtained from friendly countries including England, and international agencies which the American Government made unsuccessful attempts to block. That project had the effect of massively expanding the tourism sector.

Bernard Coard, the Minister of Finance, Trade and Planning, was the key figure in mobilizing much of the funding for the airport construction, as he was in the purchase of **Holiday Inn**, a one hundred and fifty luxury room hotel on seventeen and three-quarter acres of Grand Anse beach front. The Holiday Inn, which became the **Grenada Beach Hotel**, was bought for the EC$125, 000 overdraft which the hotel held at the **National Commercial Bank** (NCB), so no actual money had to come from the Government Treasury.

The NCB itself, the premier bank of the Revolution, was the direct result of Coard's shrewd negotiating and an amalgamation of three former banks that, at different times, offered to sell all of its local assets. The **Canadian Imperial Bank of Commerce**, the Grenville branch of the **Royal Bank of Canada** and the Gouyave branch of **Barclays** were each bought for EC$1, yes, one dollar. When they first balked at Coard's offer and insisted instead to be paid in US currency, he calmly informed them that the PRG conducted its transactions in EC currency. Later, the Royal Bank of Canada in St. George's, which became the **Grenada Bank of Commerce** (GBC) was similarly bought for EC$1.

Continental Telephone Company which became known as **Grenada Telephone Company** (GRENTEL), was also purchased for EC$1, almost as if the Finance Minister was no longer capable of counting beyond one hundred, and an Eastern Caribbean one hundred at that. Yet with cheaper services available and a doubling and tripling of real wages, many more homes were installed with phones.

Many more homes too, and small villages became electrified after the **Commonwealth Development Cooperation** (CDC), which was renamed **Grenada Electricity Company** (GRENLEC), was bought with all of its assets. The cost to the government was the inheritance of the long-term existing, modest debt of CDC. Carriacou and Petite Martinique were also electrified as a result."

By then I wanted to wake up because I needed to convince myself that I was really dreaming, yet the light, lilting voice of the hand of no particular shape, held my mind in a state of airy nothingness. I knew there was more to hear.

"The people now had services which were accessible and affordable," the hand continued. "The establishment of the **National Transport Service** (NTS) allowed for cheaper transportation cost. The **Marketing and National Importing Board** (MNIB) provided basic food items at costs which were well within the reach of ordinary people. The **National Insurance Scheme** (NIS) meant that social security was now available to all workers. Indeed, the Forty-four State enterprises, which also included NCB, GBC, **Agro Industries** and the **Fish Processing Plant**, had, by 1983, earned seven million dollars in net profit for the country.

While unemployment dropped from 49% to 12% by mid-1983, the country was saved millions of dollars by the voluntary labour of its people, who every week could be seen working on various projects throughout the island. That is how the community centers were built for example, through the mighty energies unleashed by the Revolution. Energies which were harnessed through the mass organizations of the Revolution such as the National Women's Organization (NWO), the National Youth Organization (NYO), the National Farmers Union (NFU), the Peoples' Militia and the Young Pioneers. Thousands who carried within their hearts and manifested by their actions, the spirit of the Revolution.

This spirit was perhaps best epitomized by the monthly Parish and Zonal Councils which took place in schools, community centers and other government buildings all around the island. It was participatory democracy in action. Managers of Public Utilities and other government agencies were summoned to account. National issues were discussed and recommendations were made. It was as a result of one such recommendation that the NTS was established.

Because of the poor, material circumstances and the general lack of education of the core of Gairy's support base, the PRG programmes, of necessity, would have had their greatest impact on them. Nonetheless, the vast majority of Grenadians and every one of the 21,000 households, would have benefited and would have been touched in some way or the other, by the programmes of the Revolution.

While then the 'Internationale' was being sung at NJM party functions, another song, sung with gusto, became the unofficial anthem of the Revolution:

> Forward March, Forward March
> Forward march against Imperialism,
> Forward march, forward march
> Forward march against Imperialism.
> Rupert march to Otway House
> Forward march,
> Alister marched against oppression
> Forward march
> And now Grenadians got the vision
> Would end corruption and oppression
> As we build Grenada with these very hands…"

It was at that point that I woke up, smiling more than the Cheshire cat in Lewis Carroll's **Alice's Adventures in Wonderland**. The Revolution, by the sheer magnitude of its achievements, packed so much power into its brief punch it was as if it sought to create, in its unique way, its own adventures in Wonderland. By so doing it made possible the most satisfying dream-like experience I have ever had, although I had lingering doubts that it was really a dream. But if indeed it was a dream, then one hundred thousand Grenadians shared the same dream.

Chapter 41

There was one of several persons who played a central role in the realization of that dream, and whose birth from all accounts had been normal, well, almost normal.

On the 10th of August 1944, a chubby baby boy screamed into the world and was added to the list of the thousands making up Grenada's population. His name was Bernard Coard and his parents were Flora Coard and Frederick 'Mackie' Coard also known as F.M. Coard.

He was born at the Colony Hospital in St. George's, on the same day that a rainstorm deluged Grenada. Water falling through the hospital roof gave him his first complete bath, and the nickname 'Stormy Weather" which those of his parents' generation called him, was to serve as a double reminder of his waterlogged birth and the diluvial weather conditions of that day.

The last of six boys and one girl, Bernard Coard brought up the rear just as the rest of the world was desperately seeking to put an end to Hitler's reign and his catastrophic blitzkrieg across Europe. Being a colony of Britain and with Allied Troops billeted here, Grenada was not insulated from the effects of war or from its hazards.

My Mother and I

It was around the same time that the ***Island Queen***, a Grenadian schooner, loaded with merry-making passengers and on their way to a wedding in St. Vincent, simply disappeared without a trace. Not a corpse, including that of the bride who was on board or the smallest splinter, was found. Absolutely nothing floated to the surface, not even as a mark of remembrance to those who died. It was as if the Island Queen never really existed and it was nothing more than a child's story taken out of the ***Royal Reader***.

Well, the Island Queen did exist. It was owned by Chicra Salhab, the great grandson of Captain Louis La Grenade, a Grenadian from the French Plantocracy, who fought with the British against Fedon and received as a gift of appreciation the entire Mt. Jaloux Estate.

But even from there it would not have been easy to see what became of the schooner. Grenada lies on an important and strategic sea-lane that was regularly patrolled by German U- Boats, as their submarines were also called. These undersea boats had as their policy, 'shoot first, ask no questions later,' and when their listening device picked up the heavy motor sound of the Island Queen, they did just that. The Island Queen was torpedoed out of the water, then using dragnets, the Germans collected the corpses and every fragment from the schooner, which they carried further out to sea and anchored at the bottom of the ocean.

This tragic loss impacted greatly on the small Grenadian society where family ties were close and everyone knew someone who was on the schooner. Its disappearance then only aggravated the suffering of the people where poverty was widespread and economic and social ills were rampant.

Although 'Mackie' Coard was a Civil Servant, he was a civil servant who was paid very little. His family too, living then on Scott Street in St. George's, had to bear the hardships which were common to many other families, but he sought to equip his children with the tools of success. They were made to read and read and read, to work hard and to study hard in the sound belief that knowledge and education held the key to a secure future.

At eight years old, Bernard Coard was already a student at the St. George's Methodist School. He was an active child and often participated as part of one of the two teams which engaged in hopping contests. On one leg, each team member was required to hop for a set distance. Bernard's team would always finish first simply because he was the best hopper the school ever produced. No wonder that the nickname which stuck with him throughout his life, was 'Hopper.' But Bernard Coard did not have to hop to get his first girlfriend; undoubtedly however, his hopping proficiency would have paved the way to a young female heart.

There were no girls at the World War II, barracks-built Grenada Boys' Secondary School (G.B.S.S.) which he later attended. Some may think that that may have been one of the reasons why he performed well as a student there, but Bernard Coard was fairly strait-laced and a natural with the books. He was also a Queen's Scout and a hard-nosed prefect who, during his vacations, did odd jobs at **Everybody's** Supermarket and other places. He was also a teacher.

He left Grenada in 1963 to attend Brandeis University in Massachusetts, USA, where he obtained a Bachelor of Arts degree in economics. He then moved to Sussex, England. There he worked with the disadvantaged youth and studied. He was awarded a Master of Arts degree in Comparative Politics. His thesis was on the 'Failure of West Indies Federation – 1958-1962.'

When Bernard Coard met his wife, Phyllis, at Sussex, he was thinking of a federation of another kind. They fell in love and within four months of meeting each other, they were married. Three years later their first daughter was born; that was one federation that was not going to fail.

Having signed up for his Doctor of Philosophy degree at Sussex by then, Bernard and his family had left for Central America. He spent nine months there doing research into the

Central American Common Market for his thesis in Development Economics.

While there he received an offer to teach at the St. Augustine campus of the University of the West Indies in Trinidad, which he accepted. He taught Economics and Research Methods there for two years then moved to Jamaica where he also taught for another two years at its Mona campus.

By June of 1976, Bernard Coard had completed almost all of the course work for his doctorate when his eyes did a number on him. His eyes may have decided that they had seen enough and simply shut down. He just could not see. Doctors in Jamaica diagnosed him as having keratoconus in both eyes, the bulging of the cornea. Although he received treatment and regained partial sight in both eyes, they recommended cornea transplants which he is yet to have.

When an SOS came from Maurice Bishop, he had recovered sufficiently and responded in the affirmative. He was needed to organize and take charge of the national campaign for the general elections which was expected in early 1977. As it turned out, the elections was on December 7th, 1976. Bernard Coard returned to Grenada permanently in September 1976.

It was not known whether Bernard 'Hopper' Coard actually hopped to his wife's bed, but he had been blessed with three children, two girls and a boy, evidently inheriting from his parents the ability to procreate. His father, 'Mackie' Coard, who in the 1960's had written a book which he entitled, **Bitter Sweet and Spice: These Things I Remember**, had also passed on to his son his authorship.

It was while Bernard Coard was in England that he wrote his widely acclaimed book entitled, **How the West Indian Child is Made Educationally Sub-normal in the British School System**.

Chapter 42

There was nothing sub-normal or abnormal about Mother. Notwithstanding her proliferate reproduction of men, buildings and machines, she had maintained a remarkably well-stacked, sexy figure from the time of her own birth and many lustful eyes had been on her. She was lovely to behold and had the qualities that would bewitch a lover and give a husband sleepless nights. Although she would generally be considered as big, and age appeared to have made her more bosomy than she really was, her 212, 659 square miles, within which her other vital statistics were subsumed, did not make her unattractive.

However, if 'the smaller the better' connotes beauty, then Grenada, including Carriacou and Petite Martinique, at 133 square miles and a population of 100,000 was a swan compared to the ugly duckling that was Mother. Perhaps it's an unfair comparison and one that I hesitate to make because she is my Mother, but all is fair in matters of love.

Nevertheless, if this conceptual framework of beauty were further extended, then the United States of America (USA) would have been overly short on looks and hard on the eyes. With 3, 615,123 square miles and a population of 226,504,825 it was a blot on the world while Grenada was a dot on the world map.

America may have had the characteristics that would have stopped a clock but it badly wanted to turn back Grenada's own. It wasted no time in bringing its ugliness to bear when, in the very early days of the Revolution, its ambassador, Frank Ortiz, threatened to smash Grenada's economy if it went ahead and established ties with Cuba. Other State Department and Pentagon officials accused Grenada of having a Submarine Base in Grand Etang and in Calivigny in St. George's. Various publications in the USA and Canada carried the stories and showed photos of a barbed-wired Grand Anse Beach saying that that was what existed in Grenada; a campaign that was clearly designed to discourage tourists from visiting.

"Grenada is a threat to the national security of the United States of America," declared Ronald Reagan on the campaign hustings for the 1980 Presidential Elections.

George Bush (Sr.) reportedly made similar declarations. Grenada with no airforce, no navy, no long-range missiles and a miniscule army that was barely out of diapers, was a threat to the mighty, world-power USA. It was a threat only because it stubbornly refused to bow to the dictates of the US Administration and chose to pursue an independent path to development. Reagan further sighted the international airport, which was being constructed, as a Soviet MIG Fighter Base and promised to teach Grenada a lesson, puny, underdeveloped and struggling Grenada, once he was elected.

Once Reagan was inaugurated as President on January 20th, 1981, with Bush (Sr.) as Vice President, he gave further notice of his intent. It was not the first time that the US Administration was to show satellite images of military hardware and Bases which did not exist, as it did in the case of Grenada's new airport.

President Reagan's continued menacing words and plans were much more than the shaking of a clenched fist in the face of one's enemy. His saber-rattling was to be more than saber-rattling. In that same year the USA staged military exercises called Ocean Venture '81. As part of those exercises, a military maneuver code-named 'Amber and the Amberines' was staged on Vieques Island belonging to Puerto Rico. 'Amber and the Amberines' was widely read as Grenada and the Grenadines and the maneuver was merely a rehearsal of an invasion of Grenada by amphibious landing as well as by air.

These exercises were repeated in 1982 and '83 as were the threats. On March 10th and 23rd 1983, President Reagan delivered major speeches in which he again pronounced Grenada a threat to the national security of the United States of America. By August of that year, massive quantities of medical equipment and supplies had been shipped to Barbados, enough to have lasted its Defense Force fifteen years. But Barbados had been identified as a possible staging post for an invasion of Grenada.

Along with the open, frequent and brazen violations of Grenada's territorial integrity by military planes and ships, the US Administration succeeded in spooking the Grenada Revolution for most of the four and a half years. Understandably, it became paranoid and obsessed with its own defense and preservation.

It did not help either when planted bombs came uncomfortably close to blowing away almost the entire leadership of the Revolution, including Prime Minister Bishop. It was a time-bomb planted directly beneath where they sat. Sir Paul Scoon was also there. The leaders had gathered at the Queens Park for a rally on the afternoon of June 19th 1980, to honour Grenada's heroes. Three young ladies, Bernadette, Lauris and Lorraine, were killed by the bomb and several others were injured. Strachan Phillip, a March 13th combatant who had become disillusioned with the process, was one of those held responsible for the bombing. He was killed that night in a shoot-out.

I could not be sure of exactly what DeRavinere, a former student of one of NJM's Central Committee members, and others may have had in mind when months later they were caught with a range of explosives, guns and ammunition, but no one would have wished to find out. They were deemed to be part of a plot to overthrow the government and were detained. Within forty-eight hours a rally in that connection was held at the Queens Park, and large sections of the crowd voiced their sentence, "hang them, hang them, hang them!"

They were imprisoned, not hanged. Others were far less fortunate. Four youths, Andy Courtney, Steve Lalsee and the Stanisclaus brothers, were said to be a fatal case of mistaken identity. Driving along Plains, in St. Patrick's one night in a car, they were killed by a hail of bullets, the gun-bearers believing one of its occupants to be Tan Bartholomew, an NJM Central Committee member. A soldier, Edmund Charles, was also subsequently killed in Camp Villa. Habib, Yusuf and Ayub, the believed culprits of both shootings were themselves killed by the PRA.

Others however, wanted to destroy Grenada economically and when tons of nutmegs, bagged and ready for shipment, were found to be laced with diesel or some such substance, many remembered the promise of US Ambassador, Frank Ortiz.

But the people had faith in their leaders, believed in their own strength, were imbued with revolutionary fervor and had an unconquerable spirit that seemed to emit from the Kalashnikov rifles and Makarov pistols which were everywhere. The people, uplifted by the defiant speeches of Prime Minister Bishop and other leaders of the Revolution, sang:

> "We ent giving up we mountain
> We ent giving up we sea,
> We ent giving up we airport
> That belong to we."

> AND

> "Let them come, let them come
> We will bury them in the sea.

> Let them come, let them come
> We will bury them in the sea."

The content of the songs and the chants, the assertive manner of the voices and with AK 47's and AKS's held boldly aloft, an altogether intimidating picture was painted.

The constant threats emanating from the United States against the backdrop of externally linked attempts to internally undermine the revolutionary process, meant that Grenada was in an almost constant state of high alert. Military maneuvers involving the five hundred-strong PRA and the two thousand, five hundred-strong Militia were regularly held.

At the end of which goose-stepping soldiers and militia would march, with a few dance steps added, through the streets singing and chanting and hoping that the deterrent effect of the maneuvers, the display of its military hardware and all that followed, would have been greatest on those whom it may have concerned.

> "Ah never de know
> Maneuver so nice
> Ah make up me mind
> To join the Militia."

> AND

> "Reagan have a boat
> Reagan have a boat in Barbados
> Reagan have a boat in Barbados
> When he see the AK he turn back."

Nevertheless, the upshot of all the threats, real and perceived, was to force the revolutionaries to recoil into a permanent defensive posture. If there were ever a quasi-siege mentality syndrome or some derivative thereof, then they may have been considered its unwilling victims. Nerves became taut, as tightly drawn as their impatience and unindulgence.

Every time my gates were opened to let in some poor, unfortunate soul I felt a correlative opening-up of my insides. It was the cause of much of my miserableness and sickness. I was no hypochondriac but the loud clanging sound and the banging of iron doors as persons were contemptuously thrown into and locked up deep within my bowels, brought on excruciating pain in every part of me.

The pain seemed to be most poignant in my heart from where a river of empathy burst its banks. I could not prevent, I could only accept. That was the explicit responsibility that was woven into my DNA; it was my very being. I had no say in who came or who went and at what hour. However, when I saw the sheer agony on some of the faces I knew so well, there was one thing left for me to do, cry, and I cried the Nile.

My tears were that long, and when they thought that the rainfall was just that and nothing more, it was my supplicatory tears which went up to Heaven then came back down as rain. I turned on the waterworks because they too sobbed. Their tears were not just for themselves but for the families they were leaving behind, unprotected and now without the main, and often, only breadwinner.

The emotional pain was the most difficult to bear. There can be no greater heart-breaking experience than being torn away from one's family, sometimes for no other reason than showing dissent or for being courageous enough to verbally challenge those in authority. Holding an opposing political view too strongly vocalized or seemingly questioning the right of those in 'power' to rule, was tantamount to stirring up a hornet's nest. There could hardly have been a more unconvincing plea for imprisonment, but there was.

The Revolution was zealously protective of its young self but having removed Gairy from office in the manner in which it did, it wrote the script for many of its opponents. There were various attempts to destabilize and to overthrow the PRG through violent means. Where the response was not itself violent, their purveyors were detained. Some were charged and tried, most were not, joining those who may have spoken too much.

Lloyd Noel, former NJM Political Bureau member and Acting Attorney General, was in cell No. 7. Tillman Thomas, a lawyer spoken for by Bishop when he was called to the Bar and a former employee of the Grenada office of the Caribbean Human Rights And Legal Aid Company, of which Bishop was a Director, was imprisoned. As was Teddy Victor, a founding member of NJM. Winston Whyte, leader of the UPP which joined with NJM and GNP in an electoral alliance in 1976, found himself behind bars. Ralph 'Ralphie' Thompson, a former NJM stalwart who could not be impeached for timidity during the anti-Gairy struggles, died while still a prisoner. Dr. Rupert Japal managed to stay alive, as did Kade Layne and the Trade Unionist Stanley Roberts, all of whom were also bolted in.

The Revolution brooked no 'dissident' activity, and when the 'Gang of 26,' as they were called, got around to publishing the second issue of their **Grenadian Voice** newspaper, several of them, Leslie Pierre included, were incarcerated. The local independent media was deprived of oxygen, notwithstanding the fact that the **Trinidad Guardian** and **Express** were allowed to be sold on the streets of Grenada, and unsympathetic radio stations like the **VOA** and **Radio Antilles** were easily accessible on the dial.

Not so for the four hundred political detainees whose stay within my confines was of varying length. Imprisonment meant deprivations, yet they were kept in conditions that were generally considered humane. Although the Revolution had no time for spirituality and did not even acknowledge Papa God's existence, several church officials, including Fr. Oliver Leavy of the Roman Catholic Church, were allowed to pay me regular pastoral visits and none were on record as having made complaints in that regard. Inevitably however, there were the abuses which the detainees suffered at the hands of prison officers and soldiers.

My Mother and I

Political detainees, who were held under a law modelled after one passed by the British to deal with unrest in Northern Ireland, were habitually released consistent with the policy of the Government. By the end of the revolution's tenure there were no more than fifty detainees languishing within my bowels.

Martin 'Barney' Fletcher was not one of them. Permission for his detention was not sought from him and he saw no reason to obtain anyone's permission to leave. 'Barney' had a get-things-done personality who did not believe that good things necessarily came to those who waited. 'Things happened if you made them happen' was one of his philosophical outlooks on life. Moreover, he had no idea when his release was going to come, if it was going to come, and he had neither the time nor the patience to wait to find out.

'Barney' was tall and slim. He could move fast and think fast. He spoke a lot and he spoke convincingly, enough to talk his way out of any situation, though it may have been his mouth which got him into trouble and prison in the first place. Extremely confident and bright, he had the qualities to succeed at whatever he put his mind to. Unbeknownst to the prison officers and PRA Guards, 'Barney's' mind was on escaping that day.

It was a normal morning and indications were that the rest of that day in 1981 was going to be just as normal and as routinized as the previous many days had been. I had my own rhythm that was not any different from one day to the next and for those within my care, it was the same old daily grind.

There were four strategically located guard towers which dwarfed the rest of me and had command over all that went on around me and in my immediate environs. Soldiers of the PRA armed with AK-47 and AKS assault rifles manned the towers. These Soviet-made Kalashnikov rifles had an unnerving reputation which went back to 1947. There was no landmass which had not heard of their lethal feats and every one of the prisoners had heard something of its homicidal capabilities. Almost all, then, became AK-inspired adherents of the notion that prudence was the preferred part of valour, and were waiting on their discharge papers whenever they came. But not 'Barney'. He already had all that he required that day. Well, not quite all.

When one of his fellow political detainees became unexpectedly and seriously ill that morning, 'Barney's' mind became feverish. Although his mind was churning up possibilities which were still hazy, he knew that somewhere in there was an opportunity which he could not miss. "Opportunities were equally distributed in sickness and in health," he mused.

His came, he thought, when the Hospital Ambulance was summoned to take the ill detainee to the General Hospital in St. George's. When it arrived with a Nurse and an Orderly who also doubled as its driver, 'Barney' immediately saw his opening. The ill detainee weighed plenty and help would have been needed to carry the patient on the stretcher. He was not the doctor he once pretended to be, but here was the chance to remake himself as a stretcher-bearer and an Orderly.

'Barney' moved with assured confidence and spoke with such authority that both the Nurse and the Orderly assumed he was an officer assigned to the Medical Department of the Prison. He quickly donned the white cloak which was mistakenly brought in on the stretcher and took charge. The Nurse and the Orderly were grateful for his help in getting the patient onto the stretcher and out through the gate-lodge of the prison. But as they passed, Barney made sure to keep his head bowed and his back to the officer who was sitting at the desk. The unobservant officer simply noted in the prison diary that the nurse and orderlies left with the detainee.

The sick detainee was placed at the back of the Ambulance, and 'Barney,' the assumed prison medic-cum-Orderly, slipped in after the Nurse who thought nothing of it. The doors were secured by the driver, and by the time the prison officer who was assigned to escort the ill detainee, and travelling in a separate vehicle, had arrived, 'Barney' was safely ensconced in the back of the Ambulance.

The driver made it to the main entrance of the prison in a jiffy and out the iron gates with neither the guard at the gate nor the tower guards any the wiser. With siren blaring, and moving without the constrains imposed by traffic regulations, the Ambulance was soon dislodging at the Emergency Department the latest addition to the hospital's population.

'Barney' emerged from the back of the Ambulance with the Nurse, careful to keep his head bowed and his back to the prison officer. He assisted in getting the stretchered patient to the door of the Emergency Department and then contrived a quick disappearing act, not giving the prison officer any chance to get close to him.

Using all of his daring and wit, he had made good his escape. The next time Grenada saw or heard anything of Martin 'Barney' Fletcher, was when he returned from North America in 1987.

Chapter 43

No one would have known then, except those endowed with the gift of prophecy, that in a matter of not too many years there would be more persons who heard of the revolutionary process than those who actually experienced it.

When the Central Committee (C.C.) of the NJM, its policy-making body, met to discuss the then current state of affairs in the country and in the party, it never occurred to anyone of them that that was anything other than an effort to further the cause of the Revolution; a cause to which they were staunchly devoted and a Revolution that was indestructible.

The meeting took place in September of 1983 with thirteen of the sixteen members present. Bernard Coard had resigned from the C.C. and Political Bureau (P.B.) one year before in an attempt to squash any suspicion that his frank criticisms of the party's failings, including that of Bishop, was a thinly disguised attempt to usurp Bishop as leader. Moreover, Coard wanted to break the dependency syndrome which had developed in the party. As the main conceptualizer of many of the Revolution's programmes and activities and the party's foremost organizer and theoretician, most depended on him to do the thinking.

Not much of that was required, however, to realize that things were not as they should be. All at the meeting agreed that a crisis existed. That despite the continued overwhelming support for the process and that conditions, economic and otherwise, had vastly improved since the Revolution, there was clear evidence of disenchantment among the people.

The act of drastically improving, as the Revolution did, the quality of one's life, in turn further raises one's expectations. It is one of the idiosyncrasies of life, and unless the limitations to further immediate improvement are adequately explained, as was not done, then disillusionment would set in, as happened. The poverty of the island and the underdevelopment of its productive sector could not sustain the growing expectation for more and better goods and services, unless production had significantly increased. There was dissatisfaction, for example, with GRENLEC and the electricity blackouts still experienced in some areas, while the condition of the roads was worsening.

And it was not only the roads which were not holding up. Party members, too, were falling ill from overwork and hospitalization was required in the case of some. There was a correlation, then, between the overworked party members and the fall-off in discipline which in turn affected the organizational work of the party. No surprise therefore, that the party was beginning to lose its links with the people and the attendance at Parish and Zonal Council meetings was decreasing.

While some directed criticisms at the C.C. itself, most felt that Bishop, by his loose, consensus-seeking leadership style, lack of organization and discipline, had to shoulder much of the responsibility; criticisms which Bishop himself readily accepted.

The panacea which was proposed was ***Joint Leadership*** of the party, which had nothing to do with the Prime Ministership and other State functions. It was a marrying, as it was described, of the strengths of Bishop with the strengths of Coard. Bishop had confidence-building charisma and he inspired others by his brilliant oratory. He had a rare common touch and a natural feel for others. His very personality attracted respect and admiration for the party and Revolution far and wide. Coard, though, was an excellent organizer and his discipline was the benchmark which the party aspired to. He was a strategic thinker and had a sharp grasp of political science.

Yet even doctors do not always prescribe the correct medicine and when they do, the dosage may be wrong. Further, when they do get the medicine and the dosage right, there is sometimes the added problem of patients who, for a multiple of reasons, simply refuse to take it. And as far as I know, there is no law which permits the doctor to inject medicine down the throat of a patient with or without the benefit of a gastro-esophageal tube.

It was obvious from Bishop's response that he was not happy with the proposal of Joint Leadership and that he would have taken a lot of convincing, the prospects of which were minimal since he saw the proposal as a vote of no confidence in his leadership. "...I have never had any problems with sharing power...I have worked very well with comrade Bernard over the years from school days...neither I or anybody have the right to be leader for life...I cannot inspire the masses when I have to look over my back or feel I do not have the full confidence of my comrades..."

Moreover, one member of the C.C., George Louison, was forcefully opposed to the proposal, while another had reservations, and when it was put to the vote, nine persons voted for, one against and three abstained, including Bishop. The party leader needed more time for personal reflection on the issue, and wanted to know Coard's feelings on the matter.

Bishop suggested that the C.C. hold its meeting with Coard the following day even though he, Bishop, would have been in St. Kitts attending its Independence celebrations. The meeting was held and Coard was not enthusiastic about the idea. He wanted to know whether other options were examined and why the meeting was not scheduled for a time when Bishop would have been present. He was reluctant to rejoin the C.C. and P.B. for the same reasons which led to his resignation one year before.

However, at a meeting of the entire membership of the party on September 25th, which was called to discuss the Joint Leadership proposal, a marathon meeting of fifteen hours, there was, with one exception, universal acceptance of the proposal.

The meeting was held in **Butler House**, the office of the Prime Minister. Named in memory of Uriah 'Buzz' Butler, it was formerly **Santa Maria Hotel** then **Islander Hotel**. Prior to its office conversion, its ballroom-sized dance hall was a favourite location for the many public parties and fetes which were held almost weekly. It was from there that several local bands like **Fantasies**, **Weevils**, **3+2**, **Harmony with Brass**, **Pilgrimage** and **Armand's Eight** played their way to public acclaim.

On the day in question however, it was a party gathering of a different kind and by 11.30 p.m. that night, voices broke the still of the night as they rang out in a happy and joyous rendition of the 'Internationale:'

> "Proletarians come rally
> And the last fight let us face,
> The international
> Unites the human race…"

Bishop had spoken, he had embraced Coard then each party member in turn walked by and embraced both Bishop and Coard. There could not have been a better show of unity of spirit and of will. The feeling that NJM was stronger and that the bond and camaraderie among its members were even more unbreakable than ever before, was almost palpable. The mood was definitely celebratory.

The issue was settled, all thought, as some persons drove up to Bishop's residence at Mt. Wheldale that night to share drinks with him and for a bit of 'ole-talk.' But the matter of Joint Leadership, despite what the membership believed when they left the meeting, was not yet a settled matter.

The following day Prime Minister Bishop left Grenada on a pre-planned trip to Eastern Europe to source economic assistance. George Louison would not have been present at the September 25th party general meeting because he was part of the advanced delegation to Eastern Europe. While in Hungary, Louison reportedly met with a group of NJM party members studying there, along with those who were part of the delegation, and informed them that no final decision on Joint Leadership had been taken despite the near-unanimous decision of the Party general meeting. Bishop was not at that meeting, but it was widely believed that Louison might have done all he could to get him to renege on the commitment he made to party members on September 25th.

When Prime Minister Bishop did not return via England as his original flight plan had indicated and instead went on to Cuba where he spent a few days with Fidel Castro, suspicions salted with apprehension were aroused. No one knew what Castro's fatherly advice to him may have been, but it almost certainly would not have been 'go home, behave yourself and comply with the decision of the party.'

Compliance appeared completely out of the picture when, Cletus St. Paul, the head of Bishop's personal security, telephoned his superior officer in Grenada and told him, "Dem fellas trying to F-up the Chief and it look like blood go ha to flow."

What flowed immediately was consternation-driven adrenaline as minds already wary of Bishop's stop-over in Cuba, conjured up the worst possible scenarios, and none of them were life-friendly. By the night of October 7th, Coard, as well as other party leaders, were seeking refuge in homes other than their own. Further, he was advised by security personnel in light of Cletus St. Paul's threat, not to go to the airport the following day to meet Bishop, as would have been the practice of party leaders whenever Bishop returned from abroad.

My Mother and I

Prime Minister Bishop, also accompanied by Julien Rizo, the Cuban Ambassador, returned to Grenada on October 8th, and only Selwyn Strachan was at the airport to meet him. The welcome accorded the Prime Minister then, though understandable, was far from the ideal and that did nothing to ease the tension which hung like a megaton of millstones. Over the next four days nothing was done to ease the obvious strain. Had his comrades visited him in large numbers that may well have mitigated against whatever he may have been adversely fed while he was abroad.

While then the NJM leaders could not be blamed entirely for their reluctance to go to Mt. Wheldale, Bishop was largely left to his own devices and, given his own disposition and that of the other leaders, that could not have augured well for the party and revolution.

A meeting of the NJM C.C. was held on the morning of October 12th. It was held at Fort Rupert, the Headquarters of the PRA and named in honour of Rupert Bishop. That fort had always had a military function; it was the way it was conceived by Mother which she baptized Fort Royal. It had gone through periods of bastardization but had never lost its identity and because we shared the same antecedents, nay, the same Mother, he has been my brother from time immemorial.

It was not being asked to perform a military function that morning but to serve as a temporary meeting place for the NJM leaders. The atmosphere was tense and the seedlings of animosity had taken root. Bishop told the meeting that he was no longer willing to accept the Joint Leadership decision and asked that the matter be reopened for discussion. Most of those present, with their backs already up, balked at any suggestion that the matter be further discussed. They insisted that Bishop comply with the decision of the party, a decision that was democratically arrived at and that Bishop of all persons, could not flaunt the democratic will of the party membership and its sacred decision-making mechanism of Democratic Centralism. It was one of the pillars of Marxism-

Leninism and its youthful adherents held on unwaveringly to its application.

There was no room in that youthful and politically immature approach to facilitate Bishop's personal feelings. What began as an attempt to address problems in the party and revolution, became for him a concerted effort to unseat him. Moreover, in the face of the Grenadian people, the people and leaders of the region and the world, particularly those with whom NJM shared party to party relations, this Joint Leadership to Bishop represented a humiliating fall from grace, one that his ego would not have permitted him to accept.

Shortly after the meeting broke for lunch, events took off with a speed as if, like racehorses, they were being restrained by stall gates that suddenly flew open. Bishop reportedly summoned the chief and deputy chief of his personal security, Cletus St. Paul and Errol George, into his bedroom. His instructions were clear; they were to go to persons whose names were on a list, and inform them that 'Phyllis and Bernard Coard were planning to kill him.' They were to ensure that Phyllis's name was called first. That was done out of an apparent calculation that the hostility towards Phyllis, Coard's wife and a Jamaican by birth, would be greater of the two. Errol George, who did not take kindly to this development, informed his superiors.

If the objective of that rumour mongering was to up the ante, then that had all the makings of an overdone putsch. The Coards rumoured homicidal intent spread like a roaring, devouring fire typical of the early 1970's, causing unrest and eliciting an equal amount of heat directed their way.

The C.C. meeting reconvened that afternoon as a meeting of the P.B., which both Bernard and Phyllis Coard did not attend since their own safety had been placed in jeopardy by that rumour. Furthermore, they had been extremely peeved to put it conservatively. Bishop denied any part in the rumour and made a statement on radio to the effect that all was well within the party. Cletus St. Paul too, who was called into the meeting and questioned, claimed his innocence and the innocence of Bishop. He was subsequently detained pending further investigation.

The following day Bishop was asked to remain at home by the Security Forces and had his phones removed, effectively placing him under house arrest. It was almost unnecessary to ask Coard, for his own safety, to do the same since the rumour and peoples' response to it, ensured that he did. But he was so asked. His phones however, were not removed.

When Bishop spoke at length at the meeting of the entire membership of NJM that very night of October 13th, while accepting some responsibility for the state of affairs in the party and country, he again denied having any hand in the framing and disseminating of the rumour. However, when Errol George rose, in Bishop's presence, and gave a detailed account of the rumour, its origin, spreading and Bishop's role in it, the hushed silence which immediately followed presaged the disappointment that most felt at the betrayal of their trust.

Bishop embodied everything to everybody. He was the single personification of the Revolution and all that it promised. He was admired and loved by all. Many persons then simply could not believe that that was happening. Bishop himself declined the offer to respond when he was asked to, but the party members left Butler House that night with saddened faces, heavy hearts, dejected looks and diluted eyes which collectively asked, "Where goeth thou?"

Increasingly over the next few days peoples' anger at Bishop's house arrest was going in one direction only. The other direction was road-blocked by growing hostility to the C.C. which was perceived as being responsible for Bishop's arrest. Many would have seen that brewing crisis not as the result of the immature approach to problem-solving that it was, but as an ideological dispute.

Karl Marx and Vladimir Lenin, the joint architects of Marxism-Leninism, were therefore called to account. People wanted to know who were they, "Whey dey come from?" and "Who dey dey wid?" As far as people were concerned, whoever Marx and Lenin were, they were out of place to put their mouths in Grenadians business. "Whey dey been?" one middle-aged female activist of the Revolution asked. Well, Marx had been lying far from home in a grave in Highgate cemetery in England since 1883, while Lenin's remains had been held in more opulent surroundings in the mausoleum on Russia's Red Square since 1924.

Furthermore, the people had never heard of the C.C. before since it was an internal party structure. They did not know whether it was a 'who' or a 'what,' and at best it was an amorphous entity, but whatever it was, they knew that it had to be blamed.

This would have been encouraged by public statements coming from members of the C.C., including statements aired on RFG, accusing Bishop of 'onemanism' and of being undemocratic; As well as by the visits to homes and schools by Radix, Louison and Whiteman who were attempting to persuade persons to take to the streets and demonstrate. Indeed, demonstrations, primarily of school children, had taken place in Grenville, St. Andrew's and in St. George's even as members of the C.C. were taking concrete steps to try and resolve the situation.

Bilateral meetings between Whitman and Louison on the one hand and Coard and Strachan on the other, were taking place. A search for a compromise was being vigorously pursued, but with both sides perhaps not being as flexible and as accommodating as the circumstances demanded, by October 17th it became clear that the hoped for fruit was not going to come from that tree. Regional assistance of friends of the Revolution was sought and by then one of the persons to arrive, was a leading Trade Unionist from Trinidad, Michael Als. He acted as an intermediary and that would have helped to facilitate the meeting between Bishop and some members of the C.C. on the night of October 18th.

Another meeting was taking place at the same time with some members of the party at Butler House. One of those present was Nelson Louison. He had arrived there barefooted, having to run from his home in Concord, St. John's and from his brothers in order to escape a pro-Bishop physical beating that could not have been borne standing in one place. The meeting nonetheless, urged an amicable resolution of the problems that had now engulfed the whole island.

Earlier on that afternoon, Grenadians would have heard as part of the news of the Montserrat-based **Radio Antilles**, an announcement that George Louison, Unison Whiteman, Kenrick Radix, Jacqueline Creft, Norris Bain and Lyden Ramdhanny had all resigned from the Government, which had the effect, if only in terms of perception, of worsening the crisis. Already, word of mass demonstrations expected the next day was circulating and during the course of the night both Louison and Radix had been detained. Whiteman had earlier gone into hiding after refusing to speak with Coard on the phone.

But there was still hope among members of the C.C. that, following the discussions with Bishop, the problems would have been amicably resolved by the next morning. The proposal had been that the status quo prior to the Joint Leadership decision would have been restored and that Bishop would publicly accept responsibility for the crisis. Bishop then made two requests: that he be allowed to reserve his answer until the following morning at 10 o'clock and that arrangements be made for him to speak with Louison, Whiteman and Julien Rizo, the Cuban Ambassador to Grenada, before that.

The stage had been set once more for the singing of the 'Internationale,' or so the optimists thought.

Chapter 44

When the clock on the belfry of the 18th century Anglican Church on Church Street in St. George's (once the Catholic Cathedral) struck 8 o'clock on the morning of October 19th 1983, the sun, because of an imperceptible leftward tilt of the earth, was a fraction of a degree further on than where it had been the day before.

But that did not lessen or add to its customary effulgence or the gradual upward climb of the thermometer. The sun worked like an old machine ready to be discarded by its wealthy owner; the longer it worked the more heat it gave off, almost as if its thermostat had been faulty. But it was still four hours away from high noon, four hours before the sun became its most devilish.

It was a pleasant morning weather-wise. A light wind that was at a healthy 2 on the Beaufort Scale, fluttered skirts teasingly and caressed faces lovingly. Nevertheless, the tension and sense of foreboding, which gripped the island, replaced the usual smiles of Grenadians that could hardly have been seen that morning. Persons showed up to work and children went to school although the underlying uneasiness in the air did not make it a normal day. In St. George's however, where people were expected to take to the streets in large numbers, some public workers chose to remain at home and kept their children with them. Many who allowed their children to go to school did so with a stern warning: "Stay in school and keep off from the streets."

There were signs of unusual street activity as four members of the Central Committee (C.C.) drove up to Mt. Wheldale in preparation for the scheduled continuation of their meeting with Bishop. Others went there in anticipation of the hoped for positive conclusion of that meeting. Their colleague from Trinidad, Michael Als, was also there.

Earlier on, George Louison had been taken to Bishop's home to meet privately with him as Bishop himself had requested. Unison Whiteman could not be found, and assuming that Cuban Ambassador Rizo would want to abide by the principle of non-interference, no invitation was extended to him to travel up to Mt. Wheldale.

It was not going to be long that morning before other persons, uninvited, were to be seen headed in that direction. A large crowd led by Vincent Noel, and chanting "No Bishop, No Revolution" arrived noisily at the outer gate of Bishop and Coard's residences. A few placards could be seen, one in particular boldly stated "God Bless America." "No one would wish to deny America Papa God's blessings, but where did America come in in what was happening now," I pondered.

The crowd, reinforced by hundreds more it seemed, and shoving against the iron barrier across the entrance, shook me out of my reverie. Two soldiers armed with AKS rifles manned the barrier and their futile efforts to get the crowd to move back, showed how inadequately prepared they and the Security Forces were for a frontal assault from a large crowd. They were sufficiently forewarned of street demonstrations that were expected to be as peaceful as those of the previous days had been, but none would have thought it likely that the crowd, fired-up, would have come to Mt. Wheldale. But come they did. There were many women and children in the crowd, and there were faces which all knew – relatives, friends, comrades, activists of the Revolution and some of its strongest supporters.

Even more reason why a confrontation had to be avoided. During the previous days when the people took control of the paved roads in protests, the police stayed off the streets and the PRA stayed in their barracks.

They did the same on October 19th, but when the crowd at Mt. Wheldale began making its intentions clear, Armoured Personnel Carriers (APC's) were brought in, hoping that their presence would have had a salutary effect on the people who were attempting to barge their way through.

Yet given the disposition of the crowd, the APC's could well have been sports cars. "We want we leader," they shouted angrily and continued shoving. 'We would shove our way into Bishop's bedroom if it became necessary,' was what their attitude appeared to be saying.

Lieutenant Colonel, Ewart Layne, and Major Leon Cornwall, both members of the C.C., went out to speak with the crowd. They pleaded with them for a little patience, letting them know that a meeting was going to take place and that the matter would have been resolved that day. "No way, no way!" Vincent Noel almost screamed, and when Layne and Cornwall turned and appealed to him, his response was "…all yuh go ha to kill me today."

Thus egged on, the crowd was on the verge of breaking through the barrier when the few soldiers who were there, along with the Security Personnel, were ordered to fire their AK-47 rifles into the air. At the sound of gunshots the crowd took two hasty, life-preserving steps backwards, but no one was being fired at as there was no intention to kill anyone. The crowd, once they quickly caught on to the obvious scare-tactic, regained the steps taken backwards, tore the iron barrier away from the road and rushed forward. The main gate to Bishop's residence was pulled open with ease and the people proceeded to find their leader.

Bishop, along with Jacqueline Creft who, days before, were allowed to stay with him at her request, left with the crowd. The crowd headed down Lucas Street in the direction of the city center chanting loudly, "We get we leader, we get we leader."

For those who were only interested in seeing Bishop freed from house arrest, there could not have been a happier moment. All were expecting Bishop to go to the Market Square and address the people there, the people who were prepared to risk anything for him. Indeed, Bishop was so loved and so popular he may easily have been the most admired leader in the Caribbean.

By some prior arrangement, microphones had been set up in the Market Square as if persons knew in advance that Bishop would be going there that morning. But that was not where he or the very large crowd with him went. When they got to the top of Market Hill they paused, long enough to allow a few minutes of hurried private consultation, then turned left and moved determinedly towards Fort Rupert, the Headquarters of the PRA.

The barracked soldiers, as well as the party members who were up there, watched with consternation as the large crowd, with Bishop at its head, advanced towards their location. They did not know what to make of that development. The Army Officers were too perplexed to give any instruction to the two armed soldiers who were watching over the locked gates which denied ready access to the compound. The soldiers on guard duty knew that the people had no authority to enter the Headquarters, but the fact that Bishop, their commander-in-chief, was with them, only added to their confusion. They could only stand and watch, unable to act as the gates were shoved opened, their weapons taken away, and the people made their way into a highly restricted, militarized area.

In such large numbers and having just secured Bishop's release, the crowd, unsurprisingly, were in a conquering mood and would not have taken no for an answer. However, when the crowd, led by Bishop, got to the foot of the Fort and their destination became as clear as if a seaman had shouted "full steam ahead!" several persons chose to go no further. They simply did not think it was a good idea going up to the Fort, the headquarters of the PRA. Some went back to the Market Square and waited, still hoping that Bishop would come there and speak to them.

Those C.C. members who were on Coard's veranda and watched with dismay as the crowd made its way onto Fort Rupert, were not speaking. It was as if the horror that was unfolding before them had disfigured their tongues momentarily. They would have been aware of the highly sensitive nature of the army's defense plans which were stored there. They knew of the large quantity of weapons and ammunition in its armoury, the anti-aircraft guns on its compound which could spell disaster if they fell into the wrong hands, as well as the tons of explosives, most of it for industrial use, which were kept in one of its tunnels.

They would have waited and allowed fate to have had its way if the senior security personnel on the compound, having made their assessment, did not advise that Mt. Wheldale be immediately vacated and that all move to the safety of Fort Frederick, a distance less than a mile by road.

The Coard's children were placed in a car, with a few hastily packed bags containing some of their clothing, and sent off to stay with a friend as a small convoy drove off in the opposite direction, moving along upper Lucas Street and headed for the protective arms of another of my brothers.

Bishop and several others, women among them, took control of the Operations Room (Ops Room), the nerve center of the PRA. It was located on the upper floor of a two-storied concrete building measuring about 90 feet in length and 30 feet in width. It was the only building occupying the first level of the fort and stood like a sentinel against any who may wish to breach its upper sanctum which consisted of two other levels.

From the Operations Room decisions were made and instructions were given. The soldiers were disarmed and the army officers who were on the fort were said to have been arrested and held in the Operations Room at gunpoint. Female soldiers, Chris Stanisclaus among them, were stripped to their underwear and verbally abused. The key to the armoury was confiscated and weapons, including AK rifles, were distributed to the civilians. Weapons were loaded into the trunk of a vehicle which then left. Major Einstein Louison, Chief of Staff of the PRA, was named Commander-in-Chief and armed units were being formed. One such unit on a mission went past RFG, in Morne Rouge, St. George's where soldiers were encamped and told them "We coming back for all yuh." Another unit was being sent to the Logistics Base in Grand Anse, where all the munitions of the army were stored. Armed civilians had the complete run of the army headquarters and they said and did things, including the destruction of sensitive military documents, in the spirit of the moment.

In the meantime, some of the C.C. members, Bernard and Phyllis Coard among them, who were accompanied and driven by their personal security officers, arrived at Fort Frederick and were immediately taken to its uppermost section. They went into one of its rooms adjoining a tunnel. There were a few chairs in the room but the C.C. members were looking so disoriented, unsure of themselves, gloomy and in an apparent state of shock that they probably had to be shown where to sit.

The sudden shrill siren-like sound which went off may have made some of them nervous, but it was the signal which directed the soldiers to rush into defensive positions. It was an exercise that they were accustomed to.

Fort Frederick was the base of Region One. For purposes of the PRA and the defense of the island, Grenada was divided into military regions, with each Region having specific responsibility for the defense of a Parish or a defined area thereof. There were dozens of soldiers stationed at Fort Frederick, and by the time soldiers of the Permanent Battalion, who were based at Camp Calivigny, arrived at the Fort one and a half hours after with Cletus St. Paul as their prisoner, there could have been over a hundred soldiers on its compound.

There were perhaps hundreds of civilians on Fort Rupert, many armed and not realizing the danger of their actions. Several, by the actions of others, had no clue of the danger to which they were being exposed. There were persons from almost all walks of life, nurses and school children included, and all were caught up with the sheer joy of having their beloved leader freed from house arrest and the sense of power that that would have given them. Yet there were those who were pursuing their own personal and private interests, and getting their hands on a few AK-47's and machine guns would have surely helped their cause. By the nature of the crowd it was simply not possible for Bishop, Whiteman and the other leaders there to have exerted control over all. But by their own actions they assumed responsibility for what was happening there.

When Lt. Col. Ewart Layne, the day to day commander of the army, attempted to use one of the phones at Fort Frederick, it was then that it was discovered that the phones there, and in some other military camps had been cut off. In order to establish contact with Fort Rupert it was necessary to use the phone of a neighbour. Lt. Col Layne directed a senior officer to so do.

"Comrade Uni," the senior officer said, almost pleading as he addressed Unison Whiteman who answered the phone on the other end up at Fort Rupert, "please get the people off the fort and let the negotiations continue." But it may as well have been one fort speaking to another fort.

"There will be no negotiations; is manners for all you," Whiteman replied curtly.

The sound of the phone-receiver being slam-dunked into its cradle may have struck a note of finality as far as the C.C.'s input into the matter was concerned, and could have led Lt. Col. Layne to the conclusion that it was no longer a party matter. In any case, those C.C. members on Fort Frederick could have been suffering from apoplexy or some form of paralysis. They did not appear capable of deciding anything. The situation had clearly gone beyond them and by then, a soldier who had escaped from Fort Rupert, reported on what was happening there.

It was now a military matter, the Lieutenant Colonel determined and said as much to General Hudson Austin when he called him aside and spoke with him. "Something has to be done to get the people off the fort. Unless the fort is recaptured there is just no way that the Revolution can be saved," Layne said to General Austin who himself appeared paralyzed by the situation.

At that point Layne assumed total command and dispatched a squad of soldiers, led by Officer Cadet Conrad Meyers, in two APC's with instructions to retake the fort. Weapons were to be fired into the air with the hope that its shock effect would be all that was required to get the people to leave the fort. Soldiers in a third APC followed but they were not to enter the fort. They were to intercept any who may be leaving Fort Rupert with weapons.

Fort Rupert was about half of a mile from Fort Frederick as the crow flies. But the APC's were not flying, they were travelling at a reasonable clip along the asphalt-paved roads, in no particular hurry to cover the one mile distance between the brother forts. Indeed, the almost leisurely pace permitted the soldiers on the first APC, who were not expecting any hostile fire, to sit on the outside around its turret. And as they travelled down Lucas Street and onto Church Street, they waved to persons whom they knew and called out to others.

Many of the civilians who were on Fort Rupert saw the Armored Personnel Carriers (APC's), as they made their way down Lucas Street and with soldiers sitting on top one of them, some thought that the APC's were coming to assist the comrade leader.

There were the beginnings of applause when others interjected a note of caution. They did not think so and slowly apprehension began to take hold among the people there. Some who were not crippled by its grip immediately took flight, running down the slope that served as the only exit and entrance to Fort Rupert. Others however, clutched their AK's so firmly it was as if they wanted to squeeze out of the barrels more assurance than the weapons were capable of giving. A few of them were occupying positions on the veranda of the Ops Room which allowed for total command of the entrance into the fort.

The powerfully motored APC's negotiated the slightly sloping and curving Grand Etang Road (in St. George's) with ease and went past the defunct **St. James Hotel** unaware of just how hostile the environment they were moving into was. They did not expect to see any carpet – red, green or blue – covering the concrete road which led to the first level of Fort Rupert, but they had never been treated with anything less than civility before and were not prepared for anything worse.

Yet they could not know how worse it was going to be and that is why when the APC's got to the foot of the slope, just before the gate which was opened by the crowd when they entered, the soldiers, including Officer Cadet Meyers, were still sitting on the top of the first APC.

'Bang bang bang, pah, pah!' When the gunshots rang out it was so unexpected that the soldiers sitting on the first APC had very little time to react. Warrant Officer Raphael Mason had no idea what hit him; he was shot, thrown off the vehicle and died on the spot. Other soldiers, including Private Martin Simon who received three shots to the groin area and Sergeant Byron Cameron who were also shot, though not fatally, required medical treatment. The injured were taken to the hospital while the APC's with the unharmed soldiers advanced into the fort, their own AK rifles and the heavier machine guns which were installed on the APC's, returning the gunfire as they went.

Armed civilians, three of whom were stationed on the veranda of the Operations Room, were shooting at the soldiers and it was in that direction that the soldiers concentrated most of their fire. Gunfire was also coming from one of the upper levels as well. In the exchange Officer Cadet Meyers was shot in the groin and fell to the ground. He too, had to be rushed to the hospital.

Grenada's main medical facility was kept extremely busy that day. Once the shooting began some civilians managed to make their escape through the only exit at the front. But many, including party members and soldiers, frightened out of their wits and desperate to save their own lives, jumped from the very high walls of the fort, as high as 40 feet in some places. Several received broken limbs as a result, as well as other injuries, but more sadly, a few jumped to their deaths.

The Caribs did, Fedon and some of his men did and they did so knowing that they were going to die. But the people, school children included, who leapt from the walls of the fort on October 19th, did so because they wanted to live. The choices they faced that day were as good as spinning a dice or tossing a coin. Some of those who did not jump and were unable to find a safe place to cower behind also had limbs torn away and in a few cases died from gunshot wounds. It was nothing short than a melee of lethal gunfire initiated by armed civilians.

When the firing ceased after about ten minutes and the dust cleared, though not the smoke, as vehicles were on fire, Pte. Glen Nathan was dead. Sergeant Dorset Peters was found dead at the back of the Operations Room. Vincent Noel was lying on the ground at the front of the building, barely breathing and in one of his last breaths requested some water which a soldier gave to him. Nelson 'Saltfish' Steele was dead. A few of the army officers who had been detained inside the Ops Room, made their escape by kicking out an air-condition unit at the back of the building and climbed through to safety. When the firing began, others in that room lay on the floor. That, and the prayers, would have saved most of them, but there were those who had no such luck. Ms. Avis Ferguson was lying dead, and Jemma Belmar was bleeding from the head.

Jemma was taken to the hospital and died a few weeks later. Officer Cadet Conrad Meyers, conscious of his life-threatening condition, nevertheless gave up his chance to be operated on in order to allow Private Martin Simon to go before him. Simon was saved but Meyers, previously an enlistee of the United States Army, died two hours after he was shot and three days before his 23rd birthday.

But the shooting was not yet over. Bishop, Creft, Whiteman, Fitzroy Bain and Norris Bain, all came out of the Operations Room alive. Keith 'Pumphead' Hayling, Evelyn 'Maitty' Maitland and Evelyn 'Brat' Bullen came out of the armoury. Whatever else may have happened, angry soldiers, who thought them responsible for the mayhem and for the death of their comrades, took them to the top square at the second level of the fort, placed them against a wall and shot them.

It was one of the most stomach-churning, heart-wrenching episodes in Grenada's history, indeed Caribbean history, a sickening and unjustifiable act that was made worse by the manner in which the bodies were disposed of. Later that night, those bodies, along with that of Vincent Noel, which had been wrapped in blankets and placed on a truck, were taken to Calivigny Camp where they were partly burnt and buried; partly burnt on the advice of one of the soldiers who was present at the burial ground and claimed it was the best way to preserve the bodies outside of cold-storage.

Based on what he was told, General Hudson Austin informed the people on radio earlier on that night that those persons, including Bishop, had died in crossfire. That was clearly aimed at hoodwinking the public, since, as far as the public was concerned, there could be no acceptable, rational or justifiable reason that could have explained what had occurred. It was for the same reason supposedly, that the bodies were not given to one of the funeral homes. What was left of the still functioning, perhaps dysfunctional, freaked-out leadership of the revolution, simply could not have confronted the public with the truth.

Hoping to head off any possible civil unrest arising out of the death of Bishop and others, and conscious of the fact that weapons had been widely distributed on Fort Rupert that morning, Austin went on to declare a curfew. "Anyone caught breaking the curfew would be shot on sight," he warned, another of the scare-tactics intended to keep potential trouble-makers at bay. Yet many were smart enough to know what it was. In subsequent days and in several areas people paid no heed to the curfew and could be seen hanging-out on the side of roads and in the case of the American students, were jogging on roads close to the St. George's University School of Medicine. Others went to church.

By the end of the day nineteen persons were dead, some wished they were dead and many were wounded, some grievously. Several persons had been detained, and apart from the few who were applauding Bishop's death and what was perceived as the end of the Revolution (including some detainees, others who suffered wrong during the revolutionary process, and those whom it denied the chance to line their pockets), an entire nation was weeping. Among the Cheerleaders however, would have been the American Administration and those regional governments who were envious of the enormous strides Grenada had been making.

One government which would therefore have cried itself blind, was that of Cuba which might have cursed itself for not being able to save Bishop. In a reported interview years later with then U.S. Congressman and Chairman of the Congressional Black Caucus, Mervyn Dymally, Fidel Castro admitted having received a request from Bishop on October 19th to intervene militarily, but by the time the request came Bishop was already dead.

The moral responsibility for the killings on October 19th, including those who were placed against a wall and shot, rest squarely with the surviving leadership of the revolution; and indeed, some bear greater responsibility than others.

Nevertheless, the leftward tilt of the earth and its gravitational pull on the moon may have contributed to the collective madness which consumed the Grenadian Revolutionaries; those who have died and those who have lived. Therefore, with respect to the destruction of the Revolution, the smashing of cherished dreams and the spiraling, out of controlled events which led to the catastrophe of October 19th, notwithstanding whether or not there is criminal responsibility to be apportioned, all are culpable, all have sinned and fallen short of the glory of the revolution and of history.

But such had been the negative effect of the unfettered exercise of state power and the arrogance of some young revolutionaries, steeped in ideological correctness, wallowing in the immature belief that they had all the right answers and that they were the sole repository for the blue print on the way forward. That said, they meant well.

One may say that the revolution was fated to collapse, but that the revolutionaries were otherwise too busy to recognize the warning signs; from the very attitude of several of its players that spoke of a barely concealed agenda for personal recognition and/or aggrandizement, to the intolerance shown for any opposition or opposing views. This often reflected itself in the way persons were arbitrarily detained or otherwise unjustly treated; like the unfortunate young man who did not allow George Louison the use of his table tennis racket and spent years at Richmond Hill Prison as a result.

That surely may not be the explanation for the disappearance of Frankie Bedeau, although persons connected to him are likely to believe so. Frankie Bedeau, a father and husband, has not been seen or heard of since sometime between the 9th and 10th of March, 1981, and it is a mystery occurring during the Revolution that is yet to be solved. But how can someone in such a small society like ours disappear without trace? Such disappearances have been known to occur during the height of Gairy's brutal reign and in right-wing dictatorships as in Somoza's Nicaragua and Pinochet's Chile. But here in Grenada? This too, may not have augured well for the revolutions's survival.

Chapter 45

The 5 o'clock morning sky still carried with it the vestiges of the night just past. It was not yet washed clean of the pervading blackness with which it became one. Or if it had been washed then it was with water that was previously used to launder a bag once containing coals.

The heavenly canopy on the dawn of October 25th 1983 was tinged with the darker side of gray. It was significantly lighter half an hour later however, as the monotonous drone of an unmanned aircraft overhead had eyes in military camps around the island looking upwards.

It was already sufficiently bright, and no infrared instrument was needed to verify what it was. Even without looking skywards, the soldiers' instinct and training would have told them what the sound was and what it meant. The American Government had communicated its intentions well enough in advance.

A few weeks before, the American Armed Forces staged a practice run for the invasion of Grenada at Ephrata municipal airport in the State of Washington, using some of the very troops which were later involved in the invasion of Grenada. Moreover, the American Ambassador to France was to later reveal that the decision to invade Grenada had been made weeks before. All they needed was the pretext which the Grenadian Revolutionaries blindly presented to them.

If the Revolutionaries did not oblige, for the American Administration, given their inventiveness, finding a pretext would have been Grade 1 stuff. The safety of Americans living in Grenada, in particular the American students at the St. George's University School of Medicine, was in jeopardy, they claimed, and despite evidence to the contrary, continued to assert that they needed to protect American lives. They even pressured school officials in New York to publicly claim that the students in Grenada were in danger.

Meanwhile, a fifteen-member Revolutionary Military Council (RMC) chaired by General Austin had been established. It was the de facto government but made it clear that it intended to hand over to a civilian government within two weeks. Moves were already being made to get Ambassador Mario Bullen, based in Brussels, to head that new government.

In that regard, General Austin met with the Governor-General (GG), Sir Paul Scoon, shortly after October 19th, yet the opening bars of the GG's conversation was to ask that he be allowed to stay on as Governor-General. With that taken care of, the GG turned his attention to other matters. He agreed to assist in contacting Sir Shridath Ramphal, the Secretary General of the Commonwealth, with a view to setting up an inquiry into the events of October 19th 1983. They discussed the proposed civilian government and the GG suggested persons whom he thought should be on it. A follow-up meeting was carded for October 24th, but the GG, who may have been having meetings and may have been drawing up plans of his own, was otherwise engaged.

The RMC, too, was quite busy. Although it was preoccupied with preparing Grenada's Armed Forces for the expected invasion, it did everything to forestall it. General Austin and other members of the RMC met with the vice-chancellor of the St. George's University, Dr. Jeffrey Bourne. Assurances were given and accepted that the students were not in harm's way. NTS buses were provided to take the students from one campus to another for added assurance. At vice-chancellor Bourne's request, the RMC allowed representatives of the US Embassy in Barbados to visit Grenada and hold talks with General Austin, other RMC members and the 600 medical students.

500 parents of the American students met in New York on October 23rd, and urged President Reagan not to invade Grenada. Pearls airport was opened on Monday 24th, to allow medical students who, in light of the imminent invasion, wished to leave to do so, but Barbados, in conjunction with Washington, well into the finalization of their plans to invade, refused to allow the LIAT plane to land there. The students had to remain in Grenada so that one of their excuses for invading could be preserved.

Other planes had been landing there. Barbados had become the hub of activity in preparation for that massive assault on international laws protecting Grenada's sovereignty and territorial integrity. To facilitate their illegal enterprise, the OECS Treaty as well as the Charters of the United Nations (U.N.) and the Organization of American States (O.A.S.) had to be torn up and thrown into the waste-paper basket. But then law-breakers dressed in jacket and tie and parading the corridors of power can be found in equal numbers as those dressed in the rags of the poor. However, justice is never equal and that is why some persons end up behind bars and others do not.

Although it was not itself a member, Tom Adams's Barbados hosted a meeting of the OECS – St. Vincent, St. Lucia, Dominica, St. Kitts, Montserrat and Antigua – which, at the urging of Washington, requested the United States to invade Grenada. Moreover, the actual request it is said, was drafted by Washington officials.

But George Chambers's Trinidad and Forbes Burnham's Guyana resisted all attempts to manipulate them at the Barbados meeting of Caricom shortly thereafter and, along with Belize and Bahamas, strongly opposed the invasion which Barbados and Edward Seaga's Jamaica zealously advocated.

Caricom nevertheless, placed trade and diplomatic sanctions on Grenada.

Prime Minister Milton Cato of St. Vincent however, was hoping for a less punishing way to help Grenada out of her difficulties. He spoke with General Hudson Austin by phone on two occasions following the events of October 19th. He first wanted to find out whether the General would have been prepared to meet with him and then to make arrangements for a meeting to discuss the crisis and work out solutions. A meeting between General Austin and Prime Minister Cato was tentatively scheduled to be held on Union Island on October 24th, an arrangement which the Prime Minister was expected to later confirm by phone. But no call came as Prime Minister Cato was made to follow the drumbeat of invasion.

The drumbeat intensified when on October 23rd a truck loaded with explosives was driven into the barracks of the United States Marines stationed in Lebanon, killing 241 Marines. It was embarrassing because it was their headquarters and humiliating because they were forced into a deflated exit from Lebanon. It was not one that they could easily have lived down and with President Reagan facing elections in one year's time, it was necessary to recoup lost ground.

Someone had to pay for their ineptitude and their losses and the softer the target the easier it would be to once again sing the glory of the invincibility of the United States Armed Forces, and help maintain Reagan as the presidential front-runner in the race for the White House. And if it were possible at the same time to reassert America's position in the world as the great bulwark for democracy, then that would have been like adding sugar to your favourite drink already sweetened with molasses.

Grenada in its crisis-ridden, troubled and weakened state became America's soda pop, just what the Surgeon General prescribed to make America feel manly and mighty once again. A Naval Task Force which was on its way to Lebanon was ordered to change course and head full speed for Grenada instead.

Chapter 46

If it were possible for General Austin's parents to have gotten their act together a hundred years sooner, he would have been born into slavery but nothing about his life said that he would have remained a slave for very long.

Born in Morne Jaloux on April 26th 1938 to Elliot and Elizabeth Austin, he was the fifth in a family of eight boys and one girl. Although a Methodist he attended the Morne Jaloux Catholic School and from an early age showed a thirst for knowledge. Anytime his parents missed him Hudson could be found not far away lying under his favourite tree with a book in hand. With a name like Hudson too, it was not surprising that he spent a lot of his free time, which he hardly had, in the Chemin River bathing or fishing. He may well have been named after the Hudson River. Very often as well, his parents caught up with him in the cane fields where he did odd jobs to help supplement the lean family income.

Despite being born into a family of meagre resources, unable to shield itself from the piercing wind of poverty, as a young man he worked extremely hard, determined to make something of his life. Relatively few had the opportunity to go to a secondary school, and Austin was not one of them, yet he pursued privately his Senior Cambridge from Wosley Hall in

England. He cherished the hope of becoming a Lawyer, but the money could not be found to send him off to England to study.

On leaving school he was employed at the ***Public Works Department*** where he first learnt the rudiments of road and building construction, a job which required him to travel around the island. Soon his likeable persona was also travelling, and it was not long before the name Hudson Austin disappeared to be replaced by the acronym 'H.A.' as he was popularly called. Those who never heard of Hudson Austin before knew who 'H.A.' was.

However, when Austin joined the Grenada Voluntary Constabulary (GVC) shortly after, and while still being employed at the Public Works, the acronym 'H.A.' was temporarily replaced by his colleagues. He dressed so much like Holly, the Englishman who was then Grenada's Chief of Police, and carried himself just as erect as Holly did, that 'H.A.' in the GVC uniform became 'Holly' to his friends.

But it was while working at Public Works that Holly…sorry, Austin, was transferred to the Grenada Prison Service where he rose to the rank of Chief Officer at the age of 25. He worked there for nine years and was trained in prison administration at the Golden Grove Training Center in Trinidad. His wife, Ann, had cast the magic spell of love long before that, but it was while the both of them were working at the Richmond Hill Prison, floating on the sea of knee-weakening love with Austin hardly able to eat, that they got married. Austin must have regained his appetite on his wedding night because not long after that their first daughter, Wendy, was born.

Strongly religious, he gave a lot of time to the church, church-related and other social activities. That, along with his own upbringing, may have fed his abhorrence for injustice and the things which were blatantly wrong. He became a Methodist Lay Preacher in 1964 and was head instructor at the Boys Industrial School at Madigras, St. Paul's in St. George's.

Austin returned to the Public Works Department during Grenada's Expo '69, but he did stints at the Customs, Post Office and Treasury before he resigned from the Public Service in 1972.

He then took up employment with the British American Insurance Company and remained there until 1974. But Austin loved building things, construction was in his blood and found time to pursue studies in Engineering at Jamaica's College of Arts, Science and Technology (CAST). He did much of its theoretical work with Bennett College of Sheffield, England, as well as with International Correspondence School (ICS).

Austin joined the construction firm of Gordon Brathwaite before setting out on his own. He established his own construction company called **Roads and General Construction Ltd.**, and it was while so employed at Freedom Hill, that the site became one of the training grounds and the launching pad for the attack on the True Blue barracks of Gairy's army.

Austin had overseas military training, but it was not only the military and construction that were in his blood. He is the proud father of four children, three girls and one boy which however, may lead one to the view that his personal life was not approached with the same military precision in which he was trained.

Chapter 47

When the American unmanned Drone was making its inquisitive loop around Grenada, General Hudson Austin was in the Wartime Command Center at Fort Frederick in St. George's. Like others of the Operations Staff he had already scanned the skies with zoom binoculars, located the drone and determined its mission.

Grenada had been surrounded by a flotilla of naval ships including aircraft carriers. At about 5:40 a.m., American airborne marines began parachuting onto the almost-completed Point Salines Airport in St. George's, and at Pearls Airport in St. Andrew's. The Grenadian Armed Forces had been severely weakened by the internal crisis and there was only token resistance at Pearls. The people, too, were badly demoralized, and although the curfew had been lifted in its entirety the day before and they were crawling back to a sense of normalcy, they were far too traumatized to offer any significant support to its fighting men.

Initially three thousand American troops landed in an invasion code-named *'Urgent Fury,'* as if their anger resulting from the Lebanon bombing was not well known or that there was anything secret about their manifest act of lawlessness. It was therefore in an effort to buy some legitimacy for

My Mother and I

themselves that one of their first landings was at Government House in St. George's, the residence of Sir Paul Scoon.

6.15 a.m. local time, 0 6.15 military time, AH-1 Blackhawk helicopters made their first attempt to insert a squadron of Navy SEALS onto the compound and into Government House and was fiercely repulsed by PRA soldiers armed with AK rifles and one BTR-60 armored personnel carrier. But the SEALS were determined and under cover of their own returned fire, succeeded in getting some of their number into the house.

They had to get to Sir Paul Scoon, otherwise their only hoped for fig-leaf of legality would have folded. Without any time to observe protocol, Scoon and his wife were quickly and roughly bundled into a clothes cupboard, around which armed SEALS took up guard. Their highly prized target had to be protected at all cost. A dead Governor-General could not sign the letter inviting them to invade.

Yet the Scoons were already near death with fright, especially as the SEALS were continuing to come under heavy fire from the PRA which had earlier destroyed the SEALS radio. Pinned down inside Government House and afraid to even chance a peep through the windows of the house, they had no means to call for help. But when things began getting really warm and it appeared as if the PRA were about to retake Government House, they reckoned that their options were down to one. They snatched up one of its phones and called Fort Bragg in North Carolina, U.S.A., with SOS urgency, to ask them to ask the **USS Guam**, an aircraft carrier anchored in Grenada's outer harbour, to send in support as hurriedly as they could.

In the meantime, the two thousand Marines which landed at Point Salines were seeing their 'nen-nen.' Admittedly it could have been a lot worse for them. Days prior to the invasion, the Cuban Government informed the American Government that their construction workers, many of whom had military training, would not fire at their forces if they were not fired on. And with the PRA debarred from the immediate area by virtue of an unfair stipulation by the vexed Cubans, the Americans were assured of a virtual safe landing at the point where they would be most vulnerable.

Yet the Americans could not help themselves. They were Cuban-phobic and the mere mention of the word 'Cuban' was a trigger of its own which in turn set into action the triggers of their M16 rifles and other heavy duty weapons. They sprayed the Cuban camp with bullets and received an equal and appropriate response from the Cubans. Many of them continued resisting well into the day and those who were captured were used as human shields by the Marines to cover their painstakingly slow advance. By midday when the Cubans were overcome, twenty-four had been killed and those who were alive, including the sixty who were wounded, were held as prisoners.

But there was no road-sign yet for the Marines saying 'All Clear Ahead.' The PRA had been dug in, waiting anxiously for the Marines to enter their firing sector. Armed with AK rifles, rocket-launchers and the knowledge that their actions were just, they launched into the advancing Marines with a barrage of bullets that they would never forget. Those who were able to move fast enough dived behind their tanks and armored vehicles for shelter. They sought to overwhelm the PRA with their superior firepower, and yet they were no match for the well dug in PRA soldiers. They were soon scrambling for their communication radios and as they had been doing all morning, summoned with an air of desperation, air support and reinforcements.

PRA soldiers were always encamped at RFG's transmitter site at Beausejour, northwest St. George's. As part of the preparation for the invasion more soldiers had been placed there, as it was rightly anticipated that the powerful transmitter, the Revolution's popular link with the rest of the Caribbean, would be one of the invaders primary target, and so it was.

American Marines landed on the beach about fifty yards to the back of the transmitter site. Using the surrounding foliage as cover, the marines crept up but made their presence known fairly early because their own fear of the enemy had them discharging their weapons from a safe distance. The PRA soldiers located the direction from which the fire came and greeted them with lethal fire of their own. The exchanges went on for several minutes but being more powerfully armed and better equipped, the Marines got the better of the PRA soldiers, killing several of them and capturing a few. They were made to lie flat on the floor of the building and hog-tied. Even so, the Marines were afraid to take their eyes or their weapons away from them for a second.

But they were looking in the wrong direction. Depleted units of the Militia, backed by a contingent of PRA soldiers, counter-attacked with devastating gutsiness. The Militia may have been demoralized by Bishop's death, but those who fought did so valiantly. They swept into the transmitter building with force that was so sudden and deadly, that the Marines were more focused on running than fighting. That was what their exit strategy called for. Crying "Commies, Commies" (Communists), they managed to get off a few shots of their own before scampering through the back of the building, into the bushes and unto the beach. Several were killed in the process and the few who were lucky to be alive, did as they were trained to do when death seemed imminent: get unto the communications radio and call in air support.

Resistance on a smaller scale was occurring in other parts of the island, while nests of ZU-23 anti-aircraft guns at Government House and at Darbeau in St. George's were making mincemeat of American helicopters. Marines were being killed and captured, and more and more the one day which the invaders envisaged it would take to subdue this small island, was beginning to look like one month.

Evidently, they knew nothing about the history of Grenada. They never heard of the Caribs, or of Fedon, or of the ordinary working people who stood up to the might of the British in 1951. The little they may have heard of Grenada in 1979, may have been rationalized as the product of Soviet and Cuban subversion. That would have been their explanation for the unexpected and resolute resistance they were facing. After all, invaders are never able to understand that the morally unjust and debased act of invading another man's country, arouses in the invaded an unquenchable will to resist. It matters not how big, mighty and powerful the invader is, how small and weak the invaded may be or how traumatized may be its people.

Thousands more US soldiers on troop carriers had come ashore at Grand Mal, northwest St. George's, thousands more had landed at Point Salines aboard military aircrafts, transforming there into the military base that the PRG had been accused of building, and three hundred Jamaican and Barbadian soldiers, required for police duties were brought in on an American aircraft at Pearls. But that was not going to be enough. Air strikes were ordered. The Grenadian fighters had to be bombed into submission.

The American Bombers responded to the cry for help from their near annihilated soldiers at Beausejour with a vengeance. They bombed like they were crazy, and long after the transmitter building had been largely blasted into smithereens, and there was no chance of anyone left alive, they continued bombing. They bombed the building, its immediate area and even fields of corn some distance away as if they had been overtaken by a madness of total destruction. When they finally became a little bored, they flew off to the Calivigny Camp of the PRA to the south of the island and carpet-bombed the entire area and everything in sight. And along the way, anywhere that their demons of fear told them may be mined, they bombed.

Two AH-1 Cobra gunships were sent in response to the 'please-help-us' appeal from the embattled SEALS at

Government House, but they did not fare too well. The first one was shot down by anti-aircraft fire and landed on Tanteen playing field in St. George's. The second one attempted to go to the rescue of the first and was also shot down by an anti-aircraft emplacement. The occupants of both gunships were killed.

The American Armed Forces were accustomed to seeing red, and that day was no different. An AC-130 Spectre gunship as well as an A-75, of far superior firing power, was immediately dispatched. They destroyed the anti-aircraft emplacement, but not all of the resistance at Government House.

It was only after a full 48 hours, and under the protection of massive air support, were the SEALS, backed by 80 Marines, finally able to take their leave of Government House with their priceless package under wraps.

Sir Paul Scoon was taken to the USS Guam and with all protocol long dispensed with, he was like a mammal forcibly removed from its natural habitat. After some talking to by an American Brigadier, Sir Paul Scoon was handed the fake letter of invitation to invade, which had been back-dated to October 24th and told to sign. The letter of invitation had been written by Washington officials and was typed in Norfolk, U.S.A. The first copy had been addressed to the US State Department, but that had been replaced by a second copy addressed to the OECS. Emotionally, Sir Scoon was in a bad way and came close to tears.

Despite being roughed-up, initially he had refused to sign. His own conscience was telling him that to do so would be to engage in massive fraud. "And what if the PRA somehow manage to survive despite the guns and bombs and my actions became known, what then would become of me and my family?" It was a self-tormenting question which Sir Paul Scoon repeatedly asked himself. He knew too that most of the world, including Prime Minister Margaret Thatcher of England, and Queen Elizabeth, to whom he was constitutionally accountable, had opposed the invasion. To sign, then, would be to invite a foreign power to transgress the sovereign domain of the Monarch. In the history of the British Monarchy many had been hung or shot for lesser misdeeds. If then the American invasion failed, he could be facing charges of High Treason both in England and Grenada, the punishment for which was death.

Sir Paul Scoon raised these troubling concerns with the Brigadier and received assurances that all would be safe and well, yet his conscience would not leave him alone. It was only after he was promised the carrot of continued reign as Governor-General and more of the perks, then threatened with the stick of being locked-up and other acts of misfortune if he failed to sign, did Scoon affix his signature to the fraudulent letter. He who had offered suggestions to the RMC on how to forestall the American Invasion, was now inviting them to invade, **post facto**.

Sir Paul Scoon had earned his hearty meal and was later flown to the Point Salines Guest House.

Let me be honest with you. When the bombing began, I had not eaten anything, yet I could have felt everything I had ever eaten before oozing out of me through two of my lower orifices. If naked terror could have been measured by the amount of waste deposited in a toilet bowl, then I would have needed a septic tank all to myself. I was shaking as if stricken by a combination of shingles and ague.

But I did not want to be in a hospital, I wanted a hospital or anything larger than I was, to cover me, and an otologist to temporarily disconnect my auditory nerves. I did not want to hear the sound of the bombs. It made me so scared, and it sounded as if the bombs were falling right in my backyard. I tried to block my ears, but I could not move my hands. I wanted the bombers to go away and never come back, but they kept coming and coming again, night and day, as if they were extraterrestrial aluminum bees which had suddenly discovered the sweetness of honeycomb.

Speaking of sweetness, although women had been at my disposal since 1903, the bombs had temporarily robbed me of my libido and all I wanted to do was to cower in a safe corner.

As much as I wanted to save myself, I could not duck and neither could I run. My ribs of steel and my body of thick concrete made sure of that. At that stage I yielded myself to the mercy of Papa God and I asked Him to save me and save the Grenadian people who were filling up toilet bowls of their own. I doubt many of them would have thought of stocking up on toilet paper when the curfew was lifted. Anyway, the mere sound of the bombs made their favourite hiding place below the bed seem like a spider's web at the feet of a colossal giant, but those who had a downstairs stayed downstairs thinking that the bombs would not get to them there. As petrified as they were, they too stayed put, pleading with Papa God to make the bombs stop.

Back at the Wartime Command Center at Fort Frederick, its radio communication had been taken out of action by the electronic jamming device of the invaders. Nevertheless, the High Command at the Command Center received a phone call from Cuban Ambassador Rizo, requesting the assistance of two APC's at Point Salines.

Believing that the Cubans were resisting the invaders, the APC's were promptly dispatched. They drove right past the dug-in PRA soldiers and straight into an ambush. The Americans totally destroyed the APC's and slaughtered all but two of the soldiers. The Americans later deported one of the two to Cuba as a Cuban.

But it was the super bombers which announced their savage presence when they began to strafe the area where the PRA soldiers were believed to be dug in. The Bombers were way off mark and that gave the soldiers enough time to head for safer ground.

Although the PRA soldiers had retreated, the Marines advance had been 'one today, one tomorrow,' that was the speed at which they overcame their fear of an unknown enemy. Fear that would have been made worse by the fact that earlier on Reconnaissance Vehicles had left but did not return and no, they did not lose their way. The Marines had no idea who they were fighting against. In their jittery state, quick to fire and quick to tie up one like a pig, there was no difference between friend and foe. To them all were 'Commies.' Moreover, they did not have with them the more precise grid maps often used by the military, but tourist maps not much different from the ones Christopher Columbus would have used if he had landed here. They had difficulty then finding their way, they knew where they wanted to go – the city of St. George's – but they were not sure how to get there. The prospect of 'Commies' everywhere did not make things easier for them.

Their shrapnel-spitting bombers and helicopter gunships, which had better luck locating their targets, led the way for them and provided life-saving protection. But it appeared as if, at least in one case, they were relying on the same luck to hit their target.

They pounded the immediate environs of the 18th century edifice of Fort Frederick with thousand-pound bombs, seriously injuring at least one of the PRA soldiers with shrapnel, but did not seem able to land direct hits on the fort itself. Instead, their precision bombers took out the nearby Mental Hospital, killing at least fifty persons. Another of their death-wielding bombs landed with precision on Bishop's private home on Parade, just to the back of Fort Frederick. Did they think that Bishop was somehow still alive and perhaps hiding in his home? Not likely. For them it was probably a game of 'hit and miss' knowing that civilian deaths were 'collateral damage' and there was no one to whom they were accountable.

Grenada had no navy and no air force and with no surface-to-air or heat-seeking missiles, the invaders exercised total control of the island's air and sea space. They flew sorties at will, knowing that the limited-ranged ZU 23's against their high-flying bombers, were as effective as toy guns.

They scored a direct hit on the anti-aircraft emplacement on Fort Rupert, killing soldiers in the process. RFG at Morne Rouge, one of Grenada's historical buildings, got similar treatment and was reduced to rubble. Thank Papa God that the station had been abandoned earlier on, but a repository of historical records of Grenada's past, including much of its indigenous music and cultural art forms, went up in smoke.

At all cost, no other voice other than that of the American invaders was to be heard. Initially, the American public was at best skeptical about the reasons for the invasion, and its Congress was unhappy. Washington and its operatives wanted free reign to prepare and feed them and the world with its own diet of misinformation. Having prevented the foreign press from entering Grenada for the first several days of the war, its hired chefs went to work putting together successive meals of lies.

It was in that context and in an attempt to give legitimacy to the invasion, that Eugenia Charles, Prime Minister of Dominica, was flown to Washington on the very morning of the invasion to make a sycophantic television appearance at President Reagan's side. He made efforts to convince his constituents and the rest of the world, of the concocted reasons for violating Grenada's sovereignty. 'American lives to be saved, democracy to be restored, the Soviet and Cuban influence to be gotten rid of and moreover, our actions follow the expressed invitation of the island's governor-general and the OECS,' as Prime Minister Eugenia Charles nodded her head dutifully.

The American Army's Psychological Operations Department continued its psychological warfare against the Grenadian People within the first hours of the invasion. Using a radio frequency, they sought to sow seeds of confusion, telling the Grenadian soldiers that there was no point in fighting since senior officers of the PRA and leaders of the Revolution had been captured, when they had not been.

They told Grenadians, the American people and the world that hundreds of persons had been killed on Fort Rupert on October 19th, that several mass graves filled with dead bodies had been discovered. That Grenada was a Soviet and Cuban base, and along with East Germany had provided it with military advisors. They told Grenadians that their leaders were killers who had already drawn up a list of those they intended to kill. That they were a bunch of communists who wanted to return Grenada to slavery and had already imported water-boots, hoes and cutlasses for that purpose. That food was going to be rationed and coupons for that purpose introduced. Posters of some of the Revolution's leaders, unflatteringly dressed and labelled 'killers' and 'murderers' were stuck up all over the island.

Think of any lie and the American Army psychological warfare operatives, who commandeered Marryshow House, the University of the West Indies center, as their own, told it. And Grenadians believed it. But that was somewhat understandable. As traumatized and as vulnerable as they were and with their minds appropriately conditioned by this onslaught of propaganda, they saw the invaders as 'rescuers,' 'life-savers' and 'liberators' and the surviving leaders of the Revolution as villains and worse.

Those who were able to return to their villages after the collapse of the resistance, soldiers, NJM party members and activists of the Revolution among them, were scorned and derided. They were pointed out by their own neighbours to the invading forces who strung some of them up on vehicles and drove them around their villages to be pelted with missiles.

The same finger-pointing, mouth-blabbing, whistle-blowing and snitching led the invaders to the different locations where General Austin, Bernard and Phyllis Coard, Lieutenant Colonels Ewart Layne and Liam James and Major Leon Cornwall were. The American soldiers descended, kicking down doors and brandishing almost as many weapons as the entire armoury of the PRA contained. Their numbers too, were adequate to timidly challenge the fearsome

Mongolian Army of Genghis Khan as it rode across Asia conquering all in their path.

The American soldiers approached the PRA and Revolution's leaders with the same trepidation, standing well away and shouting their orders. If Coard or Austin had chosen then to scratch their head or any other part of their bodies, that would have been the last of them. The American soldiers were that fidgety.

With all weapons trained on them they were hastily bundled up, blindfolded, handcuffed behind their backs, thrown into helicopters and flown to the USS Guam and then to the USS Saipan. There they were invasively questioned, with American agents attempting to play one against the other, threatened, locked into 'cells' and not served any hearty meals.

When they were later taken off the ships, their flight plan was not the same as Sir Paul Scoon's and their destination was different. Neither were they taken to the Point Salines barbed-wired prisoner-of-war (POW) camp in which, by the end of hostilities, three thousand Grenadians, including many women, had been kept. The camp bore no resemblance to the conditions stipulated by the **Geneva Convention** governing the treatment of such prisoners. Several were kept in 'Sweat Boxes' measuring 8ft by 8ft, and to get in or out of these boxes meant that one had to crawl on one's stomach. In one case, the box, with the prisoner inside, was lifted off the ground by a forklift driven by an American soldier. These boxes were made of ply with a slot at the top, and it was through that they were served, once per day, wishy-washy food which was passed off as meals. The extreme heat made life difficult for the prisoners, and the constant pounding on the boxes by American soldiers, day and night, made sleep impossible. Many of the other prisoners were made to sleep in the open air on the cold, concrete ground which gave new currency to Bob Marley's "cold ground was my bed at night and rock-stone was my pillow."

For forty-five of them, one bath and two weeks later, their status had not changed but their place of confinement did. They were taken to the prison with a thought to cherish.

The 'One day wonder' which the American war planners designated the twenty-four hours it would have taken to quell all resistance and seize Grenada, was ill-conceived. At least forty of their servicemen, and up to a reported many times that number, died trying to do in one day what they needed one week and twenty thousand troops to accomplish.

With an inexhaustible supply of military hardware and all of the latest gadgetry of death – aircraft carriers, helicopter gunships, bombers, fighter planes, tanks, armoured vehicles, missiles, guns of every caliber, rifles, you name it – and with a force one-fifth of Grenada's entire population, this behemoth of military might could not prevent a miniscule, ill-equipped army from getting into its face. Whatever side of the Grenadian political divide you may fall, you have to give it to them; 'dem fellars put up a real good fight!' And that was exactly what the then Chairman of the US Joint Chiefs of Staff said at the time: "We met far more resistance than we expected."

Grenada's PRA was five hundred strong which was supported by a militia grossly decimated by the effects of the tragic October events. Yet with eight BTR's, two BRDM Exploration Vehicles, twelve ZU-23 Anti-aircraft guns, Rocket-launchers and AK rifles, the Grenadian army and militia achieved a feat of 'Purple-Heart' dimensions. Perhaps in another life the victors would have recognized the bravery and resourcefulness of the vanquished. However, when days after, the Americans were still claiming that it was Cuban soldiers who were doing the fighting, then that could only have been a right-handed compliment to Cpl. Elton Thomas, Blondell Church, PFC Keith 'Rasta' Noel, Michael 'Jacks' Charles, L/Cpl. Stephen 'Blackie' McSween, L/Cpl. Keith Pierre, L/Cpl. Alstan Francis, L/Cpl. Blackette, Colin Carter, 'Kung-Fu', Roy 'Cocoa Board' Antoine, Davis 'Recce/Pecan'

My Mother and I

Mitchell, Joy 'Peclau' Mitchell, Colin Peters, Harper, Colours, Daniel Holder, Godwin McQueen, Cleveland Phillip and all the others who died and fought in the defense of their homeland.

They did not do it for General Austin, Coard or some 'foreign ideology.' They acted in accordance with the oath they made as soldiers to defend Grenada against foreign aggression and that was precisely what they did. They fought courageously and heroically, they sacrificed greatly and left behind a lasting definition of what patriotism really means.

Their many ancestors were clearly of the same view. I heard them with my own ears as they addressed the departed souls in one voice: "Yet brave sons of Grenada who left behind heart-broken Mothers and fathers, weeping children and unfulfilled dreams, in your own land, the land you gave so much to, you have found no honour. Your death and in what numbers have not even been acknowledged while a monument has been built to the purveyors of your demise.

But even in death, my brothers and sisters, we ask you to hold tight. Your names would yet be indelibly inscribed in the pages of Grenada's history, your names would be proudly held aloft and one day the example of your selfless act of patriotism would give birth to a new generation of leaders capable of honouring Grenada's own noble sons and daughters."

Chapter 48

I do not know which was worse, whether it was the rats or the cockroaches which were running unhindered all over me. Papa God Himself was so amazed by their agility and ability to avoid colliding with each other that He commissioned a new study in biodynamics. Nonetheless, as annoying as they were, the ants proved to be the greater pestilence.

If the aim of the ants was simply to harass me then that is exactly what they had been doing. But it was far worse than that. They had been launching surprise attacks, eating away at my bones, and even getting to my marrow. They appeared to love bath towels too, so when I dried myself they got into all of the wrong places. When I thought I had defeated them, they opened new and unexpected fronts, showing guile that one would not normally associate with such lowly insects. I killed a battalion and a battalion more entered the battlefield. With an estimated world population of ten thousand trillion, the ants could have afforded to attack in large numbers and with the same persistence and destructive intent associated with mobs.

They were as resolute, too, as the heat which clung oppressively. But on that particular day it had taken a definite five steps backwards. Indeed, the weather was in one of its rare funks and state of indecision. It could not quite make up its mind whether to rain or allow to reign His Royal Majesty of the day sky, almost like the point of development of the foetus where it is still possible for either chromosomes XX or XY to emerge. Indeed, both the sun and the rain were threatening to impregnate the land with their diverse, impossible-to-confuse, life-giving intrinsic selves at the same time.

It was the continuation of an eternal struggle and an almighty battle for dominance with both having equal reason to be confident of victory. They had each experienced, proportionately, the glory of success and the debacle of defeat. Yet these two lifetime enemies, despite their contentious relationship, had learnt to co-exist and to live in harmony with each other.

Détente was not a contemporary notion, the sun and rain were among its original practitioners. Neither was it a convenient idea, a stopgap measure suggested by political leaders and scientists while they quietly pursued much larger designs. It was only a new way of expressing Papa God's injunction that we live in oneness with each other and with nature. Through the medium of His divine creations He is saying to us that He expects us to be different in the way we look, in the way we think and in the way we act. That is the way He made us, but that there is no difference too big for tolerance to overcome.

However, Grenadians have allowed the things which make them unique to become greater than the things which make them one. Their differences have mushroomed into squabbles, quarrels and fights, and the foreign powers which have used Grenada as an amusement park, have exacerbated the situation to such an extent that living inharmoniously and selfishly have become as natural as the sun shining and rain falling.

Local folklore says that when these two natural phenomena occur at the same time, then 'Jumbie' is marrying, but we were never told who the unfortunate bride was.

Anyway all wedding plans had to be postponed because the bombs of the invaders had developed a universal reputation of having a fondness for wedding parties, and in any case, with so many guns around, all 'Jumbies' were inside. They knew too well that when guns are easily accessible, people were more inclined to shoot than to talk.

They saw what happened on October 19th 1983, which was followed a week later by the American invasion. In America itself where there is the constitutional right to bear arms, they witnessed the daily wasting of human lives, and in Jamaica and Trinidad, constitutional right or no constitutional right, people were getting slaughtered with guns in almost as great a quantity as the ants I killed. No one, then, they surmised, would have been in the mood to politely ask, "Mr. Jumbie, how are you and where are you off to this time of night?" So they chose to play it safe and hunkered down instead, inside cupboards, below beds, other dark places inside houses and in bushed areas.

Though gun shots were being heard day and night, the bombs had largely stopped when the political and military leaders and other activists of the Revolution were transported up to Richmond Hill in St. George's, and lodged within my innards.

As Grenada's legitimate leaders, their arrival would normally have been greeted by the singing of the National Anthem, 'Forward March' or even the 'Internationale.' But those were not normal times, and soon Mosely 'Pram' Bishop and other 'Mongoose Gang' members who were serving a prison sentence, were passing close to the block of cells where the leaders were locked up and singing a different tune, Jimmy Cliff's tune: "What are you in the House of Exile......"

Though the prisoners-of-war were not smiling, they did not think they were anywhere close to their last smile, and yet their facial expressions did not seem to suggest any belief that their next smile was as close as a few months away. Just maneuvering their facial muscles out of the contortions of anguish would have taken some time.

My Mother and I

Where I stood at a 'hard-to-miss-position' on a hill with the best views available to me, and the special role that was mine, made me a scaled-back version of the larger society, an extremely hostile environment. Although the 'Mongoose Gang' and the prisoners were soon to be reconciled, many of the other prisoners did not know why they were angry with the prisoners-of-war, but they wanted to be angry because it appeared as if everybody else were angry. When reasons were ventured by some for their vexation, then it became clear that America's Psychological Operations Department needed no paid agents. Many believed what they said, especially those who felt, and some that had good reasons to feel, aggrieved.

Scores of prison officers, too, (including two, who, during the Revolution, were detained for a few hours of questioning in connection with a prison escape)}, were angling for their pound of flesh. Some prison officers who were subsequently recruited, the son of the former Commissioner of Prison who was detained in 1979 among them, may had been for that specific purpose. The prison officers, like Grenada's occupiers and new colonial masters and their regional servants, now had an open mandate and an unperimetered berth to do with the prisoners-of-war anything that they so wished.

The prisoners' families too were abused and insulted and treated as if they too were prisoners. There were a few cases as well, of prison officers who made sexual advances at the wives and girlfriends of the prisoners when they came to visit their family members.

To further their cruel streak and thirst for vengeance, the Barbadian, Lionel Maloney, with an immense capacity for sadistic brutality, was brought in as Commissioner of Prisons. All that was missing were the gas chambers, and Richmond Hill Prison could have been a young Auschwitz or Bergen-Belsen in the making. Prisoners were regularly, arbitrarily and savagely beaten, and whether the infraction was real or imagined, it did not matter. The status of the prisoners had soon changed to political detainees, and one of them was intemperately beaten with a piece of heavy-linked chain, at the end of which he suffered three broken ribs. Almost weekly they were subjected to dietary punishment of hard, mildew bread and water. The 'offences' ranged from one prisoner wearing his glasses to another barely stepping on a drawn line which he was not supposed to cross during his fifteen minutes exercise period in the yard of the prison.

Since Maloney was sometimes the person who made out the charges and was always the 'High Court Judge,' 'Jury' and 'Appeal Court Judge,' more and more, the pursuit of justice took place in the hearts and minds of the prisoners as they lay quietly in their individual cells on uncovered fiber mattresses on wooden bunks.

The Bible was one of three books they were permitted to have in their cells which were lighted by 60-watt bulbs uninterruptedly, night and day. Pens and writing paper were prohibited articles, as were soap, toothbrush, toothpaste and spoons, plastic or otherwise. Underwear, too, had been outlawed, so, for several years, family jewels of varying size, weight and preciousness had been left swinging and unprotected.

The intentions were to emasculate the political prisoners in more ways than one, and that is why food was also used as a weapon against them. The poorest quality of 'food' that could be found, cooked in a manner a little better than the standards required for 'mange popotte' - and so tasteless, it may well have been genetically modified right there in the prison's kitchen - were dished out in dented bowls befitting hogs. These were the same bowls that some mentally sick inmates were known to urinate and defecate in. In their disturbed minds they probably thought that bowls also came from bowels, but the ***compos mentis*** of those in authority did not seem any better. The quantity of the 'food' served was such that it would have left five-year olds riddled with hunger pangs, and in hospital as well.

It was to the credit of the fortitude of the prisoners and their will to survive, that many of them were not hospitalized with food and water-borne diseases. The prison, too, like several other parts of the island, had its no-water spells and there were times when not even the Fire-Brigade was available to tote water to the prison.

But the prisoners' plastic water buckets were empty and they needed drinking water. On more than one occasion, the buckets were taken from the cells of the political prisoners, placed at the back of a van and taken to a stream or a river by prison officers. There they were filled with brown, dirty, untreated water and taken back to the prisoners to drink.

The prisoners knew that they had no fountain of justice to drink from so they went deep into themselves to summon all of their inner strength to help them stay alive, which was not what the occupiers and their flunkies desired. With the close collaboration between the prison and the court, instruments of State in the pocket of the occupiers, they formed a two-pronged attack on the prisoners and hoped, through their conniving, to bring about **Vergil**'s "...inevitable hour" of death for the rest of the Revolution's leadership.

Several of the political prisoners, with the consent of the Americans, had been taken out of the Point Salines POW camp by Barbadian policemen to be tortured. A few were handed over directly by the Americans while others, Mrs. Phyllis Coard among them, were removed from the prison by the same police officers, none of whom were Grenadians.

At least one had to do what was being asked in order to avoid having his head flushed in a toilet bowl. But mostly the prisoners were handcuffed and for hours which seemed unending, beaten in the stomach, chest, hips, thighs, head and ears with fists or pieces of pipe. One was strangled with a piece of cloth to the point of unconsciousness. Moves were being made to electric-shock a few in the genitals and other parts of the body. One actually had a piece of cord tied around his testicles and repeatedly tugged. With .38 pistols pointed at their heads, they were threatened with being shot and then it would have been claimed that they attempted to escape. At least in one case, threats were made to terrorize the mother, father, wife and children of one of the prisoners.

All of that was in an effort to get the prisoners to sign prepared statements which said that the Central Committee gave orders to execute Bishop and others and that the prisoners were either part of the decision-making or its execution. Yet, as dreadful as the consequences were for signing such incriminating statements, the greater urgency was to get out of that American orchestrated, Barbadian-operated torture-chamber.

Despite the wealth of medical records which showed evidence of physical torture, and the flagrant lies of the torturers on oath, Torturer-In-Chief, Inspector Jasper Watson, Sgt. Ashford Jones, Sgt. Ronald Bowen and Courcey Holder among them, the statements were taken as voluntarily given at a hearing before a specially contracted judge.

Hired for one specific job, Judge Dennis Byron, who was brought in from Antigua, sat on the bench with an expression of determination to earn every last cent of his estimated one million EC dollars in contract money. Guilty or innocent, these sixteen men and one woman charged with murder must be brought guilty, a decisive step in a larger strategy to get rid of the remaining leaders of the Revolution.

He had the Registrar of the High Court fired, as well as the Panel of Jurors which he, the Registrar himself had selected, and almost immediately hired a person who, up to the day before, was a Prosecution Lawyer in the very same case in which seventeen former political and military leaders were to face charges of murder. This Prosecution Lawyer then proceeded to hand-pick her own Panel of Jurors, and before one iota of evidence could be heard, they were shouting threateningly at the prisoners in open court, "murderers, criminals we go get all yuh!"

The prisoners decided that they did not wish to be 'gotten' by anybody, and that they were not going to recognize that illegality by their participation, and accordingly dismissed their lawyers. But when Judge Byron, in the furtherance of his contract, allowed the Prosecution to select a twelve-member Jury and six standbys from the same abusive and unchanged

Panel of Jurors — and to do so while he had the prisoners locked in their cells, unable to be present while this was happening — then to the prisoners the farce became absolute.

Armed foreign, military personnel were inside and outside of this specially designated Court on the compound of the prison at Richmond Hill in St. George's. American military aircraft flew constant sorties low overhead, buzzing the court with its uncoded message of power and might, enough to hold in leash the subservience of many.

The Judge sat facing his Court and the prisoners' dock with an affected air of judicial propriety. To his left sat his bodyguard, as if the Judge was saying to the Jurors sitting also to his left but at a slightly more forward position, that he was in deadly peril of these sixteen men and one woman on whose guilt they had already pronounced.

Without the constantly protesting political prisoners, the unfolding tragic courtroom drama could have been a scene straight out of America's Wild West. Some of the accused were physically beaten by police officers assigned to the Court in order to get them to accept the jurisdiction of the Court. They did not.

Week after week the Prosecution paraded before the Court suborned witnesses, with their star witness alone, around whom the conviction of ten of the seventeen accused hung, giving five fundamentally different statements. Evidence which the Prosecution had earlier unearthed and which was favourable to the accused, was kept out of Court. Evidence which should have been readily available, like the relevant prison diaries, disappeared. Documents which were seized by the invaders and which could have gone towards proving the innocence of some of the accused, were denied them despite their repeated chant "we want we documents now."

Statements which some of the accused signed under torture, were in the hands of the Press long before the Judge ruled on their admissibility, an indication perhaps that others knew in advance what the judge's ruling would have been before it was given. It showed as well the underhand collaboration that was taking place between the Court, foreign police and the Press which had total leeway to print and say whatever they wanted about the accused persons without regard to *sub judice* restrictions. Newspapers with bold, hostile headlines were even sold right in the courtroom in the presence of the Jury.

But the cherries sitting on top of the occupiers ice cream came when the Jurors were made to sign the verdict sheets indicating how they voted, a heretofore unknown stipulation for Jurors and a breach of the old dictum pertaining to the privacy of Jury deliberations. Yet the occupiers could not take any chances though that act of coercion was unnecessary. The Jurors obediently confirmed the pre-trial verdicts which they had shouted at the accused persons before the first 'witness' had been called to give evidence.

If then that was not a modern-day replay of a scene out of America's frontier period of the 18th and 19th centuries, then it must have come directly from Australia's outback. No wonder that jurists from several countries, human rights activists, European Parliamentarians, US Congressmen, local and regional observers and the political prisoners themselves, described that perversion as a 'Kangaroo Trial.' If the leaping mammals with the long, thick tails felt that they had been defamed, then they had a right to take umbrage. That was a farcical 'Trial' of immense proportions, worse than anything they could possibly have contrived. The Old Bailey wept!

But the character assault on the Kangaroo was not yet over and neither was the quasi-judicial ordeal to which the seventeen political prisoners had been subjected. Sir Frederick Smith, Rex McKay and Time Kendall, The Grenada Appeal Court Judges, were each paid one million EC dollars to hear the Appeal and to deliver a written judgment. They heard the Appeal, delivered a verbal judgment consistent with their million-dollar contracts, but the written judgment is still outstanding up to this day because the Judges have not been paid an additional six hundred and fifty thousand US dollars which they requested.

My Mother and I

Talk about bounty hunters? Some wear robes, some wear suits and others military camouflage, police and prison uniforms. The seventeen political prisoners survived them all and the special law that was immediately passed preventing them from taking their matter to the London based Privy Council, Grenada's highest Court. They endured the one thousand, eight hundred and seventeen days of especially harsh conditions on death-row and the hiring of the hangman, Mr. John Adolphus. They survived the preparation and testing of the gallows, all of which they heard from their cells, and the digging of the graves. And they prayed with members of the clergy who came to offer their prayers.

They endured, too, the making of the straightjackets and the placing of the first five of the seventeen – Bernard Coard, Lt. Col. Ewart Layne, Captain Lester Redhead, Lieutenant Callistus Bernard, and Lt. Col. Liam James who was made to replace Major Leon Cornwall – into holding cells in preparation for hanging that was only a few hours away. Don't mind that one of the seventeen lost his appetite during that period, but they all survived, Pte. Andy Mitchell, Sgt. Vincent Joseph, Pte. Cosmus Richardson, General Hudson Austin, Major Christopher Stroude, Major Tan Bartholomew, Lieutenant Cecil Prime, Johnny Ventour, Selwyn Strachan, Mrs. Phyllis Coard and Kamau McBarnette among them.

The Government of Sir Nicholas Brathwaite commuted the death sentences to life imprisonment on August 15th 1991, and there was an audible sigh of relief from the political prisoners and a chorus of 'Thank you, God!' by families and friends worldwide. Pope John Paul and Mother Theresa were among those whose strong faith and religious beliefs led them to join the campaign to save the 'Grenada 17.'

Chapter 49

Notwithstanding the fact that I grew up in a God-fearing home, and never once missed the tri-daily recital of the Angelus and Hail Marys before I began playing man and becoming set in my own ways, prayers were not one of my strong points. Yet when 'hard-times' befell the 'Grenada 17' and it appeared as if Mr. Aldolphus's hand was reaching for the lever of the gallows, I began pounding on Papa God's door as if ten devils were after me.

"Open up, Papa God, hurry, hurry! You have seventeen here to save and no one else but You to turn to!" is what the urgency of my new found faith in prayers was saying to Him, prayers of intercession which were delivered with the self-righteous conviction of a fundamentalist.

That reminds me that although the revolution did not recognize God or His presence, that does not say God was not present during the revolution. Too many good occurred despite the bad for God not to have been present. Who else could have inspired the establishment of NIS or MNIB or the House Repair Programme and countless other caring and uplifting programmes? You cannot say to God "Look God, this is our turf so keep away!" Or "God, would you please stay out of our business, this does not concern you!" Or worse yet,

My Mother and I

"Mind you own business, you too damn farse!" Man's business is God's business and vice versa! You cannot wish God away and your non-belief in God does not make God non-existent nor is it going to restrict His activities! One cannot execute a Detention Order on God!

So given the amount of prayers that was going Papa God's way, with hanging imminent, and the speed at which they were being dispatched, He must have had at His disposal the finest voice-mail machinery that could ever have been created. That would have allowed Him to listen at His own convenience and when He was least harassed.

Papa God may not have considered Mother one of His harassers and being a devout Roman Catholic she prayed real hard too. But she was also a staunch defender of the rules of fair play and the requirements of justice and would have been appalled at the speed at which apparently normal persons were willing to strip off their clothes and get into bed with the worst of human indecency.

The political prisoners may have survived but not the Court as the revered institution it once used to be, not the Parliament, the Police nor the Prison, institutions of State that have been desecrated by the invaders, their clients and politicians and turned into instruments of political persecution. These respected bodies once thought to be beyond the reach of corruption and held on a pedestal by all, have become, potentially, as malleable as a baby's bottom and are often used to further the ruling party's grip on political power.

And yet, when it was happening to the political prisoners many, in a land of numerous 'Christians,' kept silent, too afraid to speak out or did not believe that it could possibly happen to them. In Germany too, when Hitler began his pogroms many reacted in the same way until it was too late.

In the atmosphere of fear, therefore, and the 'it-could-never-happen-to-me' attitude, the brigands and bounty-hunters got much of their own way with the 'Grenada 17,' like a woman who, despite resisting as much as she could have, could not prevent herself from being gang-raped while the neighbourhood looked on and did nothing.

There were doctors who looked on, judges, lawyers, church leaders, police officers, prison officers, politicians, educators, journalists, civil libertarians, community and other interest groups and even a few former comrades. They looked on and did something: they co-operated with the occupiers and their lackeys and, in some cases, played an active role in this atrocious public rape. Yet those who did something by not doing anything may have been just as accommodating. Others simply sought to take advantage of the 'Grenada 17' and their families in their weakened, relatively impotent and vulnerable state.

Many too have shown scant regard bordering on criminal negligence for the families of those who died on October 19th 1983. It is difficult to understand one's pain unless one is in the actual circumstances of the sufferer, but the things which make us human are the same things which make it possible for us to commiserate with the suffering of others.

The anguish of these people would have been made far worse by the manner and particulars of the death of their loved ones. But the refusal to recover the bodies for a proper burial would have sentenced the families to a hell of eternal torment.

Nine bodies were buried in a single grave in October 1983. On or around November 9th 1983, a grave registration team of the US Army led by Captain Forde, unearthed these same bodies, partly burnt and decomposed. They were then taken to the St. George's University School of Medicine to be examined. Subsequently, at a sitting of the Court, the Jamaican soldier and member of the Caribbean Peacekeeping Forces, Cpl. Earl Brown, Barbadian Police Officers, Sgt. Colin Brathwaite and PC Courcey Holder, led evidence with respect to the unearthing of the bodies. One was definitely the body parts of a woman, and another believed to be that of Bishop given what he was wearing. Family members of the deceased were called into Court to identify the personal effects, including rings, pendants and watches, recovered at the grave. Photos were also produced in Court showing the grave, personal effects and body bags said to contain the deceased.

It is therefore the most well-known secret that the Americans took control of the bodies, so why the conspiracy of silence thirty years later? The families and friends of the deceased should be made to suffer for the rest of their lives because the Americans do not wish a shrine to be made of Bishop's grave thereby giving him as much power in death as he had in life?

Where are Grenada's political leaders, its church leaders and community leaders? Why are they not saying anything? Why are not questions being asked? Are they hoping that the quest for the bodies would become as dead as the bodies themselves? Is it that they are simply afraid to rock the American boat? Or is it that they are more comfortable with sacrificing the well-being of Grenadians at the altar of political expedience? Perhaps it is that they believe that for as long as they can keep the mystery of the bodies unresolved, the longer it would be available to them to use as a political tool to keep Grenadians divided and from moving on. Witness the way some persons were quick to shout "the bodies, the bodies" when the issue of the release of the 'Grenada 17' came up for discussion, and, after that, total silence until the issue came up again.

But the question remains, were the bodies completely destroyed? Were the skulls of the deceased crushed to smithereens after the bodies were recovered so as to make identification virtually impossible? If not, where are they? Should Sir Paul Scoon, the person who exercised executive authority, ostensibly or otherwise following the invasion, not have been called on to account? Why haven't the United Nations, OAS and other international bodies petitioned for their assistance?

Isn't it ironic that, following the invasion, the Psychological Operations Department of the US Army claimed that mass graves with hundreds of bodies were discovered, and yet thirty years later not one body from a single grave can be produced? Believe me, if they were American bodies, the offending country would have had hell to pay.

It was the same hell that was levied on the political prisoners when they were put through the wringer of subhuman prison conditions. Mrs. Phyllis Coard was held apart from her other sixteen colleagues and the way she was dealt with by the female prison officers was simply atrocious. The fact that she has survived, albeit with severe psychological and other medical problems, speaks to her own inner strength.

Her male counterparts, on the other hand, were kept together and were therefore able to rely on each other's hardiness in their determination to stay the distance. The 'Grenada 17' was something like the ants; they simply were not giving up! Individually and collectively they found ways to pass the time and to preserve their sanity.

Cosmus Richardson was one of the political prisoners. On March 13th 1979 he was a member of the Grenada Voluntary Constabulary (GVC) and was based in the St. David's Police Station. He was one of several men who had been sent to the True Blue army barracks that morning when they received reports of a fire. It was a fire yes, because the 'Green Beasts' barracks had been torched by the revolutionary fighters, but the picture was much larger than that.

Just how much larger, the GVC, including Richardson, was unaware as the bus which transported them sped along the True Blue Stretch. It was the same bus which was held-up by one of the revolutionary fighters with an empty pistol. Four and a half years later, the bearer of the empty, magazine-less pistol became Richardson's co-defendant and colleague.

Richardson was detained on the morning of the Revolution and was subsequently taken to Richmond Hill Prison where he spent five months as a detainee. In 1981, in less than two years after his release from prison, he joined the Peoples' Militia and a few months later joined the PRA. By

My Mother and I

1983 Richardson was a First Class Private and held the same rank when the occupiers detained him in January 1984.

His body may have been detained but never his mind. He loved singing and with his strong religious background, many of his songs were religious. There were two others who also loved singing but, for their fellow colleagues, their singing was more of a secret weapon against the heat than anything else. In fact, one only asked them to sing if one were in the mood for 'hold-you-belly-and-roll-on-the-ground' daylong laughter.

When Richardson's mournful, cultured singing-voice rang out from his cell in the early hours of the morning, during the day or in the quiet of the night, it did one or two things to his colleagues who were housed in individual cells on death-row in close proximity to him. Some became depressed, others became uplifted. Even I was not insulated from feelings of melancholy despite my heart of concrete.

> "I don't want to cross Jordan alone
> And I know He will be waiting for me
> When my Savior arise
> I will be waiting for Him
> I don't want to cross Jordan alone."

But when Richardson sang one of his father's compositions I felt amused. Richardson's father had been a policeman for 21 years, and participated in calypso competitions held among the police.

> "Linda wash up you bowl
> Linda wash up you bowl
> Every night I coming to eat
> I smelling you bowl quite out in the street.
> I just left you and went away
> Only just dey I didn't go to stay
> But now I come back to you
> You bowl even smelling worse than the zoo."

I could not imagine Richardson singing about any other bowl except the aluminum, dent-ridden, weather-beaten ones in which meals were served and those needed detoxification. In any case, I had already washed up mine because I was tired and was ready for bed.

In the meantime, the weight of the shared responsibility on the shoulders of the political prisoners for the demise of the Revolution and the horrific events which preceded it, have made the past thirty years a living purgatory.

Their more than two decades of imprisonment has largely been one of atonement. They have gone out of their way to assist the other inmates at the prison academically and otherwise. They have given similar assistance to prison officers, among them those who once brutalized them and enthusiastically subjected them to the worst possible inhumane prison conditions. The prisons authority too, found the 'Grenada 17' to be remarkably resourceful and constantly relied on them for their help and support.

In that regard the political prisoners, by their discipline, hard work and respect for others, have been a positive influence on the rest of the prison population. It is no wonder, then, that Richmond Hill Prison has been the most stable prison in the region, and perhaps too, the most forward thinking.

Unfortunately, the rest of the society appears to be in as much need of rehabilitation as the prison. With the collapse of the Revolution, backward-thinking politicians threw out the gold nuggets with the dust and cultivated instead a culture of lies, lawlessness, graft, get rich by any means and moral turpitude which have overrun every aspect of Grenadian life. 'Anything goes, anything accepted' seems to be the new standards to which Grenadians aspire. The 'fast-food' mentality is taking people who were once God-centered, family conscious, respectful, caring and nationalistic nowhere fast, and the examples that are being given to the young people in particular, do not augur well for Grenada's future. Unless its leaders stop talking their examples and instead start living their examples, our young people are headed unerringly up to Richmond Hill Prison.

Where all of that would take Grenada's people only Papa God really knows. It does not look too good from here, but the glass is not yet half-empty. Grenada's history has gone through cyclic bittersweet periods. The bitter parts always appeared longer than the sweet parts but sometimes the bitter parts carried with them moments of sweetness, and likewise the sweet times were themselves bearers of bitter moments.

But these are matters to be pondered on another time. I have already told you one story and although I have a thousand more stories to tell, I am tired and I am hurting all over.

For me, 'Aches' of whatever kind could have been my real name. My joints have been made arthritic from all that I have had to endure. The load of all I have had to carry has weakened my limbs. My stomach has become ulcerated by the uncountable poor souls that have been jammed within my insides. The early signs of glaucoma are in my eyes from the pain of all that I have had to witness and from the shed tears for the many for whom I have wept.

My head no longer feels like my own from all the bullets and bombs that have come my way, from the shrapnel wounds of war and from all that I have had to remember. My ears are hurting from the innumerable sad stories of suffering and poverty that I have had to listen to, and from the many sounds of conflict; while my heart has been sapped by the troubles of Grenada and its people.

My sister Jeudy once called me a bitch and she was probably right. I would have had to be a tough bitch to have survived all these years. Believe me, I do not know how I, Richmond Hill Prison, despite the battering, survived more than a century of so much pain, injustice and hardships; but, as angered as I am and as likely as my function is to change yet again, I intend to remain standing as a symbol of Grenada's historical past.

Did I hear you ask, "Who is my Mother?" Is that what you are asking?

GO TO FRANCE!

GLOSSARY

Chapter 1

1. **Aldous Huxley** - (26 July 1894 – 22 November 1963) was an English writer and one of the most prominent members of the famous Huxley family. Best known for his novels including *Brave New World*, a book that was often banned for its sexual content etc. and a wide-ranging output of essays. Huxley also edited the magazine *Oxford Poetry*, and published short stories, poetry, travel writing, and film stories and scripts.
2. **Cardinal Richelieu** - born in 1585 and died in 1642. Richelieu dominated the history of France from 1624 to his death as Louis XIII's chief minister, succeeding Luynes who died in 1621. Richelieu is considered to be one of the greatest politicians in French history.
3. **Mazarin** - **Jules Mazarin** (French: [ʒyl mazaʁɛ̃]; 1602–1661), born **Giulio Raimondo Mazzarino** or **Mazarini**,[1] was a French-Italian[2] cardinal, diplomat, and politician, who served as the chief minister of France from 1642 until his death. Mazarin succeeded his mentor, Cardinal Richelieu.
4. **William, Duke Of Normandy** - **William I** (circa 1028[1] – 9 September 1087), also known as **William The Conqueror** (*Guillaume le Conquérant*), was the first Norman King of England from Christmas 1066 until his death. He was also Duke of Normandy from 3 July 1035 until his death, under the name **William II**. Before his conquest of England, he was known as **William The Bastard** because of the illegitimacy of his birth.
5. **Joan Of Arc** - **Saint Joan of Arc**, nicknamed **"The Maid of Orléans"** (French: *Jeanne d'Arc*,[1] IPA: [ʒan daʁk]; ca. 1412[2] – 30 May 1431), is considered a national heroine of France and a Catholic saint. A peasant girl born in eastern France who claimed divine

guidance, she led the French army to several important victories during the Hundred Years' War, which paved the way for the coronation of Charles VII. She was captured by the Burgundians, sold to the English, tried by an ecclesiastical court, and burned at the stake when she was 19 years old.

6. **Marshall Pétain - Henri Philippe Benoni Omer Joseph Pétain** (French pronunciation: [petɛ̃]; 24 April 1856 – 23 July 1951), generally known as **Philippe Pétain** or **Marshal Pétain** (*Maréchal Pétain*), was a French general who reached the distinction of Marshal of France, and was later Chief of State of Vichy France *(Chef de l'État Français)*, from 1940 to 1944. Pétain, who was 84 years old in 1940, ranks as France's oldest head of state.

7. **Marshall Foch - Ferdinand Foch** (French pronunciation: [fɔʃ]), GCB, OM, DSO (2 October 1851 – 20 March 1929) was a French soldier, military theorist, and writer credited with possessing "the most original and subtle mind in the French army" in the early 20th century.[1] He served as general in the French army during World War I and was made Marshal of France in its final year: 1918

8. **General Charles De Gaulle - Charles André Joseph Marie de Gaulle** (English: /ˈtʃɑrlz/ or /ˈʃɑrl dəˈɡɔːl/; French: [ʃaʁl də ɡol] (1890–1970) was a French general and statesman who led the Free French Forces during World War II. He later founded the French Fifth Republic in 1958 and served as its first President from 1959 to 1969.

9. **Napoleon Bonaparte** - (15 August 1769 – 5 May 1821) was a French military and political leader during the latter stages of the French Revolution. As **Napoleon I**, he was Emperor of the French from 1804 to 1815. His legal reform, the Napoleonic code,

has been a major influence on many civil law jurisdictions worldwide.
10. **Louis XVI** - (23 August 1754 – 21 January 1793) ruled as King of France and Navarre from 1774 until 1791, and then as King of the French from 1791 to 1792. Suspended and arrested as part of the insurrection of 10 August during the French Revolution, he was tried by the National Convention, found guilty of high treason, and executed by guillotine on 21 January 1793 as a desacralized French citizen known as *"Citoyen Louis Capet"*. He is the only King of France ever to be executed.
11. **Marie Antoinette** (French pronunciation: [maʁi ɑ̃twanɛt]; baptised **Maria Antonia Josepha Johanna** (or **Maria Antonia Josephina Johanna**[1]); 2 November 1755 – 16 October 1793) was an Archduchess of Austria and the Queen of France and of Navarre. She was the fifteenth and penultimate child of Empress Maria Theresa of Austria and Emperor Francis I.
12. **"Let them eat cake"** is the traditional translation of the French phrase *"Qu'ils mangent de la brioche"*, supposedly spoken by "a great princess" upon learning that the peasants had no bread. Since brioche was enriched, as opposed to normal bread, the quote supposedly would reflect the princess's obliviousness to the condition of the people.
13. **Louis XIV**- (5 September 1638 – 1 September 1715), known as **Louis the Great** (French: "Louis le Grand") or the **Sun King** (French: *le Roi-Soleil*), was King of France and of Navarre.[1] His reign, from 1643 to his death in 1715, began at the age of four and lasted seventy-two years, three months, and eighteen days. As such, it is one of the longest documented reigns of any European monarch.

14. **Louis XV-** (15 February 1710 – 10 May 1774) ruled as King of France and of Navarre from 1 September 1715 until his death. After he succeeded to the throne at the age of five, his first cousin twice removed, Philippe II, Duke of Orléans, served as Regent of the kingdom until Louis's majority in 1723. Cardinal de Fleury was his chief minister from 1726 until his death in 1743, at which time the young king took over control of the French state. Louis XV was a member of the House of Bourbon.
15. **Colbert- Jean-Baptiste** (1619 – 1683), French statesman and financier.
16. **De Tocqueville- Alexis-Charles-Henri Clérel de Tocqueville** (French pronunciation: [alɛksi or alɛksis də tɔkvil]; 29 July 1805, Paris – 16 April 1859, Cannes) was a French political thinker and historian best known for his *Democracy in America* (appearing in two volumes: 1835 and 1840) and *The Old Regime and the Revolution* (1856). In both of these works, he explored the effects of the rising equality of social conditions on the individual and the state in western societies.
17. **Jean-Paul Sartre- Jean-Paul Charles Aymard Sartre** (French pronunciation: [saʁtʁ], English: /ˈsɑrtrə/; 21 June 1905 – 15 April 1980) was a French existentialist philosopher, playwright, novelist, screenwriter, political activist, biographer, and literary critic. He was one of the leading figures in 20th century French philosophy, particularly Marxism, and was one of the key figures in literary and philosophical existentialism.
18. **Marie Curie- Marie Skłodowska Curie** (7 November 1867 – 4 July 1934) was a Polish–French physicist–chemist famous for her pioneering research on radioactivity. She was the first person honored with two Nobel Prizes[1]—in physics and chemistry. She was the first female professor at the University of

Paris. She was the first woman to be entombed on her own merits (in 1995) in the Paris Panthéon.

19. **Proclaimers of Liberté, Egalité, Fraternité**- *Liberté, égalité, fraternité*, French for "Liberty, equality, fraternity (brotherhood)",[1] is the national motto of France, and is a typical example of a tripartite motto. Although it finds its origins in the French Revolution, it was then only one motto among others and was not institutionalized until the Third Republic at the end of the 19th century.[2] Debates concerning the compatibility and order of the three terms began at the same time as the Revolution.

20. **Bastille** - The **Bastille** (French pronunciation: [bastij]) was a fortress in Paris, known formally as the **Bastille Saint-Antoine**, and for most of its history used as a state prison by the kings of France. The Bastille was built in response to the English threat to the city of Paris during the Hundred Years War.

21. **Dante** - **Durante degli Alighieri**, commonly known as **Dante** (US: /ˈdɑːnteɪ/; UK: /ˈdænti/; 1265–1321), was a major Italian poet of the Middle Ages. His *Divine Comedy*, originally called *Commedia* and later called *Divina* by Boccaccio, is considered the greatest literary work composed in the Italian language and a masterpiece of world literature.

22. **Robespierre - Maximilien François Marie Isidore de Robespierre** (IPA: [maksimiljɛ̃ fʁɑ̃swa maʁi izidɔʁ də ʁɔbɛspjɛʁ]; 6 May 1758 – 28 July 1794) is one of the best-known and most influential figures of the French Revolution. He largely dominated the Committee of Public Safety and was instrumental in the period of the Revolution commonly known as the Reign of Terror, which ended with his arrest and execution in 1794.

23. **Descartes** - **René Descartes** French pronunciation: [ʁəne dekaʁt]; (31 March 1596 – 11

February 1650) (Latinized form: *Renatus Cartesius*; adjectival form: "Cartesian")[3] was a French philosopher and writer who spent most of his adult life in the Dutch Republic. He has been dubbed the 'Father of Modern Philosophy', and much subsequent Western philosophy is a response to his writings, which are studied closely to this day.

Chapter 2

1. **Du Parquet** - The French governor of Martinique, Jacques-Dyel *du Parquet*, purchased Grenada from a French company in 1650 and established a settlement at St. George's
2. **Santa Lucia** – The Spanish name for the island that was known to the Caribs as Hewannora – 'The Land of The Iguana. Today the island is known as St. Lucia.
3. **Caribs** - The name that was given to the Kalinago people by the Spanish, means cannibal. The Lesser Antilles were settled in 1,000 AD by the Caribs, a far more combative people than the Arawaks. The Caribs believed in a remote supreme God but they had several deities with which they related.
4. **Hewannora** - The Land Of The Iguana. The name the Caribs gave to St. Lucia.
5. **Carib Beer** – A fermented alcoholic drink found in several Caribbean Islands.
6. **Kalinago** - Carib, Island Carib, or Kalinago people, after whom the Caribbean Sea was named, are a group of people who lived in the Lesser Antilles islands. They are an Amerindian people whose origins lie in the southern West Indies and the northern coast of South America.
7. **Aztecs** - The **Aztec** people were certain ethnic groups of central Mexico, particularly those groups who spoke the Nahuatl language and who dominated large parts of Mesoamerica in the 14th, 15th and 16th centuries. Often the term "Aztec" refers exclusively to the

Mexica people of Tenochtitlan (now the location of Mexico City), situated on an island in Lake Texcoco.
8. **Mayas** - A Mesoamerican civilization, noted for the only known fully developed written language of the pre-Columbian Americas, as well as for its art, architecture, and mathematical and astronomical systems.
9. **Incas** - The largest empire in pre-Columbian America. The administrative, political and military center of the empire was located in Cusco in modern-day Peru. The Inca civilization arose from the highlands of Peru sometime in the early 13th century. From 1438 to 1533, the Incas used a variety of methods, from conquest to peaceful assimilation. The official language of the empire was Quechua.

Chapter 3
1. **Granada** - A city and the capital of the province of Granada, in the autonomous community of Andalusia, Spain. The city of Granada is located at the foot of the Sierra Nevada mountains.
2. **Camerhogne** - 'Spiritual Home' – of the Carib people. The name the Caribs gave to Grenada.
3. **Atabeyra** - The earth Mother, and guardian of moving waters and childbirth; one of several deities of the Caribs.
4. **Priapos** - The Greek God of procreation
5. **Arrowroot** - A large perennial herb found in rainforest habitats. It is cultivated for a starch obtained from the rhizomes (rootstock); it is chiefly cultivated in the West Indies, where the native Arawaks used its powder; it has small white flowers and fruits about the size and form of currants. The rootstocks are dug when the plant is a year old. They are yellowish white, jointed and covered with loose scales.
6. **Agouti** - A burrowing rodent of the genus *Dasyprocta*, native to the West Indies and tropical America and

usually having brown fur streaked with gray. They are related to guinea pigs and look quite similar but have longer legs. The species vary in color from tawny to dark brown with lighter underparts.
7. **Manicou** - They are also commonly called *possums*, noted for feigning death when in danger; esteemed as food in some areas. They make up the largest order of marsupials in the Western Hemisphere.
8. **Iguana** - *Iguana* is a herbivorous genus of lizard native to tropical areas of Central and South America and the Caribbean.
9. **Zemies** - The images of the Carib's many Gods- made of clay, shell or cotton, and with which they decorated ceramic pots.
10. **Arawaks** - Amerindians who were driven to establish new settlements on the larger islands.
11. **Ceiba** - A type of wood the Carib's used along with silk-cotton to build sturdy, ocean-bound, wood canoes, measuring between forty and ninety feet.

Chapter 4
1. **'Eat and sleep."** - Refers to the feeling one gets after eating large amounts of food. Often associated with the need to take a nap after eating.
2. **Pepperpot** - A West Indian stew of vegetables and meat or fish, flavored with cassava juice, red pepper, etc;
3. **Yocahu** – 'Giver Of Cassava'- a male God residing in volcanoes, another of the Carib's deities.
4. **Spanish bolero** - A form of slow-tempo Latin music associated dance and song. Dancer Sebastiano Carezo is credited with inventing the dance in 1780. It is danced by either a soloist or a couple.
5. **Carbet** - Were huge oval-shaped community houses used for social events.

6. **'Shak-shak'** - The fruit of the flamboyant tree when shaken the seeds inside transformed it into a kind of musical instrument.
7. **Zanzas** – Wooden or stick-like instruments cut to specific dimensions.
8. **Pitapat** - To move with a series of quick tapping steps; to make a repeated tapping sound.
9. **Boogie-Woogie** – A style of piano-based blues that became popular in the late 1930s and early 1940s, but originated much earlier, and was extended from piano, to three pianos at once, guitar, big band, and country and western music, and even gospel. Whilst the blues traditionally depicts a variety of emotions, boogie-woogie is mainly associated with dancing.
10. **Kaierouanne** – The Carib Chief
11. **Griot** - A West African storyteller. The *griot* delivers history as a poet, praise singer, and wandering musician.

Chapter 5
1. **Abettor** - To approve, encourage and support.
2. **Saboteur** - Someone who engages in sabotage.
3. **Abzocky** - Awkward
4. **Pantomimed** - Communication by means of gesture and facial expression

Chapter 6
1. **La Diablesse** - A woman whose poise, figure and dress make her appear to be beautiful; her hideous face is hidden by a large brimmed hat. Her long dress hides the fact that she has one human foot and one cow's hoof; also she walks with one foot on the road and her cow's hoof in the grass at the side of the road. She can cast spells on her male victims and she leads her unsuspecting victims into the forest. When in the forest, she disappears

and the man, confused, lost and scared, runs around the forest until he falls into a ravine or river and dies.
2. **Jumbie** - A type of mythological spirit or demon in the folklore of some Caribbean countries. Jumbie is the generic name given to all malevolent entities; however, there are numerous kinds of jumbies, that reflect the Caribbean's complex history and ethnic makeup, drawing on African, Amerindian, East Indian, Dutch, English, and even Chinese mythology
3. **Mamamaladie** - The restless ghost and/or crying of a woman who has died in childbirth and has been buried with the child still inside her. Her cries are said to be heard for nine nights after her death as her spirit moves between the grave and the house in which she died.
4. **Loupgaroo** – (French for werewolf) a human who changes into a wolf at his/her own will.

Chapter 8
1. **Bananaquit** - (*Coereba flaveola*) A species of passerine bird of uncertain relation, on the island of Grenada in the West Indies; has a plumage color polymorphism in which individuals are either yellow and black or all black.
2. **Flamboyant tree** – The national tree of *Grenada*. Tropical tree having showy yellow to orange-red flowers; sometimes placed in genus Poinciana; it is also called Royal Poinciana; the scientific name Delonix Regia.

Chapter 9

1. **Le Compte** – Du Parquet's cousin. After his death in 1654 he was replaced as Governor of Grenada by 'Louis Cacqueray de Valminière'.
2. **Agoraphobia** - Anxiety about being in places or situations from which escape might be difficult (or embarrassing) or in which help may not be available.
3. **Caribphobia** – Fear of the Caribs.

Chapter 11
1. **Armed to the teeth** - Having many and powerful weapons.
2. **Punji sticks** - A sharpened, often poisoned, bamboo stake planted in a series as a barricade or planted and concealed in a hole, ditch, etc. as to cut or impale an enemy; a type of booby trap.
3. **Pois-gatee** – French patois: Pois means peas and gatee means scratching. A tropical plant with barbed hairs that cause severe itching. **Cowitch** is another common name by which it is known but **Mucuna pruriens** is its scientific name. The plant is said to have multiple health benefits including as an aphrodisiac.

Chapter 13
1. **Obiyel Wa' obiran** - The Carib's deity attending the souls of the dead.
2. **Macabre** - A grim or ghastly atmosphere.

Chapter 14
1. **Cawing, hooting and cooing** - The call of the seagulls
2. **Le Morne de Sauteurs** – 1652: the last of the defending Caribs rather than be ruled by the French, threw themselves into the sea from a precipice that the French christened *Le Morne* des *Sauteurs* or translated means Leaper's Hill.
3. **Port Royal** – present day St. George, first established by the French.
4. **Fort Royal** - present day Fort George, built by the French.

Chapter 15
1. **La Grenade** – French for Grenada: The name given to Grenada by French Colonizers.
2. **Machiavellian** – Cunning, duplicity or bad faith.
3. **Armageddon** – A decisive battle (See Rev. 16: 14 – 16).
4. **Morne Jaloux** – French meaning Jealous Mountain; the name of a village on the outskirts of the capital that retains its name from the French.

Chapter 16
1. **Stiff-necked** - Grenadian colloquial/local vernacular for the condition of having muscle soreness or stiffness in the area of the neck.
2. **Bis peccare in bello non licet** – (Latin): One must not blunder twice in war.
3. **Thatcherite** – An advocate of Thatcherism or believers in the policies former British Prime Minister Margaret Thatcher articulated.

Chapter 17
1. **Julien Fedon** - Fedon, a freed coloured Grenadian, was a descendant of a French expatriate. Fedon led a Rebellion/Revolution (March 2, 1795-June 19, 1796) that almost duplicated the success of the Haitian revolution. Like the Haitian revolution, Fedon's rebellion/revolution was ignited by the tenets/principles of the French revolution-Liberté, Egalité and Fraternité.
2. **Toussaint L'Ouverture** - also **Toussaint Bréda**, (May 20, 1743 – April 7, 1803) the 18th century self-educated slave with no military training drove Napoleon out of Haiti and led his country to independence. He was the leader of the Haitian Revolution. His military genius and political acumen led to the establishment of the independent black state

of Haiti, transforming an entire society of slaves into a free, self-governing people. The success of the Haitian Revolution shook the institution of slavery throughout the New World.

3. **Jean Jacques Dessalines** - (born c. 1758, West Africa—died Oct. 17, 1806, Pont Rouge, near Port-au-Prince, Haiti), emperor of Haiti who proclaimed his country's independence in 1804. Dessalines was brought to the French West Indian colony of Saint-Domingue (Haiti) as a slave. He worked as a field hand for a black master until 1791, when he joined the slave rebellion that broke out in the colony amid the turmoil caused by the French Revolution. In the decade that followed he distinguished himself as a lieutenant of the black leader Toussaint Louverture.

4. **Henri Christophe** - Henri Christophe was born in 1757 on the island of Grenada. He was an adolescent when he arrived in Cap-Francais in St-Domingue. In 1778, he fought as a volunteer in Savannah, Georgia, for the independence of the United States of America. He was only 21 years old. Henri Christophe, a lieutenant of Toussaint, who fought the army of Napoleon during the War of Independence, is very well known for his influence in the northern section of Haiti, where he built monuments, palaces and forts.

5. **Alexander Sabès Pétion** - (born April 2, 1770, Port-au-Prince, Haiti—died March 29, 1818, Port-au-Prince), Haitian independence leader and president, remembered by the Haitian people for his liberal rule… Pétion served in the French colonial army before the French Revolution and then joined the revolutionary troops of Toussaint Louverture and, later, those of the mulatto general André Rigaud. Fleeing to France after Toussaint defeated Rigaud, who had set up a mulatto state.

6. **Jean Pierre Boyer** - a native of Saint-Domingue, was a soldier, one of the leaders of the Haitian Revolution,

and President of Haiti from 1818 to 1843. He reunited the north and south of Haiti in 1820 and also invaded and took control of Santo Domingo, which brought all of Hispaniola under one government by 1822. Boyer managed to rule for the longest period of time of any of the revolutionary leaders of his generation.
7. **Fedonists** – Allies and supporters of Julien fedon.
8. **Belvedere** – The name of the estate owned by Julien Fedon, one of the largest plantations in Grenada and with it many slaves who were responsible for its large production of cocoa and coffee.
9. **Victor Hughes** - (born in Marseille July 20, 1762 and died in Cayenne August 12, 1826) was a French politician and colonial administrator during the French Revolution, who governed Guadeloupe from 1794 to 1798 emancipating the island's slaves under orders from the National Convention. With an army composed of White, Mulatto and ex-slave soldiers, Hughes worked to export the revolution to neighboring islands, including Dominica, Saint-Martin, Grenada, Saint Vincent and Saint Lucia.
10. **St. David's** – The name of one of the six parishes on the mainland Grenada situated in the southeast.

Chapter 18

1. **C'est la guerre** – French for 'that's war, it cannot be helped'.
2. **Fedon's Camp** - The historic mountain hideout to which Julien Fedon retreated following the collapse of the rebellion he led against the British in 1795. A densely vegetated area that stood 2,509 feet above sea level.
3. **Jacques Chadeau** - One of Fedon's lieutenants.
4. **Cherry Hill** – A village on the northwest outskirts of the capital city.

Chapter 19
1. **Conseil Souverain** - A political body appointed by the King of France and consisting of a Governor General, an intendant of New France who answered to the French Minister of the Marine. The members of the council were chosen as part of the French nobility.
2. **Lothario** – A man whose chief interest is seducing women.
3. **Tête-à-tête** - Without the intrusion of a third person; in intimate privacy; A private conversation between two persons.
4. **Lugubriously** – Exaggerated or affectedly mournful; with feeling of bitterness or grief.
5. **Engagés** - Indentured servants recruited in France for service in the colonies.

Chapter 20
1. **Abyssinia** – The name used by Europeans to refer to Ethiopia.
2. **Province of Kaffa** – A province in Ethiopia named after the Kingdom of Kaffa (c.1390–1897)
3. **Hottentots** – The name given to the native Khoikhoi people of Southwestern Africa by immigrant Europeans. Today it's considered a derogatory term.
4. **Bantu** – The general label for 300-600 ethnic groups in Africa.
5. **Tsetse fly**- Large biting flies resembling house flies that lived in mid-continental Africa between the Sahara and the Kalahari deserts.
6. **Filigreeing** – Ornamental work especially of fine wire of gold, silver, copper and of a delicate or intricate design.
7. **Fretwork** – Wood or metal usually designed geometrically in an interlaced decorative design that is carved or cut in low relief.

8. **Leitmotifs** - An associated melodic phrase or dominant recurring theme that accompanies the appearance of idea, person or situation.
9. **Lingua franca** – A common language that was spoken in Mediterranean ports consisting of Italian mixed with French, Spanish, Arabic and Greek.
10. **Chimerical** – Existing only as a product of unchecked imagination; something of a fantasy.
11. **Kismet** – Fate/Fortune/Destiny.
12. **Insouciance** – Lighthearted; unconcern.
13. **Diurnally** – Recurring everyday.
14. **Phantasmagoria** – Shifting series of illusions or deception produce by magic or the like in which figures increase or diminish in size, pass into each other or dissolve.

Chapter 21
1. **Alcupa** – A worm medicine of old.
2. **Bight of Benin** – Wide bay in West Africa, the Western section of the Gulf of Guinea.
3. **Cornfish** – Fish salted or seasoned after it is cleaned, then sundried.
4. **Biltong** – Dried Salted fish which originated in South Africa; strips of lean meat cured by salting and drying.
5. **Mersey** – River in Northwest England flowing into the Irish Sea near Liverpool.
6. **Big Ben** – A large bell in the clock tower of the Houses of Parliament in London.
7. **King William 1V** – King of England who reigned from 1830 – 1837.

Chapter 22
1. **Mens rea** – Criminal Intent or prior intention to commit a criminal act, with the knowledge that the act is a crime.

2. **Force majeure** – an unexpected event that prevents someone from doing something they promised to do; a force that is impossible to resist.

Chapter 23
1. **Serbia** - Officially the **Republic of Serbia**, a landlocked country located at the crossroads of Central and Southeast Europe. Following World War I, Serbia formed Yugoslavia with other South Slavic peoples. The capital of Serbia, Belgrade, is among the largest cities in Southeast Europe.

Chapter 24
1. **Masantoe** – or **Masanteau,** A torch; refers to the bottle filled with kerosene with the wick at the mouth made of cloth. Whereas the Flambeau, which is French for flame, is often made from bamboo.

Chapter 25
1. **Moyah** – A village in the parish of St. Andrews.
2. **Dunfermline** – A Village in the parish of St. Andrews next to Moyah.
3. **'Hand-me-downs'** – Worn clothing passed from one sibling to another, usually from a older sibling to a younger.
4. **Saville Row** - A shopping street in Mayfair, Central London, famous for its traditional and exquisite tailoring of men's clothing.
5. **Gascoigne Blaize** – One of Eric Gairy's chief lieutenants and the cousin of the late Herbert Blaize who later became Prime Minister of Grenada.
6. **Rupert, John & Roy Bishop** – All brothers. Rupert was the father of Maurice Bishop and both John and Roy were his uncles; Roy was another of Eric Gairy's chief lieutenants.

Chapter 27
1. **'Jook'** - Grenadian colloquial/local vernacular for poking or jabbing someone with a finger, usually the index finger, or piercing with anything that has a point.
2. **Mibone** – A **Grenadian** wasp that has a formidable sting.
3. **Sky-red** – Major fires which engulfed Grenada during the Eric Gairy led, 1951 social revolution.
4. **Soukooyah** – or **Soukooya** or **Soucoyant.** A vampire which takes the form of an old woman by day and at night becomes a flying ball of flame sucking blood. The Soukooyah is said to be notoriously compulsive and can be caught by sprinkling salt, rice or sand at entrances. The vampire would feel compelled to pick up every grain.
5. **El Dorado** – (Circa 1596) A city or country of fabulous riches thought to have existed in South America by 16th century explorers.
6. **William Galway Donavan** – A newspaper editor and federationist who was well known for his principle that "A naked freeman is better than a guilded slave". He went to jail rather than withdraw his public criticism of what he considered to be an unjust decision of a corrupt Judge.
7. **Guy Fawkes** – (13 April 1570 – 31 January 1606), also known as **Guido Fawkes** and **John Johnson.** Speak of the Gunpowder Plot of 1605 and you speak of Guy Fawkes, who, along with others, planned to assassinate King James 1, by blowing up the Parliament building with gunpowder, and restore a Catholic monarch to the British throne. The plotters secured the lease to an undercroft beneath the House of Lords. The Westminster Palace was subsequently searched during the early hours of 5 November, and Fawkes was found guarding the explosives. Over the next few days, he was questioned and tortured, and eventually he broke. Found to be guilty of High Treason he was hanged,

drawn and quartered. Fawkes has become synonymous with the Gunpowder Plot, which has been commemorated in England since 5th November 1605. His effigy is burned on a bonfire, often accompanied by a firework display. It is also commemorated in Grenada, notably at Morne Jaloux.

Chapter 28

1. **Bois Bandé** – (French for "hard wood") is the bark of a tree famed in parts of the Caribbean for its properties as an aphrodisiac. Benefits include strengthening and increasing sexual power, desire and the ability to perform sexually. Large doses may lead to uncomfortable and long lasting erections. Unlike Viagra, Bois Bandé is a totally natural product which has been used for generations since the days of the Kalinago people. It is grown in Grenada.
2. **Sqandermania** – (1961) Allegations of corruption made against Gairy, known to Grenadians as Squandermania, which led to Gairy's removal from office.
3. **Ton-Ton Macoute** – Haitian Secret Police created in 1959 by President François 'Papa Doc' Duvalier. In 1970, the militia was officially renamed the **Milice de Volontaires de la Sécurité Nationale** (Militia of National Security Volunteers, MVSN). Haitians called this force the "Tonton Macoutes," after the Haitian Creole mythological *Tonton Macoute* (*Uncle Gunnysack*) bogeyman who kidnaps and punishes unruly children by snaring them in a gunnysack (Macoute) and carrying them off to be consumed at breakfast.
4. **Carte blanche** – The authority to do as you wish.
5. **Harambee** – An East African Swahili word meaning "Let's Pull Together" or Unity." The festival included lots of food, drumming and social interaction.

Chapter 29

1. **Cocoa, Nutmeg & Banana Boards** – These were statutory bodies which ran the affairs of the respective commodity cooperative. The produce was bought and marketed by the Boards and the farmers were in turn paid for their produce.

Chapter 30

1. **Stucco** - A material made of an aggregate, a binder, and water. Stucco is applied wet and hardens to a very dense solid. It is used as a coating for walls and ceilings and for decoration. Stucco may be used to cover less visually appealing construction materials such as concrete, cinder block, or clay brick.
2. **'The New Jewel'**- NJM flagship newspaper; and in its heyday had the largest circulation of newspapers in Grenada.
3. **Duvalier – François Duvalier** (April 14, 1907 – April 21, 1971) was the President of Haiti from 1957 until his death in 1971. Duvalier first won acclaim in fighting diseases, earning him the nickname **"Papa Doc"** ("Daddy Doc[tor]" in French). His rule, based on a purged military, a rural militia and the use of a personality cult, resulted in the murder of thousands of Haitians and an ensuing "brain drain" from which the country has not recovered. **Jean-Claude Duvalier**, nicknamed **"Bébé Doc"** or **"Baby Doc"** (born July 3, 1951) was the President of Haiti from 1971 until his overthrow by a popular uprising in 1986. He succeeded his father, François "Papa Doc" Duvalier, as the ruler of Haiti upon his father's death in 1971. He presided over a reign of terror in which many thousands were killed or tortured and many more fled the country.
4. **Pell–mell** - Disorder or in a jumbled, confused manner; helter-skelter.

5. **Bull-pestle** or **Bull pistle** – Grenadian colloquial for a tough, long whip made with the penis of a bull; reputed to have a sobering effect on anyone unfortunate to be whipped with one.
6. **Innocent Belmar** - Innocent Belmar hailed from Birchgrove, St. Andrew's in Grenada. He entered the Grenada Police Force in 1956 and was a Constable for 13 years. In 1969, Belmar started a series of advancements from Corporal/1969 to Sergeant/1970 to Inspector/1972 and to the commissioned rank of Assistant Superintendent (ASP) in 1973. He played a leading role in Gairy's reign of terror in 1973-1974 and despite the ruling of the Duffus Commission of Inquiry that he was to be excluded from holding any public office, Belmar ran for and won the St. Andrew's northwest seat in the 1976 General Elections on a GULP ticket.

Chapter 31
1. **Sounder** – A movie based on a young adult novel by William H. Armstrong. It is the story of an African-American boy living with his sharecropper family. Although the family's difficulties increase when the father is imprisoned for stealing pork sausages and ham, the boy still hungers for an education. "Sounder", the dog's name, is the only character name used in the book.
2. **Bata Shoe Store** - A large family owned shoe company based in Bermuda but currently headquartered in Lausanne, Switzerland, operating 3 business units worldwide – Bata Metro Markets, Bata Emerging Markets and Bata Branded Business. It has a retail presence in over 50 countries and production facilities in 26 countries. It no longer operates in Grenada. In its history the company has sold more than 14 billion pairs of shoes.

3. **Committee of 22** – An umbrella body comprising of 22 church and civic organizations which spearheaded the strikes and demonstrations against Prime Minister Gairy in November 1973- January 1974.
4. **Dame Hilda Bynoe** - **Dame Hilda** Louisa Gibbs **Bynoe**, DBE (born in Crochu, Grenada, on November 18, 1921). She is well known throughout the Caribbean as the first woman Governor in the British Commonwealth and the first native Governor of her island home of Grenada (1968 – 1974).
5. **'Babash'** - Locally fermented spirits. An extremely potent overproof rum with a fearsome reputation. It is sold under-the-counter (illegally).
6. **Mongoose Gang** – Gairy's Secret Police.
7. **Asafa Powell** - (born 23 November 1982) A Jamaican sprinter who specializes in the 100 metres. He held the 100 m world record between June 2005 and May 2008, with times of 9.77 and 9.74 seconds respectively. Powell has consistently broken the 10-second barrier in competition, with his personal best of 9.72 s being the fourth fastest time in the history of the event.
8. **War of Jenkins' Ear** – (1739-1748) A war between Great Britain and Spain. Its unusual name, coined by Thomas Carlyle in 1858, relates to Robert Jenkins, captain of a British merchant ship, who exhibited his severed ear in Parliament following the boarding of his vessel by Spanish coast guards in 1731. This affair and a number of similar incidents sparked a war against the Spanish Empire, ostensibly to encourage the Spanish not to renege on the lucrative *asiento* contract (permission to sell slaves in Spanish America).

Chapter 32
1. **Boomsie** or **Bamsee** – Grenadian colloquial for buttocks.

Chapter 33
1. **WIBS** – A regional broadcasting network with headquarters in Grenada, inaugurated in 1955. The establishment of the station and the running costs for the first few years were provided by British Colonial Development and Welfare Funds (CDW). The Windward Islands of Dominica, Grenada, St. Vincent and St. Lucia shared the air time throughout the day. It enabled much closer communication and news information exchange. In the late 1960s Premier Eric Gairy decided that he wanted his own national government radio station and WIBS fell apart with each island going its own way.
2. **Donkey's years** – A very long time.
3. **Empire Cinema** – Located on the Carenage in St. George's, Grenada, one of two major cinemas, Empire Cinema held a special place in Grenada's cinematic history. It was for many decades an entertainment icon and featured from time to time, local and overseas singers, bands and other performing artists.
4. **Grenada National Party (GNP)** – The party was founded in 1955 and took its support from the urban middle class and landowners. A conservative party led by Herbert Augustus Blaize. It first contested national elections in 1957 when it won two of the eight seats.
5. **Herbert A. Blaize** – (February 26, 1918 – December 19, 1989) born in Beausejour, Carriacou, was a Grenadian politician and leader of the Grenada National Party. When Grenada was still a British Crown Colony he served as the first Chief Minister from 1960-61, and again, from 1962-67. He became the first Premier of the autonomous Associated State of Grenada briefly in 1967.

Chapter 34
1. **Le Pigalle** – An area in Paris around the Place Pigalle, on the border between the 9th and the 18th

arrondissements. It is named after the sculptor Jean-Baptiste Pigalle (1714-1785). Famous for being a tourist district, with many sex shops on Place Pigalle and the main boulevards and prostitutes operating in the side streets. The neighborhood's raunchy reputation led to its World War II nickname of "Pig Alley" by Allied soldiers.

2. **Duffus Commission** – Set up following the violent incidents in Grenada (November 1973-January 1974). The Commission was chaired by Herbert Duffus, with leading members H. Aubrey Fraser and Archbishop Samuel Carter. The "Duffus Report," which it produced, was a work compiled by many people, working endless hours. Its official title, signed off by the authors 27 February 1975, is "Report of the Duffus Commission of Inquiry into the Breakdown of Law and Order, and Police Brutality in Grenada.

3. **Inter alia** – Among other things.

4. **Green Beasts** – The name aptly given to Gairy's army because of the colour of the camouflage they wore and their capacity to act violently.

5. **Sancho – Fernando Sancho** (January 7, 1916 – July 31, 1990) A Spanish actor, born in Zaragoza, Aragón, Spain. He was often typecast as a Mexican bandit in paella and spaghetti westerns, including *The Big Gundown* (directed by Sergio Sollima), *A Pistol for Ringo* and *Return of Ringo* (directed by Duccio Tessari), *Arizona Colt* (directed by Michele Lupo), *Minnesota Clay* (directed by Sergio Corbucci), and *Sartana* (directed by Gianfranco Parolini). Though invariably given the same role — a Mexican bandit chief — Sancho was a strong actor, and became one of the icons of these films.

6. **Montezuma** – (1466–1520), Ninth Aztec Emperor, ruler at the beginning of the Spanish conquest of Mexico.

7. **Siberia** - An extensive region constituting almost all of Northern Asia. Comprising the central and eastern portion of the Russian Federation. Siberia remained a mostly undocumented and sparsely populated area for a very long time. During the Soviet Union era there were many penal labour camps there and many were deported or exiled to Siberia.

Chapter 36
1. **Expo '69** – (April 5 – 30, 1969) A regional trade and cultural fair, held under the auspices of **Carifta**, the Caribbean Free Trade Area, the forerunner to **Caricom**. Grenada was the first Caribbean Island to host such an exposition which attracted visitors worldwide.
2. **Easter Water Parades** – (Circa 1976), These took place on the Carenage in St. George's, Grenada at Easter time. The Carenage was decorated and a shoreline was created and filled with beach sand. Activities included boat and swimming races, art exhibitions, cultural displays, music, games etc.
3. **Bootstring** – **(1978)** An ambitious development programme, launched by Gairy which he called **"Operation Industrialization and Employment Bootstring.** Operation Bootstring appears to have been Gairy's version of the Puerto Rican model of development.
4. **Kerry Parker Series** – **Kerry Francis Bullmore Packer**, (17 December 1937 – 26 December 2005) was an Australian media tycoon. The Packer family company owned controlling interest in both the **Nine television network** and leading Australian publishing company **Australian Consolidated Press**, which were later merged to form **Publishing and Broadcasting Limited** (PBL). At the time of his death, Packer was the richest and one of the most influential men in Australia. Outside Australia, Packer

was best known for founding World Series Cricket. In 1977 the Nine Network cricket rights deal led to a confrontation with the cricket authorities, as top players from several countries rushed to join him at the expense of their international sides. Packer was famously quoted from a 1976 meeting with the Australian Cricket Board, with whom he met to negotiate the rights to televise cricket. According to witnesses, he said: "There is a little bit of the whore in all of us, gentlemen. What is your price?"
5. **Carib Factory – Carib Breweries,** where the alcoholic drink, Carib, is brewed. Located at Maurice Bishop Highway, formerly True Blue Stretch, St. George's, Grenada.

Chapter 37
1. **Pro bono** – For the public good.
2. **Beverly Flats** – Family apartments owned by the Bishop family and located in the south of the island of Grenada.

Chapter 39
1. **Valentino – Anthony Emrold Phillip - 'Brother Valentino,'** a Trinidadian calypsonian also known as the People's calypsonian. *Stay Up Zimbabwe* was one of his well known compositions as was *Dis Place Nice*.
2. **Flagrante delicto** – In the act of committing a misdeed; red-handed.
3. **Sheila Joseph** – (born April 9th, 1963) A female soldier of the People's Revolutionary Army (PRA) during the Grenada Revolution who was accidentally shot and has since been confined to a wheelchair.

Chapter 40
1. **St. George's, St. Mark's and St. Andrew's** – three of the six parishes that make up mainland Grenada.

2. **Sandino Plant** – The name of the concrete blocks and house building plant established by the revolution and located in the south of Grenada, named after Augusto César Sandino, the Nicaraguan nationalist and revolutionary.
3. **NISTEP- National Inservice Teacher Education Programme** - The teacher education program initiated during the Grenada revolution aimed at revising and upgrading teacher training, efficiency, effectiveness and the charting of a new course for the education system.
4. **CPE – Center for Popular Education** – The national literacy programme established by the Grenada revolution.
5. **PRG – Peoples Revolutionary Government** – The Grenada Government which was appointed following the March 13th, 1979 revolution.
6. **'The Revo Milk'**- Milk obtained during the revolution from the European Union which was widely distributed free of cost.
7. **Bernard Coard**- Deputy Prime Minister, Minister of Finance, Member of the Political Bureau and Central Committee of the New Jewel Movement during the revolution.
8. **NTS – National Transport Service** – Established by the revolution following a suggestion which came out of a Parish Council Meeting.
9. **MNIB – Marketing and National Importing Board** – Set up by the revolution and was primarily engaged in the marketing of farmers products and the importation of basic food items which had the effect of significantly reducing the cost of such items.
10. **NIS – National Insurance Scheme** – The first such scheme, established by the revolution to provide for the social security and well-being of Grenadians.
11. **NWO – National Women's Organization** – A mass organization for women during the revolution.

12. **NYO – National Youth Organization** – A mass organization for youths during the revolution.
13. **NFU – National Farmers Union** – a trade union established to represent farmers during the revolution.
14. **NJM – New Jewel Movement** – (JEWEL – the acronym for 'Joint Endeavour for Welfare, Education and Liberation') – the party which led the Grenada Revolution, formed on March 11th, 1973.

Chapter 41

1. **Island Queen** (August 5th, 1944) - A Grenadian schooner, with 67 persons on board, disappeared on its way to St. Vincent during the Second World War.
2. **Royal Reader - The Royal Reader** - The six volumes of the Royal Readers were a graded series of textbooks ... First published in the 1870s by Thomas Nelson & Sons of London. They were widely used in primary schools in Grenada (Circa 1930 – 1960) and imparted Victorian values and morals.
3. **Chicra Salhab** – Owner and captain of the Island Queen; He was the great grandson of Captain Louis La Grenade, a Grenadian from the French Plantocracy who fought against Fedon on the side of the British.
4. **Keratoconus** - The bulging of the cornea.

Chapter 42

1. **UPP – United People's Party**, whose leader was Winston Whyte, former Parliamentarian and Minister of Government.
2. **GNP - Grenada National Party**, led by late former Prime Minister, Herbert H.A. Blaize
3. **'Gang of 26,'**- So named by the leadership of the revolution; a group of persons who was considered dissidents or counter-revolutionaries, some of whom were incarcerated.

4. **Grenadian Voice** – Now a leading Grenadian newspaper, was first published during the revolution by the socalled "Gang of 26". Its editor, Leslie Pierre, was incarcerated during the Grenada revolution.
5. **Trinidad Guardian and Trinidad Express** – The name of two of the main newspapers published in Trinidad and sold in Grenada.
6. **Voice of America (VOA)** – Owned by the Federal Government of the United States. A widely listened to radio station, with a distinctive American and Western bias, reporting the daily news and carried other programmes as well.
7. **Radio Antilles** - A radio station founded in 1963, located on the island of Montserrat. The station operated at 930 kHz AM and covered the entire Caribbean region. Radio Antilles was shut down, abandoned and later buried completely by lava and pyroclastic flow deposits after the start of the Soufriere Hills volcano eruption in 1995.

Chapter 43

1. **Central Committee (C.C.)** – The supreme policy-making body of the NJM formed after the March 13th, 1979 revolution.
2. **Political Bureau (P.B.)** – The body which carried out the day to day supervision of the NJM's party work and was established following NJM's formation in 1973. It consisted of some of the most senior members of the party.
3. **GRENLEC – Grenada Electricity Company,** so named after it was bought from the Commonwealth Development Cooperation (CDC) during the revolution.
4. **Joint Leadership** – The ill-fated attempt to marry the strengths of Maurice Bishop and Bernard Coard in shared leadership of the NJM; the proposed panacea for what was then seen as weak leadership of the party.

This was at the core of the October 1983 political crisis. One may say, ironically, that this was a tragic case of an acrimonious and violent divorce before the consummation of the marriage.
5. **Butler House** – The office of the Prime Minister during the revolution and named after Grenadian, Uriah 'Buzz' Butler, well known regional trade unionist.
6. **Whey dey come from?** - Grenadian colloquial/local vernacular for asking "Where have they come from?"
7. **Who dey dey wid?** – Grenadian colloquial/local vernacular for "Who are they with?" **Meaning**: "who is his/her girlfriend/boyfriend?" or "who is his/her woman/man?"
8. **Whey dey been?** – Grenadian colloquial/local vernacular for "Where have they been?"
9. **Radio Free Grenada (RFG)** – So named immediately following the revolution; it was Government owned and operated and Grenada's only radio station at the time. Formerly Radio Grenada.
10. **Radix, Louison and Whiteman – Kenrick Radix, George Louison and Unison Whiteman:** Ministers of Government during the revolution and leading members of the NJM. Indeed, Whiteman was one of two leaders when the NJM was formed. Whiteman was one of those killed on October 19th, 1983. Radix and Louison have since passed away.

Chapter 44
1. **Anastasio Somoza Debayle** – (5th December – 17th September 1980) President of Nicaragua 1967 – 1979; the last of the Somoza family to be president.
2. **Augusto Jose Ramón Pinochet Ugarte** – (25th November 1915 – 10th December 2006) President and Dictator of Chile 1973 - 1990

Chapter 45
1. **LIAT** – Leeward Islands Air Transport headquartered in Antigua.
2. **OECS** – Organization of Eastern Caribbean States.

Chapter 47
1. **Urgent Fury** - Codename of the US-led invasion of Grenada in 1983.
2. **To See Your Nen-Nen** – Grenadian colloquial/local vernacular to describe unusual difficulty or hardship.
3. **Gutsiness** – Marked courage; daring or pluckiness; to have gumption or cojones.
4. **'One today, one tomorrow'** - Grenadian colloquial for slothful; to move at an unusually slow pace.

Chapter 48
1. **Mange popotte** – French patois: Manger means to eat and popotte is a little thing. In patois it is best translated to mean some little stupidness! And in the context of the story, food prepared without regard to quantity, quality, appearance, taste and smell.
2. **Compos Mentis** - Sane in mind; being of sound mind, memory, and understanding.
3. **Sir. Nicholas Brathwaite** – Former Prime Minister of Grenada 1990-1995.
4. **Vergil – Publius Vergilius Maro** (also known by the Anglicised forms of his name as **Virgil** or **Vergil**); (October 15, 70 BC – September 21, 19 BC) was a classical Roman poet, a master poet and one of Rome's greatest; best known for three major works— the *Eclouges* (or *Bucolics*), the *Georgics* and the *Aeneid*.
5. **Sub Judice** – A latin phrase meaning: 'Under judicial consideration; before a judge or court of law'. This restricts the extent to which judicial proceedings can be reported or dealt with in the public domain.

6. **Old Bailey** – London's Central Criminal Court, seen as the mecca of the English justice system. The Old Bailey is located about 200 yards northwest of St Paul's Cathedral, just outside the former western wall of the City of London. It is named after the street on which it is located. Over the centuries (1673-1913) the building has been periodically remodelled and rebuilt in ways which both reflected and influenced the changing ways trials were carried out and reported.

Chapter 49
1. **Pogrom** – To exterminate as in Hitler's crusade against the Jews.

*Sources include: ***Wikipedia Encyclopedia; Webster's Ninth New Collegiate Dictionary; Britannica; Dictionary of Caribbean Langauge -Jeanette Allsop et al;** Merriam-webster.com; Latinlaugaugephrases.com; Urban dictionary.com; www.answers.com

Bibliography

The following works were consulted and drawn upon in the creation of this docu-novel. I am particularly indebted to W. E. B. DuBois's book, herein listed, which was heavily relied upon with respect to the writing of Chapter 20.

Brizan, George. *Grenada: Island of Conflict, From Amerindians to People's Revolution 1498-1979*. Zed Books Ltd. 1984

Coard, Bernard. *Grenada: 1951-1983: Notes For CXC/O'Level Students of History and Social Studies*. 2003

Victor, Teddy. *Twenty Years Ago: The Jewel*. Grenadian Voice, March 7, 1992.

DuBois, W.E. *Th-e World and Africa*. International Publishers. 1976

US Navy Seals web page

Made in the USA
Charleston, SC
14 March 2014